God's Rebel

Changed Heart Series #1

Michelle Janene

God's Rebel

Changed Heart Series #1

Michelle Janene

STRONG TOWER
PRESS

Sacramento

Strong Tower Press
Sacramento, CA
strongtowerpress.com

Publishers note: This is a work of fiction.

Names, characters, places and incidents are either products of the author's imagination or used factiously. All characters are fictional, and any similarity to people living or dead is entirely coincidental.

Editor: Paige Duke

Cover art: by D's Concepts and Designs

breaks: Lighted Sword: image # 42422439 idimair, Map Font Underworld by hmeneses

Cover: Shutter Stock image Kiselev Andrey 67878571, Shaiith 246642865, and Patryk Kosmider 92425513, Font: MacHumaine by Bill Horton

Scripture quoted or paraphrased from Geneva Bible ©1599

To family who support, encourage, help and love on me.

To writing sisters and brother who share our lives in our words.

To all who love an adventure.

To those who seek the truth wherever it may be found.

KINGDOM OF
VERONIA
PLEASANT LOCH
DUSKMOOR RIVER
BRANDY RIVER
MISTY RIVER
SIMMERING TIDES

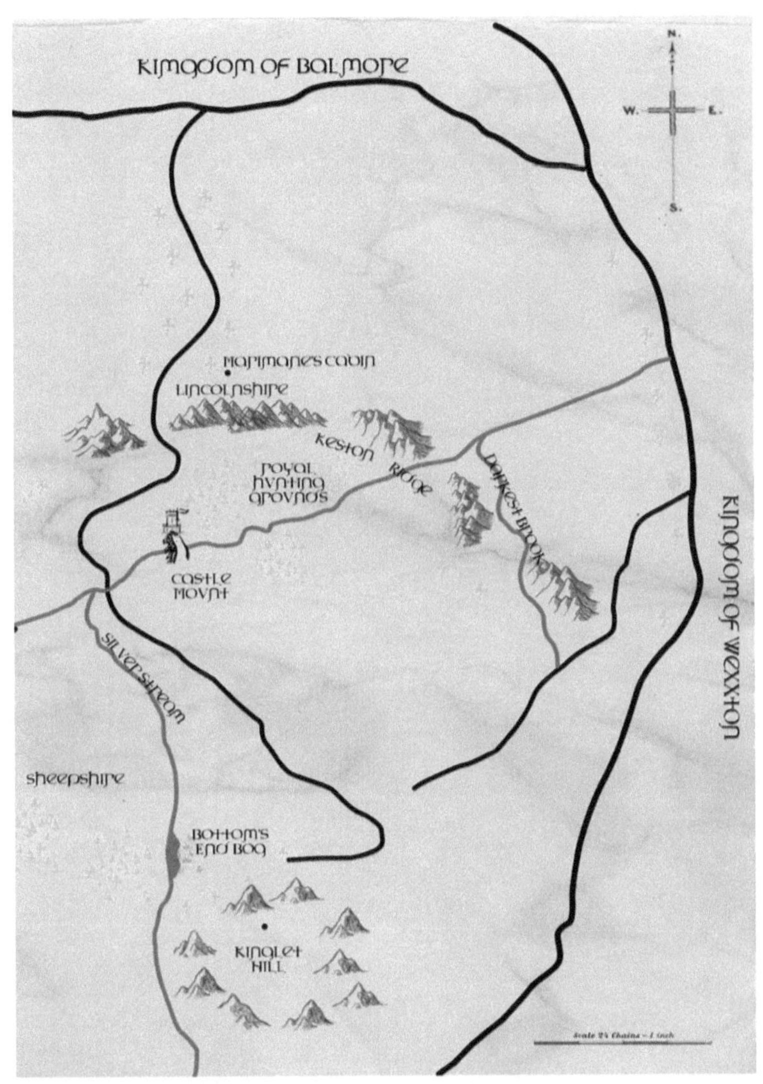

KINGDOM OF BALMORE
N.
W. E.
S.
Marimane's Cabin
Lincolnshire
Keston Ridge
Royal Hunting Grounds
Darkest Brooke
Castle Mount
Kingdom of Wexxton
Silverstream
Sheepshire
Bottom's End Bog
Kinglet Hill
Scale 2½ Chains = 1 inch

Chapter 1

A low growl rumbled through the air between them as she hunkered down in the rear of her cell. It grew with intensity as he drew near.

"Ah, ya're soundin' well, my pet."

She bared her teeth as the growl swelled to a roar, vibrating her insides.

Jarel laughed, raking the end of his torch along the bars as he cooed to her. "To touch yar skin and pull ya close. Ya could delight any man."

She scooped a handful of the cool filth from the floor. It oozed through her fingers as she hurled it at him, but she remained well out of reach.

"Ya wretched beast!" He slammed the torch against the metal, showering her with embers.

"Jarel, sir? The foreign knight has returned to view the merchandise," a guard called from above.

"I am not finished with you, wench," he said.. He hollered up to the man as he stomped away, "Fetch me a clean tunic."

Halton left the freshness and promise of a fine spring day behind and entered the slave market. Glancing down on the man swaggering toward him, he scowled.

"Good mornin', sir. Mighty fine day to buy a mite of human flesh, isn'n it?" Jarel, the slave master, flashed a toothy grin. His beady eyes hidden under bushy brows that threatened to meet in the center, were set deep in his narrow face. This man was not to be trusted.

Halton recoiled a step. He did not belong here. He should go back to the foreign king's hall, and bathe. *Lord, why have You sent me to this place?* He sighed at the silence but held to the thought that any he purchased this day would be well treated in King Edgar's court. They would be given a chance for advancement and possible freedom for their loyalty and faithfulness. They could never hope for similar treatment if sold to a Balmorian.

Squaring his shoulders, Halton swallowed the bile flavoring his throat. "We will see if I can stomach you long enough to rescue any of these poor souls."

Jarel's face filled with a joyous smile and his keen eyes glinted, making Halton's stomach tighten as he followed the avaricious man toward the cells.

Purchasing servants—the very idea revolted him. He should not have come. He tried to avoid it even now, the muscles in his back twitching to turn, his feet eager to carry him away. But God had brought him to ease the pain he'd heard yesterday. As the market closed for the night, Halton had made arrangements for early this morning.

Lord, is this Your will? He served a wondrous God. The reluctance of his flesh settled into a familiar peace. Halton trusted God would lead him to the one He wanted brought from the slaver's cells. Only God knew for what purpose.

Following the quick slaver, they crossed the courtyard where the most profitable slaves would later be displayed for potential customers. Jarel rubbed boney hands together and turned to look up at him. "I've seen naught of ya 'bout Sangborgh before. Ya new here 'bouts?"

"I hail from Veronia. King Edgar's thane. My king commissioned me to speak with your king on a matter of equal concern to both Veronia and Balmore."

"Ah, ya met with our repugnant king then, did ya?"

Halton straightened and narrowed his gaze. "I have been pleased to meet with your honorable king, aye. I found him to be an admirable man among loathsome characters."

A guard unlocked the final gate to the cells with a reverberating *clank*, and the door swung open with a nerve-grating creak. Jarel and Halton passed through before the guard followed them inside and slammed the door.

The reek of sweat and refuse hit Halton with the force of a jouster's blunted lance. He staggered back a step, eyes watering, and choked down bile. He did not dare take another breath. Then the moans of the captives flooded his ears and crushed his heart.

"The pungent strength will fade in but a short moment." Jarel flashed a grin, his jagged teeth like the fangs of a hungry wolf. "I smells naught but profit." He inhaled deeply.

Halton's stomach rolled and sweat beaded on his skin. He closed his eyes against the stinging and prayed. His jaw locked, and his fists balled tightly. *Do not retch.* He took a shallow breath and trudged through the stinking, cramped corridor between the rows of unwashed men and women imprisoned behind steel bars.

"What seek ya this day, sir? Strong backs?" Jarel grabbed a trembling arm and pulled a man to the bars. "Or sweet wenches?" He leered at a woman on the other side, and she shuddered.

Halton's heart crumpled under the weight of the eyes peering at him from behind the bars. "My home does not traffic in human flesh. But I am sure the Good Lord will reveal which desperate souls He wishes freed from your dark dungeon," Halton whispered.

Jarel stumbled both in step and words. "Ya have no servants?"

Halton kept his voice low. "Servants a plenty, but no slaves. All in service are paid and can earn their freedom."

"Amazin' it 'tis, and quite absurd. Think of all the dentris ya could keep in yar pouch if ya but owned slaves?"

"A human life is of far greater value than any number of coins."

Jarel sneered and continued through the cramped corridor.

Halton straightened as they approached the more crowded cells. He must open his heart to God's leading yet steel himself against the fact he could never hope to free them all. His heart rent in two.

"But, sir, human flesh is most valuable indeed." Jarel again rubbed his hands together.

Halton pointed to one possibility, a tall dark-haired man with hollow eyes. "Shall we begin? Name a price."

"Twenty dentris."

"That is the price of a draft team of six horses. I will not go higher than ten." Halton crossed his arms over his aching chest. Prudence told him the shrewd, voracious peddler would never deal fairly with a novice. The first price would be far higher than what Jarel would in fact settle for in payment. If he could lower the price, he could afford to rescue more than one from the deplorable conditions now assailing him.

"I couldn't open the cell for less than eighteen."

"Twelve."

Jarel shook his head, his straight locks flopping about his face like a dying fish. The poor man being haggled over stared blankly in the void between him and Jarel, so Halton moved on.

Jarel pointed out another man with short blond hair, who looked more warrior than slave. "Thirty for this strong back." Jarel puffed his chest, and Halton took a step to continue.

"I swear my fidelity to you and your master, sir. I vow to serve well and without complaint." The slave spoke articulately and held Halton in a steady gaze. His firm jaw and straight back further convinced Halton of the depth of his assurance.

Halton considered the man for another instant, "Fifteen."

"Ya're daft! He'll fetch fortys or more in some markets. He's the finest flesh in my collection."

"I would never so waste the King of Veronia's gold on a practice he has outlawed. Eighteen is the most you shall receive from me, and if you persist on refusing my price, mayhaps I would be best served to leave at once."

Jarel's chin rose and his head tilted. A bony finger tapped an odd rhythm on his jutting jaw line. A faint hum drifted through the stilled cells. Did the man weigh the profit of this one soul over the potential of numerous sales?

He finally nodded his consent to the price and turned to the guard who followed them. "Remove him and take him to the preparations room to clean." Turning to Halton again, he said, "A new tunic will be five more dentris."

"I can buy them for half as much in the market." Halton turned as if to leave. "It is past time to be done with you."

Keys rattled a cheerful jingle, and the heavy steel door creaked with the sound of freedom.

"Very well, very well." Jarel looked back over his shoulder at the guard, as he ushered Halton back into the dungeon. "Give him a clean tunic. He'll wait in the holding room till I send for him. When ya're done, come get the others." His gaze held Halton's as he grinned and raised a brow.

The guard led the blond man away. "I swear my oath of allegiance to you and the king of Veronia. Thank you, sir. I will serve you well. Thank you."

"I will collect him and any others I purchase at first light on the morrow."

Jarel nodded, and they proceeded between the noisy throng of hopefuls.

A filthy hand seized Halton's sleeve. His gaze followed the arm up until it met watery, red eyes. The man holding him fast, moaned. "Please, sir, I'll serve your king faithfully."

Halton gently pulled free and tried to step clear of the man's grasp only to be seized from the other side.

"Choose me, sir. Please." The woman begged, tears carving muddy trails down her cheeks.

Halton regretted—too late—stating he served the King of Veronia. Each soul within these walls now vied in desperation to serve in Veronia's palace as well.

Halton sought God and steeled his heart. He next selected a heavyset man farther down the corridor for a few dentris before descending the stairs into the fetid underbelly of the lower cells. The chambers above had been deplorable; these were beyond all imagination. Halton slogged through ankle-deep refuse, as it came from slaves in these cells and ran through cracks in the mortar from those above. The few flickering torches struggled against the windowless dark, and added a sulfur flavor to the putrid stench.

The slaves here, little more than rag-covered bones, moaned and pleaded, filling Halton's ears until he feared he would drown in their pain.

"Help me."

"Take me, please."

"I can still work."

"I'll serve."

Little flesh hung on many of the malnourished bodies, and most looked too frail to lift their own head, let alone their hands to service. The noxious oozing of festering sores made Halton want to turn away, but he looked nonetheless. He could be their last hope. He continued. Then God prodded him forward with a whispered nudge. The Lord sought someone here.

Jarel raked the shaft of his torch along the bars of the cell to his right, and a menacing coo hissed across his lips, "Hello, my pet. Are ya better?"

A low, wild growl erupted from the figure huddled in the dark corner of the polluted cell. The head turned, and Halton realized a woman with black matted hair was snarling at the slave master. As Jarel thrust the torch through the bars, her deep-green eyes bore into the foul man with tangible hatred and her savage growl grew, revealing her fierce teeth. The hair on Halton's neck rose.

A cruel laugh rumbled through the slave master.

The woman turned her hard gaze on Halton, and the pain and fear he saw there caught at his heart. Her stare pierced him deep as any sword, and the quiet voice in his soul whispered. *This one, My son.*

"What?" In shock, Halton couldn't stop the word.

"She's a tough one." Jarel's gaze caressed the full length of the woman. "Many has tried to tame her, but she's as wild as a polecat and claws her way about till they return her. Been here near five years. No one wishes such an unruly beast." Jarel laughed as she turned back to him growling. "I only keeps her around to have somethin' to play with." His suggestive tone and repulsive sneer made Halton shudder.

He turned to the woman again and asked silently, *Are you sure, Lord? You want me to take this one?*

Yes, she is My precious daughter. Take her from this place and teach her of Me.

A lone woman on the long journey home with his knights and those he'd already purchased could prove challenging. What would his king say? Did the palace have need for her? God pulled on his heart again. God had a purpose for her, and Halton needed to be obedient. He nodded. "She is coming with us. I will give you eighteen for her, same as the warrior."

Jarel leered at the woman. "I tell ya true, sir, ya don't want this one. She's wild and unwilling to serve."

"She will come with us or none of them will."

The slaver sighed. "Yes, sir, as ya wish."

As he turned to leave, Halton selected one more of the men in the lower cells for a fraction of the rest. Then he climbed into the clean air of the slave compound and filled his lungs with the freshness of the newly budding trees beyond the walls. "My men and I will arrive at first light and inspect our four additional companions again before I make payment."

"Agreed."

Halton escaped the slave market and made straight for a public bath to rid himself of the filth left on him by the odious merchant and his compound. He followed that with a visit to the tonsor for a shave.

Later Halton met his men on the Balmorian streets. They waved as he approached, "Hello, sir, what have you been about all morn?"

"Rescuing souls from the slaver's dungeon."

Halton considered the four knights who had accompanied him on this mission. Corin, the eldest, served as second in command. His red hair flamed bright in the sun as his eyes grew wide. "You bought slaves?"

"Rescued." Halton attempted a smile, but weariness flattened it. "I but followed the request of the Lord."

The oddness of his actions left his men silent and gawking at him. God wanted the woman—though Halton could see no clear purpose for her. He closed his eyes again, searching for direction. No answer came. Had he chosen correctly?

"Eldon, I have purchased a woolen riding skirt, under-tunic, linen jerkin, and shoes. Please deliver them to the slaver for the woman." He held a bundle out toward the knight.

Eldon had proven himself an able fighter in recent skirmishes, and though his jaw slacked, the slender knight eventually took the items and obeyed without comment.

"You bought a woman?" Corin stammered, the hint of a smirk turning his lips.

Heat slithered into Halton's cheeks and he huffed. "She is not for me, and I did as I was called to do. Now, we will need more horses, four to be exact. Take Bray with you to purchase them. I shall take Shaw and collect provisions.

"We require flour and salted meat…" Halton stomped toward the market, forcing Shaw to quicken his steps to keep up.

With preparations in hand, Halton returned to the foreign king's hall. He struggled to attend to the conversations around him as he pushed his food about his plate. Later as he lay back on the rush-covered hall floor, he stared into the black abyss of the smoke-stained rafters. *Lord, go with us.* He sighed. *A woman. What is the Lord about?* The new day would see new beginnings for more than those being freed, he feared.

Chapter 2

Halton and his men arrived at sunup to collect their new traveling companions. A three-week journey south to Veronia stretched out before them. They found the men in a preparation room near Jarel's office. The three men stood in the empty room, clean and ready to ride. A narrow desk sat under the window, and an anvil and hammer sat on a low stone shelf built into the wall nearby. The woman did not accompany them.

"She refuses to don the clothes ya sent, sir," Jarel stated with a satisfied smirk.

Halton growled fiercely at the wicked little man, now seeing the wild woman in a whole new light. Murmurings and unintelligible grunts were the vile man's native language. He snarled, and Jarel led him to the woman's putrid cell without further comment. The clothes sat piled on a stool above the filth just inside the cell door.

"See? I tolds ya, she's an untamed beast who will not do as she's told."

Halton turned on the depraved flesh-peddler. He stalked toward the little man, grinding words between his teeth. "You would force her to change in front of hundreds of leering eyes, while you escorted the men to private chambers to clean and dress? I do not know anyone—civilized or not—who would allow themselves to be degraded in such a hideous fashion. Prepare a room for her needs at once."

As Jarel fumbled for his keys, Halton added with a roar, "The price you will receive has now gone down."

"Sir, we've signed the papers, ya can nay go changin'—"

Halton stepped into him, grabbed him by his crusty shirt, and pulled him off his feet.

Jarel fell silent.

"Open. This. Cell." Halton choked a furious staccato. A tremor ran through the slave master he still held. Halton dropped him and the door creaked open. Stepping in, Halton picked up the stack of clothes and approached the cowering woman. He reached a hand to her as he spoke in a tender whisper. "My lady, you are leaving this awful place. Please, come with me to an area where you can prepare in private to depart."

The woman's head spun around, and she stared at him with wide eyes, making him wonder if anyone had ever addressed her with kindness. She held his gaze for several moments before she rose, ignoring his outstretched hand. Halton noted she stood nearly as tall as he, but her confinement in the slave master's dungeon left her gaunt with a vacant stare. Her soiled and tattered kirtle hung loosely about her, and he feared the garments he purchased would do likewise. At least they would be clean.

He led her up, out of the lower prison confines, to a room on the main level next to where the men waited. Directing her inside, he did not follow but handed her the clean garments from the doorway. "You may change in private, then we will leave. I will post my guard to see you are not disturbed. There is no need to rush, but the sooner you are ready, the sooner we can put this foul place behind us." Unease twisted his middle, but he offered her a slim smile as she took the clothes. Halton shut the door with a solid thump and backed into Jarel to allow Corin to step forward to stand guard.

Halton returned to the waiting men. They startled as he entered, and their eyes darted about as they sifted their weight from foot to foot. The tall blond attempted a smile, but his tight lips drew more of a straight line. He approached the strong-looking man, remembering his instant vow to Veronia's king. The man breathed rapidly. His bright blue eyes flashed with what Halton perceived as intelligence. He straightened under Halton's gaze, and his well-toned muscles rippled under his new tunic.

"What is your name, sir?" Halton asked.

"Cynric, sir, but most call me Cy."

"How did you come to find yourself in this place?"

"I am a hired man-at-arms and allowed myself to be commissioned to a nefarious rogue. This is my punishment and rightly deserved." His face reddened, he dropped his gaze, and he cleared his throat.

Halton moved to the next man, who came from the lower cells. Dark hollow eyes set deep in his shrunken cheeks made them appear lifeless. His mousy hair drooped over his face, and his new tunic hung on his emaciated body.

"And you, sir?"

"Darrel, my lord. I served as the assistant to the steward of an earl in the north and fell into misfortune for bringing dishonor on my master. I fell in love with one of his wealthy neighbor's daughters."

The other slave, taken from the upper cells, was stocky and obviously well fed; it was clear he had not been captive long enough to lose much of his girth. Halton again wondered what made him choose the rotund man. But the man's round face brightened with a huge smile as Halton approached him. He spoke with unrestrained cheer. "I am Garrick, sir. My extensive debts forced me to sell myself to pay back my creditors. I am greatly obliged for the rescue, sir, for my hunger has become powerful strong in these last days."

Halton frowned for a moment, but the jovial man did not suffer under his disapproval. He stepped back and considered them again before speaking. "As of this moment, you are bond servants of His Majesty King Edgar of Veronia. You will serve him in whatever capacity he deems you worthy and until such time as you are relieved of duties by death or freedom."

Eyes danced, and the men glanced sideways at one another. Cy and Garrick smirked past the more solemn Darrel between them. They nodded their understanding.

Halton held up an iron shackle before them. "Until your diligence earns your freedom, you will wear this iron band around your wrist so all will know you belong to the king. You will be returned to him should you attempt escape."

Halton addressed the men with stern directness, so he was startled when Cy shot out his right arm to have the band placed on it. "I will work with unwavering diligence, sir, and look forward to the day I might earn the king's favor, that I may fight alongside him with honor."

Shaw placed the band around Cy's wrist and directed him to rest his arm on the anvil. Halton watched as the young knight carefully positioned the heavy rivet in the hole of the first protruding tongue of the band and drove it through the second hole, securing the band so only a blacksmith could remove it.

As the ringing faded from the room, Shaw motioned Darrel forward. The man raised his arm with slow resignation, and he sighed deeply as he set his wrist in the band on the anvil. When it sat secure on his arm, Garrick waddled forward. Shaw attempted to fit the band, but it would not go around the man's stout wrist.

Shaw stepped back, rubbing his chin. At last, he picked up the remaining band and held both together as one larger shackle. He ran a hand through his wavy hair, loosing some of it from its knot. He looked at the two bands again, and after another moment he fastened them together on one side. He placed them over Garrick's wrist and secured the closure on the other side. Though loose, they would not fall off.

No band remained for the woman, Halton realized, but his ears rejoiced at the silence of the infernal clanging.

With the men now informed and banded, they waited another half hour before the woman joined them. Halton turned, allowing his eyes a quick scan from the top of her head to the tips of her leather-covered toes. The garments did not fit her well, but they were a good deal better than her tattered kirtle. Her face and hands were now clean, and her hair lay stunningly straight about her stiff shoulders, the beauty of it flowing from her head like a river of onyx until it splashed about her. Halton stood captivated. A gust of wind passing between the window in front of her and open door behind caught several strands. Halton stepped to Garrick and removed the cord, intending to draw the top of his tunic closed. But it lay untied, unable to encompass his girth. He handed it to the demure woman. "Lash this about your hair, my lady. It may be less bothersome then."

Compelled to make her more comfortable, he kept his words soft. "Well, dear lady, I hope you feel as refreshed as you look." Halton offered her an easy smile. "What is your name?"

She made no attempt to speak but continued to stare at the floor near his feet. Her shoulders slumped.

Jarel stepped forward, puffing himself up as large as his slim frame would allow. He used his club to raise her chin until she looked at her new master. "She has a tongue." He clouted her on the jaw.

She narrowed her gaze as she twisted to look on her abuser.

He pressed the stick into her jaw, dimpling her skin. She opened her mouth and stuck out the small pink appendage. "But she has ne'er done more than growl and snarl. Dumb creature."

Halton jerked the club from her trembling face. "Perhaps she saw no point in wasting her intellect on a worthless piece of dung such as yourself!"

Jarel stumbled back several steps.

Forgive me Lord, for I know You call us to love our enemies, but I hate this man.

Turning to Corin, Halton struggled to form words as every muscle clenched. Heat radiated through him, and his heart drummed. "Pay this foul man so we may leave without further delay."

Halton stomped from the room as coins rattled. Jarel's giddy laughter filled Halton's ears as he stepped into the courtyard well clear of the building. He came into the full light of the sun rising above the city walls.

The woman came abreast of him and closed her eyes. She raised her hand to shield her face. Slowly her arm slid to her side, and she turned her face toward the warm spring sun with her eyes still shut. Her skin bathed in the amber radiance gave her an angelic hue. The Spirit within him stirred as her countenance glowed, not entirely from the sun.

Halton allowed her to savor the warmth of her freedom as he moved past her to their horses.

"The gelding is said to be particularly docile, so I would put the woman on him," Corin advised Halton before turning to Cy. "The bay there is spirited. Can you handle him?"

"Aye." Cy's wide grin filled his face, and he elbowed Darrel, "We are leaving this pit, we walk not to Veronia, and we may yet earn freedom. This is better than we could have dreamed."

"If they have food, then it will be better still," Garrick said, rubbing his belly.

Cy mounted with an ease that spoke of familiarity and time spent in a saddle. Darrel groaned as his spindly arms pulled him up on a sedate gray horse. The woman joined them and sat in her saddle before anyone could assist her. It took a strategically placed box and many grunts for Garrick to struggle awkwardly atop his horse. Halton pondered what they would do the next time the giant needed to remount.

Halton and his knights joined them, but before they could spur their horses forward, Jarel stepped in front of them and handed Halton several lengths of rope. "Ya had better secure at least the woman. She'll bolt on ya at the first opportunity. And as wild as she is, she'll disappear and ya'll ne'er see her again."

Turning, Halton saw her stiffen. Her darting green eyes never caught his gaze. "I trust you know the dangers, better than most, of what atrocities can befall a woman on her own, wild or not. I hope you understand we are here for your protection and that you will not try to flee."

Jarel snickered, "As ya wish, but ya'll be regrettin' it."

Corin leaned down and took the ropes, placing them in the leather pouch behind his saddle.

They formed a tight group with Corin and Halton in the lead, while Shaw and Bray rode on the outside of Cy and the woman. Garrick and Darrel followed them, and Eldon served as rear guard. Due to their delay, the streets of the capital were crowded. Merchants hawked their wares as they trudged through the throngs of people beginning their day.

The wide city gate stood open to all traffic coming and going from the city. Once beyond it, the crowds thinned and the travelers expanded the distance between them allowing for more comfort and increased speed. Corin echo his satisfied sigh at finally beginning their journey home.

Halton settled into the comfortable rhythm of his horse, but his mind rattled with concern for the woman riding stiff behind him. A forbidding whisper of wind brought the hairs on his neck to attention. Halton studied the rolling hills. Coming to the crest of a rise, he scanned the distance to the far-flung border. A thin black fog snaked between the distant peaks. Halton's warrior heart trembled. Evil lay crouched there.

Lord, go before us and protect us.

Chapter 3

The familiar rhythm of Halton's charger stirred a well-known peace, and the peace ignited hope of an uneventful and joyful homecoming.

"Where is everyone?" Garrick asked, pulling Halton from his reflections.

"Few shires and villages mark the land between the Balmorian capital and our shared boarder. Balmore is a cold, windswept land."

Cy chuckled. "It lays knee deep in snow over half the year. Cold does not begin to describe it."

"I hear Veronia is warmer," hope rang in Garrick's voice.

Halton loosened his cloak in anticipation of the warmer southern lands. "Aye, Veronia stretches across the summer lands." Halton turned his attention to the colonnade of trees of every kind adorned in fresh spring leaves and a few lingering blossoms and imagined he walked across the bailey of his home.

Alertness hummed at the edge of his senses. He searched the areas where men bent on nefarious adventures might lurk. Halton took a deep breath, his gaze flitting to the sky, and rested in his God's mighty hands. *I take pleasure in riding in Your open spaces, Father. For on horseback I can think and pray and worship surrounded by my Maker's creations.*

Halton sought to commune with his Lord, but the tranquil ride he envisioned did not present itself. Their pace dragged, and the still air became choked with unending yammering.

"Do we stop and eat soon?" Garrick whined.

In frustration, Halton closed his eyes and ground his teeth. The jolly and good-natured man from earlier in the day had dissolved into a petulant curmudgeon.

"Come, we have ridden for hours on end. We must stop to eat. A fellow can waste away in this saddle."

Grunts and groans wafted through the air telling Halton that Garrick's prattling was wearing on everyone's nerves. Garrett rambled of things he had done, places he had seen, and, most importantly, foods he had tasted. He did not endeavor to engage someone in mindless conversation, for the man enjoyed the sound of his own voice far more than any response his fellow travelers offered. Only the pressing need of his stomach interrupted his monologue.

Halton craned his head around to Bray. "We will eat in the saddle."

"We do not stop?"

"Fie, man, can you think of nothing other than your stomach?" Shaw said.

"Actually, I thought of my behind."

Now Cy spoke next, his words tight. "I would think you have enough natural padding to cushion such a delicate rump."

Halton's words hissed between his teeth. "We are trudging along slower than a lame man. If we eat not in the saddle, a month shall fritter away before we arrive home."

Garrick mumbled his disapproval. "Well, may we at least do so now, sir?"

Halton nodded his head toward Bray, and the curly haired knight retrieved a bag from behind his saddle, which contained biscuits and dried venison. He distributed their portions, reaching back and offering the big man his first.

"Mayhaps with something other than your tongue flapping in your mouth, the rest of us will have a few moments of peace," Cy groaned and thanked Bray for his share.

Their reprieve proved short lived, as the gluttonous man devoured his share with a revolting slottering before most of the others received their portions.

"Is there naught more?"

"Oh, by my sword, man, shut your mouth or I will shut it for you!"

Halton raised a brow and stared at Eldon. Never had the knight erupted in anger. Inwardly, though, Halton rejoice at the instant silence.

Bray encouraged his horse to draw alongside of him. Halton accepted his meal as he caught a movement over the younger knight's shoulder. Too late to stop the woman's wild dash, he dropped his food. Popping his horse in the ribs, he gave chase. They flew off the road and down an embankment to a narrow field.

Once her horse found his footing in the tall grass, she steered him for the tree line a short distance in front of her. She lashed the reins on the horse's sides and pumped her heels into him, forcing the mount to greater speed. Over the pounding of hooves, Halton bellowed for her to stop, and Corin yelled at her from just over his left shoulder.

Halton's strong charger swung wide, closing the distance between him and the woman, and veered to block her path.

She jerked her horse to avoid a direct collision. As she turned, their legs became crushed between the two mounts. She lashed out, whipping at Halton with the ends of her reins.

Halton grabbed the intended weapon, and his arm suffered a sharp jerk when the horse came to the end of his lead and an abrupt stop.

The sudden halting of her horse sent the defenseless woman

headlong over her mount's right shoulder, as though launched from a trebuchet. She landed with a hard thud and rolled several more feet, disappearing into the green blanket of grass.

Halton growled as he dismounted and threw the reins of both horses to Corin. His long pounding strides sank into the soft turf. He did not know which galled him more: that the slave master spoke true, as he endangered his men in the impromptu chase down the steep embankment and across the uneven field, or that the headstrong woman could have injured herself and his reputation.

He approached where she lay sprawled on her back.

She rose to her elbows and shook her head with a whispered groan. The dazed women turned to face him. Her brows rose high. She glanced from the dirt beneath her, to the grass waving at her shoulders, up to him as he continued to advance. She crawled backward, away from him. Her eyes grew wide, and her lower lip disappeared between her teeth. She lashed out as he reached for her, clawing and kicking at him.

Halton managed to take hold of her, and he yanked her to her feet.

She jerked one arm free, cringed, and covered her face.

His fury melted like icicles dangling in the hot sun. She expected a beating. Shame filled him, for he had been of a mind to oblige her with a sound lashing. Now the very thought frightened him. He looked on her again with fresh eyes.

She cowered before him trembling. He drew in a long slow breath, allowing it to calm him as he prayed. *Forgive me Lord. Help me reassure her she will not be harmed.*

Peace washed over him. He turned to her and spoke gently, "Are you hurt, my lady?"

She dropped her arm and considered him through wide eyes as her shoulders relaxed down from her ears. She flinched as he moved to brush the dirt and grass from her garments. He took care to move with slow purpose and only touch her with tenderness. She stilled.

Taking hold of her, more gently this time, he led her back to her horse. When she struggled to raise her arm for the pommel to pull herself up, Halton ran his hand over her right shoulder. She squeezed her eyes closed and squirmed under his close examination.

"You must have landed on this shoulder. 'Tis not broken, but is sure to smart and blacken in the days to come."

She brushed him off and straightened, her chin jutting out as she tried for her saddle again. This time a faint gasp of pain escaped her lips. Halton bent, cupped his hands, took her foot, and boosted her into the saddle. He turned to Corin's horse and removed Jarel's ropes. He bound her hands together and lashed them to a hole bore through the pommel of her saddle. Corin had paid little for the damaged tack, but now Halton acknowledged God's provision.

Taking her reins, he mounted his charger. "I truly hoped never to bind you, my lady, but you have left me no alternative. I will not risk my men and horses to chase after you." He leaned near, holding her gaze. "And I would never leave you to your fate, alone in this wild land."

She lowered her head, and they rejoined the others waiting on the road. Halton mused aloud. "I pray you will not require me to bind you thus for the entire trip. It would be most unpleasant for all of us."

"Is she hurt?" Cy asked, looking the woman over as she took her place beside him.

"She is no doubt blackened with bruises, but I found no serious injuries."

Cy flashed the woman a kind smile before turning his attention to Halton as they resumed forward movement. "May I ask, sir, what brought you to Balmore? Surely you did not travel such a great distance for some tattered and unruly slaves?"

Halton paused to consider his response, but the impetuous young Shaw blurted the words as though discussing crops. "We are on a mission from our king."

"To send his thane and a band of knights to a neighboring ruler, something of great import must be raising our king's concern."

Halton looked at the man again. He had judged right in his assessment on first meeting the warrior. He possessed a quick mind and even now comprehended the situation. If he allowed Cy to continue, he would most assuredly conclude the full purpose of their mission.

Halton chose to be plain with the inquisitive warrior. "You are quite right. We came seeking a treaty as brothers-in-arms against a common enemy."

"The Black Knight," came Cy's hushed and tense reply.

Corin turned to look squarely at Cy. "What do you know of him?"

Cy shrugged. "Little, I fear. I know he terrorizes the border villages of both Balmore and Veronia. I thought I signed on with a war band to fight him and his black army but instead ended up raiding my own people."

"He is evil itself, and a black plague follows his horde," Shaw said. "Because he is on our common border, King Edgar wished to seek alliance with King Harthacnut of Balmore. We have engaged in a few minor skirmishes but never seen the knight himself. His forces are strong—"

"Unnaturally so," Bray interrupted.

"King Edgar believes our small army will be no match against him and hoped Harthacnut would assist," Shaw continued.

Cy shifted. "I have heard tales around the campfires of demonic occurrences. Unholy shrieks to make the blood freeze and the desecration of bodies. Did Harthacnut agree?"

"Readily so." Halton tipped his head toward Cy. "Though he confided he fears even our combined forces will do naught to halt this formidable enemy."

Shaw finished his dried venison. "King Edgar thought likewise, for he commissioned others to the kingdoms south and west at the same time he sent us."

"Not likely they will get involved until the problem is at their own door. Shortsighted fools!" Cy barked.

Halton again turned and gazed on the man. Cy saw the truth of the situation. "I look forward to talking around our own fires, for it seems you have experience of such fools."

"I can weave a good yarn. Should keep us entertained most of the trip." Cy offered an easy smile.

They rode much of the rest of the afternoon in blessed silence until Garrick could no longer hold his tongue. "Surely you do not intend to make us ride all night, sir?"

Cy turned. "Is your tender arse raw?"

Darrel spoke for the first time all day. "I have to admit my *skinny* rump could do for a rest. We are simple household servants, not hardened warriors, sir. Mayhaps a time on our feet would do us well."

Halton shot a glance to Corin beside him, and they agreed with a nod it would be best to call it an early night. They turned from the road and meandered about a half a league into the forest, finding an open space large enough to make camp among the oaks. Halton pulled the woman's horse near. Her emerald eyes cut into him with the lethal intent of a pair of daggers. *It is going to be a long trip, Lord.*

Chapter 4

"I'll gather firewood." Eldon set his saddle on the ground and turned to the tree line.

"May I assist him, sir? An extra pair of strong arms could be useful for all the wood we might need," Cy asked with a raised brow.

The men dismounted, and Halton untied the woman from the saddle and lowered her to the ground. Halton turned to judge Cy. The blond warrior continued to voice his eagerness to redeem himself of his past mistakes. What a stark contrast to the straight-backed, locked-jawed woman beside him. He gave the fidgeting warrior a quick nod, and the two men disappeared as he turned back to consider the lady.

"The anger flashing in your hard gaze does little to persuade me to unbind you, my lady. In fact, I believe I will take the added precaution of tethering you to a tree." The steel shackle, secured with its cotter and heavy length of rope, would not prevent her from escaping, but it might slow her long enough to alert one of them.

Once he secured her, he watched as she slumped to the ground, hands lifeless in her lap and head hanging. Like a defeated soldier, the battle now lost, no fight remained. Did she yearn for death as such a warrior often did? *Lord I pray she does not desire such an end.*

Turning from the gloom of her countenance, Halton shook his head as he watched Garrick still struggling to dismount his horse. When at last he worked his leg over the back of his mount, he fell to the ground with a thud that reverberated through Halton's leather soles. Garrick sat there for several moments stretching and rubbing his stiff appendages before he fought to his feet with great grunts. He staggered a few steps away and plopped his bulk on a fallen log near where Shaw and Darrel gathered rocks and cleared leaf litter in preparation for the fire.

Garrick rubbed his chubby hands together and licked his lips. "Supper."

Halton handed him a pot, "If you wish to eat, you must help. There is a stream in that direction," he pointed. "Follow the sound and fill this. Look for roots as you go." Halton shoved the pot into his hands before the glum man pushed himself up and lumbered away. Halton did not fear him running off. His great belly tied him to their food supply.

Darrel gathered tinder, and the slender young Bray struck the flint and coaxed an infant spark into a bright flame. Twigs snapped in the deep shadows. Cy and Corin materialized from the dusk, arms laden with fuel for the growing fire.

"Just in time," Bray cheered. "Dump your loads here."

"Looks as though we shall be warm this evening," Cy said as he brushed bits of bark and debris from his tunic.

Garrick lumbered toward the fire. "Sir? I only managed to find a couple of wild turnips and an onion. Will this meager amount even help? There are a lot of us men around the fire."

"Fear not, my big man," Corin said with a heavy sigh. "We have plenty of other ingredients to mix with these fresh vegetables. You will get enough to sustain you."

"Aye, well done, Garrick." Halton took the items to the woman. "Please clean these so Bray can cut them for the meal."

Without rising, she spun away and straightened her defiant back.

He took a deep breath, filling himself with the peace of his God. "If you provide no help, you will not eat." She sat like stone. Halton walked away and did the task himself.

Bray added the collected ingredients to others from their supplies and created a simple but hearty stew. It bubbled in the pot dangling over the flames, filling the air with the aroma of venison. Several stomachs voiced their eagerness. Halton turned to the woman, wanting to invite her to join their meal. He did not intend to make her go hungry, especially considering she missed her midday meal due to her adventure catapulting off her horse.

The lady lay curled as far from the fire as her tether allowed. Her back to them, she did not move. As the others sat around the fire to enjoy their meal, Halton retrieved a blanket, covered her, and offered her a steaming bowl. She flung both aside, and he walked away.

Later, as he stretched out near the fire, he noticed the warm covering wrapped snuggly about her. He lay his weary head down, staring into the flames and asked, *Lord, are You sure of this?*

An affirmation and the word "patience" came to mind. His muscles relaxed, and his breath came in slow, even sighs. *Yes, of course, Father, she is the one You have chosen, and I must be patient with her. My single day of kindness will do naught to wash away years of cruelty and abuse. Only Your love and kindness will soften her heart. Thank you, Father, for all the forbearance You have shown me.*

Halton stole a last quick glance at her.

The chirping of linnets and the cooing of doves pulled Halton from sleep. He rolled on his back and noticed the woman had move sometime in the night to be nearer the warmth of the fire. Satisfaction teased his lips to smile.

The others stirred. Bray rose and grabbed the supplies to mix dough. He set small lumps of it on a narrow tray to fry them for the breaking of the fast and the midday meal they would take in the saddle.

"I will go for water," Garrick said.

Halton marveled at his willingness.

"If it pleases you, m'lord, I will join him to fill our waterskins for the day," Darrel mumbled and Halton gave quick consent.

"We go to scare up some game," Corin said as he and Shaw swung their bows over their shoulders.

Cy stood glancing around and shifting from foot to foot. Halton understood the restlessness of a warrior forced to sit idle. Halton tossed him his own bow. "You any good with one of these?" Cy snatched it from the air and nodded with a foolish grin.

"Go set your hands to helping those hunters."

"Yes, sir." Cy disappeared before Halton could change his mind.

Next he approached the woman who sat with her arms wrapped around her knees pulled tight to her chest. "Good morrow, my lady. I wager you are hungry. Why not attend to the cakes for Bray? We should eat soon."

When she remained as still as a statue, he took hold of the ropes at her wrists and pulled her to her feet.

Her gaze narrowed on him. Actual flames seemed to flash in her vibrant green irises, but he resisted any thought of chastising her. Stepping aside, he motioned her toward the fire and the waiting cakes.

She looked at him a second more, stomped to the frying biscuits, and using her unbound foot, kicked the tray into the fire.

"Oh, my lady! What have you done?" Bray scrambled to rescue as many as he could. "Our day's meal. Ouch! Fie, nearly half are inedible now."

Halton looked at her in sober silence and watched her grow more straight, shoulders pushed back as if steeling herself for the coming blow. He did not strike out but shook his head sadly. She shuddered for an instant, and her eyes darted in a nervous flutter. "I regret you made this choice, my lady. We will have little to eat if the men fail to capture any game. I hope we are not all too weak to sit our saddles."

Her shoulders sagged and her head dropped, but Halton did no more to scold or discipline her. Finally, she turned away from him, stumbled to the end of her tether, and slumped to the ground—the picture of misery.

"No success, sir," Shaw announced as the three hunters returned.

"'Tis unfortunate," Bray grumbled.

"What happened?" Cy asked as his eyes went from the smoldering black nuggets in the fire to the woman crumpled in the leaf litter.

"A mere misstep, nothing to fret over," Bray said, and Halton stood a little taller at the kindness of his young knight.

Cy offered some of his gruel to the dejected woman. She shrugged away and refused, though her stomach's loud protests echoed in the clearing around the fire. Halton watched as first Cy, then Bray, and later Shaw's head rose at the sound, and they gazed at her with furrowed brows.

With the meal completed and the fire doused, they climbed into their saddles. Garrick led his stout dapple to stand near the fallen log and strained into the saddle. Halton moved to offer the woman a boost, but she mounted unaided. She bit her lip until tears pooled—a clear sign to Halton that she injures incurred in the fall pained her.

Halton lashed her to the pommel. "I have found a name for you, my lady," he said with eagerness. "Until you tell us otherwise, we shall call you Mariamne, for it means rebellious. And if I have ever met a *rebellious* soul, 'tis you, Lady Mariamne." He gathered her reins and returned their group to the road.

"Mariamne. I like it." Cy drew his horse beside her. "'Tis a good and proper name." He smiled at her, but Halton watched as she turned to face the road ahead, staring glassy-eyed and unfocused.

"How did you know Mariamne means rebellious, sir?" Cy asked.

Halton could not suppress a joyful grin. "My grandmother was of God's people, a Jew, and she taught me a great many things."

Garrick held his tongue for much of the day, though he still assured the midday meal commenced exactly at the sun's zenith. With biscuits lost to the fire, they ate the remaining stale cakes with their staple of jerky. Mariamne refused to eat from another's hands.

"Sir!" Corin announced causing everyone to look up. "There are early ripe raspberries there."

"Berries!" Garrett sang out, urging his horse toward them.

"We will dismount and enjoy God's provision for us." Halton sighed.

"I will stay on my horse and get the higher ones," Garrick offered. Berry juice already stained his fingers and ran down his chin.

Halton released Mariamne from the pommel. She slid from the saddle but stayed near her horse. Then, as though her raucous stomach overruled her pride, she shoved handfuls of the bright berries into her mouth.

When they turned to remount, Halton chuckled at her stained fingers and mouth. In that moment he could almost see the wild beast within, covered in some creature's blood. He wet a small strip of cloth handing it her to clean before she remounted.

The journey resumed, but less than an hour later, Mariamne started retching over the side of her horse. Bray tried to pull his mount to a safe distance.

Halton stopped as she lost more of the blood-colored berries onto the dusty road. "Oh Lady Mariamne, forgive me."

She straightened and tried to wipe the vomit from her mouth onto her shoulder, but again she flinched in pain.

Halton reached and gently cleaned her face with the cloth. She lowered her gaze, and her pink cheeks deepened to crimson, yet she lifted her face to encourage him to finish.

"Dear Lady, I did not consider how long it must have been since you ate a proper meal or I never would have allowed you to gorge on the berries. Your poor belly knows not what to do with so much after suffering without. The hard seeds are further multiplying your discomfort."

She jerked over her horse's left shoulder and expelled the last of the hateful fruit.

Again Halton wiped her face and offered her a little water to cleanse her mouth.

She shrugged him off, the berries at last banished. She settled and they continued.

They rode until near dark, when Garrick's whining grew intolerable and they set camp. Mariamne approached the fire unbidden and cleaned the night's roots. Though she remained tethered, Halton loosened her bindings enough for her to assist with the preparations of the stew.

Halton approached her. "Here you are, Lady Mariamne. This bit of broth should provide you with nourishment but not cause the upset of the berries."

She took slow sips from the wooden bowl.

Later Cy reached for her bowl and refilled it. "Well, it seems as if it is going to stay down. Why not try a little more?"

She ate all they gave her.

Chapter 5

Mariamne stirred as Halton approached the next morn. His feet crunched the leaf litter in a slow, purposeful pace. He took a knee before her, tenderness caressing his face. "I am amenable, my lady, to unbinding your hands—though the tether will remain—if you are keen to assist with the cakes."

An empty numbness consumed her like a dragon devouring her from within. Naught remained open to her but to comply. It mattered little her antics and her attempts to escape, for these odd men remained kind and considerate of her. She loathed recalling how she had retched from her saddle the day prior. Heat stung her sunburned cheeks.

The others lent a hand to the making of camp or preparing of meals and earned praise and gratitude for their efforts—no matter how small. Could she expect like treatment? No, not for her. Everything differed for her. But her current rebellion only served to confine her all the more. Mayhaps it would be worth trying to behave, if only to prove she would not receive the same favor as the men.

She lifted her hands. Once freed, she moved to the fire to turn the cakes until they glowed a golden brown.

"These are wonderful," Cy praised her.

She brushed aside his continued kindness—such sentiments would not last.

"Best I have ever eaten," Garrick agreed, licking the crumbs off his fingers.

She turned from the man who found any food to his liking then sat and nibbled on a cake as she stared into the fire. When their praise persisted, she walked to the end of her tether and turned her back on them. She too received praise and thanks for her small part in their simple meal—yet the foreign experience set her heart pounding and her muscles clenching. She trusted not these men—or any man. On the rare occasions kindness had been employed, 'twas for the purpose of wooing her into compliance. She would not bend to their desires. It mattered little the kindness showered upon her—she would bend to no man's will.

Sun, oh glorious sun. As they rode clear of the deep forest onto the open road, she turned her face to the radiant light and drank in its warmth. The light and heat bit at her exposed skin, but even this limited freedom—out of the dark cell and in the sun with the hawfinches calling welcome to her—oh, 'twas beyond marvelous. Were she not soundly tied to her saddle, she could imagine running through the fields, hands raised in reckless abandon, joining the bright birds' songs.

Halton increased their speed, and she shifted as her mount set a steady rhythm on the hard-packed road. This man, Halton, pushed them harder each day. He appeared as eager to reach their destination as she dreaded the same. Her horse settled into a canter, and she dug her heels into the stirrups for more comfort. Her hands scraped against the coarse ropes and stung fiercely with the sunburn covering her exposed skin after she had languished so long in the dark underbelly of the dungeon. While unbound this morn, she noticed her hands darkening where the ropes did not hide them from the sun. The bound area of her skin remained ashen white.

She lifted her shoulders and let them fall as an exasperated sigh fluttered over her tongue. She could not run free, for the rope held her in bondage. Still a slave, bound for some unknown fate, she despaired of ever knowing freedom. Her jaw locked, and her teeth ground together as reality settled on her with the weight of the approaching mountains.

Her head shifted from the welcoming sun, her eyes opened to the endless road before them, and she met Halton's gaze as he glanced over his shoulder at her. She avoided his tender stare as he inclined his head to her again. Once he turned forward, her eyes followed his gaze into the unknown stretching before them. Her mind leapt like a drunken rabbit from one notion to the next.

Mariamne. She considered her new name once more. She found it wholly more pleasing than many of the vile things she remembered being called. She could not recall ever having a proper name. *Slave Girl* remained the kindest designation ever afforded her. Again her shoulders rose. A painful twinge rumbled down her right arm before they dropped in another deep sigh, but a wry smile fought to break through her hard shell and dance on her lips. *Mariamne.* The pleasantness of the name belied its meaning. She found it a fitting name indeed, for her own outward appearance told nothing of the deep-seated rebellion hidden beneath. She favored this new epithet and intended to keep it—come what may in the days ahead.

Five years! She fought a rumbling deep growl. Her heart staggered anew at the possibility of being the property of the horrid little Jarel for such a time. Was it possible to have been imprisoned so long? It would not be beyond the slave master to say five years when in truth only two had passed. She searched her memory to recall how many solstice festivals she overheard the guards discussing. After several moments she tossed her head in frustration, a tiny bubble of disgust escaping into the still air. With two celebrations occurring each year and no light in the underbelly of the slave market to distinguish the long days from the short, she could not be sure how long he had held her.

Were it five, would this mark her twenty-fourth year? No, the newly leafed trees and blooming flowers spoke of spring, and her birth occurred in the cold of winter, thus making her twenty-five—if Jarel spoke truth. How was it she could not recall a father or mother, yet she knew beyond doubt that her birth came in winter? Again frustration overwhelmed her. She wanted to shake off her bounds and scream to the heavens. No manner of life deserved the unknowing emptiness of this existence. Tempests of emotions raged within her, heating her insides as the sun did her flesh.

She pushed aside the old angst and picked up the trail of her length held in captivity. Twenty-five years and nothing but a nightmare of a life to note its passing. Sour fumes touched the back of her tongue. In her earliest memories, she was a girl of about ten; she vaguely recalled working on a farm. *Was it my family's farm or one I served on as a common laborer?* Flashes of harvests and winters at the spindle and loom flittered through her mind with the speed and color of bright hummingbirds, but the people of her memories had no faces or names. They remained blurs in a sea of hazy recollections. She resented their obtuseness and efforts to stay hidden from her.

The next recollection to present itself found her in her early teens. She had been sent—*or was I sold?*—to a manor house. She worked in the fields for a few years before being brought into the house as an attendant for the daughter of the lord. Her hands fisted beneath her bindings. The pampered girl required naught—not another servant or another bobble. It had been the lecherous master who desired another conquest. Her muscles went rigid as stone. How she hated him! She had endeavored never to find herself alone with the lascivious man. She straightened, pride filling her. She had been successful for a time. But then Lord Hasomoth found her in the library returning a book for her sniveling mistress—the girl could not read her own name! A shudder raged through her at the memory of what happened next. Her wrists scraped against her coarse bindings, adding their discomfort to the pain she stirred by the memory. Her vision filled with it.

Hasomoth again stood blocking her escape. She blinked to clear her sight as her heart pounded louder than the gait of her horse.

"Please my lord, allow me to pass. I must return to my mistress," she had pleaded.

"You are such a delectable treat. And I have waited far too long." He seized her roughly and pinned her to the divan under his weight. As he released her arm to raise her skirts she shrieked and raked his cheek with her sharp nails.

"You filthy wretch!"

All these years later, the agony returned fresh as she remembered how his fist drove deep into her ribs. She remembered the sound of bones cracking, and she trembled.

"You will pay."

Mariamne closed her eyes. Her only relief had come when the lord's wife entered the room.

"What in heaven's name?" Lady Hasomoth stammered.

Mariamne smoothed her skirts with shaking hands.

The wise lady's eyes darted from her faithless husband to the frightened slave and then back again. Her eyes narrowed on her husband. "You are a wretch, Rupert. At least she has the decency to resist your unwanted advances." She crossed her arms. "You may send her away or sell her to a slave trader if you wish, but you will not bed her—and I forbid you killing her."

Lord Hasomoth opened his mouth to protest, but his wife whirled on him. "Remember how you acquired your title, my lord. Think long and hard on it before you defy me."

Mariamne escaped the manor, but Lord Hasomoth exacted his revenge in the only manner his wife would permit. Though spared an assault, she suffered the debilitating agony of a whipping.

She opened her eyes and straightened as the misery flooded her mind and stung her long-healed back. The punishment left her barely able to stand by the time they threw her in a cell on the upper level of Jarel's compound. The slave master had been away when she arrived, but he found her soon enough upon his return.

"Well, well, what a pretty thin' you are." He licked his lips as he entered her cell. "I should think it wise to sample these goods. I could then better advise potential buyers of the quality of this product."

When he approached her, she tried to pull away, but the pain wracking her body proved intolerable and deprived her of the strength to do more than take her next breath. He touched her and she moaned with such gut-wrenching agony he withdrew his offending hand.

He stepped from the cell and secured the door with a heart-crushing clank.

"What is it, Master?" a guard had asked just outside the door.

"She growled like some fearsome beast," Jarel stammered.

"The man who sold her said she clawed her master's face until none could unrecognized him."

By some unforeseen miracle, Jarel never came at her again, limiting his abuse to words and a passing brush thereafter. But her continued snarls and growls kept him at bay. He had spoken the truth, however, when he told Halton others had purchased her and attempted to *tame* her.

A smile tickled her lips as she recalled how she had left each would-be master bloodied before he returned her to Jarel's cells.

Now here she sat with a new group of men. New, yet unlike any man she could recall. She watched them with a hawkish gaze born of constantly being threatened, but in these two days she found no evidence of any of them leering at her or even taking much notice of her. Halton and Cy looked on her more than the others, but there was something different in their gazes. She knew naught of what this unfamiliar glance meant, but it stirred unease for reasons she could not comprehend. Regardless of what it meant, she did not care for it.

Truly, Halton made no sense at all. She shifted her gaze toward him again and noticed his straight back and broad shoulders. The sun sparkled off the tips of his short-cropped hair as he rode in front of her. What was the man about? What did he want? All men wanted something. He made no overt actions to force himself on her—nor did any of the others. But all men wanted such things.

She sighed again. He had never yelled—though he possessed skill in the art. Again a smirk toyed at the corners of her lips as she remembered how Jarel cowered under his unbridled wrath. While he was more than capable of berating, no harsh words had yet passed his lips toward her. He oft sounded more sad than angry.

Her jaw tightened and her teeth snapped together to the rhythm of her mount. What a distasteful feeling his disappointment stirred. She knew well the sting of a hand and the cut of a whip, but his displeasure unsettled in a way she resented more than all the others.

Just strike and be done with it. She harbored a silent rage at him. *Show not your disapproval and expect change to spring forth.* She drew herself up tall and unbending as her jaw became locked in a vow. *I will change for no man.*

Chapter 6

"We have fallen into a predictable routine, m'lady. Is it not good to be out of that pit?" Cy rolled her blanket into a small parcel. He offered her an easy smile, and his merry whistling commenced once more.

Mariamne watched him, her middle twisting into profound knots. But his eyes never left hers, conveying everything of friendship and kindness, and nothing of lust.

As he turned and saddled her horse, the pressure simmered inside her, making her head feel like it would soon explode. Her teeth grated together as her jaw seized shut. Perpetually merry, the men enjoyed all manner of freedoms. Yet, Halton kept her restrained, and chastised her. A shudder ran through her as she recalled the previous evening.

Halton had stirred in his sleep. "Lady Mariamne, it is well past midnight. Where do you hope to go in the dark of night?" he asked before she could grasp the cotter to free herself from the shackle tethering her. He sat up. "I can sleep in the saddle, my lady. I will sit here and watch over you to assure you come to no harm."

Mariamne swiveled on her rump, gave him her back, and stamped her feet in the leaf litter, causing it to crackle and crunch her disappointment.

"Problem, sir?"

"No, Cy, Lady Mariamne fancied a pre-dawn walk, but I have prevailed on her to remain."

"It would be my honor to take the next watch. I give my oath no harm will befall her." He stated the words with a conviction that caused her to look at him. He held her glance—steady and unwavering in the low firelight. Why did he swear to protect her? She closed her eyes and turned away, for his gaze seemed to bore into her heart.

Halton yawned as he answered. "I will wake you in two hours."

"Aye, sir."

Mariamne's clenched her fist, recalling the event. While Cy, Darrel, and Garrick where permitted to wander unguarded, they barely allowed her the kindness of a sheltered moment to relieve herself. The inequality boiled like a kettle left unattended over a flame.

Halton's words interrupted her seething.

"Corin? Do we carry an extra blade?"

"Aye, sir. Two in fact. Shaw carries one and I the other."

Shaw untied the weapon and approached Halton. The fire burning within Mariamne erupted as the older man accepted the sword in its sheath and approached Cy.

"You are well liked by my men, Cy, and I trust you. We are nearing the border, and I would welcome another blade to defend us should the need arise."

Cy took a knee before the man. "It would be my honor to serve, sir. May I continue to be found worthy in your eyes."

As Cy strapped the long weapon to his side, Mariamne glared at the favored man. Visions of running them through with the blade danced in her head.

Bray slapped Cy on the shoulder. "You are now more guard than guarded. Sir Halton is not one to give unwarranted praise. You can be assured, we are fortunate to have you among our number."

"Aye," the others echoed.

Mariamne picked up a rock near her feet and hurled it at them with a choked shriek. The men ducked the projectile and turned to her wide-eyed.

As the men opened their mouths to offer their heated objections to her unruly behavior, Halton stepped between them, a deep scowl twisting his kind face with displeasure. "It is past time we resumed our journey. To your saddles."

The men moved to their mounts, narrowing their gaze on her.

The group took the road and settled into a loping gait as the sun crested over the distant mountains. The men bantered cheerfully as rumbles of disgust rolled in Mariamne's chest.

Cy turned to address the man riding the horse behind hers. "Darrel, it has scarce been a week, and already you are looking twice the man you were."

"Do I look half the man I was?" Garrick asked with earnest hope.

"It may take another week to reach such a lofty goal, Garrick," Shaw said.

"Oh, do not whimper so, man," Darrel chided him. "It is far simpler for a destitute man to gain than the reverse."

"Oh, aye, we have time yet before we arrive in Veronia. We will all see the difference by then," Halton said. "Remember you are limber enough to mount your horse now."

"And your whining has improved as well, Garrick," Bray offered with a sharp chuckle.

Mariamne closed her ears to the men's verbal jousting. Not a single bit of cheer could she find, bound as she was to her saddle. She refused to hear them. But without their banter, her mind became occupied with Halton's ominous behavior and troubling words.

Each day he increased their speed and pushed them longer. This morn he armed the blond slave next to her. Halton confounded her. He treated the slaves as friends, and it played havoc with her understanding of the world.

When night descended and they made camp, Halton offered her a small dagger to assist Bray in preparing the meal. Her mind filled with the sight of ramming it into him. But the smile he offered acted as a firm staying hand covering hers. He left her and dropped to his knees in a posture of prayer.

"Sir Halton, which God do you serve?" Cy asked.

"There is but one God, the Father, of whom all things are." Halton spoke with an assuredness Mariamne failed to comprehend.

And neither could Cy, apparently, for he pressed, "But, sir, how can you say there is but one God, when all Balmore worships a great multitude?"

"'Thus saith the Lord the King and redeemer, the Lord of hosts, I am the first, and I am the last, and without me is there no God.' 'And rent your heart, and not your clothes: and turn unto the Lord your God, for He is gracious and merciful, slow to anger, and of great kindness, and repenteth him of the evil.'" Halton's firm voice resonated, leaving no room for question.

Cy leaned forward, "Will you teach me of this one God?"

Darrel and Garrick affirmed the request.

Mariamne glanced at Halton as he turned toward the men. She became stone, as an inner glow filled him. Delight flooded his face, his lips disappeared, and his teeth shown within the most enormous smile. "It would be my greatest honor to instruct you in the wonders of the Mighty God."

Something stirred in Mariamne—a hunger born not of her stomach but somewhere deep in her soul. She shook to free herself of it. When it would not release her, she moved her hands closer to the flames until the pain drove away the unwanted thoughts.

I will no more follow some invisible God than a man. The gods give me nothing, and I will afford them no penance or adoration. She wiggled around until the tip of the dagger dug into the palm of her hand. Drops of blood appeared before the yearning fled.

Chapter 7

Subtle changes overtook the men. Halton went to his knees more frequently and for longer periods of time. He made her dizzy with his repeated circuits around their camp muttering protection over them.

"Lord Almighty, protect us. Set Your angels about us. Guard us from the evil one."

He came to the fire to eat, his face ashen. "Shaw, Corin, Bray, Eldon, and Cy, tonight we take turns standing watch. No more than two hours each. We need our rest as much as protection. We dare not fail in either."

Mariamne shuddered at the growing trepidation. What stirred the fear? The tree-lined road before appeared identical to the tree-lined road behind. They passed shires filled with happy people, unaware of any unseen dangers.

The men's anxiety fed her fear just as Bray's meals nourished her flesh.

Snap! Her eyes again focused on their surroundings, and her heart lodged in her throat. Eldon's horse faltered on the uneven branch broken under his hoof. Gray clouds boiled above, and yet long shadows snaked out toward her. The trees hid their bright colors. The men's easy chatter choked to tense silence.

As they turned off to make camp, Mariamne noticed the deepening of the creases about Halton's face. His brows furrowed until they all but touched. This night he only stopped his circling prayers to speak blessing over the food.

"Lord Most High, Provider and Sustainer, we come before You this night and thank You for Your continued sustenance and protection. We have delighted in the tender care of Your hand, and we ask for Your protection again this night. Send Your angels to surround us and hide us from the evil one and those who serve him as they seek to root us out, to kill, and to destroy. We thank You in advance for Your answer. In the precious name of our Savior, Jesus Christ. Amen."

Mariamne sat in rapt wonder at such an odd prayer. The entreaty was deeply personal and intimate, so unlike the mindless rote petitions so many uttered in the dark cells of the slave compound. He spoke with assurance he would be answered.

The words of the prayer stirred her emotions. The ominous words of being hunted by things wanting 'to root out, to kill, and to destroy' initially quickened her heart, and great torrents of fear crashed within her. But yet, Halton's trust in his God and the protection He provided calmed her like nothing before and washed away the fear. He did not pray timidly or hopefully. He was confident and certain they would be safe. Nevertheless, Halton continued his circuits, stopping to sleep only when another took his place.

Mariamne woke several times in the night to sounds in the forest beyond the light of the well-tended fire. Once she caught a glimpse of what looked like white eyes shining in the flame's glow. An eerie chorus of whispering voices called to her. She shuddered and moved closer to Halton, who lay behind her.

Before first light, the whispers of the men drew her out of her fretful sleep.

"They came close last night," Bray muttered.

Shaw threw a log on the fire, sending sparks into the pre-dawn light. "A great number of them, by the sound of it."

"We are unharmed. They could not cross the barriers our God

placed around us." Halton appeared calm, but the furrow continued to crease his forehead as he turned and checked on her. "Let us eat and be on our way. The faster we move now, the sooner we will be out of these enspelled woods and safely in Veronia."

Mariamne listened, but no one spoke of hearing voices calling to them, and her stomach twisted in tight knots of dread.

They galloped much of the day, pausing only to rest the horses. Every voice became as mute as Mariamne's as a strange malevolent mist snaked between the numerous trees. Gooseflesh covered her. Mariamne tried to shake it off, but she conceded the forest possessed an almost oppressive weight surrounding them. She looked to Halton for guidance and saw his head bowed in prayer.

Whether due to his prayers or something else, the mist never reached the road. But it grew thick and black among the trees. Its sinister darkness blocked the setting sun.

Corin drew near Halton. "We must make camp…"

"'Tis early yet," Halton said.

"We cannot proceed safely without torches."

Halton sighed. "We will camp there." He pointed to a clearing a half a league ahead.

"It is small, sir, but the trees should be far enough from the center to give us warning if anyone—or anything—approaches." Cy sounded confident, but as Mariamne turned to him, she noted the deep lines now etched in his face. "We will watch over you, m'lady," he assured her.

Fear stifled their appetites, and Mariamne lay by the large fire trying to sleep as Eldon took first watch. She wrestled with her blanket as sleep eluded her, only to be awakened at near the same instant she captured a moment of slumber.

A sweet voice cooed to her. It used a name she could not fully comprehend, but it beckoned. She rose, stretching her arms high above her head, and arched her long back. Dawn had come and gone with midday close in its approach. The day shone clear and bright with no oppressive fog. She glanced around in disbelief at the men still fast asleep.

"They are overtired by the fear Halton is stirring in them. They need their sleep. Come to us," the voice invited. "We promise you a place of peace where no man will ever hurt you. A place where every need will be provided for and you will lounge in unimaginable comfort."

She hesitated, her insides divided between longing and dread.

"Come to us. You will be *free*."

Caution lost its grip on her, and she mindlessly reached for the dagger Halton had foolishly left with her the night before. She cut through the rope tethering her to the older man as the voices cheered her success. With the men snoring, she stood and walked toward the enticing voices as cheerful cries joined it, filling the still air with their celebration.

"Yes, you are free. Come now before they wake."

Mariamne stopped. Apprehension twisted to doubt. She turned back to the camp, and her eyes opened to the truth. The light of day vanished, and cold reality kissed her skin with gooseflesh. Deep night still blanketed the land, but a brilliant light reaching to the heavens surrounded the men. The warm light welcomed her and offered true safety. She took a step back toward it and the truth it held.

A hand seized her arm. She struggled to free herself of the grip as she looked down onto the form of a shriveled man covered in black mud leaving only the whites of his eyes to be seen. She lashed out as terror gripped her. Another dark figure grabbed her other arm, and they pulled her toward the trees.

Chapter 8

Halton bolted to his feet as if the Lord Himself shouted his name. "Shaw, Darrell, build the fire!"

Who stood guard? He scanned around him as the others scrambled to their feet in the dim glow of the embers. Shaw, Darrell, Corin, Garrick, Eldon, and Cy—all present. Bray. No sign of him. He would never leave his post. Halton moved his foot, but when it came too easily he knelt and collected the tether rope at his ankle until he came to the severed end. Straightening, he cast a wide glance toward the tree line as the flames leapt to life with a pop behind him.

"Mariamne!" he bellowed as his innards twisted painfully.

"Cy, Eldon, Shaw—watch for Bray, but remain and secure the camp. Garrick and Darrel—mind the fire. Corin—with me." Halton barked as he drew his sword and raced for the woman.

His captain's blade slid from its sheath, and his heavy footfalls kept pace with Halton's as they sprinted for the forest. "Lord, protect her and help us."

The moment Halton and Corin entered the dark woods, the holy light they carried within them filled their blades and made them glow a brilliant white. The swords' light lit deep ruts created by Mariamne's new shoes as her captors had dragged her away.

Undergrowth rustled as the horde fled from the truth in the light. A woman's voice cried out to their right. "Save me, sir."

The men gave it no attention.

A more frantic plea wafted through the still night air, followed by several more desperate wails. They sounded from various points around them, but Halton and Corin followed the tracks.

Mariamne's trail became lost in rocky ground. Their slow progress grew intolerable, and Halton called to the heavens. "Please, Lord, aid us in saving Your daughter."

A shriek—like that of a cornered polecat—rent the silence, and the men raced toward it.

Mariamne tried to jerk free of the blackened hands. She saw Halton on his feet. Terror filled his bellowed cry. More little men joined the two and followed as those securing her took a zigzagging path among the trees. The creatures spread out and started to call to Halton in a woman's voice. Something within her rejoiced in the realization these foul little men did not know the truth of her silence. Nor would the men coming to her rescue be fooled by their attempts.

The breath fled her lungs as they slammed her to the ground. She lay on her back, fighting to recapture air. One cackling creature held her arms above her head while the other fought with her skirt. She kicked at it.

When it could not gain access, it straddled her and rent her bodice. She shrieked.

More cloth tore.

Another violent scream burst from her lungs.

Radiant light filled the tiny clearing where she lay held on the moist earth. A flaming sword burst through the creature sitting atop her. The beast bellowed and vanished in a puff of gray smoke. The one holding her hands tried to flee. His small head toppled from his body, bouncing once before it too vanished into vapor.

Mariamne shot to her feet, flailing.

Hands reached for her.

She pulled away and stumbled.

Something seized her wrists, saving her from the fall.

She lashed out, but her wrists were pushed to her chest, and a strong arm encircled her. She wiggled and writhed in the tight hold. A whisper tickled her ear, but fear stole the words. Another hand cradled the back of her head, and the whisper brushed her face again.

"Peace, Mariamne. Shh. You are safe, my lady. No one will harm you. I have you, Mariamne, and you are safe."

Halton—he held her secure.

"You are safe, my lady."

The fight ended—her strength fled with her next exhale. Her knees buckled, and she slid to the ground, still wrapped in Halton's comforting embrace as he descended with her. She gripped his tunic. Desperation drove her to never want to be separated from him again. Hot tears slid down her cheeks and wet the cloth as he stroked her hair.

He held her a moment longer. "My lady, we must return to the clearing and the protection of the others."

As she pulled away, the temping voices filled her thoughts. They called her to her doom, and her hands flew to her ears.

Halton must have understood. He covered her hands with his own, raised his eyes to the fog-hidden stars, and spoke a prayer she could hear even through the muffle of both their hands.

"Mighty God, come swiftly to the aid of Your daughter. Make her deaf to the call of the evil ones. Shut their mouths so they hold no power over her. In Your name, Jesus Christ. Amen."

His gaze dropped to hers again, and she became aware once more of the light surrounding him. He removed his hands, and she did likewise, marveling at a forest utterly devoid of sound—save a nearby trickling stream.

Halton kept his eyes level with hers as he pulled off his cloak and wrapped it around her, covering her damaged clothes. Though she was not totally exposed, very little remained to cover her. Heat filled her cheeks as she tried to gather up the tattered pieces. She looked back at Halton's gentle face and marveled to see the man taking no advantage. He covered her completely before his eyes ever left hers. She stole a glance at Corin, who occupied himself scanning the darkness for more enemies.

Unwanted tears pooled again, and her head dropped uninvited to Halton's chest as they continued to sit on the forest floor.

He put one strong arm around her and took her hand, helping her to stand, "You will feel better once we are out of these evil-infested woods and near the warmth of the fire."

Halton offered Corin his sword. "Captain, lead us."

"Aye." Corin lifted both weapons and lit their way with the strange glow.

She drew strength from Halton as he wrapped her in a steady arm to prevent her from stumbling.

The others raced to greet them when they emerged from the trees. Garrick brought her water, and Cy handed her a blanket, both of which she accepted with a newfound gratitude.

She watched as they stole glances at Halton. He shook his head and reassured them, "She is unharmed."

They breathed a collective sigh of relief. It rattled her insides, set her heart to pounding, and pulled hot tears from her eyes again. She staggered under the weight of their compassion. Her knees grew weak once more, but before she could unwrap her hands to catch herself, Cy cradled her. Like Halton, his touch said nothing of desire and everything of kindness, increasing the flow of tears. She did not understand these men.

As Cy set her near the fire, Halton approached her with a boyish smile and something small in his strong hand. Kneeling before her, he said awkwardly, "I could not reckon why I would grab a needle and thread when we left near a month ago, but God knew there would be a need. May I repair your garment, my lady?"

She pulled the blanket and the borrowed cloak about her. Without a word, Garrick stood, collected his blanket, and held it in front of her. Turning his back to her, he spread the blanket wide between his hands to shield her. Cy, Shaw, Darrel, and Eldon did likewise until they completely surrounded her within a protective wall. Someone approached, and an over tunic appeared between the blankets.

After a few moments, she tugged on a couple of the blankets, and the wall evaporated as silently and respectfully as it appeared. Cy smiled at her with an approving nod. "The knight's tunic becomes you, m'lady." He moved to the other side of the fire and sat watching her.

Mariamne lay in the warmth of the fire and the kindness of these men and drifted to sleep.

Chapter 9

Hands rested on Mariamne's shoulders. Their grip tightened and proceeded to shake. Fear churned inside her, but her eyes would not open, as though a weight anchored them closed.

The grasping hands became more desperate and then came Halton's voice. His words wafted far away, garbled. An icy hand rested on her face, and she managed to pry one eyelid open. She moaned at the sun's weak light.

The evil fog now lay dense around the clearing. Her pulse quickened. A tremor shuddered through her. The men stood around her as Halton knelt and cradled her face. A gasp and murmur rolled among them.

"Eldon, Corin—search for Bray," Halton instructed as his lips drew to a sharp line.

Mariamne stirred lazily as if the oppressive fog had settled within her head. Halton called her name and his hand rested on her shoulder, but she could not pull from of the mental haze engulfing her.

She blinked and the other lid opened, but he looked hazy. As she stared up at him, his lips almost disappeared in their tight strain across his face. His gaze held her with an intensity that set her waking stomach to twisting. The vein in his neck bulged.

He grabbed the borrowed tunic covering her with one hand and his dagger with the other. "Forgive me, Mariamne, but I need to look for wounds."

The fabric rent as he exposed her to a few inches below her

collarbone. She would have fought him, but the horrified gasp of the men still standing over her turned her to stone.

Her thoughts turned to a muddy river bottom. What concerned them? What did they plan to do to her? A nightmare engulfed her of all of them coming at her. Coils of fear wound through her. But even as the panic worked at clearing her haze, the alarm in their eyes sent her apprehension spiraling in a new direction.

Halton spoke to Garrick and Shaw. "Gather the coals and remaining wood and get the fire hot." Next he directed Cy. "Give every dagger and knife we have to Shaw." He rolled up his sleeves and turned to Darrel. "Find pieces of cloth. Wet them and bring them to me with the remainder of our water."

As he knelt beside her barking orders, Mariamne looked and found great dark snaking web-like tendrils under her pale skin. They emanated from long furrows of deep black. She gathered enough strength to move her stiff arms in an attempt to brush away the charred marks.

Halton captured her hand, "I am so sorry, my lady," he moaned, his voice etched with dread and his words strangled. "It is the sickness, a poison of the evil one, and I must remove it before you are lost."

Mariamne forced her eyes to focus as she fought to escape her mental fog. Gazing at the growing flames and pile of daggers, her heart lurched. She looked back to the man towering over her. He intended to cut the blackened flesh out with hot blades.

Another thought slammed into like raging floodwaters. The creatures last night were not covered in mud. Their bodies were filled with this poison. Fear choked her and she shuddered violently. She struggled to sit up. *Get away. Escape.*

Halton glanced up at Cy standing at her head and nodded.

Her head and shoulders had barely risen off the ground when Cy dropped to his knees and pinned her flailing arms to the ground on either side of her.

She tried to jerk free as Corin secured her legs, and her eyes flew to Halton as her lungs turned to stone and her heart hammered. She thrashed within the men's grasp.

Tears threatened to tumble over Halton's lids. He lay his hand on her cheek and spoke in a raspy whisper, "I am so sorry, my lady. I never intended to hurt you, but this poison must be burned out now, or all will be lost."

She thrashed in vain against the men holding her. Cy and Corin would not yield. She could have moved more if a whole house collapsed on her.

She jerked from Halton's comforting hand.

"I vow to make quick work of it."

Darrel returned with the cloth and water. Halton rent and wet it. He tied a piece over his nose and mouth. "Darrel and Garrick, tie one over Cy and Corin's faces."

Next the others stepped several feet away and prayed audibly over them.

Halton placed a final damp cloth over her face. She shook it off. He picked it up, his voice calm but earnest, "It would be far worse to breathe in the dying spores, for there is no way to remove it from the lungs." He replaced the cloth.

She stilled. Her heart pounded She fought for breath.

As the first hot blade approached her flesh, loud screams erupted in her skull. The evil within sensed its impending doom. It filled her head with such a cacophony of noise her stomach lurched with the nausea. A searing blade pressed onto her skin. Agonizing pain. A scream tore both from her lungs and from the evil dying within.

The cooled blade lifted, replaced by a searing one. Halton moaned miserably, "Forgive me." The torture continued as five more blades pressed against her skin in rapid succession, giving her no time to recover. The torment paused, and the cloth slipped from her face.

Halton whimpered as he tenderly brushed away some of the tears cascading back into her hair. "My lady? Can you look at me?"

She could not move. She drank in the respite and refused to think the pain could continue.

He commanded her. "Mariamne, look at me—please."

She struggled to comply. Her pain blurred his face in her tear-filled vision.

"Is it done?" Cy groan.

"I see yet another black spot in her iris. I still have not rid her of it. Did they touch you anywhere else?" he asked, the words muffled by the cloth over his mouth and nose.

Her strength gone, sleep beckoned like a long-lost friend, and her eyes slid closed.

Halton grabbed her shoulders and shook her back to awareness. "Are you hurt anywhere else, my lady?"

She stared at him, not caring over minor hurts. She longed only for the blessed comfort of nothingness.

Halton shook her again, and a moment of clarity filled her as she remembered where the poisoned-filled men intended to place their spore. A horrified shudder stole her breath. Her thoughts clear, and she had kicked the creature from her before he could…

Clarity dawning, she wiggled her left arm under Cy's grasp. He released her arm and she hoisted it to Halton.

He rolled the sleeve until it exposed three puncture wounds and their webs growing up her forearm. He sighed, and his eyes slid closed for a moment. He covered her face and placed Cy's hand lower on her arm to secure her again.

More burning. Another look at her eyes. Pressure eased when Cy and Corin released her. A splash of water cooled her inflamed collar and arm. She welcomed the bliss of unconsciousness, allowing it to wrap her in comfort.

She jolted awake. Four of the men rested around her. One man lay before her, another behind her, another at her feet, and the last at her head. The other three stood beyond them, facing out, further encircling her.

Halton's short hair poked out of his cloak pulled high over his face. Fearing she may be drawn away again, she gripped the cloth and willed—no begged—for the protection he had prayed over her.

Sleep captured her again.

Chapter 10

The cloak pulled from her hand and ripped Mariamne from a blissful sleep. She reached out, trying to grasp its comfort.

A tender hand covered hers and Halton soothed, "All is well, my lady. Fear naught. We are here. You are safe."

After many attempts, she managed to pry her weary eyelids open and look into his gentle face. His lingering smile reassured her. "May I check your wounds?"

She gave half a nod as she flopped onto her back. She did not possess the strength to fight him or even refuse him.

He removed the cloth covering her arm.

She feared the wound she would find and blinked in disbelief. Little evidence of the punctures, and none of the black poison, remained to give testament to the attack. Her skin, while red, bore no sign of welts or raw, damaged flesh. Even in her haze she knew she should see the wounds suffered by having repeated hot blades pressed against her skin. She closed her eyes, fighting to make sense of what her eyes and skin testified. But even this simple mental effort taxed her limited strength.

Halton brushed the skin, stirring a dull sting.

She looked again at where the black tendrils had snaked across her skin but a few hours ago. Halton nodded and cocked his head to one side. "It is an odd thing. The burning serves only to affect the poison and not the flesh containing it." He exhale and his high-perched shoulders fell as he looked at her.

"If the poison is caught early, it can be burned away with no permanent injuries or scars, but the more flesh that is infested, the greater the trauma to the poor soul infected."

Mariamne looked again at her arm, seeing her skin virtually untouched.

Halton sat back on his heels. When he spoke, sorrow tainted his strong voice. "More victims die from the burning than from the poison itself. As the spore dies, it seems to suck away the victim's life. Those who survive the cleansing are oftentimes left bedridden for days or weeks, too drained of their vital strength to lift their heads."

Mariamne nodded, feeling exactly as he described.

Halton removed the cloth draped across her front.

The flesh there showed marked healing. There were no open or raw wounds, only red skin warm to the touch.

"I regret to inform you, Lady Mariamne, you will not be afforded the comfort of many days abed to regain your strength."

She followed his gaze to the malevolent fog now so thick Mariamne could no longer see the tree line a few paces away. Somewhere her body summoned enough strength to shudder. She choked on her next breath and coughed for a few moments. The effort only served to drain her of the little strength she possessed. Her head fell back against the blanket covering the hard earth beneath her, and her eyes slid closed.

Halton spoke, drawing her back into the waking world once more. "We must leave this place. It grows more dangerous. Veronia is less than half a day's ride, and another day beyond the border we should be clear of these woods and the evil possessing them."

Mariamne attempted to push to a sitting position, but her limbs shook and would not lift her. She looked at Halton, choked by her feebleness and angry at needing his help. She smashed her fist into the ground as she fought to keep her eyes open and remain awake. A familiar growl rumbled low within her. Unwanted emotions tangled with the reality of her situation. Her greatest desire—to be free of all men and their claims on her life and body—slammed against her new need to be protected by these men. A tremor grew, starting deep in her toes and traveling up to her head as the war within ensued.

Seeing her struggle for breath, Halton rested one hand high on her back and held her hand with the other. With a gentle tug he helped her to a sitting position. Her head spun, which made her stomach tumble and the internal battle flee.

Garrick knelt next to her with a cool, damp cloth. With tenderness she did not expect, he wiped away the beads of sweat forming on her brow and upper lip. He swept her hair aside and laid the refreshing coolness on the nape of her neck. "Give it a minute and the sickness should abate, my lady."

Her stomach pitched and heaved, like some unruly beast lurked within. A foul taste invaded her mouth before it calmed. The uncomfortable waves of sickness subsided, and Garrick offered her a sip of water. She pushed it away.

"Please, my lady, you must take a little."

He held the waterskin to her lips. She swallowed a small sip, and when it did not spring back up, he urged her to take another. She refused a third, and he let her be.

The men left her resting near the fire as they made preparations to leave. She followed their movements with weary eyes. Eldon sat preparing the food at the fire. Mariamne rose up on one elbow to glance at all the men around her. She saw everyone at work, except Bray. She reached out to stop Shaw as he passed. She possessed no words to ask nor even strength enough to open her mouth. Would the young knight understand her silent question?

Shaw followed her gaze toward Eldon and sighed. "Bray is not with us." He pulled from her, and she reached out for him again.

Cy caught her grasping hand instead. Her vision filled with Cy's kind face as he knelt before her. "Eldon and Corin went in search of him at first light yesterday, m'lady. They returned after Halton finished your treatments, while you slept." Cy took a slow breath. His gazed searched hers. His eyes closed as he inhaled and released the breath with equal measure. He swallowed audibly. "He is dead. The horde killed him and one of the horses."

Mariamne shook. Cy rubbed her uninjured arm, but memories of the curly headed knight who loved to laugh haunted her. The others would miss him, for he lightened their burdens with his jovial spirit. A tear slid down her cheek, and Mariamne admitted she would miss him too. Cy slipped away as grief flooded her spirit. She grew uncomfortable in her sentiment for a man. She tried to brush the unwanted emotion aside like leaves blown on an ill wind. She turned away from the activity to consider other matters. Anything would do.

Those evil men had forced her to the ground, shredded her clothes, and infected her with poison. These same creatures set upon Bray. She lived, but they killed him—and a horse. Why? Why poison her? Why kill him? Why only one horse? If they could killed them all, their prey could not escape. Her questions made her dizzy, which served to stir her belly into uncomfortable waves yet again.

She tossed her head, stirring her dizziness further, and braced for the pain of the coming retch. It did not come. She turned her contemplations to something else.

The men prepared to leave. The porridge gurgled over the fire, but it smelled different—burnt mayhaps. Bray never burned their food. She had been the perpetrator of the burned biscuits.

She clenched her fists and dug them into the soil beside her. Grass and dirt collected under her nails. All her attempts came to naught—she missed Bray. And she hated herself for it.

A half an hour later, Darrel approached with his blanket and her repaired bodice and jerkin. The others arrived, and her dressing screen reappeared. She set about willing her leaden arms to pull off the tunic and don her own garment. It took her longer than seemed reasonable, and when she finished she doubted her arms still had the strength to alert the men of the task's completion. But the blankets lowered, and the men set about packing them.

Garrick approached her again. His round face looked drawn. He attempted a smile, but only one corner of his mouth rose. "My lady? I know it may not seem appealing, but you need to eat a little before we leave. It will help you today, even if it is only a couple of bites."

Mariamne crinkled her nose as her stomach set to rolling again.

"Will you try, please, to take a little porridge?" he held a small spoonful before her and tipped his head encouragingly.

She sighed, prying her mouth open. She was too weak to take the wooden utensil from him.

Garrick managed, with great care, to get four spoonfuls in her before she refused any more. He stood, his head held high and chest puffed out. Was he proud at her effort or his own aid?

Cy came next as the others brought her horse and doused the fire. "Do you think you can sit a horse, m'lady?"

She looked up at him with doubt, but he nodded his belief. He placed his great hands around her waist. His thumbs touched in the front and his fingertip met in the back. He drew her to her feet, helping her stand on wobbly, uncooperative legs. She instinctively grasped his forearms to keep from falling.

Cy's hands grew in strength about her. "I have you, m'lady. I will not allow you to come to harm."

He waited a moment for her to gather her bearings as he held her steady. With unimaginable gentleness, he turned her until she faced the horse and supported her from behind, his thumbs resting against her spine. He lifted her while Shaw and Eldon manipulated her nearly lifeless legs over the saddle and into the stirrups.

With all these men touching her, Mariamne should have been terrified, but their collective tender touch only left her with the fear she may retch on one of them. Garrick offered her a cool cloth, and her stomach settled, though it took longer this time with the porridge adding to her discomfort. Halton looped the reigns over her horse's head and handed them to her.

She struggled to raise her gaze to him through half-open eyes. Of all times, this should be the day to take the reins and lash her to the pommel. She possessed not even the strength to hold the thin leather strips. She closed her eyes. *Please can we not stay a little longer so I might sleep?*

But Halton pulled her from any thought of rest. "Forgive us, my dear lady. I know you are weak and tired, but the danger forces us to move. We cannot afford to lose any more men. Who would see to your safety if such a loss occurred?"

His eyes spoke of trust, a confidence that she no longer wished to be out of arms' reach, let alone out of sight of these men. She took the reins with trembling hands.

They turned for the road. Shaw slipped forward to take poor Bray's position on her right. His loss pricked her again. What had become of her over these few days to transform her so she cared for a man—any man? The pain tightened her throat. She struggled to breathe, and hot tears welled up to blur her vision.

The formation closed in so tight around her the horses swatted one another with their tails and their riders frequently bumped knees. She sat secure and safe among these unusual men. The light of their God kept the evil fog at bay and allowed a spot of sun to peek through above them. A deep and unfamiliar peace settled on her as she rode untouched through the surrounding sea of malice. She released her thoughts to the winds, focusing every ounce of her remaining strength on staying upright atop her swaying horse. Fearing it would prove too much for her, she pressed her free hand into the hole in her pommel.

Chapter 11

The slow clop of the horses' hooves echoed as they trudged at an unbearable pace for Mariamne's sake. Halton worked the muscles, forcing them to unclench. She tottered at every jostle but didn't fall. Danger beyond their vision caused the hairs to rise on his neck and arms. Hidden in the fog was the horde of the evil knight. The had killed Bray and sought to infest Mariamne. A rare shudder danced down his spine. What evil did the horde intend for this woman?

Doubt toyed with him. *Naught can be done to save her. It is too strong.*

"Lord God." He spoke aloud so evil could hear. "I call on the name of my Savior, The Christ, to save Lady Mariamne and the rest of us. For my God is mighty to save."

The nagging fear and doubt fled the truth. He increased their pace.

"Sir, we must slow, or mayhaps even stop. Our lady can go no further," Cy said. "She has almost fallen. Only our quick hands have managed to steady her and hold her safe."

Halton reined in. "I dread the idea, but agree. We must allow her a short rest."

Cy carried her to a small patch of grass where Garrick laid a blanket and Darrel covered her with another.

Halton prayed. "Thank you, God, for these men I now call friends."

"Sir!" Cy's shout ripped Halton from his prayers.

Less than an hour had passed. Cy yanked Mariamne out of sleep and into his arms with such sudden force a small yelp escaped.

Two black snakes slithered through the tall grass toward Cy and his charge.

Shaw's sword filled with holy light and cut one snake in half.

The second snake moved to climb Cy's leg as it sought to reach its prey he cradled. Cy jumped away as Corin killed it with a quick strike.

Mariamne's eyes grew wide, and Cy pulled her closer, "Sorry, Lady Mariamne. Wee snakes approached in the grass."

Cy forced a smile to his tight lips, but as his fear-filled gaze met Halton's, it betrayed the seriousness of the incident.

Mariamne dropped her head to his shoulder, and Cy spoke in a voice calmer than Halton thought possible. "I think the time is nigh we resume our journey, m'lady."

She gave a single nod, and he placed her feet back on the ground.

"Why not partake of a few bites before we continue?" Garrick offered the cold gruel.

"It would do you good, my lady," Halton said. Corin, Eldon, and he stood watch as Cy held her steady. Garrick and Darrel plied her with food and water.

She pushed the items away and wiped her mouth with her forearm. Mounted, they set out once more. Their speed carried them across the border into Veronia by midafternoon, but the fog again slowed them to a near standstill. It encased them. The unearthly sounds emanating from within the darkness set the horses to prancing and tossing their heads.

They covered a half a league at a slow trot. It was forward movement, aye, but too slow. Three great black hawks burst through the fog overhead. The sliver of light surrounding the travelers momentarily disoriented the powerful birds. They made erratic circles no more than two sword-lengths above.

The menacing birds dove toward Mariamne.

Halton drew his sword as sharp blackened talons reached for her head.

Cy's powerful hand pulled her out of the first's reach.

Shaw blocked the next attack with his mail-covered arm.

Corin shot the third down with his crossbow, causing the others to flee as it landed still alive and screeching in rage.

Leaping from his saddle, Halton ran it through with his flaming sword. "Check everyone for wounds!" Halton kept his eyes to the sky.

"No injuries, sir," Corin said a moment later.

"I have Bray's chain mail," Eldon offered, pulling it from a saddlebag.

"Cy and Shaw—help place it on our lady," Halton ordered.

Cy took the armor. "'Tis heavy, sir. Mayhaps beyond what she can bear in her weakened state."

Halton motioned for him to continue. "Even so, she still has need of the protection."

They had to move.

If nothing else, the ride helped clear Mariamne's muddled thoughts. Why did these attacks focus only on her? What did this evil want? Fear coursed through her like a raging river. Her heart drummed an erratic beat.

She had been lured into the woods but not to be torn apart like Bray and the horse. The evil creatures who had captured her sought to make her like them—enspelled, evil, damned. She fought for breath.

Cool sweat covered her skin. She trembled.

Likewise, the snakes had come at her, not the men standing guard. There could be no mistake, the hawks also directed their attacked at only her. The intent so single minded that they saw naught of the men with their weapons.

Her mind reeled and her heart raced. Halton and his knights had traveled this road less than a month ago. Yet they had not experienced anything like the fog, the oppression, or the danger.

A violent tremor surged through her causing Cy to wrap his cloak about her. What did this evil want? What had she ever done to warrant the single-minded threat against her and the destruction of her soul?

The trembling escalated into violent shaking. These men could spur their horses to a gallop and abandon her. She gulped air into her constricted lungs. The others would be safer without her. A terrifying dread consumed her to the point she could no longer breathe. Every muscle of her body clenched, adding to her discomfort. She glanced at the men, knowing they might even now be plotting to flee to safety. But they sat as alert to coming danger as ever.

Fear flooded her, stirring irrational emotions. *Kick the horse and charge away.* Better to die of a broken neck on her own terms than be abandoned to the vile black creatures. Aye, it made the most sense. *Lash the horse. Dash away. Now!*

Her shallow breaths came in ragged gasps. Fear overwhelmed all thought. Her muscles shook with accumulating tension, waiting to be unleashed into the reins and her horse's flanks. *Now. Must go now.*

Halton turned, catching her in his stare. The fear melted with the awareness of the lie meant to separate her from her safety. Her muscles cramped and ached as she fought not to run. She must stay. Remain with these men. Or perish as a loathsome creature. She leaned forward, still caught in Halton's gaze, and handed him her reins. She could not trust herself or the impulses making her vulnerable to the evil.

Halton's hand covered hers. His touch served as a lifeline pulling her from the abyss. His strength and the truth within him stilled her, and the longing to escape evaporated. Peace returned. Her breathing calmed, and as swiftly as the battle ended, her strength vanished. She slid from her saddle toward Halton. Cy seized her and pulled her straight again.

"Hold," Halton said. "We cannot afford another stop, for the evil one is intent on claiming Lady Mariamne and keeping her from a great destiny."

Cy stepped his horse closer to hers to pull her from the saddle.

"Allow me, friend," Darrel drew his horse between Halton and Cy. "We need your sword, Cy. I am no use in a fight. I will carry our lady. We can continue together on Bray's strong warhorse."

Halton saw the prudence in the offer. Cy continued to steady her until Darrel cradled her, and they wrapped her in a blanket.

They resumed their arduous journey.

Corin raised his torch high, "If we do not get out of the reach of this evil soon, we never will."

The last of the sun was barely visible before she stirred in Darrel's arms.

"How do you feel, my lady?" he asked.

Halton drew them to a stop. "Lady Mariamne, you slept through the night and much of the day. We must increase our speed. Can you sit your saddle?"

With a quick nod, they helped her onto her horse.

As she slid her feet into the stirrups, Halton barked sharp orders.

"Cy, Shaw—watch her. We will cover the remainder of the ground out of the border woods with haste."

Mariamne and the others followed when Halton spurred his horse to a gallop.

Hooves rumbled over the packed earth, rattling Mariamne's teeth. She leaned further forward as anxious as the rest to be free of the evil.

"Halton, sir!" Cy said.

A tight bunch surrounded Mariamne. She sat straight and calm. She moved as Halton neared to see past him better.

"She pulled her horse up short, nearly causing a collision with the rest of us," Eldon said.

The men's stares covered her like a sodden wool cloak, but Mariamne's eyes focused on a spot in the road several paces ahead.

"'Tis merely a fallen tree, my lady. The horses will clear it with ease. Fear naught," Halton said.

The unsettling feeling of a lie stirred again. They did not see the truth. Corin drew his sword at a sound in the surrounding darkness.

"Please, my lady, we must continue," they urged.

In the sword's light she saw the truth.

She did not understand the light, where it came from, or how they wielded it, but it held power. The light held the peace and kept them safe. The light came from the men, not their weapons. It struck her then. 'Twas the light of their God. He surrounded them and inhabited them all at the same time. Their God was truth. With His light infusing their swords, she could see the reason for her unease.

She urged her horse a couple of steps ahead, coming abreast of Corin. She grabbed the wrist of his sword arm and pointed the tip of his blade at the fallen tree.

Gasps filled the air as they followed the light. The obstacle seemed to melt away anywhere the light touched and revealed a real log beyond the illusion.

"Thank you, Lord," Halton said. "We would have cleared the deception with ease. but would have lacked the time to jump the actual hazard."

"We would have been killed," Garrick muttered.

They turned to her with a mixture of awe and gratitude fluttering over their faces.

The knights, including Cy, pulled their swords and filled them with the power of the God within them. With the blades aglow, they proceeded less recklessly, avoided several similar traps, and rode on unobstructed until first light. The forest thinned, and the hateful fog melted away. The sun's warmth eased Mariamne's aching muscles, and added to her weariness.

By midday the men struggled to stay in the saddle as much as she.

As exhaustion overtook them, Halton turned from the main road and led them to a small shire a few leagues to the west. He approached the first farmer he came to and spoke in quiet whispers. The man pointed to a large barn in the middle of the shire. Halton motioned for them to follow.

As several young boys rushed to tend their abandoned horses, Mariamne and the men staggered into the barn and collapsed into the hay.

She slept unmoving until the grumbling of her empty belly roused her. A deep inhale and the smells of food greeted her.

Halton rose stiffly and left first. She followed with the others moments later. In the brilliant light of the new day sat several food-laden tables. Young girls placed wooded trenchers and tin cups as a bearded man motioned them to come and sit.

One of the women curtsied to Halton as he approached, "Good morn, sir. You must be famished. Please come and eat, for all has been prepared."

Halton's brows knit together as his head tipped to the side.

"We recognize the king's guard, sir, even on the far-flung border. A mission of great import must have bee place on you to come through the evil lurking thick as sheep's wool at shearing time—and with a lady."

Every woman fixed her gaze on Mariamne.

Halton turned to Mariamne and his knights, "The good people of Wiltonshire have seen we are well fed. Come, eat your fill."

As they took their places, Cy and Shaw sat guard on either side of Mariamne. They nodded at her and dove into the welcome sustenance with great enthusiasm.

A smile tickled. Halton forgot to pray over the meal. Mayhaps the need no longer remained as they traveled safe beyond the fog.

Chapter 12

"We remain in Wiltonshire till we regain our strength. I wish to collect news of the evil we passed through," Halton said.

Mariamne lay on the hay and listened to their concern-tainted conversation.

"They say there has oft times been a strange mist in the area," Eldon said.

"Aye," Corin added. "And the occasional ravaged wild animal. But the villagers spoke of a great change as the dense black fog rolled in a few days ago."

"They also report more animals killed, including livestock," Eldon said.

Halton rubbed his jaw and neck, listening closey. "Several of the men have agreed to escort Corin and me to an observation point established atop a rise north of the barn. They set up a rotation of volunteers to keep constant watch from there." Halton left the barn, Corin close on his heels.

She caught a bit of movement. Cy sat with his back against a stall a short distance away.

"Sleep, m'lady. I will keep watch over you."

She curled onto her side in the straw, drifting off to sleep in the silence left in the men's absence.

Voices woke her. Cy stood near the door with Shaw and Eldon

talking in excited whispers.

"When Sir Halton and Corin joined the day's guards, the men reported the fog reverted back to a scattered mist the previous dawn and has remained unchanged. Sir Halton is convinced the fog pursued us, or more specifically our lady. He says all our movements corresponded with the villager's description of the fog's behavior." Shaw said, as a chill skittered up Mariamne's spine.

Cy ran his hand along his collar. "Though I saw it with my own eyes, hearing this makes the hair on my neck rise. Where is Sir Halton now?"

"He sought solitude to pray," Eldon said.

Cy's next words commanded the others. "We must follow his example."

All three dropped to their knees.

Mariamne watched and listened. She wrapped her arms around her knees.

The men shared prayers round their reverent circle.

"Lord, there is still far to travel, and the evil is great. How are we to survive?" Cy pleaded.

Eldon spoke next with eyes closed, but a great smile filled his face. "The Scripture says, 'Yea, though we walk through the valley of the shadow of death, we will fear no evil: for You are with us; Your rod and Your staff, they comfort us.'"

Cy slipped back onto his heels. He looked at the young knight. "Truly, the Holy Words of God say we will walk through evil and not be afraid?"

"Aye, it does, and so much more, my friend," Eldon said.

Their prayers forgotten for the time, the three men sat in the straw and talked of all the ways this unseen God took away fear. Mariamne reclined again on her soft, fragrant straw and allowed many thoughts to drift through her weary mind like a gentle stream in a parched land. Sweet peace wrapped around her like a warm blanket, and more of the Holy Words of this unusual God caressed her.

"For God hath not given us the spirit of fear; but of power, and of love, and of a sound mind."

This God behaved like no other. She yawned, and sleep enveloped her.

Life proceeded around her, but Mariamne spent most of their first two days in Wiltonshire in peaceful, restorative sleep. She only rose for meals, but whether she ate or slept at least two knights escorted her.

This protectiveness started the tongues to wagging among the shire's women. As she approached the barn doors to join the midday meal, she caught the excited chatter of three women standing outside.

"King Edgar has finally found a queen. I told you he favor not any of the pretentious highborn ladies of Veronia. They are much too haughty and pampered for our sensible and straight-thinking king," the first woman said.

"Aye, King Edgar would never suffer his wife taking more than her due, especially at the expense of their subjects," another agreed.

The third woman joined in. "She is an exotic beauty. Do you not agree? Raven hair and rich-green eyes. From where could she hail? It cannot be Balmore. Their women are dull and pale, but hers has such warm sun-kissed skin. Falkness mayhaps, or from the Asterie Islands into a Balmore port?"

The first woman agreed, "Thus the reason she never talks among us, for our tongue is still difficult for her and she wishes not to make a poor impression on her future subjects."

The other two ladies, kin on the idea, helped the wild contrivance quickly become regarded as fact. During the meal, the retelling closed around her like Jarel's chains. The entire hamlet became convinced she came by ship from these islands to seal a treaty with some distant king through marriage to Veronia's King Edgar.

Mariamne all but choked on her fowl at the absurdity. How disappointed they would be when they learned Halton had purchased her as a wild slave. She tried to brush their grand scheme aside, knowing how gossipmongers liked to gad about. But she caught Halton staring at her from the next table.

A strange look of knowing twisted her insides. The tale lapped in unwelcome waves from all sides as she considered his behavior throughout their arduous journey. He, from the beginning in the cells, called her a lady, something wholly improper for such a lowly woman. He never abused her nor spoke harsh. But then, one would loathe to mistreat a woman who would one day be his queen. In such a high position she could exact ultimate retribution. Had this been the whole point of his kindness—simple self-preservation?

What a ludicrous notion—her as queen. Common slaves never aspired to more than peasant freedom. What king would accept such a bride? Or did Halton not plan to inform his liege of these important facts?

Her willful spirit ignited. Her jaw clenched and her teeth grated until her head ached. She would be no part to such a conspiracy. Her mind flamed with secret plans. She set her thoughts to ways of ruining the king's acceptance of her. Even if the rumors held a hint of truth— she would not be queen. To be so chained to a man and a position would be worse than living out her days in Jarel's fetid cells.

She stomping from the table, her food left. Cy, her faithful shadow, followed at her heels without sound. Shaw scrambled to snatch a couple of rolls and hastened to join them.

She burst through the front of the barn, plodded through its middle, and stomped out the back into the bright sunlight. Here she found isolation, save her two guards, who kept their distance. Mariamne filled her lungs with the scent of newly opened flowers. The long grass swayed in the gentle spring breeze, which carried a smattering of fluffy white clouds across the sky.

The familiar comfort of her rebellion embraced her like an old friend, and she set to plotting her fall from grace. She would avoid the hateful crown no matter the cost. Her steps slowed, taking a meandering path to allow her mind to travel the well-worn trails of defiance. A satisfied smile turned her lips as the plan came to life. When supper arrived, her course lay set and well rehearsed.

As she retraced her way back with mischievous eagerness, she spotted Halton kneeling under a tree. His hands were raised, entreating his God to some great action. Back rigid and jaw tight, she glared at him. If he thought to get his God to make her be his queen, the heavens help him. Not even this powerful God could make her carry such a heavy burden!

Halton had watched Mariamne storm off, and he feared for her. He too excused himself and again sought sought his Lord. He knelt in moist earth under an ancient oak and pleaded with his Maker.

I know well Your comfort, guidance, and protection, Lord. I am Yours, and You have promised to never leave me nor forsake me. But what of Mariamne? I fear for her. She knows naught of You, Lord.

The wind stirred, and with it came the silent truth. *She knows Me, for she sees Me in you and the others who carry My light. She feels My touch and hears My tender care. Remember, she saw the trap you failed to recognize. She felt My absence and knew to use My light to reveal the truth.*

The breeze twisted and swirled around him, tossing loose leaves into his face, and the message came again—more powerful.

My son, I hold her in the palm of My hand, as I do you. Your fear lies somewhere else, not in losing her to the evil but in giving her to your king. She belongs not to you, Beloved. Turn not from the path I have given you—and her.

Halton's eyes shot open, and he dropped back on his heels as if hit with a physical blow. He sat gasping for the breath driven from him. As coherent thought returned, he confessed to his all-knowing God, who saw his heart, that he loved Mariamne.

Shame flooded his soul, for God had revealed Mariamne's destiny at the beginning of their journey. She belonged to his king. Yet over the trial-filled days, he had allowed the longings of his flesh a foothold in his heart. He could not allow his enemy to fan the flames of this unholy love. It could be used to keep her from God's purpose as surely as if the black poison's spores filled her.

Oh Father, forgive my betrayal. Oh wretched man that I am! Who shall deliver me from the body of this death? I will cast my burden upon my Lord, and You shall sustain me: You shall never suffer the righteous to be moved. Lord, help me to follow You and You alone, and protect me from the fiery arrows of the evil one.

Peace washed over him in comforting waves, and he savored the tender presence of his merciful God. He reveled in the holy communion, wanting to cherish it forever as it filled every corner of his soul.

With her plan formed, Mariamne joined the evening meal. When all were gathered, she would overturn a table and screeching like a crazed animal. And if Halton stood near, she intended to slap him to remove this horrid notion from his feeble head.

As she approached the place reserved for her, anticipation bubbled. Cy stood behind his seat, waiting with a deep frown. He could not know what she intended.

Clovis, a woman in her thirties with a great brood of children, stepped between Mariamne and Cy. She held a package outstretched toward Mariamne.

Clovis offered a deep curtsy and passed the simple cloth-wrapped package bound with a bit of twine to Mariamne with respect and awe.

Mariamne stopped cold.

"It is but a humble token for you, my lady. I hope it will be to your liking. Many hands have labored on it," Clovis said, her eyes cast to the ground between them.

Mariamne glanced to Cy standing behind the kind woman, and he gave her an encouraging nod. Yet she struggled to take the item from the woman's hands. Never could she remember receiving a gift, not even as a child. Now these simple women offered something made of their own hands. Mariamne trembled.

A hand pressed against her elbow. Cy stood beside her now, helping her raise her arm to take the gift. She never saw him move, but with his help she took the bulging package. It shuddered before she placed on her empty trencher. A beautiful patchwork velvet bodice over a plain white linen chemise lay inside. Shiny wooden toggles adorned the front, and a fine braided cord graced the back of the bodice. Embroidered embellishments covered the lovely fabric.

Mariamne gasped. Never had she seen such a beautiful garment, and she struggled to imagine where these humble people could have gathered such expensive materials. They had sacrificed these treasures to honor her. Her rebellious heart seized until it quivered.

"Is something wrong, my lady? Do you not like it?" Clovis's voice quaked.

Tears tumbled unchecked. Gratitude overwhelmed her. Mariamne startled the woman with a fierce hug. Mariamne regained herself, giving Clovis and the women gathered around her a deep curtsy. She ran her hand lovingly over the garments as more tears came.

"Would you have a place where Lady Mariamne might change?" Cy asked. As Clovis led her the way, Cy whispered in Mariamne's ear. "Well done, m'lady."

His obvious pride made her float along the lane following the excited Clovis until they reached her long house. Cy and Shaw trailed her protectively, and Clovis chattered the entire time, though Mariamne heard not a word. She walked with the precious gifts clutched to her breast, unable to control her grateful tears.

Clovis showed Mariamne inside the simple home to a place near the pallet across from the byre. "You may change here, my lady." Clovis left her to change.

She emerged from the home to spin euphorically as all admired the work she wore. They returned to the tables, and Mariamne ate with joy in her beautiful garments.

Not until she lay in the straw to sleep did the thoughts of howls and spilled food venture across her mind. She sighed, thankful for being distracted from behaving so foolishly. Somehow, she did not want these people to see the ungrateful child she could be if left to her devices.

Mariamne's heart still railed against the mere thought of being queen, and she intended to prevent it by whatever means her rebellious mind could concoct. But a tiny part of her savored the genuine respect and love these people offered at the possibility she could be their queen. Truth lay in what she desired least.

Mariamne shook and flopped to her other side. She shoved the idea away as one thought regained her attention. To be queen necessitated marriage to the king—and she would be bound to no man.

Chapter 13

"Godspeed on the remainder of your travels," the villagers called. Mariamne sat with the men atop their rested mounts at first light.

Halton set a quick pace, and they made good time in the warm spring weather.

Mariamne's resentful rebellion would not be contained, however. Before the sun reached its zenith, she saw a way to begin to avoid the crown. She spotted a lone apple tree not far from the road with a few good apples still in its upper limbs.

She reigned enough to slip out of her protective circle behind Shaw. With slow purpose she walked her gelding toward the tree.

"M'lady?" Cy called.

Without acknowledging him, she brought her mount under a low-hanging limb.

"Lady Mariamne, what are you doing?" Shaw shouted as the others drew near.

Before they could reach her, she stood, balanced on top of her saddle, and climbed into the tree. She scampered to the highest limbs, plucked a succulent red fruit, and sat on a branch to eat it with great relish.

"My lady, please come down," Halton asked.

She would not look at him.

"Lady Mariamne, come down here this instant!" he ordered.

Not a muscle budged in her stubborn resolve.

"Come down!" he bellowed.

She glanced at him, and a mischievous grin tickled her lips.

The man watched her in stunned silence. Then he turned away, and his shoulders rose and fell with a heavy sigh she could not hear.

Halton dismounted. "We might as well eat until the good lady chooses to come down. We cannot continue until she is ready."

Cy shook his head in exasperation. "Rebel indeed!" He moved to position his horse closer to the tree. It seemed he intended to ascend her perch and join her. She tilted her head. Whatever would he do once he reached her?

Before he could get a handhold to hoist himself up from the saddle, Mariamne hurtled an apple past him. It grazed his shoulder.

His head shot up, and his brows drew together as he narrowed his gaze on her.

Mariamne covered her mouth as a forgotten laugh threatened to burst from her. She held another apple poised in her other hand and waited until he settled back onto his mount. She dropped it to him.

Cy tossed it to Shaw, and she dropped several more. She reached behind her and collected more there. She dropped enough for each of them to have two. Then seeing one last tantalizing orb, she balanced on the tip of one foot and leaned out, setting the apple to spinning with a brush of her fingertips.

"Take care, m'lady. You reach too far!" Cy yelled.

She leaned farther.

A strange wind whipped about her, shaking the tree. Her toes slid off the branch, and she crashed through several limbs. She caught herself a second later. Planting her feet on a wide branch, she held tight. Frozen for several moments until the tremors stopped, she took two deep breaths to collect herself. She turned and lowered herself the rest of the way.

Cy pulled her from the tree onto his saddle. His gaze was hard, and a disapproving frown twisted his lips. "You are bleeding, m'lady," he whispered through a clenched jaw as he wiped her chin. "'Twould be a pity to ruin your fine gifts for a foolish jaunt."

A smile toyed on her lips again, and she slid to the ground with a playful toss of her head. She mounted her horse, munching contentedly on the apple she had managed to hang onto in the fall.

Halton frowned at her as she led her horse past him and back to the road, while the others scrambled into their saddles.

As Mariamne treasured her success at proving her unworthiness to be queen, an unwelcome thought vexed her. For some inconceivable reason she wanted to please Halton and Cy. The revelation she could give a wit as to what any man thought of her kept her from any further frolicking the rest of the day.

Though her thoughts captured her, Mariamne did note Halton's gaze fell on her less with each mile. His tender looks never brushed her face. A distance grew between them, and she fretted over her unruly behavior. Had she at last gone too far? The silent rebuff distressed her, and she struggled to be obedient. And yet at the same moment, she resented her compliance. A war ensued within her.

"Our pace will slow some as we ascend the first of two mountain passes before we reach King Edgar's keep in the wide valley beyond," Shaw told Cy.

"How long until we reach the keep?" Cy asked as he smiled at Mariamne between them.

"A little over a week, God willing."

A handful of days stood between her and some unknown fate. Mariamne grew restless. Wild thoughts of what awaited her in King Edgar's palace assailed her.

The narrowness of the trail forced them to move single file, and Mariamne took the opportunity to flaunt her rebellion. Spying another, more risky trail above, she turned her horse from the safety of the wider path. Her horse twisted and turned as he switch-backed several times before gaining the trail several feet above and walked parallel to them.

"Lady Mariamne, it is not safe up there," Garrett called.

"You are putting your horse in danger, m'lady. He has been good to you," Cy scolded.

Shaw pleaded. "Lady Mariamne, please come down."

Halton refused to turn and look at her.

Mariamne smiled at them, uncaring as her mount moved with precision along the steep rim. A commotion to her left caught her attention. She looked up as a boulder careened past her. The poor gelding slipped and slid for several steps until it found a sure foothold and shook its head, snorting irritably.

She whirled to see the men on the path below her. Her strangled heart pounded its relief to see them unharmed.

"Darrel, are you well?" Cy called.

Darrel rode behind him. Beads of sweat glistened on his brow in the sun. A shudder ran through him, and he gulped for air. "Aye, but that stone came mighty close."

Mariamne's stomach soured and bubbled. She could have caused the sweet man's death. He never failed to treat her with kindness. He did not deserve to die for her antics.

She glanced up the ridge, scanning the mountaintop. Did she see a small black form duck out of sight? A shiver ran through her. The unseen enemy was using these frolics as an attack. He continued to try and separate her from the safety of these men. If they died, evil would have her.

She eased her mount to fall back into line and once again committed to constrain herself to docile behavior for the next few days.

Three days later, in the long narrow valley between the two mountain ranges, restlessness again overcame her. She bounded from her horse to run into a field full of flowers like a child, twirling around with her arms outstretched and her face turned joyously to the cloudless blue sky.

She spun and spun while the men sat watching her with great smiles. None stopped her. Did they somehow know she had never been afforded this simple privilege? Did they want her to know joy as much as she needed to experience it? Or had there been a moment long ago? A memory danced at the edges of her thoughts, but she could not capture it.

She let her thoughts go spinning until dizziness tingled her weary mind, and then she allowed herself to fall back into the thick grass. She lay there only a few seconds when a great boisterous brown hound came leaping into the field yapping to share the joy. It licked her all about her face with its great slobbering tongue. Mariamne rubbed it about the neck.

A moment later, the dog stepped past her, snarling with intimidating growls and bellowing with harsh barks of alarm.

The men came to her aid in a heartbeat.

Cy grabbed her off the ground while Eldon and Corin decapitated another pair of black snakes poised to strike her.

Mariamne shuddered and returned to her saddle, and the dog ran off. This hunt would not end until it claimed her.

The next day Halton turned down a lane of a large village. "It is too late to start across the ridge this day. This is Lincolnshire, the last shire before the great Kestron Ridge. We will stay here tonight and refresh ourselves and our supplies."

They led their horses into the stables of a spacious alehouse and left them with the squire.

"We need three rooms," Halton told the lanky innkeeper.

Corin paid the man as Halton instructed them, "Men, divide yourselves to share two rooms, and place Lady Mariamne in a room between."

Halton turned back to the innkeeper and dropped several more coins on the counter. "The lady will have a hot bath, and she will require a serving girl for the evening."

Mariamne's head whirled. She could not remember the last time she indulged in such a luxury—mayhaps while she served the lord's daughter. Many times she had accompanied her mistress to an event where she bathed before hand. She shook off the old memories and climbed the stairs with eagerness.

The serving girl of no more than ten, with unruly wheat-colored hair and a dirty kirtle, led the way. As Mariamne sat on a simple chair, a stream of lads brought in buckets of steaming water to add to the great wooden tub. The girl remained to assist Mariamne in undressing, but Mariamne waved the girl out of the room.

She slipped out of her garments and laid them thoughtfully on the bed. She turned to glance at her back in the reflecting glass hanging on the wall. The raised white welts left in her dark flesh sent her to trembling. The ugly, hateful scars sent her mind racing forward to what awaited her over the ridge. How would she be treated at journey's end?

She shook her head, allowing her loose hair to cover the scars, as a tear escaped her eyes. She pushed away the nightmares of the past and resisted the nerve-rattling imaginings of the future as she sank into the tub's welcome indulgence. She let the warm silky comfort wash her mind of all its concerns.

The young girl returned while she soaked. Seeing the garments on the bed, she said, "I will take these to be laundered. Here is a kirtle to wear until they are ready."

Mariamne made no protest as she slid under the water, drawing strength from its silent embrace. When she surfaced, she reached for the soapwort root mixture left beside the tub. When she finished, she dressed herself before the servant returned. Mariamne allowed the girl to brush her hair. The girl added scented oil before plaiting it and binding it with the leather thong.

Lightness filled her step, raised her chin, and curved her lips, even in the simple borrowed garment. She left her room to join the men for supper. The soft padding of her leather shoes whispered in the still hallway. Darrel escorted her, and she smiled at him as he offered her his arm to lead her down the narrow stairs to the main room.

Mariamne sat in contentment, listening as the men talked with the villagers on all the happenings in their absence and again savoring a meal she had no hand in preparing.

"Corin," a newcomer called as he entered.

The knight stood to greet the man by name. The villagers knew these men, and laughter filled the room in their familiar surroundings.

"In honor of our special guests, I have secured entertainment for the evening," the innkeeper announced.

As the bard took a seat in the middle of the room and strummed his psaltery, Mariamne caught the trailing words of a small group nearby.

"… the future queen."

"Can it be?"

"'Tis true. Look at how the king's thane and his men guard her."

Even here, they imagined her to be their long-awaited queen. Eyes clamped shut and her fists clenched in her lap, as a snarl built in her belly. Before one song concluded, she stomped to her room. They did not leave her alone to ponder. Eldon followed her and took the first watch at her door, and the servant girl darted inside before Mariamne could slam the barrier to the hopes of those outside. The girl moved to a small pallet in the corner.

A slave with her own personal servant! How ludicrous!

Mariamne's agitation led to fiery pacing in the small space between the door and the bed. She could not be still.

How old and gnarled was this King Edgar that everyone sought him wed? They all conceded he tarried too long. Was he some shriveled ancient thing? Or a brute? Or a hideous monster? Would none of the local nobles consent to marry their daughters to him? Why must she be the one to marry him?

Her pacing grew into stomping as an insuppressible desire to throw something filled her. She reached for the hairbrush and caught a glimpse of her poor cowering servant. She stilled. Her dark emotions had swept her into danger yet again.

She sighed in exasperation, replaced the brush, and turned to the washbasin. She splashed cool water on her heated face. As she dried, she took a moment to stare into the polished surface on the wall again.

After so many days in the warm sun, her skin had darkened to the color of honey, which highlighted her hard green eyes. Her long onyx-colored hair, now clean of road dust, gleamed like a polished gem. Her cheekbones were high and regal beside her small straight nose, and just above her petite chin her vibrant lips held an unflattering pout.

She ran her hand over her face. The reflecting glass did not show the girl of her memories. When had she changed? Had she always looked so? She sighed again and walked to the slim featherbed. She plopped down with resignation and fell back across the quilt. *Will I never have a choice in what happens to me? Must I always be controlled by another's opinion of who or what I should be for them?*

Despair washed over her as tangible as the water on her skin earlier. Her tears finally erupted. Turning her face into the pillow to keep the servant from hearing, she cried herself to sleep.

Chapter 14

The men's laughter increased. The excited chatter flew from man to man as they neared their destination. Yet Mariamne's dread grew. Escape eluded her. Journey's end would find her a worthless slave, or bound to a man and a position she could never bear. If she dared run, the evil and a far worse fate would overtake her. As her stomach knotted and threatened to bring up her dinner, her mind filled with images of being chained behind strong bars until she took her last breath.

The height of their joy compared to the depth of her despondency threatened to crush her. Anguished tears rolled unbidden. She pulled up the cowl of the warm wool cloak Halton had provided her. The expanse of fabric blocked the cold wind and hid her hopeless tears.

Cresting the high summit sprinkled with patches of snow, Halton pointed to the king's keep. A narrow shaft of the day's last rays highlighted the lone structure rising high above the flat valley.

The image caught Mariamne and stirred something unfamiliar in her tormented spirit. A profound sense of yearning struck her. Part of her longed to race down the hill and charge straight into its gates.

A warm gentle breeze swirled, caressing her moist cheeks and carrying with it an almost indiscernible whisper. *Come home, Daughter. Here you will find unimaginable joy.*

Mariamne gasped as peace enticed her. It lulled and wooed her as it seeped into her bones. She clutched at the peace. She reached out to the welcome. Her spirit hungered for the promise the fleeting whisper offered. Could this be a place to call home? The wonder of the possibility filled her with an excitement she had never known.

She wanted to make the feeling a part of her. To embrace such peace would wipe away the horror of her life. But her old fear reasserted itself, reminding her of her pain, doubts, and the evil deeds of men. The strangling remembrance sent a shudder through her entire body and drove the hope away, like birds in a meadow set to flight. Her limbs trembled, dizziness danced around her head making her nauseous. She held her breath and hoped the tears wouldn't come again, as hope lay crushed under what would come in the next days.

They slept near the peak in a shallow cave before descending the ridge the following day, Mariamne continued to reach for the promise, but her inner tumult kept it out of her grasp.

In the valley late the next evening, the golden pinks of the setting sun glowed through the thinning trees, and the group caught glimpses of the rocky outcropping on which the king's keep stood.

Their destination still lay too far to reach before nightfall, so they made camp one last night to grumbles, yet no one so loud as Mariamne's.

Come to us. Blackened men called to her from the shadows of her dreams. In her nightmares, she stood in the open—alone. Twigs snapped around her. Voices hidden in the foliage cackled and taunted.

In the dark of her dreams, she screamed at the top of her lungs. "I will never be one of you!" She turned to find herself standing in the aisle of a church. A wrinkled man with shaggy gray hair only contained by a crown sat on a throne. He waved her forward to the chair beside him. Another crown sat upon its cushion.

Mariamne turned, but the chains attached to cuffs on her wrists and ankles held her fast. Dressed in an elaborate gown, she thrashed and squirmed. When she looked, the old king gathered the chains, and pulled her toward him. "No! I will never belong to you!"

She stood alone in the void of her dreams.

Beloved.

Never had the rising sun brought her more relief. Not even on the glorious day she stepped from Jarel's cell. A strange calm settled on her, like the sea after a storm.

They ate quick bites as they packed, their eager footfalls stirring dust. The horses whinnied as the men flung saddles over their backs. Were they as impatient to return home as their riders?

From atop her mount, Mariamne watched the growing keep with a mixture of fascination and trepidation. The craggy rock jutted out of the ground like some ancient being thrust from the belly of the earth, the king's fortified dwelling, the crown on its head scraped the sky.

Only one path wound to the gates. The narrow lane allowed but two riders side-by-side.

Cy sat nearer the rim next to her, commenting in awe. "Those curtain walls have to be nearly thirty feet high, and I wager more than ten feet thick. What necessitated such a strong structure when it is nearly inaccessible by more than a handful of enemy soldiers at a time?"

"Mural towers." Cy pointed in uncontained excitement.

Mariamne didn't know whether he talked to her or to himself.

"Half round to improve the field of fire. I wonder what they use them for? Worship houses, living spaces, kitchens, maybe prisoners in the basements? This is no keep, but a proper high king's castle."

As they passed through the gatehouse, Cy pointed to each of the formidable gate's components. "'Tis so big," he said breathlessly of the bailey. "Hawks. Hounds. Armory. Blacksmith. Alehouse," Cy listed the various structures with awe and wonder flavoring his words as they proceeded up a small incline.

Inside the inner gate, they entered a small ward, and their eyes fell on the king's home, built against the rock wall that towered over it.

Another warm breeze greeted Mariamne, carrying the fragrant scent of roses, corn cockles, forget-me-nots, and daffodils. As Cy prattled on about the castle, the still voice whispered to her again. *Welcome home, Beloved.*

She gasped.

"Aye, m'lady, 'tis the largest castle I have ever seen as well." He turned, waiting for Shaw, and asked him a multitude of questions.

Mariamne availed herself of his distraction and led her horse toward the bright blossoms of a garden nestled next to the stone structure Cy called the castle.

A booming voice interrupted her respite. "Ah, Halton, my friend, you have returned. We worried over you. The others returned weeks ago, and I feared I would need send men to learn of your fate." The large man wrapped Halton in a gruff hug the moment his feet hit the ground.

"Your Majesty," Halton said with a bow when the king at last released him.

Before he could continue, Cy leapt forward, and took a knee at the king's feet. In one continuous breath he swore his fidelity. "By the Lord before whom this land is holy, I, Cynric will to King Edgar of Veronia be true and faithful and love all which he loves and shun all which he shuns, according to the laws of God and the order of the world. Nor will I ever with will or action, through word or deed, do anything which is unpleasing to him, on condition that he will hold to me as I shall deserve, and he will perform everything as it was in our agreement when I submitted myself to him and chose his will."

Mariamne saw the king straighten. Not an old man—not young either, mayhaps a score older then her—mayhaps less. He cast a furrowed glance toward Halton.

Halton opened his mouth, but Darrel and Garrick knelt and swore their fidelity as well.

Only after each said their peace did Halton have a moment to explain. "Led of the Lord, Sire, I went to the slaver's compound. God Almighty directed me to purchase these men from the putrid dungeon. They have proved to be faithful in service, Your Majesty. Being invaluable in the aid they rendered along our journey, I count them friends, Sire."

Halton indicated each man. "Darrel is a man of learning with the ability to read and write. He is quick of mind and eager to assist. Garrick is a man of humor, who lightens the spirits even in the darkest of situations and is kind to the depths of his soul. And my comrade Cy, a warrior with a strong and sure arm and a heart as loyal as the day is long. He will never fail you, Your Majesty."

Halton turned to the king. "God blessed me with their aid. I shared my burden with these faithful men and brothers in Christ. Each is a man of courage and noble character, and I would have been in need without them after the tragic loss of Bray."

Mariamne looked on from a distance, her heart pounding, as the three men remained kneeling before their new sovereign while Halton's words of praise showered them.

Edgar turned to the three men, and stroked his chin for a moment. He accepted their oaths. "It is right that those who offer to me, King Edgar, and my people unbroken fidelity should be protected by our aid. Cynric, Garrick, and Darrel have proven themselves faithful ones of ours, by the favor of God coming here, and have seen fit to swear trust and fidelity to us in our land, therefore we decree and command that for the future Cynric, Garrick, and Darrel be counted with the number of Veronians. And if anyone perchance should presume to kill any of them, let him know that he will be judged guilty by the laws of this land, King Edgar, and his people."

He placed a hand on each head, saying, "As it is not the habit of my thane to give unwarranted praise, I hereby release you of your bond status and free you to find gainful employment anywhere within my realm."

Mariamne dismounted and took a step toward them, hope springing up like a grand fountain.

Cy remained on his knees, and his voice quavered. "It is my greatest desire, Your Majesty, to join your men-at-arms so I may fight by your side in the coming battles against the evil threatening our land."

Edgar glanced to his knights, who gave a quick nod of their eager approval, and he granted Cy's request.

She took another step, anticipation strangling her heart and lungs.

Likewise, the king granted Darrel's request to assist the king's chancellor.

Another step.

"And you, Garrick? Where would you go?"

"Your Majesty," Garrick said with a grin splitting his face. "I request to become a tanner's apprentice, for no other reason than the position appeals to me."

The king cocked his head to one side, but he granted the request also. "Come, let us break bread together and share a cup of welcome and friendship. After, go to the blacksmith and have those servant bands removed. Come, you are welcome, friends," the king said with a sweep of his great hand.

Mariamne moved to make herself known.

King Edgar stood beside Halton as the others led the way into the king's home. The king, only taller than Halton by a hand-width but with broader shoulders, turned his back without seeing her. His muscles rippled under his tunic and jerkin. The ends of his light-brown hair bent in the breeze. His features were sharp as though chiseled of stone, yet softened by his close-trimmed beard and mustache. But his smile melted away any apparent hardness.

She quickened her steps, remembering his ready acceptance of the men, welcoming them as his own. She started to run as he climbed the stairs.

Halton appeared in her path as the king's back disappeared through the double doors.

Her heart stuttered as her mind filled with only one thought. *Will he free me too?*

She darted around Halton and raced toward the king.

The king almost stumbled as she curtsied to the floor before him. He afforded her a slim smile before turning to join the men. "What news do you bring?"

Mariamne's heart dropped to the souls of her feet. All breath fled her lungs, and thought evaporated with all her hopes of a new life of freedom from obligation.

Halton pulled her upright and led her into the kitchens to the left of the hall while the men sat with the thoughtless king to the right.

"Lady Mariamne, wait for the food and bring it out. I assure you, when the time is right, I will speak to the king on your behalf."

Mariamne could not keep a deep pout from twisting her lips. But as she waited in the noisy kitchen, her ire woke. Like a dragon uncoiling from a long sleep, it raised its head and belched out its hatred. She stood, tapping an irritated rhythm with her foot as servants hastily placed food on trays for her to deliver to the men. Resentment boiled. Every man who ever ignored her needs sprang to her mind, fueling the flames. She stomped each step to the waiting men. The trays quaked.

She plopped down the first trays but received no acknowledgment. Her breath came in quick hot puffs as she returned to the kitchen for others. The fleeting uninterested glance of the king pricked a nerve, stirring old rebellion to the surface with such force it filled her cheeks with searing heat.

She seized the next tray half full and stomped to the boards again. She approached the king where he sat among his men and paused for him to look at her. When he turned his eyes to her, she dumped the carved meats and accompanying juices into his lap.

Choked gasps echoed through the hall as she tossed the tray to clatter on the table.

Edgar looked at his soiled garments and glanced at Halton. He said not a word as he slowly rose and returned the food to its tray. He raised his head to her.

Mariamne stood defiantly, steeling herself for the slapped rebuke. At least that would prove he knew she existed.

Instead Edgar turned from her to address Halton in a calm low tone, "She will not do."

She will not do? The words reverberated in her heart as she stared at the back of his head. Her outlandish action flooded her mind. She had allowed the evil to overrule her common sense. She had ruined everything.

Chapter 15

Images of her blatant attack on the king flooded Mariamne's thoughts. Panic gripped her, turning her insides to stone. She spun on her heel and ran from the hall, tears blurring her vision.

She raced for the only open door in the ward—the royal stables. Constructed against the tall rock wall upon which the castle perched, there was no exit. She staggered to the rear, collapsing in a heap of tears.

She sat with her face buried in her hands. Shuffling straw and heavy footsteps alerted her that others approached. She looked to see Darrel, Garrick, and Cy.

Garrick sat, draping his arm tenderly around her, while Darrel wrung his hands and paced. Cy leaned cross-armed against the stall post beside her.

"Oh, my lady, 'tis not so bad," Garrick said. "Once Sir Halton explains, King Edgar will understand."

"Such may not be the result, Garrick. Her affront insulted the king to his face," Cy's remark carried an air of doom. He grunted. "Oh, m'lady, you are forever acting as your own worst enemy. Why must you always be the rebel? Is there never a time to be at peace, dear woman?"

"Harsh words, sir," Darrel whispered.

"You know I speak truth and say it not to injure, but to make her see the harm she does herself."

"Aye," Garrick groaned. "Mayhaps King Edgar will see fit to

forgive her? He seems a kind man," he added hopefully.

"He is a man of God," Darrel offered.

While they debated her standing with the king, Mariamne continued to cry. The king's words echoed through her skull. *She will not do.*

He did not say, "*This* will not do," or "*Her service here* or *in this fashion* will not do." But "*She* will not do." He had rejected her. He did not want her. Not as a slave and certainly not as his queen.

The nightmares of an unfulfilled destiny beset her afresh, and the empty dark void engulfed her again. Evil had won. Even after all she survived during her journey, it used her own hand to achieve her end.

"Sir," each man acknowledged Halton as he approached the stall where she sat sobbing.

"Please return to your meal, gentleman. Allow me a moment with the lady."

They nodded and filed out as Mariamne's tears strangled her every thought.

Silence choked the air. The horses stilled.

"Lady Mariamne," he stated softly.

She launched herself into his arms.

He grasped her wrists to stay her advance and stepped back from her. His eyes were wide, and his brows rose nearly to his hairline. He became rigid and kept her at arms' length.

"No, my lady. 'Tis not proper." He swallowed slow and purposefully and drew in a long breath, releasing it as she watched his throat bob with the effort of clearing it to speak. "You are not for me. You have been chosen for another."

Mariamne staggered from him. He let go of her, and she plopped back on the hay. His words held her as firm as his hands had a moment ago. Like standing in a bell tower when the clapper struck, she reverberated with them. Her hand flew to her throat, grasping at it to open and allow the life-giving air back in.

You have been chosen... her thoughts repeated in an endless drone. She was chosen. Now the voices of the evil ones calling her the night they dragged her into the woods became sharp—distinct. The name they used—*Chosen One*. They called her chosen, and lured her to her doom.

Chosen. Halton knew it. The evil knew it. But who chose her, and for what purpose? Had she already failed? A thousand questions bombarded her at once, and the sting of Halton's rejection lay forgotten. Her head spun and her stomach tumbled.

She blinked and saw Halton's image clearing as he still stood over her. His mouth moved as though he spoke, but no sound entered her thoughts for several moments.

"So not all is lost, my lady. The king has allowed you to remain as a chambermaid. He will not punish you, but I would not hazard another outburst. The king's patience does have its limit, and you have already reached it."

Halton's firm tone drove the seriousness of her plight into her stubborn brain.

"Come, my lady. Let me show you your duties and your sleeping chamber, and we will pray the God of redemptions can make something beautiful of this mess."

She staggered behind him, across the ward, through the deserted hall, and up the stairs to the second floor.

"These are the guest apartments for King Edgar's noblemen and their families. They need a good cleaning and dusting, including airing the linens."

She nodded, and he led her past the rooms and up a tiny back spiral staircase to the third floor.

"All the rooms on the west side are the king's chambers. Those on the east have served as the queen's chambers. Most recently, the king has bestowed the honor of their use on some of his more deserving dukes. They also need cleaning.

"You are not to enter the king's chambers. Better yet, approach him not at all. Most days he is out with his men or attending to business, so there should be no reason for concern." His gaze narrowed on her.

There would be no reason for concern. She nodded.

He turned to the relatively small door to their right at the end of the queen's suite and opened it.

"This served as King Edgar's nursery until he came of an age to take one of the apartments on the second floor. There is a small pallet in the corner where the nanny slept. Uncover it and remove the dusty linens. This is where you will sleep until such a time as the Good Lord sees fit to move you."

Again Mariamne nodded, though it seemed an odd place to house a chambermaid. She glanced at the cluttered and neglected room. It was crammed to the ceiling beams with the castle's unwanted, yet priceless furniture.

Halton left her, saying as he closed the door. "I will return with clean linens, water, and a proper skirt."

She shimmied carefully to the back of the chamber. The buried pallet lay shrouded in thick dust. Further back and partially hidden by a tall wardrobe, a filthy window blocked the light. She took care as she removed the items from the pallet and folded the bed linens back on themselves containing the dust within. She repositioned several chairs, a desk, and a divan and forced the wardrobe further down the wall. Taking a small bit of cloth, she worked to clean the window.

Halton returned, laying the clean linens and dark skirt on her bed before setting a bowl and pitcher on the desk.

She splashed water from the pitcher over the rag and removed the remaining film from the window. She stood admiring her work until a throat cleared making her turn.

Halton stood waiting for her. He motioned to the soiled linens, "I will show you the laundry, my lady."

She collected the items and hastened to follow. She remained close behind him, her quick steps padding across the smooth stones. They proceeded down the back stairs, past the second floor, to the hall, and out through a narrow hallway between the kitchen and the rock wall. They exited the building and crossed a small open space to the laundry facilities. No servants lingered about as he told her where to bring the dirty items and where to collect clean ones.

They left, rounded the front of the kitchens, and he showed her the castle well and around the grounds of her new home. She listened dutifully before he released her to return to her borrowed quarters and clean before supper.

She paused for a moment, looking out the inner gate. What if she left? She obtained her goal. She would never be queen. Why did it now cause her pain? *Chosen One.* Who would want such an ungrateful beast? A tear slid down her cheek. The scent of the garden brought the memory of the welcome that called this her home. She turned and trudged up the stairs.

Mariamne did not return to the hall for supper that evening. Until dark engulfed her small room, she spent the hours rearranging the various homeless pieces of furniture until a clear path emerged from the door to her pallet and the window. She placed the desk under the bright portal to the outside and set the pitcher, bowl, and a hairbrush upon it. She found a small looking glass among the discarded items. She hung it from the wardrobe's decorative finial. A beautiful blue satin high-backed chair she placed between the door and her bed. She dared not sit in the lovely thing until a clean length of cloth covered it. Finding a chamber pot beneath a small table, she placed it in the far back corner.

The dying sun hid its light from her darkened room, forcing her to feel her way to her pallet and abandon her work for the night. As she lay there alone, the darkness took on a physical presence. It battered her with the regrettable events of her day, forcing her to face her shame and disappointment. Unbearable pain jabbed her heart like the blade of a broad sword, until deep sobs wrenched from her. *Unseen voice who called 'Welcome,' forgive me.*

Stillness washed over her aching spirit like a gentle rain on a withering flower. Comfort filled her, surrounded her, and cradled her in a night full of pleasant dreams.

The first rays of the day streamed into her little room. She dressed, collected supplies, and returned to the second floor and the first of the many apartments Halton instructed her to clean. She folded the linens, placing them near the door to be carried to the yard and shaken free of dust. She wiped the furniture clean and, from her hands and knees, she scrubbed the floors until the stone titles shone.

She worked from the furthest corners toward the door. The rhythmic swish of the brush over the tiles also served to clean her mind of its contradictory thoughts. The splash of water reminded her of the peaceful touch of the whispered voice. Her heart hungered to feel it again.

Distant steps disturbed her quiet reflection. Rapid steps pounded down the back stairway. Door after door along the hallway opened and slammed shut as the frantic steps grew louder. The door in the adjacent room did not open, but the sound of running footfalls filled the hall.

Mariamne looked up from her scrubbing as Halton bolted into the room, nearly tripping over her bucket of soapy water.

"Oh, thank the Lord above!" He gulped deep drafts of air, leaning forward to brace himself on his knees. His shoulders relaxed as he stood to look on her again. "I did not see you at the breaking of the fast, and when I came for you and found you not in your chamber, I…"

Mariamne nodded. He feared she had run away, but she swept an arm about the room to indicate her hard work. His tight smile did not give Mariamne an impression of approval.

"Yes, I can see now I need not have feared. You have been diligent in your duties. But, my lady, 'tis the Lord's Day.

She stared blankly at him. What was so special about this day? Was it one of his God's sacred days?

"We do no work on the Sabbath, as He instructed us. Instead we meet in His house to hear the Holy Scriptures taught."

She cocked her head at him. Surely Halton, and his God, knew she did not hold to his faith. Why did it matter if she cleaned on this day?

Halton waved at her to follow. When she did not move, he squared his shoulders and extended an arm of escort to her. "Please allow me to show you the way, Lady Mariamne."

As he led her to the chapel, he explained in hushed tones, "The rumors of an exotic beauty in the king's castle have already stirred the tongues to wag. As have the grossly exaggerated tales of your refusal to marry King Edgar. Apparently you expressed your great dissatisfaction in loud rantings before throwing a silver tray at his head." His voice rang with a mixture of merriment at the outrageousness and irritation at the inaccuracy.

"Everyone is eager to get a glimpse of the king's long awaited bride, so mayhaps it is for the best you remained unseen this morn, for I know such a notion is abhorrent to you. I will show you the way to the upper gallery in the chapel. There you can sit and listen in shadowed anonymity."

They entered the vestibule, and Halton steered her to the left. "Take the stairs to the gallery, my lady. Sit in the pews there."

He continued through the double doors in front of them, leaving her alone.

Chapter 16

Standing at the base of the stairs leading deeper into the foreign house of worship, Mariamne considered turning and exiting. The ornate structure captured her, but the sound of music enticed her up the stairs to the small space hanging above the people gathered below. She chose the first of the small pews and peered over the railing at the faithful singing a melodiously of the power of their God.

Peace saturated the place, stirring the hunger again. Though she could not grasp meaning of the words, she enjoyed them. Following the songs, a priest in fine robes stepped forward and spoke.

He prayed, and Mariamne startled afresh at the personal tone of the prayers to this unseen God. Everyone who spoke of Him, or to Him, seemed to be on intimate terms with Him. This closeness further stirred an irrepressible longing. Part of her wanted to know this God in the same manner.

But as the priest read from the Holy Book, Mariamne's mind wandered. She could not comprehened the meaning of the words. "For every creature of God is good, and nothing ought to be refused, if it be received with thanksgiving. For it is sanctified by the word of God, and prayer." Yet the same passages held those seated below as if they fed on the very words themselves.

At some point in the long-winded speech, a light caught Mariamne's attention. It flowed through the high stained-glass window. The faint light touched the priest, drawing her gaze. He glowed with the same holy light that fill the swords. The aberration shimmered and shifted, and though she could still see the priest he seemed to be a silhouette within the light. The holy man seemed unaware of the radiance. She glanced at the worshippers, but they likewise appeared not to see the manifestation.

The growing intensity of the radiance drew her attention once more. Another face took shape in the light. It looked up at her, and she felt the warmth of its glow. Mariamne watched as both the priest and the face in the light spoke as one, as if for her alone. "'For I know the thoughts that I have thought toward you,' saith the Lord, 'even the thoughts of peace, and not of trouble, to give you an end, and your hope.'"

The light vanished, and Mariamne shuddered. Those words echoed the promise from the mountain. Her heart soared like a bird loosed from his cage. A realization struck her with a tangible force. The whispering voice belonged to the God Halton and all those in the nave. This God, who they spoke to so personally, in turn spoke to them—and, in fact, spoke to her. She sat unmoving as questions danced in jubilant circles.

Lost in thought, Mariamne remained in the cool darkness. She sat hidden in the gallery until the silence reverberated off the tall stone walls. Glancing down, she realized the worshippers had all left. She slipped from her seat and descended the steps with only a whisper of her skirt. Looking around to assure no one lingered, she crept into the nave.

Something drew her toward the altar and drove her to her knees. Awe filled her until she almost burst from it. She bowed her head. *What do You want of me?* Her heart pleaded for answers she was not sure she wanted to hear.

Serve your king, My Daughter, the familiar whisper told her soul.

Warmth filled her as nothing before. Would He speak to her

again? When it became apparent there would be no more, she rose and went to the kitchen without hesitation.

Mariamne seized a tray before she could be stopped and strode with single-minded purpose into the great hall filled with men-at-arms, knights, and the king's officials. She strolled past all the tresses without seeing those gathered and approached the dais where King Edgar sat. The hall fell deafeningly silent as she curtsied humbly and set the tray before him with care. He nodded his approval, his rich-brown eyes shining pleasantly. She stepped off the high place and returned to the kitchen.

As she walked, she barely noticed the hushed whispers springing up all around her. Her spirit filled with the pleasure of the One who told her to come. Her lips turned in a long-forgotten smile as contentment engulfed her. Retrieving two more trays, she brought them to the others gathered for the meal. She made several such trips before she slipped into the dimness at the side corner of the hall. She sat with some of the serving maids and other servants and ate for the first time since her arrival.

When the meal concluded, Mariamne helped return the trays, trenchers, and other items to the kitchen. A group of serving maids set about scouring them clean, but they refused to allow her to join them.

"Please, my lady, 'tis the Lord's Day. Go and enjoy your new home, and we will see all is completed. You may come and inspect our progress later. There is no need to supervise."

Mariamne turned to conceal the wry smile twisting her lips, and she now experienced Halton's frustration with the rumors swirling about her. The gossipmongers had already visited the kitchen.

She left the hall and climbed the stairs of the nearest tower.

Cy and Darrel approached her as she ambled on the inner walls.

She savored the peace swirling within her.

"Well done, m'lady," Cy said, his head held high and his chest puffed.

"Yes indeed, Lady Mariamne. We are all very proud of you."

They offered her bright smiles as they fell silent beside her. After so many wordless hours in the saddle, a silent walk seemed like the most normal form of camaraderie, and they strolled thus for over an hour.

They parted as Mariamne turned into the royal garden. She remained until she returned to the kitchen to serve at supper and again the following morn.

Following the meal, she hid herself away as she set about cleaning the guest chambers until they gleamed. As day followed day in the same simple routine, she was surprised by the joy she found in the labor of her hands. The bright sun smiled through the windows of the western apartments, and she was overwhelmed by a sense of profound fulfillment.

Slow, purposeful footsteps echoed their approach, and her peaceful heart skipped a beat. Things would not remain this simple for her, she feared.

Chapter 17

Mariamne pulled herself from her quiet contemplation when
Halton appeared in the doorway of the queen's chambers. She sat back
on her heels as he interrupted her scrubbing and studied him.

He stood rigid, and opened his mouth to speak, but no words
ushered forth. It snapped shut, and he turned to his right, skulked two
steps, spun, and marched back across the space inside the threshold.

Mariamne waited, her heart rate increasing with each circuit he
made.

He stopped, turned with a raised finger and his mouth opened
again. Strangled sounds escaped, and he started to cough. He paced
again.

The deep furrow in his brows stirred Mariamne's belly, making
her nauseous.

He stopped abruptly. "My lady, the day I feared has come sooner
than I anticipated, and I have a terrible burden to place upon you." The
words spewed out in one long stream, and he shifted from foot to foot
after they erupted into the air.

She waited, holding her breath.

"Lord Richards and Lord Stanley will be arriving on the morrow,"
he said, as if this made the matter clear.

She stared at him.

"They are the king's dukes from the south. They are the most
vocal in their disapproval of the king's unwed status."

Mariamne's heart dropped to her knees and lay still. Now she understood where his thoughts carried him.

"They have long demanded King Edgar take a bride, but last year at the council of high lords, they gave him an ultimatum. He is to be wed by his thirtieth birthday or they will seek to remove him from the throne. The king's birthday is in two weeks," Halton explained without emotion. "I believe this kingdom will not stand without King Edgar, and furthermore I propose God has chosen you to be his queen."

She shook with uncontrollable tremors as he stared at her.

"I understand this is not something of your own choosing, Lady Mariamne, but for the sake of our kingdom and all the lives entrusted to King Edgar, I must insist you *pose* as his queen. It would only be for the benefit of these pesky lords. Nothing would change for you. It would be a marriage in word alone."

Her cheeks grew hot beneath Halton's intent gaze. Fear rattled within her like a wild beast.

"My lady, you must stand beside the king and allow us to say you are his queen. These men will be gone in a few days, and life will return to the way it is now. I know it is a terrible burden to place upon you, Lady Mariamne, but it is the only way I can see to save Edgar and his kingdom. Please, come with me."

Mariamne closed her eyes as he took her hand and pulled her to her feet. Her shoulders slumped, and her head dropped as her soul clamored to reclaim the peace of only moments before. But erratic fearful thoughts raced inside her head like hornets.

"We must now convince King Edgar," he added ominously as they stepped into the hall. Leading her to Edgar's study, he barely waited for his knock to be acknowledged before opening the door.

"Oh good, Halton, I have been discussing with Tye the arrival of…" Edgar's words trailed off as his glaze eyes lit upon Mariamne.

"Your Majesty, I do not think you have been formally introduced to the Lady Mariamne," Halton said.

Mariamne watched as Edgar shot him an irritated look, "Lady? I thought her to be a mute slave."

Mariamne's head dropped, and heat flooded her entire body. Beads of sweat formed above her lip.

"I may have rescued her from a slaver, Your Majesty, but she is every bit a lady." Halton's tone was firm and laced with anger. "And she is to pose as your queen!" he finished with a curt flourish.

Mariamne startled. No man addressed his better in such a bold tone—and this man spoke to his king.

Edgar's hard gaze shifted from Halton to her, and back again.

"I cannot say as she appears a good choice for a queen, even in these desperate times," Edgar said, leaning back.

Tye stood from his place opposite the king's desk and motioned for her to sit.

Fearing she might collapse, she welcomed the respite. She dropped into the seat and clung to the arms.

"You agree with this absurdity, Tye?"

"I not only agree with it, Sire, I asked Halton to bring Lady Mariamne here to be a part of our decision. There is already talk in the castle and through the countryside that she is your treaty queen, Sire. They are eager to see you married and your kingdom secured from all the noblemen's schemes."

"But you say she is only to *pose* as my queen."

"It is out of kindness to the lady, Sire," Halton interjected with more calm. "It is my impression she has not been well treated by men in the past, and marriage to any man would be unbearable, I fear."

The king slid his glance back to her, and she trembled under his keen stare. Her gaze plummeted back to the floor. "But to lie?

Gentlemen, does not our God tell us such things should never been done? It would be better to tell the truth and let Him make a way for us."

"This is the way He has made, Sire," Tye reassured.

Edgar sighed and pushed back his great wooden chair, causing it to scrape on the stone floor.

Mariamne startled.

He walked around his desk and rested back on the nearer edge. He reached out a tender hand and raised her face to look on her. Brushed by the intensity of his scrutiny, she dropped her gaze to the floor once more.

"Forgive my harshness, my lady. I meant no disrespect. I am grateful you would even consider this wild scheme. But I have to ask you if you really want to be a part of deceiving my dukes, and in turn my people? They have long awaited a queen, and if they learn this is but a ploy to keep my throne, they will turn on us both." He released her chin and straightened with a sigh. "Somehow I fear you appreciate far better than I what horrors await us if my people discover this deception. I respect you for your tenacity to attempt it anyway, but I cannot ask you to bear such a burden. It would not only be unfair to you, but also to my people."

He turned to his men, "God will provide us another way." He moved to return to his chair.

Halton blocked his path. "Sire, this is the only way. You know Richards and Stanley and what they are capable of. They will tear the kingdom apart. You must consent to this..." His voice trailed off, and he leaned in, seeking the king's ear. Though he hoped to keep the knowledge from her, the whispered words still reached her. "I believe God has chosen her as your true queen, Ed. You must see..."

Edgar turned back to her. He leaned against the desk again, and his head tipped, as he seemed to consider her with more interest.

"Lady Mariamne, will you consent to pose as my queen? You are free to choose. There will be no repercussions against you."

Her head shot up, and she stared boldly at him. He gave her the choice. To agree or not. The freedom in the simple question touched the depths of her battered spirit.

She looked away as the memory of the quiet whisper washed over her afresh. *Serve your king.*

She savored the peace the familiar words brought for another minute before raising her head, though she avoided looking directly at the king. Without fear or hesitation, she nodded her agreement.

"Thank you, my lady. You honor me and my people. May God bless us in spite of what we are about to do."

"Tye, I believe there are still some of my mother's gowns in one of the wardrobes in the queen's chamber. See if any might be suitable for our new queen."

"Yes, Your Majesty." With a quick observance, both men turned to leave.

Mariamne stood, curtsied, and followed them.

"God be with us," Edgar mumbled as she passed through the door.

Chapter 18

Edgar stood, rubbed his aching neck, and stretched to loosen the muscles. He worried over his hasty decision. What would his people think? Would they accept Lady Mariamne? A moment of merriment tickled him. How would it be to have a mute queen? The queen saw to the education of the squires and the order of the home and the servants. It seemed unlikely this lady could fulfill the role.

He venturing out of the confines of his study. Many already gathered within the hall. The air vibrated with excitement. Everyone greeted him with a great giddy grin.

Word had already spread. His priest was not there to pray, as they had agreed upon. "Shall we give thanks and break bread together, my friends?"

"Aye!" they sang out as one man.

"Heavenly Father, we thank You for Your gracious care. We give You the honor for every blessing. Prepare our hearts and our hands for the battles to come, and bless our bodies with the bounty of Your land we share this night. Amen."

"Amen!"

Edgar watched as serving maids scurried from the kitchen to the boards and back. Mariamne did not appear among them. For the briefest of moments, he worried.

No one served him, and he motioned to get a maid's attention when Mariamne bound from the back stairs. Though her attire remained the same, she was profoundly changed; she stood a taller, and she held her head erect.

She acknowledged him as she hurried. She emerged from the kitchen moments later with his tray. A sweet smile graced her face, and her eyes fell on him again as she approached.

The room hushed as she leaned close to him in a way speaking of familiarity but not disrespect.

He smiled. She understood her new role with exceeding clarity. Edgar laid his hand affectionately over hers. "I feared you changed your mind, my queen," he whispered.

She continued to smile and gently tipped her head nearer. A small movement, yet done in such a way everyone seated behind her would believe she spoke or laughed, though she did neither. But her attention shifted for an instant. Her luscious green eyes, the color of deep emeralds, engulfed him, telling him more clearly than words that she stood beside him in this, come what may.

Gratitude filled him, and he squeezed her hand gently.

Her eyes dropped slightly again, signaling that she remained his humble servant.

His heart ached as he remembered how he had failed to free her, and the harsh words he had spoken both to her and about her.

She took her place at the back of the hall.

Edgar followed her movement until the room hummed to life again. The merriment and raised cups spoke of his men's approval. Could this really be so easy?

The meal concluded, Edgar stood to retire to his study, but Mariamne caught his eye.

She stood near the door.

She smiled coyly and curtsied at his approach, offering him her hand.

Without thought he raised his arm, and her light touch steered him outside. They strolled toward the royal gardens.

Many of his men and servants clustered in various groups about the ward, each stopping to watch them with bright smiles and hidden giggles. Of course, the people needed to see them together.

Mariamne only had eyes for him. No one who saw them would dare believe she did not love him.

Looking into her adoring gaze even gave him pause. Not until they reached the depths of the garden, hidden from prying eyes, did her gaze drop. She sat on a narrow bench beneath an ancient white willow.

A somber look washed away the amorous feelings she obviously imitated.

His heart ached. He wanted it all to be real. But he knew he could not ask that burden of any woman. He stared a second longer. "May I sit with you, my lady?"

She peeked at him, and a smile that spoke much he did not understand parted her deep-red lips. She nodded.

They sat in silence for several minutes. "You are amazing, Lady Mariamne."

Her brows rose, but her gaze never met his.

"You seem to know instinctively what needs to be done. Your actions in the last hours have convinced the entire castle of our union. You are brilliant."

She considered a bright cluster of pansies. Were there tears pooling?

She sat still then raised her left hand and traced an imaginary wedding ring on her finger.

"Oh aye, of course, my bride. How dull of your husband to forget your ring."

She smiled, almost in roguish agreement.

It made him laugh. "May I never fail again to meet your needs."

Again she stared without looking at him.

He stood and offered her his arm, "Shall we return to our waiting public, my lady?"

She rose with silent grace and placed her hand on his arm as her loving persona returned and they exited the garden.

Even more of his people waited to catch a glimpse of them together now. They wound through the packed inner ward, greeted by smiles and congratulations.

Back in the hall, they parted and Mariamne continued to the stairs.

Edgar found Mariamne later as she finished cleaning the last of the second floor apartments.

She curtsied with her eyes cast to the floor, once again his dutiful slave.

"Please, my lady," sadness hugged his words.

Her head rose slightly, and she lifted a slim black brow.

"Your kindness to me and my people is beyond measure. Please, whether we are in public or in private, do not see yourself as anything less than my equal."

Mariamne's head shot up, and she swayed on her feet.

Somehow her astonishment cut him. "I have never seen you as a slave, my lady." A mischievous smile tickled his lips. "Not even when you dumped a tray of meat in my lap."

Her cheeks flushed, but he reached out and placed his hand on her arm.

"It was no less than I deserved for neglecting you so and offering you not the same freedom I offered your friends." He shrugged. "I cannot fault you for your disappointment, my lady. I should have told you then you were free, as you are now. You may stay or leave," he said soberly. "I did not know Halton set you to working up here. You are not a slave or a servant, Mariamne. You are nothing less than the king's most honored guest. And I pray you choose to stay a very long time." Oh, that she would stay by his side until the end of his days. Halton had stirred his hope, and now it would not be silenced.

His words elicited tears to slide down her cheeks.

He brushed one aside with his thumb and smiled at her. Taking her left hand, he slid a ring on her slender finger.

"It is not a traditional wedding ring, for the multi-stoned monstrosities are entirely unfit for such a lovely and noble hand as yours, my lady." A strange playfulness washed over him. "And we can hardly say we have a traditional marriage."

She returned his smile with an impish one of her own, and his laughter echoed in the hallway.

A servant appeared at the top of the stairs. The woman bowed near to the floor, with a knowing smile at having caught the couple alone. "Forgive me, Your Majesties. I need to clean the apartments before your guests arrive."

The king turned to stand beside Mariamne and raised his arm for her. "There is no need, Audrey. Queen Mariamne has already seen to the preparations."

Before the stammering woman could collect herself, they had climbed halfway up the main stairs to the third floor.

"Pleasant dreams, my queen," he bid her with a bow and entered his suite.

Once the king's door closed, Mariamne proceeded to the nursery and plopped onto her simple pallet.

She was free to come or go as she pleased. *She* was free to come or go as *she* pleased. She was *free*! The very thought made her addled and a little lightheaded. Like a child overflowing with excitement, she kicked at the bed and smashed her fists into it. Where would she go? A kaleidoscope of ideas raced through her mind all at once. A quiet mountain cabin, a hovel on the beach, the possibilities swirled about her like a twisting wind.

One memory halted them. *Come home, Daughter. Here you will find unimaginable joy.*

Every thought of leaving evaporated. She raised her left hand and looked at the carved gold band encircling her finger. Its engraved leaves and swirls held a bright emerald in the shape of a pear. It sparkled in the fading light.

Finally free—yet she could not leave. The irony awakened her rebellion, but she closed her eyes and thought of the pride in Edgar's voice when he called her his queen. The anger cooled. His actions were kind, giving her the choice, praising her actions, and showing her deep gratitude. His harsh words now melted away in his tenderness and his promises of freedom. These thoughts prevented her from wanting to leave him in his time of need. He called Cy, Darrel, and Garrick her friends—and, indeed, she did think of them as friends.

But freedom still wooed her. She would wait until the dukes were satisfied and returned home before she considered herself and her own plans. Then it would be safe for Edgar when she did choose to leave. Though, as the slipped off to sleep a small part of her dared consider the incredible possibility of staying.

Chapter 19

Mariamne rose before first light. She slipped from the nursery into the queen's chamber. She trembled at the thought of making the space hers. She only posed as queen; she was not King Edgar's true queen. No vows would be said. She remained free to stay or go. She stamped down her fear and moved through the luxurious decorations and beautifully carved furniture of the private sitting room. Tabletops and floors gleamed from her cleaning, and the rug smelled of the fresh spring air from its beating outside to rid it of a layer of winter dust. At least the room looked like someone occupied it.

Another tremor of misgivings rumbled through her as she stepped inside the queen's bedchamber. Her gaze skimmed over the bed and moved to the wardrobe.

The king's seamstress worked quickly to alter two of the dresses once worn by Edgar's mother. She added extra embellishments to the hems to account for Mariamne's greater height, and she tightened seams to hug her slimmer frame. The queen had not been a large woman, but Mariamne's time in a dungeon had left her with quite a different figure from a woman in a home of plenty.

She pulled both gowns out and considered them. She frowned at the priceless materials and craftsmanship, knowing they held too much value to drape over her lowly frame. She hung both up with trembling her hands and set to pacing the open area between the wardrobe and the bed, double the size of her slave cell.

Collect yourself, woman. 'Tis a dress—fine though it may be—it is a garment to cover you when you meet these irksome dukes. Put one of them on. Take care when you wear them. This will be over in a few days, and these gowns can be returned to their chest—to await their true owner.

She finished the last button as a small knock came at the inner door. She opened it to see one of the serving girls, Olivia.

She bowed her head and slipped into a low curtsy. "Good morn to you, Your Majesty."

The title raced over her skin like an infestation of insects, but she managed to stifle the shudder. She raised a brow.

"The lords have yet to show their fulsome faces. If it would please you, I have been sent to help you prepare for the day."

She waved a hand over her garment, indicating she had already dressed.

The girl's cheeks pinked. "And your hair, Majesty?"

Mariamne ran her hand over her plaited braid, which she had not touched since she rose. She smiled sheepishly and nodded to the young woman.

"May I arrange it in the latest Veronian style?"

After a moment's consideration, Mariamne waved the girl inside and sat while she fixed her hair in a myriad of swooping braids, pearl strands, and clips. Sitting as Olivia fussed over the best drape of the strands, Mariamne worked to still her pounding heart. Today would test her resolve in more ways than she could even imagine.

Chapter 20

"Enter." Edgar's heart thudded as the knock sounded on his study door. He glanced toward the window and gauged the hour to be mid-afternoon. He had spent much of his day worrying over Lady Mariamne. How many times had he read and re-read the same portion of the document in front of him? He leaned back and rubbed his neck.

Is her fitting complete? Does she have second thoughts about agreeing to this pretense?

A young blond squire poked his head in the door with a quick observance. "Sire. Lord Stanley, Lord Richards and his priest, and the dukes' families have arrived at the main gate. They insist on an immediate audience with you, Your Majesty."

Edgar sighed and set aside his work. "Find a maid to inform Queen Mariamne of our guests' arrival. Then escort the dukes to the hall."

"Aye, Your Majesty."

Edgar moved to his throne on the dais and waited to receive them, his fingers drumming on the arm of his chair. Mariamne took her place in the shadows behind him with a gentle swish of fabric. He should call her forward to the chair beside his, but he smiled to himself.

She chooses the better. Remaining hidden and allowing me to announce her would confound these men's plans in a grand fashion. He held surprise on his side.

The men stomped into his presence, dusty and disheveled with their weary families in tow.

Edgar took a slow deep breath. *Thank You, Lord God Almighty, for bringing Mariamne to me, for such a time as this.*

The lords gave the barest of observances and blurted out almost in unison, "Your time is near complete, Your Majesty."

Edgar considered them as he bit down on his tongue and waited for control.

Lord Richards, a rough man even on his best days, stood puffed up, several strands of gray hair hanging loose from his warrior's knot, his face covered in stubble. He looked more overfed and sloppy than ready for the battlefield. His eyes narrowed and filled with loathing for his king.

Edgar shifted his gaze to the shorter Lord Stanley. With his thinning, wispy, light hair and boyish face, Stanley struggled to carry the same authority as his counterpart. Being scrawny and overly dressed in satin breeches and doublet with a great ruffled shirt gave him an unflattering effeminate appearance.

Restraining the smile tugging at his lips, Edgar sat still under their threat. When he spoke, his voice rumbled with steely determination. "Is this why you two have stormed into my castle without so much as a proper greeting? To see your ultimatum fulfilled or your threat enforced?"

"You know well all the lords are agreed, Majesty," Richards announced, his chin rising even more. "Our land is in need of a queen and an heir." He turned toward his daughter, who stood trembling a few feet behind him. Barely of marrying age, the slender flaxen-haired beauty had grown more pleasing than when Edgar saw her last. "Since you have not yet chosen—"

"But I have chosen, Richards." Edgar freed the smile to turn his lips.

Every eye fixed on him as a few mouths gaped open in their

disbelief.

"You have selected a woman to marry, Sire?" Stanley muttered.

"I have not only selected her, gentlemen. She is here with me now." His hand swept out to his right, and Mariamne stepped forward.

She moved to his side with quiet elegance, poised in a regal stance with her head held high, and let her hand light on his open palm. She wore a rich burgundy gown with a low-scooped neckline and bodice accented in gold, which caressed her every curve. Her glistening black hair hung braided in multiple small strands gathered loosely with a pearl clip, the long ends dangling down, brushing the nape of her neck.

Edgar stared, smitten by her beauty and poise. He sighed contentedly and turned to savor the envious, slack-jawed gawking nobles.

Mariamne gave a small curtsy to them with a diminutive incline of her head.

"This is Queen Mariamne of the Asterie Islands." Edgar relished their bewilderment, for few people knew anyone from the far-off southern islands. People from the islands were known for darker skin, like Mariamne's, however. And with so little knowledge of the place, the dukes would be unable to challenge his claim.

Edgar turned with an adoring look, allowing himself the pleasure of her stunning beauty. Finally he said, "These are my southern dukes, my dear. Lord Stanley, Lord Richards, and their respective wives, Lady Roanne and Lady Elizabeth.

She inclined her head. "It is a great pleasure to welcome you to our home."

Edgar was grateful to be seated when he heard her utter the simple words. Like warm honey to his tongue, her rich voice—a little ragged from lack of use—came to his ear sweetened with a lilt, adding credence to her foreign origins.

Edgar's eyes fell on poor Tye and Halton where they stood behind the lords as the dear men tried desperately not to react to hearing Mariamne speak for the first time. Fortunately, all focus rested on her, and no one noticed their shock.

Richards narrowed his gaze and found his voice. "Your Majesty, how did you arrange this in such haste? Surely you have not signed the treaty to make this union legal, for we would have heard of it."

Mariamne seemed irritated by his tone, for she spoke to him with authority. "I can assure you, Sir Halton signed the contract on King Edgar's behalf. Likewise, he exchanged all appropriate formalities to secure my legal presence here. The king paid the price agreed upon and afforded my representative all the rights which come with such a union in the king's name." She extended her arm gracefully toward Halton in the back of the room, and the light caught on her ring. "You may confirm this with Sir Halton himself, or the knights, chancellor, or the personal friends who accompanied me on the long journey."

"The contract to be wed may have been signed, but it still does not mean you have been married to the king in the sight of God, *my lady*," came Richards's sharp retort.

Edgar opened his mouth to challenge the man's mocking tone, but Mariamne handled the situation with great flare.

Mariamne brought her hand to her breast with an offended gasp, and Edgar bit his tongue to keep from laughing. Her tone indignant, she spoke again. "Surely, sir, you do not think so little of King Edgar as to imply he would take a woman to his bed without the blessing of Almighty God by the administration of His ordained priest?"

"No, my lady, I never intended to imply something so unbecoming of the king," Richards grumbled.

Edgar noticed Halton now as he too struggled to suppress his laughter at seeing the infuriating man so flustered.

"But, Sire, why did you not allow the people to come and celebrate this joyous occasion with you?" Stanley pleaded, trying to turn the conversation away from Mariamne.

Edgar became distracted from the answer as the welcome warmth of Mariamne's hand returned to his. "I am afraid, gentlemen, upon our arrival and report of the troubles on the border, the king came to understand the urgency of the matter. He deemed it necessary to wed before the coming battles." Mariamne's voice danced around him.

Edgar allowed the men to shift nervously under his keen gaze as he closed his hand around Mariamne's and kissed it with growing affection. "Though she has been here but a handful of days, I have found the Lady Mariamne to be a rare treasure. I could see no reason to delay."

Edgar stood and stepped near the edge of the dais. "We will have a grand celebration in the fall, before the deep snows, to commemorate our joyous union and formally crown Lady Mariamne queen."

Stanley's brows scrunched together. "The fall, Sire? Why do you wait so long to inform your people of this blessed event?"

"Royal announcements are being carried by sandesman to all the provinces as we speak. But there is no time for revelry when the fate of the kingdom is at stake, Stanley."

Mariamne spoke, fear shading her words enough to draw the dukes' intent gaze. "There is a great threat poised on our borders, and I experienced it first hand. It must be dealt with at once or there will be nothing worth celebrating and no one left alive in the land to make merry."

"Indeed, gentlemen, Lady Mariamne speaks the truth. In fact, I thought you came here today to tell me the number of men you are committing to bring with you to the battle."

The lords shared a sideways glance.

Edgar knew the two smug men never considered battles or war strategy. They pushed the rumors of the impending danger from their minds, intent only on forcing his hand. They continued to steal glances, furrow their brows, and shift the weight between their feet. Clearly they did not wish to think on it even now.

"May we settle our families, Your Majesty, before we sit to discuss matters of graver concerns?" Stanley asked, his head bowed and his ruffles looking as limp as his countenance.

Edgar smiled, more at the duke's discomfort than out of friendliness. "Certainly, Stanley. Make your families comfortable, and we will meet at the conclusion of supper to confer on the matter of the impending war… and your involvement in it."

Edgar returned to Mariamne's side.

Each nobleman placed a stiff arm across his middle and bowed to a respectful bend, while the women pulled out their broad skirts and dipped in a curtsy.

As the subjects righted themselves, Mariamne laid a gentle hand on Edgar's arm and smiled with a tilt of her head toward him. Oh how she made his heart soar. "My lords, it is the custom among my people for the noblewomen to serve at the lord's tables. I have already put the tradition into practice in King Edgar's hall. Can I expect your wives and daughters to join me this evening?"

The two dukes remained silent, and the women swayed as they straightened from their observance.

Edgar bit his tongue once more. These men would find the very thought of their noble wives and daughters serving like common servants repugnant. The dukes stood speechless; they could do nothing but clear their throats, as they look frantically around the room as if they were trapped. The wives pressed close to them and reached for their husband's arms, their eyes pleading. Would they dare refuse Mariamne and thus offend him more?

"Aye, my lady," they acquiesced. Lady Elizabeth yelped as though she had been poked with a sword, and it looked as if Lady Roanne clouted her husband in the back as she bit her lip.

Mariamne's smile brightened. "I am so delighted. It will be good to have other ladies to dine with this night, my king." Cheer danced on her words as she gazed into his eyes. He could get lost in them.

The noble families made their way across the hall to the stairs.

Mariamne stepped demurely away from him.

Edgar turned to her, about to explode with excitement, but she placed a finger in front of her luscious red lips. He followed her surreptitious glance over her shoulder toward their departing guests. One servant disappeared up the stairwell, and a final footman struggled with an overly large trunk.

Mariamne leaned in to whisper, "There are still many hungry ears about, Your Majesty. Please be mindful of your words."

He took her hand and kissed it, he watched as her eyes grew wide and a hint of color brushed her lovely face. Edgar could not bring himself to release her hand but turned and led her and his two men into his study.

Edgar spun when Halton secured the heavy door behind them. He placed both his hands tenderly on either side of her face and kissed her forehead with an elated smack. "You brilliant lady!" He released her when her breath caught and a wave of fear filled her eyes.

She stepped away from him, trembling.

He walked around the desk as Tye indicated she could sit in the far chair, while he took the nearer one and Halton remained standing. The chair was barely under Edgar when words tumbled from him again. "I never, in all my lifetime, could have imagined a confrontation with those two scoundrels proceeding so well. And it is all to your credit, dear lady."

"More amazing still, Sire, every word she said…" Halton paused at the word to turn and flash her a large smile and wink at her, "every word she spoke held the complete truth. Yet it left a complete falsehood for them to accept. Well done indeed, my lady."

"I have never seen Stanley and Richards more confounded," Tye chuckled. "I welcomed the discomfort of not reacting to your stunning beauty, poise, and surprising ability to speak, my queen, to bear witness to the momentous event."

As Edgar and his men prattled on about the success of the announcement and introductions, they showered her with praise. But Mariamne sat staring soberly at the floor. Her bewilderment left Edgar to wonder whether anyone ever afforded her a kind word. She seemed quite overwhelmed.

Mariamne remained rigid and silent as her eyes bore a hole in the floor's stones. When she did speak, her grave tone tempered their joy as if she had splashed cold water on them. "This is only the first salvo, Your Majesty. They are most assuredly not convinced, and they will be seeking to find any weakness in the front lines of our tale until they leave. We must remain on our guard, or this momentary victory may all be for naught."

Edgar sat back admiring her afresh. "You are an amazingly intelligent and perceptive woman. Of course, my lady, you are correct in your assessment of my lords, and you expressed it with quite an accurate military illustration." He allowed his gaze to rest on her, taking in all her fine qualities and reconsidered her suitability as his queen. His respect for her was growing by the moment.

Her blush deepened under his continued praise.

"We will remain vigilant at all times," he said.

"There are matters to attend before supper, Your Majesty. If I might be excused?"

Edgar and Tye stood with her, and she curtsied low.

"Of course, my lady. I look forward to seeing you at the meal," Edgar said.

She bowed her head and floated from the room.

Chapter 21

Mariamne stumbled from Edgar's hall. Her head swam with such uncommon adoration for her and her actions, it stole all thought. She spoke when the men addressed King Edgar. She told them things with no plan to speak aforehand. She allowed the king to press his lips to her flesh—three times!

She gasped and struggled for composure. She wandered, until she blinked and found herself in the chapel.

She avoided the altar and climbed on shaking legs to the dark gallery. She slid into a pew in the shadows and closed her eyes. Her mind tumbled with the events in Edgar's hall replaying over and over again.

She had never intended to speak when she stepped beside the king as his queen. A strange merriment bubbled, for after so many years she didn't even believe words would form on her tongue. Oh to be sure, she could growl, snarl, and howl—but speak? Impossible. Yet words flowed as if not her own.

She put her elbows on her knees and let her head drop into her hands. If she acted thus after but a few hours as queen, the heavens help them all should the dukes tarry too long. Her boldness could see her forcing King Edgar off his royal steed and charging into battle in his stead.

Her breathing slowed and her thoughts calmed. A gentle air swirled.

"The heart of a man purposeth his way: but the Lord doth direct his steps?"

She straightened at the strange words. Where did the voice come from? A soft thud reverberated below her, and she moved to peer over the railing. A dark robed man stooped to collect his book.

"Fie, I have lost my place again. Lord, how am I to prepare for the sermom with these constant annoyances?" He bent a knee at the altar before continuing to the room beyond.

A pleading question sprang forth. "This is Your doing, God of this land? What do You want of me?"

The gentle whisper touched her heart. *Come to me, Precious Child. For I know you are weary and heavy laden, and I will ease you. In Me, you will find rest.*

The bell in the steeple at the far end of the building jarred her from her respite. Supper was a half hour hence. She crossed the bailey to the alehouse and prepared for the skirmish awaiting her.

Chapter 22

The women sat at one of the king's boards near the kitchen. "We are here as you ordered." Lady Elizabeth grimaced and crossed her arms over her expansive bosom.

Elizabeth's daughter, Lady Ingrid, rose while Stanley's wife, Lady Roanne, remained seated next to her young daughter.

Mariamne cleared her throat of the chuckle rumbling within.

The mothers rose, but they snorted and refused to curtsy. Their glaring looks brought heat to Mariamne's cheeks. Deep scowls marred their faces, and Mariamne smiled at their tame form of rebellion. Did her face ever look so unpleasant?

The men gathered in the hall, and Elizabeth's arms dropped to her sides, fists clenched tight. "Well, are we to stand about all evening, or are there tasks we must see to?" The small features in her large square face puckered as if she ate lemons.

"Of course, ladies, please follow me." Mariamne waved her arm toward the kitchen and watched as the women's jaws clenched at her cheerful words. "It is an honor to have such noble women join me this eve. The thoughtfulness you show will not be forgotten."

Did Elizabeth growl?

Mariamne cleared her giggle-prone throat again.

"Your Majesty, good eve," the cook sang, dipping low.

"Good eve, Esther. The Ladies Roanne and Elizabeth and their daughters have agreed to assist with serving at the boards this night. Is it not a joy to have hands to share a task?"

She watched as the tall cook struggled to contain her own giggle. Her gaze fell on the sour women. "Oh indeed, Majesty, a very great— *joy*." Esther clapped her hands, and the serving maids brought forth the prepared trays.

Mariamne collected two and presented them to Elizabeth.

The woman's arms stuck to her sides and her gaze narrowed. "And what am I to do with *those*?"

"Place them on the furthest board. One tray between the second and third man and the other in the middle of the table."

Elizabeth seized them and spun with such force that some of the meat juices splashed onto Mariamne's gown. The noblewoman smirked before completing her turn toward the door. The slap of her shoes echoed as she thudded through the door.

Mariamne stuffed down her growing rage mingling with her worry over the gown she had borrowed. Closing her eyes, she remembered the soft-spoken Edgar and released the breath. She turned her appraising gaze on Lady Elizabeth's daughter, reminding herself that Elizabeth had expected to be the mother of the queen only a few short hours ago.

Her plaited hair, no long constrained in the tight bun, now softened Lady Ingrid's beauty. Ingrid would make an impressive queen, but the young woman seemed grateful not to find herself in Mariamne's position. Ingrid no longer trembled; her shoulders were relaxed, and her gaze sat gentle on Mariamne's face.

"I am grateful for your service. Thank you for honoring my traditions."

Ingrid took the next two trays without comment.

Mariamne turned to her last two helpers. Lady Roanne's round cheeks flamed, but she attempted to form a smile under her haughty nose. She took the next trays, also spilling some of its contents—

though it landed on the ground and not on Mariamne's gown.

Roanne's young daughter danced, her curly blond hair bouncing around her smiling face.

"And what is your name, precious girl?"

"Erika."

"You are very pretty, Erika."

"I know."

Mariamne smiled and handed her baskets of bread.

Erika eagerly accepted the baskets and raced off to her new adventure.

Mariamne straightened. At least one of them did not yet look on it as being beneath her station to serve.

Mariamne collected the tray for the king's table with another. "Esther, have the girls wait until the nobles have made a couple of trips first."

Rich laughter filled the kitchen. "Oh aye, Your Majesty."

Mariamne noted the raised brows and smirks as the men watched the noblewomen drop trays on the boards. She placed one tray as the women stomped to the kitchen and proceeded to King Edgar. She set his tray before him, laying her hand near his as she leaned to capture his ear. "I requested more wine sent up from the alehouse, Your Majesty, and secured the services of mummers. I hope I did not presume too much."

Edgar kissed her hand, sending heat up her arm. "Quite the contrary, you acted perfectly queenly, my lady. You have had the foresight to think of everything." His gaze dropped from hers, and a wry smirk turned his lips. "Mayhaps with a queen in the castle, the king's gatherings will cease to be the great bore they are oft claimed to be."

She could not contain a small bubble of laughter, and hurried away to continue serving. A quick scan of the hall showed her that the women sat as the maids now saw to the work. She stopped one of the girls taking a tray to them. "Serve them last."

"Aye, Your Majesty," the girl giggled.

Stanley's three boys, Clifford, Doyt, and Loudon, were traversing between two boards and smashed into her with such force that she lost her footing. Steadying hands encircled her waist. A red-faced and wide-eyed knight worried the corner of his lip as he struggled to release her without allowing her to fall.

She smiled as she found her balance and his hands dropped away. "Thank you, sir. You saved me an embarrassing fall."

He nearly choked and bowed his head. "Think nothing of it, Your Majesty."

The two younger boys pushed past her in wild merriment once more, and she stepped back into the knight again.

He seized the leader by his ruffled shirt. "Your unruly behavior endangers Queen Mariamne," he announced in a loud, angry shout that drew the attention of the boy's father, and the king. "Apologize and sit before you cause real harm."

"Unhand my son, man!"

Edgar's voice rumbled before the knight could comply. "Not until he has made his expressions of regret to his queen."

The boy muttered a halfhearted contrition.

"I heard you not, boy!" Edgar leaned forward, glaring at Stanley.

The nobleman looked to the king and back to his son and inclined his head.

The boy harrumphed his displeasure. "I am—*sorry—My—Lady*."

The knight looked to Edgar and released him, but he and his brothers resumed running among the tables before Mariamne finished.

The ladies sat in humiliated silence, picking at their food. Only

Erika greeted her. "Hello, Majessy." She struggled with the word through the gap in her front teeth.

"Hello, Erika."

Mariamne watched as Ingrid's eyes wandered over the men with interest.

"Is there a knight you fancy, Lady Ingrid?"

She flushed with color.

"My daughter will never be wed to a common knight."

"I spoke nothing of marriage, dear lady. But there are many fine beaus at King Edgar's tables. Any girl would be blind not to notice."

"Well, well, I… I never. Such things are beneath us."

"As is serving the meals, but you did so this eve," Mariamne quipped. Turning her attention to the more pleasant Erika, Mariamne said, "I wish I had curls like yours."

"Oh, but Your Majessy, you have suss pretty black hair, and it is so s'iny," the girl babbled.

"You are most kind, Lady Erika."

"Did your mosser have black hair too?"

"I do not remember," Mariamne stammered.

Erika leaned forward to whisper tenderly, "Did see die, Your Majessy?"

With the women's eyes boring into her, Mariamne nodded and turned their conversation away from herself. "What interests you, Lady Erika?"

The girl babbled and the women gleaned little more of their new queen.

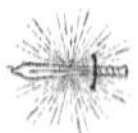

Servants cleared the boards of all but the wine and ale as the mummers took their place near the center of the room and performed a few short skits to the accompaniment of a pleasant harp. They performed a Veronian favorite before the lords excused themselves to follow Edgar to his study and the hall cleared.

The long day wore on Mariamne, and she turned to the main stairs seeking the comfort of her pallet. In the middle of the third floor, she froze at the sound of laughter in the queen's chambers.

Footfalls sounded behind her, and the voices of talking servants came up the back stairs before her. All escapes were blocked. The nursery door lay too far away. Those approaching drew nearer. They would be on her in moments. She was trapped. Her pounding heart drowned out all thought, and she stepped into Edgar's sitting room. Alone, she fell back against the door and tried to breathe. Gulping air into her startled lungs, she waited for the sounds of the servants' footfalls to fade, so she might leave unseen. But the hallway outside filled with laughter and running as Stanley's brood raced up and down the corridor.

Chapter 23

Mariamne wandered to a divan in the center of King Edgar's sitting room and crumpled onto it. Her anxious thoughts whirled and her head ached at the evil men's intentions. She must stay. Their trap had been sprung, and she sat in it. There would be a confrontation this night, and all could still be lost if she could not overcome her fear and play her part.

The decision made for her, she summoned her feeble courage and stood on quaking legs. Gulping air into her constricted lungs, she entered King Edgar's inner chamber.

His great curtained bed filled the center of the room to her right, while two smaller rooms lay to her left. One appeared to be a library, while the other tiled room with its enormous iron tub obviously served as the bathing chamber. She considered them but concluded neither area would be suitable for sleeping.

She turned back to the sleeping chamber with determination and spotted the king's travel mat peeking out from under the bed. Her eyes scanned the furniture, and a plan formed.

She relocated a couple of small tables and then went to the opposite wall and retrieved an ornately carved wooden screen and placed it between the bed and the wall. She yanked the mat free, pounded out the dust, and laid it in the corner behind the screen.

Her sleeping accommodation secured, she turned to his dark dresser. Her entire body quaked, her panting echoed through the room, and her heart pounded. Closing her eyes, she tried to inhale slowly, and released the breath with a whisper, "Forgive me, Your Majesty."

With as much haste as she could manage without destroying the order in the drawers, she rifled through the king's unmentionables. Her tattered linen undergarments would be inappropriate either in Edgar's presence or those who planned to catch them together.

Finding something suitable, she snatched it from the drawer and slammed it closed. Her face flamed hot with her embarrassment and gall. She stepped behind the screen—lest the king return—and slipped out of her gown and into his long winter nightshirt. She looked at the new borrowed garment, knowing it an unsuitable length for a lady's night rail but better than any of her alternatives.

Next, she further covered herself in his cloak. She moved to the bathing room, stood before the looking glass, and worked at length to let down her hair. With no brush, it lay in bumpy ribbons down her back.

Beset with worry and unable to sit still, she took a small lamp, increased the wick to brighten it, and walked the length of the narrow library. The numerous bound parchment volumes filled the tiny space with a pungent odor.

The queen's door banged closed across the hall. She jumped and nearly dropped the lamp. Stanley must have returned. Edgar would soon arrive to his own bed. She trembled and grabbed a shelf to steady her. After some time, she absently removed a thin volume and took it to a cushioned seat below a window. Wrapped in the warm cloak, she tucked her bare feet beneath her. Her heart pounded and her breaths came in constricted gasps.

The outer door sounded, and every muscle in her body went rigid.

Then King Edgar entered.

She bolted to her feet, terror sweeping over her. She had placed herself in a vulnerable state, leaving him to think or do anything. She panicked. The room spun. Mariamne dropped back to sit.

He turned abruptly, averting his eyes and stuttered. "My lady?"

"Lord Stanley has taken the queen's suites," she told him in a rough voice, which spoke as much of her fear as her strained throat.

"What!" Edgar reached for the door.

"Your Majesty," Mariamne called, and he paused without looking at her. "'Tis all part of their plan and our test. We must remain and prepare for whatever they intend." She sighed as his shoulders dropped and his hand moved from the door. "I have been well educated in the schemes derived in the hearts of wicked men. 'Tis no accident Lord Stanley awaits across the hall. Though Richards is more vested in proving your marriage a farce, it is Stanley here, which speaks clearly to a plan. Your Majesty, they must find us properly attired for bed."

"I am so sorry for all of this, my lady," he groaned. "'Tis much more than you ever agreed upon. I must end it."

He again reached for the latch, but she called out with more calm. "Sire, everything has succeeded thus far. Please throw it not away on my account. Your kingdom is of greater value than my comfort."

He rested his forearm on the door casing and leaned his head against it. "You are a dear lady. I fear when our trials with the dukes are complete, I will be unable to adequately repay your overwhelming generosity."

"Let us win the victory first, Majesty."

He straightened and took a step into the bedchamber without looking toward her.

A loud bang accompanied by squeals of laughter sounded at the outer door.

Edgar turned as his inner door flew open and Clifford ran full force into him. A moment later, Doyt collided with them both.

"By my sword! What is the meaning of this?" Edgar bellowed. He regained his balance and stepped between her and the children, shielding her from their wandering gazes.

"Boys? Where have you gotten to now? Come. Time for bed." Stanley yelled, unconcerned and acting as though unaware of their whereabouts.

The boys giggled as they raced from the room.

"Someone sent them," Mariamne hissed.

Edgar reached out a stiff arm to slam the door closed, but Roanne stepped into the doorway, and her distrustful gaze washed over them both.

"Forgive me, Your Majesties, I do apologize if my boys disturbed you."

"My lady, if you are incapable of controlling your spawn, several attendants can be assigned to manage them." Mariamne's curt words had no effect on the woman.

Roanne rose on her toes to look at Mariamne, but Edgar blocked her view. "That will not be necessary."

As the woman still did not leave, Mariamne stepped one leg forward but remained well hidden behind Edgar's broad shoulders. "And another thing, madam—have a servant girl retrieve my night rail from the third drawer of the dresser, my green gown from the wardrobe, and my brush from near the washbasin." She thought, grateful of all the cleaning she'd done in queen's chambers in the last few days. Her muscles relaxed.

Lady Roanne's eyes flew to hers. "Oh heavens, we did not know you stayed in those chambers…"

The king straightened to his full imposing height and leaned forward as he spoke, his words slow and measured. "They are known to all as the *queen's* chambers, woman. Surely the name alone should have marked them for the *queen's* use—even to dolts like you and your husband."

"We will vacate them immediately, Your Majesties," the woman stammered, but she still would not leave.

"Upset not your family, madam," Mariamne said, projecting a playful, amorous voice. She stepped a little to the side of the king, allowing the cloak to open below her knee. She watched as Roanne's eyes drifted to her exposed shin below the hem of the king's nightshirt. As Roanne locked eyes with her again, Mariamne raised a delicate hand and placed it on the king's chest, smiling first at him and then back at Roanne. "These accommodations are not so undesirable. I think we can be obliged to suffer and endure them until your departure."

Her mission apparently accomplished, Roanne's nose tipped up and she turned to leave.

Heat radiated from Edgar as Mariamne pressed against him, and his heart thundered under her hand. She feared she had inflamed his passion and took two great steps away.

He reached out and slammed the inner door shut.

She startled. A gasp escaped her parched lips as she trembled.

Edgar stood riveted in place as though turned to stone. His fists clenched so tightly they turned white.

Her fear grew until her legs again would not hold her. She dropped to the seat once more and hugged the cloak tight about her.

Strangled words at last ground between his clenched teeth. "Might our tests finally be complete?"

A great breath slipped from her as she crumpled into the window seat. It was not passion but wrath that consumed him.

"I venture they will seek not to invade your inner chambers again, Your Majesty. Though they may sneak into the outer," she added as a warning.

He did not move.

"Majesty, I told little Erika my mother died when I was young."

Edgar's tense shoulders dropped. He turned, though his gaze studied the tapestry hanging on the wall to her right. "Good, for Richards inquired after your parents. I too told him your mother was dead and your father could not leave the islands to escort you, as I could not leave Veronia to greet you."

She tipped her head back against the window, her breaths and heart slowing.

He turned to the bathing room, and water splashed in the porcelain basin. "We should discuss more of your background," he said, running a towel over his face as he stood in the doorway.

"Yes, Your Majesty. If we are to falter now, 'twill be with our own words."

A light knock sounded on the outer door.

Edgar flew to it in two angry strides that boomed off the walls.

Mariamne watched from her perch on the window seat as a poor servant nearly melted under his menacing demeanor. He grabbed the garments, and she flew from the room, dropping the queen's silver hairbrush in her haste. He bent, picked it up, and returned to the bedchamber. He laid the items on the bed. "I will step into the outer chamber, my lady."

Moments after the door latch sounded, glass shattered to bits against the wall in the outer room.

Mariamne hid behind the screen and removed Edgar's shirt with its musky sent that made her head swim. She would never be able to capture sleep incased within it. She changed into his mother's night rail, folded his shirt, laid it on the dresser, and opened the door before returning to the bench to brush her hair.

Edgar entered momentarily, and she could tell by the set of his jaw he still thought of Stanley. But as he walked further into the room, his eyes caught on the screen in its new position in the far corner. A quick glance at the floor and he broke into a bright smile. "You are the clever one, my lady, and your mind is always at work. You have devised a most excellent solution. I will gladly sleep on the floor for the chastity of such a fine woman."

"No, Sire," she said, springing to her feet. "The mat is for me."

Now he did turn and look at her, though his gaze never wandered from hers.

She held herself still. "I could nay take your bed, Majesty."

"And I would never allow such a fine lady to sleep on the floor."

"Your fine bed is no place for a slave, Majesty."

After a low grumble she amended the statement. "Or even a former slave."

"But it is the place for the woman who has saved my kingdom and my throne—how many times this day?"

"Please, Your Majesty, I have slept on far worse, and a clean soft mat on the king's expensive rugs will be grand enough."

"And a proper feather bed would be an expression of your king's great favor."

She opened her mouth to protest again.

"Are you always so stubborn, my lady?"

Her head dropped and her cheeks heated, "I fear so, Majesty."

A good-natured chuckle graced his words. "I will bear this in mind in the future, but for tonight the king will have his way."

He stepped behind the screen only to reappear moments later still in his breeches and untucked linen undershirt. "Do you like to read?" he asked as he sat in the chair to pull off his boots.

She crinkled her brows at his odd question.

He nodded toward the book beside her.

She looked down, having forgotten she pulled the slim volume from the shelves and shook her head. "'Tis hardly the thing a master teaches a slave, Sire."

"But such is part of a lady's education." His stocking feet padded across the room, and he pulled a blanket from a trunk. "Mayhaps Hugh, or even your friend—Darrel, is it not?—can see to some private tutoring."

Tears stung her eyes. "Thank you, Your Majesty."

He settled on the mat, saying with a yawn, "Dear lady, 'tis the very least I can do. If you have need or want of anything, you have but ask."

She slipped off the cloak and slid into the bed, unable to put proper words to her gratitude. "Do you wish the lamp blown out, Your Majesty?"

"At your pleasure, my lady," he said through another yawn.

Soon his slow deep breathing filled the room assuring her he slept. She lowered the wick, dimming the light. It took her considerably longer, but she did sleep surrounded by his heady scent. Her dreams beset by worries of the day to come, she tossed much of the night.

Chapter 24

When Edgar rose at first light, he found Mariamne already gone. The open bed curtains revealed the straightened covers, but her sweet honeysuckle scent lingered in the room. As he sat on the bench near the window to pull on his boots, he paused to pick up the book she had pulled from the library. A book of love poems. He smiled.

He left his chambers. The ruckus banging from inside the queen's chambers battered his nerves. The children's laughter grated, and he stomped down the stairs as though outrunning a vicious beast.

Edgar thundered across the ward. "Ready my horse," he called to a squire. "And send to the barracks for Halton, Cy, and any others who wish to hunt."

Spotting Tye, Edgar delivered a short message for his lords and joined the others.

The men talked excitedly as they filled their quivers and swung their bows over their shoulders. The day dawned bright, and Edgar hoped to release his raging anger in a good chase on worthy game.

As she oversaw preparation of the breaking of the fast, footsteps pounded through the hall. She peeked out to consider Edgar as he stomped across the rushes. Shoulders thrown back, fists clenched at his side, he did not glance to the right or the left.

She stood for a moment longer in the doorway and pondered him. He was an uncommon man. Edgar knew the names of every person within his castle and treated them each with kindness. He took no regard for station, addressing a chambermaid, an imposter queen, or a duke's wife with the same respect.

She shook her head and returned to the kitchen, remembering his earnest apology. No one ever sought her absolution. King Edgar could become enraged, as he had last night. But even in his seething wrath, he did not lash out. His anger never stormed out of control. What gave him the power to rein in his emotions? Was it the unseen God, and if so, how did worshipping Him endow His followers with such restraint?

"Your Majesty?"

Drawn from her contemplations, she lifted her head. "Yes, Esther?"

"Corliss picked some early berries yesterday. I have cut them to place on your bread, Your Majesty. I know King Edgar also favors them."

"You are very sweet, Esther. Thank you, I will enjoy them, but the king has gone. I know not where, but he looked determined as he passed through the hall a short time ago,"

Esther rubbed her hands together. "Then I will plan for venison stew. King Edgar and his men never fail to bring down at least one deer."

Mariamne stared at her, trying to understand her words.

"He goes to hunt. If he leaves the castle early—you will find him in his hunting grounds."

Mariamne nodded as she arranged the breads on the many trays and considered those bustling about her. A smile pulled at her lips, and an odd flutter ran through her heart. The servants honored her with exceeding kindness and treated her with the utmost respect.

These new foreign feelings pulled at her rebellious spirit. They laced around her, binding her to King Edgar, his castle, and an unwanted destiny. A nervous shudder raced through her, and a cool chill slid like a drop of winter rain down her spine.

Shaking off the darkness, she turned to gather the trays. Without Stanley's boys, the meal could proceed peacefully.

Richards lumbered his bulk to stand next to the overly adorned Stanley. They arrived in riding clothes, and their wives sat at the back of the hall.

Tye approached them, speaking loud enough for all to hear. "King Edgar has no desire of your company. After your deplorable behavior last night in his bedchamber, you may never again be afforded the king's favor. When King Edgar returns from hunting, he expects you will be out of the queen's chambers, Lord Stanley. He further expects both of you will greet him with an appropriate act of contrition." Tye turned abruptly and took his seat.

Mariamne bit the inside of her cheek, as the two men stood red-faced in the middle of the hall. Richards's deep scowl creased his plump face, while Stanley's pink cheeks only added to his ridiculous appearance. They refused to join the others. Richards snarled something to his companion. They both turned and collected their families with a snap of Richards's finger and returned upstairs.

At the end of the meal as Mariamne helped clear the boards, she turned to a serving maid. "Corliss, whatever is the matter?"

"The lords and those children, Your Majesty."

"You mean Stanley's spawn?"

The petite freckle-faced girl covered her giggle with a delicate hand. "Aye, Majesty. They demanded food be brought to their room. But what everyone else ate was not to their liking. They demanded

cheeses and jams, next they wanted wheat loaves and not barley rolls."
The girl sighed heavily, and her shoulders slumped.

"Have they finished eating?"

"Aye, Majesty."

"Good. I will see to the problem before the next meal."

Corliss curtsied deeply. "Thank you, Your Majesty."

As midday bells rang, Stanley's servant slunk toward her, head hanging low. "Lord Stanley and his family plan to dine with Richards's clan in the queen's sitting room."

"Do they now?"

"Aye, madam, they require their meal be brought to them. The maid said I must speak with you."

Hot rage burned her cheeks as her nails dug deep into her palms. She fought to follow Edgar's example and not take her wrath out on the servant standing before her. Head low and eyes half open, he shifted nervously before her.

Maids exited the kitchen with the special trays ready for their horrid guests. "Corliss. Dawn?"

"Aye, Your Majesty?"

She managed a smile for the serving maids. "Would you please do me a great kindness and deliver a message, instead of the food, to *my* chamber?"

They curtsied, returned the food to the kitchen, and came to stand before her with Stanley's servant. Smiles of satisfaction graced the maids' faces.

"Please tell all those gathered above that they may not eat in the queen's chambers, for I do not wish any of the priceless things soiled by their carelessness. There is food available in King Edgar's hall if they care to join us, but none will be provided for them at any other place or time."

As the three turned to deliver the message, Mariamne entered the kitchen. "Esther, please make all the staff aware that no food is to be taken to the lords in the apartments nor may they come get any. And no one is to prepare a special meal for them if they come to you later."

"Aye, Your Majesty," she replied with a giddy smile.

Mariamne groaned as the families skulked down begrudgingly for midday. She avoided eye contact with them as they sat together in the back of the hall. All except for the boys, who raced about even more wildly than before.

At one point, Mariamne nearly tripped over Clifford and Doyt. Losing her patience, she cuffed them both about their ears, and they yelped. She grabbed them by the collar and pulled them to within an inch of her face. A low menacing growl rumbled as she ground out words through a locked jaw, "You will sit or you will leave."

"Boys, come here," Roanne called in alarm, and Mariamne released them.

They stood unmoving for a moment, eyes wide, before taking a few slow steps from her. When she did nothing more, they sped back to their mother and cried their woes into her skirt. Unfortunately, their somberness did not constrain them for long, and too soon they raced among the many tables. They carefully avoided Mariamne, however.

While the lords ate at the boards, Mariamne approached the steward. "Sir Tye, will you kindly see to it Stanley, his brood, and their belongings are removed from the queen's suite and the linens changed?"

He wiped his mouth, "Aye, Your Majesty. It will be done at once, and guards will be posted to assure they do not return."

"Thank you."

After the meal, Mariamne kept busy with any task and did not afford herself the time to socialize with the sour ladies, had they even been amenable to it. She knew the duty of wives of any household was to entertain all the noblewomen under her roof. But she could not persuade herself to pretend to be nice to these women.

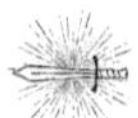

Edgar sauntered in triumphantly with his hunting party. The chase of worthy game allowed his blood to pound the memories of last night's affront from his mind. He missed everything he launched an arrow at, but others saw to filling his storerooms. Now as he cleared the inner gate, he noticed Mariamne filling water from the well. Emotions jarred him as if he had been thrown from his horse. He hadn't considered her needs all day. She suffered more than he last night, yet she raised her head and smiled at him wearily.

Leaving his mount with a squire, he approached her with halting steps, his stomach twisting into knots. "Good afternoon, my lady. How did you fare this day?"

She hefted her burden onto her hip and turned toward the hall. Sunlight caught on the pearls in the snood holding her ebony hair, and it reminded him of stars in a midnight sky. She blew a loose strand of hair from her face.

He stepped into her path, took the bucket, and reached out to tuck the stray behind her ear. "You look tired, my lady." The knot in his middle grew more painful.

She pulled from his touch, and her cheeks colored. "I fared not as well as the king, since he escaped his foul dukes and their nauseating brood for a time."

The smile slipped from his face at her soft rebuke, and the shamed tremor of his heart forced him to set the bucket down. Some of its contents slopped onto his boots. "Oh, my lady, I am so sorry. I never thought… I never thought about *you* as I fled from them. Please forgive me."

Her gaze rose to his, her lower lip captured in her teeth and her brows drawn together. "Forgive my complaining, Majesty. As I have said, I am not worthy of the thought."

A dagger pierced his heart. How could he have been so thoughtless? "Tell me of the trials of your day, please, so I might find a way to make amends."

She told him everything, and his anger flared to the surface afresh.

"Those miscreants struggle to even sit through an entire meal. You are the king, Sire, and this is your home. Must you suffer them another moment?" Her head dropped, and she nearly moaned. "Forgive me, Your Majesty. It is not my place to question."

He reached out a finger and raised her chin. "You above all others have this right."

She dropped her gaze, though he still held her chin.

"I need their military commitment for the coming war," he said in exasperation.

She pulled from his touch. "Why, Your Majesty? If these men cannot come to the aid of the king to whom they have sworn fidelity, they will be left defenseless if he falls and they should never receive the king's aid again should he succeed. For after your great victory, you will be too busy showering your allies with honor and favor to concern yourself with any threat of them." Her lip disappeared between her teeth once more.

Edgar considered her patiently. "But I have loyal subjects living in their provinces, my lady."

She looked into his eyes once more. She opened her mouth to speak but snapped her jaws shut and closed her eyes with a small shake of her head. She took a deep breath and tried again. Her jaw trembled. At last, words burst from her, "Let it be known King Edgar will not defend these two louts, and the people are free to move anywhere within your land to remain under your protection. Like creatures escaping a sinking vessel, the people will run without a second thought from anyone so out of your favor. The dukes will lose their tenement holders. There will be no one to bring in the crops and no one paying dues to support their outrageous lifestyles. They would be left begging for scraps as you grant their lands to others more deserving."

He stood in awe as the truth of her words rang like the great steeple bell.

She raised a quizzical brow to him as her lips drew a tight line.

He took her hand and kissed it with a grateful smile. "I am continually amazed, my dear lady, for your outward beauty is only surpassed by the exquisiteness of your intellect."

She stepped from him, blushing as she showed him a quick observance, collected the bucket, and returned to the hall.

"Halt!" Mariamne's sharp tone brought Edgar up short. His gaze quickly moved from her steeled stance across the room. Seeing Stanley's brood hurtling toward her, he took the bucket and set it on the floor. Lord Stanley stepped from the stairs behind his wild boys and approached with his chin hoisted high.

"Lord Stanley, I have assigned these squires to attend your miscreant children." She pointed to three nearly grown, stout men who stood to join her. "Since you are obviously unable to control them yourself, these men will stand behind your reprobate offspring and see to it they remain seated at boards until everyone has concluded their meal."

"And if I refuse, madam?"

Edgar stepped toe-to-toe with Stanley, making the lord crane his neck to meet his king's gaze. "She is your queen, man, and you will address her as such. If you are unwilling to accept your queen's chaperones, I will see to it your degenerate spawn are removed to the stables, tethered, and fed from the troughs with the rest of the beasts."

Stanley attempted to puff himself up. "You dare not."

Edgar leaned into him further and ground his words between his teeth. "Test the mettle of my words and see if they are not as strong as the steel in my blade." He moved his hand to the hilt of the sword at his hip. "I could, by all rights as your king, do far worse."

Stanley shuddered, tipped precariously on his kitten heels, and almost fell. His eyes went wide and he gasped. He stepped back with a silent bow.

The squires stepped forward and followed the children as they exited the hall.

Stanley stepped carefully around the king and trailed behind.

"Thank you," Mariamne breathed gratefully.

Edgar turned to her. Her chin rose a little higher. Her eyes danced in the flickering light of the torches. He collected the bucket, offered her his arm, and escorted her to the third floor, where they separated to freshen before the evening meal.

Chapter 25

Edgar plodded across the hall an hour after his confrontation with Stanley. His men gathered as he straightened his doublet and stomped onto the dais without speaking to anyone. They sat in hushed conversation. Were they also waiting to see if the dukes would apologize?

The lords and their families came last to the hall, and when they arrived they went to the boards in the back without comment.

Mariamne stepped from the kitchen with the meal trays.

Edgar held up a hand. "There will be no food until I have heard from my lords."

She inclined her head, dipped a simple curtsy, and returned the food. She reappeared to stand outside the kitchen door. Her gaze remained on him.

All eyes turned toward the dukes. The room hushed. No one spoke. No one moved. After several minutes, Edgar wondered if anyone still breathed.

Richards sat straight-backed, staring through a narrowed gaze at Edgar. He spoke not a word, but challenge screamed in his eyes.

Stanley shifted uncomfortably. He opened his mouth once, but Roanne seized his arm.

The weight of the silence in the room grew.

Stanley looked to Richards, but the older man did not acknowledge him. Finally he freed himself from his wife's grip and stepped forward. His stomach growled in the soundless room. "I ask,

Your Majesty, for forgiveness on behave of my wife and my children. They committed an unforgivable affront to you and the Lady Mariamne when they barged into your chambers while you prepared for bed."

"Stanley—" Roanne choked.

A huge gasp rippled through those gathered in the hall, drowning out Roanne's response.

Edgar noted his admission lacked his responsibility in it.

"She. Is. Your. Queen!" Edgar spoke each word with a depth of conviction that reached to the soles of his feet. "You are to leave my castle at first light, Lord Stanley, and you are not to return until you are invited to do so." Edgar reined in his fury, his tone flat and cold.

"What of the war host, Majesty?" Stanley stammered.

"Since you have refused to promise me any such host, I did not expect you to be accompanying them. If you have reconsidered and plan to join your king on the battlefield, you may yet regain his favor. If you prove yourself the coward, I will gladly award your title and your lands to those more deserving when I secure my kingdom."

Another cry went up from his wife, and all the color drained from the duke's face. He bowed slow and deep and returned on stiff legs to his seat.

The hall erupted as dagger hilts thumped on wood and filled the room with his men's approval.

Edgar raised a firm hand, and they fell silent. They followed his gaze. Each man remained transfixed on Richards as Edgar waited for his act of contrition.

The duke bellowed from his place. "Because I had no part in the affairs of last night committed by Stanley and his sons, I will not apologize."

Edgar stood, his hand on the hilt of his sword. "We are all quite aware you advanced Stanley's actions to take the queen's chambers and concoct a way to get his woman into my rooms. For Stanley is too dull to orchestrate such an elaborate plan. I know your great hopes to get me wed to that sour-faced primping daughter of yours.

"You, sir, and your puckered women will leave my home immediately, for I will not suffer your insubordination any longer. You will be escorted to Wellfort Manor by my knights to collect what heirlooms you may possess, before you are evicted and stripped of your title, your land, and your holdings."

Richards rose slowly to his feet. He advanced on Edgar and drew a small dagger from his belt. He held it menacingly.

Edgar jumped down from the dais and met him in two great strides. He drew his long blade and held it at the man's throat. "Accept your fate, or I will see you hanged before the meal concludes."

Richards stood unmoving. He spun the small blade. His eyes narrowed as he looked from it to the tip of Edgar's blade. Richards's muscles tensed. His lips drew a harsh line. His breathing quickened.

Did he plan to try and take his king in hand-to-hand combat? Here? Now?

Richards dared a glance around the room and stepped back from the sword tip, lowering his dagger. "You will live to regret this, Edgar." He raised the dagger as if to throw it.

Edgar brought his blade up, cutting a deep gash in Richards's arm. The dagger dropped.

Several knights sprang to Edgar's defense and secured the enraged man.

"But you, Richards, will not live to regret what you have done!" Edgar turned his head only a degree and shouted over his shoulder. "Halton, take him to the executioner. He has threatened the life of the king in his hall, in the presence of all these witnesses."

As Halton and a handful of knights pulled the bellowing man to his doom, the hall filled with a cacophony of screaming women and shouting knights as they confirmed their witness to the man's treachery. With Richards no longer in the hall, thumps of dagger hilts on the long boards accompanied rousing cheers.

When the din subsided, Edgar turned to Elizabeth and Ingrid. His gaze leveled on them as he slid his sword back into its sheath. "Get out!"

The crying women fled up the stairs.

"Tye, take some maids and a handful of men and assure they take only what belongs to them." Edgar returned to his seat.

The thumping of the daggers continued and was joined by the men's shouts. "Long live King Edgar! Long live the king! Huzzah!"

At times, he doubted his men's loyalty. But not after tonight. They would follow him into battle. He sighed in relief and looked to Mariamne. *Lord, You have so blessed me by bringing her here. You have surely sent her here to save this kingdom. Look what her simple question about my tolerance of my men's behavior has accomplished.*

She stood with her shoulders thrown back and her chin held high. A smile graced her face, and she inclined her head when their eyes met.

Edgar's heart fluttered like a caged bird before an approaching snake. Was Mariamne proud of him? His pounding heart leapt to his throat. His thoughts failed him.

She tipped her head to the side and raised an eyebrow.

He swallowed the hard lump in his throat, wondering why the admiration of one woman he had known but a few days should affect him more than the approval of his men.

Her hand moved tentatively toward the kitchen door.

He managed to raise his hand, beckoning her to begin the meal.

She disappeared beyond the door, and Edgar struggled to capture breath. She reemerged with a trail of maids on her heels and proceeded to his table. Laying his tray, she spoke in a pleading whisper. "No matter how your stomach turns, you must eat tonight of all nights. Do not show regret or thought of the man—not now. Linger over your meal as if it is any other."

Edgar watched as she returned to the kitchen. His gaze washed over his men as they raised their cups to him. He looked down at his plate, tore off a haunch of venison, and forced it down into his knotted stomach.

His meal complete, Edgar stood. Daggers rapped their applause, and a smattering of huzzah's rang out once more as he walked with slow steps. He moved out of the hall and toward the dungeon and the man whose death he had ordered. Entering the dark confines of the barred space below the inner tower, he approached a small man in a brown robe. "Have you met with him, Father?" Edgar asked Father John, Richards's personal priest.

"I accompanied him here, Your Majesty."

"Has he shown any remorse? Has he recanted his threat or his behavior?" Edgar hoped the hard man would yield, that he would yet be able to spare his life.

"To the contrary, Majesty, Lord Richards has hardened his heart. He will not listen to instruction. He will not even allow Holy Scripture read over him. He rants and raves and continues to make bold threats against you, Sire—you and your new bride." Father John's narrow shoulders heaved. "Richards is lost to us, he will meet his end unshriven."

"Thank you for your efforts, Father." Edgar turned from the priest and instructed his men to prepare for the execution. He trudged up the steps. His stomach twisted into a hard knot nearly doubling him over in pain. A small contingent of men took their places, and Edgar regretted following Mariamne's advice, for the food he consumed now threatened to return.

Richards emerged from the tower, squirming between two guards. "You will fail, Edgar. All is lost. Can you not see? He is coming, and he will devour your kingdom. Your weak and pathetic rule will finally see its end." He cackled madly as the noose slipped over his head. "You think you will win by killing me, but your day is coming. Soon you will meet your own end on the end of his bla—" Richards flopped at the end of the noose, abruptly silent.

As he died, the illusion surrounding him evaporated, revealing a shriveled black corpse.

Edgar staggered back a step and rocked unsteadily on his feet. He blinked and shook his head, hoping to clear his vision. This could not be true.

"He is consumed by the hateful poison of the horde," a knight gasped in horror.

"This is where my enemy is gathering his troops—from my own people." Edgar groaned to Halton standing beside him. The realization shook him, and his voice echoed the trembling of his heart. "If the evil can easily infest our good men, and then be hidden so thoroughly from us, what chance of victory do we have?"

Halton drew his sword and raced back to the castle.

Edgar followed close on his heels, "What are you doing?"

Halton met Elizabeth and Ingrid as they loaded bags into their carriage. He filled his blade with holy light and turned it so he bathed the women in its righteous glow. The illusion surrounding them evaporated, revealing the extent of their exposure to the venom.

"Elizabeth is consumed. She too is lost to us," Halton stated with dread. "The Lady Ingrid is seriously infected."

The creature left in Elizabeth's stead screeched in the holy light and lunged at Halton with deadly intent. He skewered the vile thing on the end of his sword and it writhed in agony from the light filling it for a moment before exploding in a puff of dust.

Ingrid crumpled in a pool of tears as she tried in vain to brush the poison from her skin. She looked up at Edgar with great pleading eyes as she fell prostrate at his feet. "Please, Your Majesty, spare me."

Stirred by compassion, Edgar moved forward.

Halton stepped protectively between them, sword still raised. "I will have her taken to the physician, Your Majesty. By God's grace and our prayers, she may yet be saved."

Edgar nodded, and two knights assigned to escort her home secured her. He listened to her desperate wailing as they led her to Carrington's house near the outer gatehouse. Edgar stopped Halton as he moved to follow. "How did you know the light would reveal them?"

Halton smiled. "Queen Mariamne taught us as we ventured through the dreadful fog, Sire. I have no idea how, but God Himself must have made it known to her."

Halton informed those within the king's walls of the events. He instructed the knights lingering about to draw their swords and bathe all in holy light. They closely inspected any visible skin and every eye for any sign of infestation. Only Stanley could be found with the poison. "Escort him to the Carrington and continue to examine all within the castle walls," Edgar ordered.

"Sire?" Stanley blubbered, tears tumbling down his face.

"Your exposure is not great, Lord Stanley, you should be cured."

"Forgive me, Sire," Stanley sobbed as they led him away.

Chapter 26

Mariamne entered the physician's two-story stone structure and followed the sounds of weeping. The structure stood against the outer curtain wall, with treatment rooms on the ground floor and personal apartments for the physician and his wife above. The glowing fire where two knights inserted daggers into its coals drew her gaze and she shuddered.

Carrington and Halton greeted her. "Your Majesty," they said as one.

Ingrid lay strapped trembling to a bed.

"I will not lie to you, Lady Ingrid—this will be a terrible ordeal. But you are young and strong, and you will be restored."

Ingrid calmed.

Mariamne spoke to Carrington, "Sir, might your wife and I be allowed to remove her clothes and only expose the poison? It will allow the poor girl a small portion of her dignity."

"I am a physician, Your Majesty."

"It is still degrading to have a man see you in such a bare state, even if it is for your aid."

The doctor opened his mouth.

"Please, sir, if only as a favor to me."

He inclined his head and stepped from the room. Footfalls sounded on the stairs.

Halton looked at her, his arms crossed and his gaze hard.

"She is terrified and wishes to be free of the evil. It does not yet possess her, sir."

"I will not leave you with the possible threat, Majesty."

"Will you graciously avert your eyes?"

He nodded as Sarah, Carrington's wife, entered.

"Sirs, please leave us," Mariamne said.

The knights and doctor left, and Halton turned away, but his hand rested on the hilt of his blade.

Ingrid's lips trembled, and her puffy red eyes locked on Mariamne's. "Thank you."

Mariamne nodded, unbuckled Ingrid's bindings, and helped her remove her elegant gown and fine linen undergarments to expose the poisonous webs.

Seeing no black webs on her breasts, Sarah and Mariamne wrapped Ingrid in a strip of clean cloth. After Sarah draped another wide piece of cloth from Ingrid's waist to her knees, Mariamne motioned for her to return to the bed.

Ingrid sat looking at her infected skin, as great sobs racked her body.

Sarah helped her lay back, "Peace, my lady. We are here."

Ingrid allowed them to restrain her once more and looked at Mariamne with tear-filled eyes.

Mariamne met her gaze evenly and told her the truth. "The poison is very advanced. It covers most of your upper body and lower legs. It will take a great deal of burning to be rid of it. The only way you will survive is to focus on the light of your God and know, with all certainty, the pain will end and you will be left whole. Are you convinced of this, my lady?"

She nodded weakly.

"You must say it, Ingrid. Tell the spawn inside of you that you will survive and be left whole."

The girl licked her trembling lips. "I will survive and be left whole." Tears gushed.

Mariamne made her repeat it until the girl yelled the words. Then she covered her with a sheet and laid a tender hand on her cheek. She leaned near and encouraged Ingrid, "Keep saying it, no matter the pain or the fear or the doubt. I will look in on you as oft as my duties allow. Be strong."

She pulled Halton outside with Carrington. "You may tend the blades and fire now, sirs," she said to the warriors.

The two knights reentered.

"Healer, how much do you know of this condition?"

"The poison must be burned completely, and only when the eyes are clear is it gone. As dark as her eyes are now, she will be like the others I have treated and die from the treatment without ever being free of the toxin."

"She will if you try to burn all of it from her at once," Mariamne said.

Halton's arms crossed again. "But it will continue to grow if it is not all removed, Your Majesty."

"Have you ever been infected, sirs?"

They glanced at one another and shook their heads.

"I have, and I can tell you it is an intelligent evil, not a toxin. It invades the body and the mind. Before a blade ever touched me, the evil screamed out in terror. It sensed its impending end. It retreated in on itself as the heat approached my flesh, and it tried to hide from the burning.

"This is my suggestion, good healer. Begin the burning, but only use a few blades. I withstood eight burnings and rode a horse for a time the following day. I believe I am stronger than the delicate Ingrid, so mayhaps only four or five burns should be done, until you can judge her tolerance. After the burnings, allow her to rest and get her to eat before you resume. But as you allow her to rest, continually bring the hot blades to within inches of her skin. It will not further injure her, but it will chase back the spawn and keep it from reasserting itself."

The doctor's head tipped to one side. "It is an intriguing treatment, Your Majesty, I doubt anything like it has ever been tried. I will attempt to do as you have suggested, we should know its effectiveness within a few days."

"Thank you, sir. I will come to look in on her at first light on the morrow." She gave the men a quick curtsy and stepped into the last rays if the setting sun.

She slipped into the church, but she found Edgar within. Mariamne left without disturbing him.

Edgar knelt before the altar as his men searched his home with holy light. He intended to pray for Ingrid, Stanley, and the lives of his people, but his mind would not focus. Regret for having killed a man stole his breath and crushed his spirit. This man had supported his father, and even his own reign in the beginning. He searched his mind for a sign or any hint he should have seen. Mayhaps if he had noticed sooner, Richards could have been spared. The unseen opportunities burned in the back of Edgar's throat, constricted his chest, and clouded his thoughts until he slumped before the great altar.

I would have no man to perish, My son. Richards chose freely whom he would serve—and it was Me. His blood is on his own head.

Edgar moaned, "Oh Lord, the enemy is so strong."

Be strong and of good courage, fear not, nor be discouraged for I the Lord thy God will be with thee, whithersoever thou goes.

Edgar lingered for a long time and let those words wash over him, fill him, and strengthen him. Finally he returned to the castle and slept, deeply cradled in his God's peace.

Mariamne served at the first meal while Edgar remained sequestered in his study. The empty dishes had long since been cleared when a contrite Stanley and his better-behaved family entered the hall from the rooms above. They prepared to leave.

He took a knee. "Your Majesty, I humbly beg your forgiveness for the great disrespect I have shown you and my king. I will not cower behind the poison found in my veins, for my rebellion allowed it a foothold in my soul. I am once again your humble servant, Your Majesty, and I will do whatever you and King Edgar command, including surrendering my life, for it is the least I deserve."

Memories filled her of the times since leaving the slaver's cells when she expected—and deserved—punishment. She recalled afresh the great relief when reparations never came. That repeated grace softened her heart and made her want to do all the more for the person who gave it.

She placed a gentle hand on the man's small head. "Your heartfelt apology has been accepted, my friend, and you are free to go in peace. I would ask you to pray for your king, and his kingdom, and supply the men he needs to be victorious in battle so he may return unharmed to his throne."

The man trembled and started to weep. "I have already sent one of my knights ahead of my return to prepare the majority of my forces to aid the king immediately. I have further secured lodging for them in town until King Edgar is in need of them. My king has but to send one sandesman to me and I will be here to fight by his side and die to save him, if I may. Until that day, I will seek God for His forgiveness and His blessings on my king and queen."

He stood and bowed as Mariamne thanked him.

Before midday, Edgar stepped from his study and motioned for a maid to come close. "Please find Queen Mariamne and ask her to come to me."

The girl curtsied, "Aye, Your Majesty."

Soon a gentle rap sounded on his door.

"Enter."

She gave him a deep observance, and sat in the chair he motioned her toward.

"Thank you for coming, my lady." Her gaze wandered to the warm sun outside the window. Offering his arm, he led her into the garden. His lips parted in his first full smile in days as she raised her face to the sun.

She stood with her eyes closed for several moments as she drank in the warmth after several days filled with gloom in the castle. Finally she opened her eyes and looked at him with such contentment he feared saying anything to disturb her.

But she spoke first, "Lord Stanley gave you a very earnest apology before he left, Your Majesty. He has promised most of his knights will arrive to an inn in town before the end of next week. He also promised to bring all his fighting men at the least word from you. I accepted on your behalf, but if you would have him do otherwise, I am sure a fast squire could reach him."

"There is no need, your acceptance is my own. Thank you again, my lady." He smiled. "I am surprised he is well enough to travel, after his treatment."

"The poison had not progressed far, and he rode home in a carriage with his family."

She sat on the bench and indicated he could join her.

He stared off at the wild rose vines covering the outside of his study, and sighed several times.

"Something troubles you, Majesty?"

He did not turn. "It has been an arduous few days, and now that I may take my rest and possibly get to know my queen better, I feel I must leave."

She looked at him but did not speak.

"I will take half my men and visit the rest of my lords. I need to see if any of them are likewise infected. I also feel the burden to explain Richards' fate. I will collect their pledges for the battles to come and see for myself the condition of my lands and border."

He took her hand. "You are free to go or stay at your pleasure, my lady. It is my prayer you will choose to remain as my queen, but I will not request this of you. I have asked enough, and you have blessed me abundantly." He sighed and turned back to the roses. "I fear how our people will respond if we both leave at the same time, but you must follow your own heart.

"I will ask but one boon of you, my lady. Halton says the warrior Cy attended you with great care while remaining diligent to your protection as you traveled here. I intend to ask Cy to be your personal guard. Please go nowhere without him. I fear for you, Mariamne, but Halton said Cy would give his life to protect you. I should accompany you, if you choose to leave."

He admired her beauty. "My lady, will you accept this final request of your grateful king and would-be husband?"

"Aye, Your Majesty." Her words, little more than a whisper, carried as much awe as they did promise. "I will go nowhere without the blond warrior."

Edgar leaned back against the tree trunk they sheltered under. "I have also received Hugh's consent to teach you to read our language. I told him you can read your own tongue but wish to read ours. Should you stay, he will meet you in my study after first meal, and to all within the castle it will appear as though Tye is briefing you on the state of the castle in my absence while Hugh dutifully records the information."

"Thank you, Your Majesty. You have been most generous and kind." Her words cracked.

"It is my greatest pleasure, dear lady." He returned to staring at the wall. "I will be gone at least a month, mayhaps closer to two, depending on what I learn." He rose. "Be well, Lady Mariamne." He dared not say more, for his next words would seek her promise to remain.

"I must seek Cy now. If you will excuse me."

She rose with such grace his heart skipped a beat. "I will again look in on Lady Ingrid. Thank you, Majesty." Her last words seemed to catch, and he noted the tears pooling.

He bowed, and they stepped from the garden to go their separate ways.

Edgar called to a squire, "Have Cy come to me."

Cy entered his study with a deep bow, and Edgar indicated he could take a seat.

"How are you faring in your short time here, Cy?" he asked.

"Your Majesty has been exceedingly generous, so I am quite well, Sire. Your men have accepted me and have helped me refine my skill with all manner of weapons. I greatly look forward to fighting alongside my king."

"I am glad you are well treated. My knights and captain have nothing but good reports concerning you, and I understand your desire to fight beside me. I will eagerly welcome your mighty sword when the time comes. But until such time, I have a special duty to ask of you, though I fear you may find it much less desirable."

"I am yours to command, my king," Cy said, moving to the edge of his seat.

Edgar leaned back. "The Lady Mariamne is not my wife," he said honestly. When Cy did not react to the news, Edgar raised a quizzical brow.

A whimsical smirk turned his lips. "Sire, I traveled with the woman for over a fortnight, and while she is far better than the day of her release to Sir Halton's care, I truly did not believe her heart could be won so quickly. Though you, Sire, have produced by far the greatest change in her. But there is a great deal of hurt still within that woman."

"Yes, you truly see the matter clearly, Cy, which is the point of your assignment. I have freed the Lady Mariamne, as I did you and the others, and while my great desire is for her to stay, I fear she will not. I charge you as her personal guard. Go where she goes and see to her safety at all times. Do not stop her or attempt to dissuade her, for she must be free to choose." Edgar raked his hair. "So, Cy, will you do this great service for your king?"

Cy took a knee and placed his right fist over his heart. "It would be my greatest honor to be entrusted by my king with the life of his queen."

Edgar pulled the man to his feet. He grasped the man's forearm. "Thank you, friend. You have put my mind at ease."

Chapter 27

Carrington greeted Mariamne with a tired but happy grin. "Your Majesty, she endured five blades last night, and the poison has been cleared from her neck and shoulders. She slept soundly for a time, and Sarah gave her some stew at first light. Your treatment has proved effective, Your Majesty. I have driven the spawn back from her collarbone to a small area above her breasts, and a couple of patches on her arms were banished—all with the threat of the blade alone. It should only take a few blades to burn these areas away now, rather than the six or more I feared.

"I have likewise reduced the size of the infestation at her stomach, and I am now working on her legs. I do not know the extent of her back, but I hope to turn her after the next burning." He beamed triumphantly. "If your treatment continues to be effective, I will send word to all the kingdoms, and many more lives will be saved from this evil—thanks to you, Majesty."

"You are very kind, Healer. I am grateful it appears to be working. Please bear in mind, sir, the evil does not wish to die and it will try to deceive you into believing you have succeeded when you may not have completely wiped it out."

Carrington nodded.

"Sir, I believe you have been up all night. Please go rest for a spell. I will see to her needs and the beleaguering of the evil."

"Oh Majesty, I could never—"

"It would truly give me great pleasure to see to the spawn's discomfort, sir, and I fear I owe the Lady Ingrid for my unkindness."

The doctor passed her a fresh white-hot blade and left the room. Some time later, Shaw and one of the other knights came and relieved those who sat guard and kept the fire hot.

Shaw grinned at her and bowed low, "Your Majesty."

She turned to trade her cooling blade for a hot one, heat filling her cheeks at his seeming pride in her.

After a time, the doctor returned, rested and fed, to continue his duties.

"When do you plan to resume treatment?" Mariamne asked before she left.

"This evening, to allow the coolness of night for her rest."

She bowed her head and returned to the hall.

As she walked from the doctor's chambers out into the sun, Halton fell into step beside her. His features drawn, he lacked his normal calm.

"My lady, I am not comfortable leaving you here alone. I will ask his majesty if I could remain behind—"

"There is no need, sir."

"I would feel better—"

Mariamne stopped and considered him. "Truly, sir, there is no need. I am safe within the king's walls, and should I choose to leave, King Edgar has asked Cy to remain with me as my personal guard."

"Cy? Do you favor such an assignment, my lady?"

"I thought you trusted the man. You yourself armed him within days of adding him to your company. You praised him to your king. Why would you doubt him now?"

He shifted his weight on his feet and scanned the yard with a quick glance. "I do trust him, my lady. I would feel better if I also remained close."

She started walking once more. "And I, sir, would count it the greatest boon for you to attend your king as he has requested of you."

He bowed as he moved away. "As you wish, my lady."

Edgar and his men, including Halton, rode from the castle at first light. Mariamne saw them off with many of the castle residents. The king looked down at her from his warhorse and said softly, "I hope to see you before the turn of summer, my lady." He did not allow her time to respond as he led his men through the gates.

Pulled by some all-consuming force, Mariamne moved to the nearest tower. She climbed to the top when the king rode through the inner gate. She traversed the inner battlements until they joined with the outer curtain. Her feet moved of their own accord, and an unrecognizable feeling swirled within her. Faltering steps carried her along the outer battlements until she stood over the front of the castle walls. Her fluttering thoughts would not be captured as she watched the men wind down from the castle perch to the valley and off to the north. A strange mixture of feelings she could not understand washed over her in waves. Could she be experiencing pain at seeing the king leave? Why would she care if the king came or went? And why did she already look forward to his return?

"It is a most extraordinary notion to miss someone you have but only met, when they have been gone for but moments," a warm voice mused next to her.

She startled and turned on the intruder.

Cy stood leaning on the crenel between two merlons not far from her. He flashed her a great roguish grin.

In two quick steps, she reached him and slapped him angrily on the upper arm. "The king entrusted you, sir, to guard me. I do not believe the king would favor your spying on me and scaring life from my body."

He laughed boisterously. "Oh, m'lady, 'tis good to hear your voice, even when it spouts harsh rebukes."

Laughter bubbled out of her for the first time in years, joining his merriment of her own foolish behavior. She leaned back against the merlon nearest him, crossed her arms, and looked over the inner bailey. "I beg you accept my profound regret for the king having harnessed you with my care, sir. I know your deepest desire is to fight at his side."

Merriment faded as a serious timbre filled his voice. "King Edgar has seen fit to entrust the care of his most valuable treasure to a foreign man-at-arms. What greater honor could there be for a man like me, dear lady?"

Mariamne refused to look at him. "But I know well you understand the true nature of things in the castle, sir, and..." unable to finish her thought for the strange pain in her chest, she could only look out over the bustle below.

"I see naught but what is meant to be, and what will one day be— the truth," he whispered.

She turned to stare at him unbelieving.

"Give it time, m'lady, you have been here not but a week. You too will come to see matters as we all do. You are the rightful queen of this land."

She shuddered and turned back to looking out over the town at the foot of the castle. They stood for several moments before she moved to the nearest tower and descended the stairs to step into the bailey. Cy trailed her as near as her shadow but remained outside Ingrid's room.

Ingrid rested on her stomach as Carrington worked to beleaguer the spawn on her back. "She withstood more blades than the night before, and her front appeared clean when I turned her this morn."

Mariamne trembled to see how widely the black tendrils of the spawn covered her pale skin. She feared they only labored to chase the evil around and not really rid Ingrid of it.

"Have no fear, Majesty. I expected her back to be worse since it remained untreated for two days. But the treatment is proving most successful."

"I hope you speak truth, Healer. Is there anything I can do?"

"Pray, Your Majesty."

The odd stirring returned to her insides, and she stepped from the treatment room and ran square into Cy.

He stepped aside and waved out a strong arm for her to proceed ahead of him. Cy remained on her heels throughout the day. She nearly spilled a tray trying to avoid him outside the kitchen, and later she tripped over him among the boards. She found herself stumbling over him constantly, as he was forever close at hand. Her irritation with him only served to draw him nearer.

As she climbed the stairs to her chamber later in the night, he followed her. "I am but going to my bed, sir," she called over her shoulder, quickening her steps.

"I intend to sleep at your doorway."

She spun on him at the top of the stairs and nearly pushed him down them. "By the sword, Cy! I give you my solemn vow: I will not think of leaving the castle without you."

He stood on the first step, looking straight into her eyes. "I will take you at your word, m'lady, for it is my honor at stake if I should fail to attend you wherever you go."

The seriousness of his tone drove out the anger. "You have my vow, sir. I swear to rouse you, regardless of the hour, should I have need of you."

He nodded to her with a kind smile and returned to the hall, where she found him sleeping each morn at the foot of the stairs.

"Your Majesty."

"Carrington, you are in good spirits."

"It has taken three more nights of burnings, but I have at last succeeded in expelling all the spawn." He sighed with satisfaction. "I waited until after she roused to eat before I examined her under the holy light of a warrior's sword."

"Did you find any evidence of the evil?"

"One black spot remained in her pale-blue iris. After she ate, we searched the full length of her body under the light until I found the last tendril on the inside of her upper arm. I burned it immediately and left my wife to dress her in a night rail before moving her to a comfortable bed."

"May I move her to the second floor of the castle, sir?"

"I would prefer to keep her here under supervision for a few more days. When I am sure there are no signs of the poison, she may be moved, Your Majesty."

She nodded and wandered from the house with a deep sigh. In Edgar's absence, Mariamne found little to do and she had hoped attending to Ingrid would help her to occupy her idle hours.

As her days unfolded now, she attended reports and reading lessons every morning but failed to grasp the written word. There seemed a great many squiggly lines, and each carried a different sound and name, and she was forever mixing them up.

"How grateful I am King Edgar is not present to see me flounder and fail so profoundly, for it would make him face the truth of how dull I really am," she told Cy as he accompanied her to the well.

"Patience, m'lady," he soothed.

But only a few days passed before she stumbled from Edgar's study nearly in tears and fell into Cy's arms. "I continue to fail to grasp what children learn." She seized his arm. "I wish to go for a ride, sir. Will you please allow me an afternoon outside these walls?"

"I will accompany you anywhere you would care to journey, m'lady."

She sighed in relief and contained her threatening tears. "Thank you. Please see to the horses, and I will don the riding skirt."

She returned within moments, and as the squire handed her the reins of her horse, the captain of the garrison approached with his brows drawn tight together. His turned to scowl at Cy.

Mariamne stepped forward. "Fear not, I am going for but a short ride. I need some time away from these walls, please. I promise to return before supper."

A relieved smile filled his face. "Pell, go to the garrison and tell Nyle, Robert, and Wells they are to accompany the queen."

The squire darted off as a groom started to prepare the additional mounts.

"Thank you, sir."

"Enjoy your ride, Majesty."

Soon Cy led them around the east side of the castle and into Edgar's preserve. They did not take the hunting trails but instead trotted their horses along the great paths carved through the trees.

At one point Mariamne glanced at Cy mischievously and spurred her horse to speed. He understood the look. She laughed at him thundering down the path beside her. It took the remainder of their escort a few minutes, however, to catch up with them.

She slowed and turned to another path Cy said would eventually turn them back toward the castle. They rode in near silence with only a few glances exchanged between her and her faithful guard, yet it seemed those glimpses held a thousand understood words between them.

Mariamne glanced at him now, and he dismounted to assist her before she fully reined in. She ambled around collecting wildflowers then stood utterly still as a young fawn struggled to its wobbly legs to follow its mother. She turned back to the men filled with excitement when the deer slipped from sight.

As they returned through the town a few hours later, Mariamne caught sight of a dress mannequin in front of a small shop. She had but to glance at Cy, and he turned and led them to it. He dismounted, as did the men, and while two stood guard outside, Cy escorted Mariamne into the shop. It sat deserted except for the young woman sitting and stitching on a length of sky-blue cloth. She looked up with a greeting as Mariamne looked at another garment hanging within.

"Good day, my lady."

The displays of simple skirts, fine chemises, and bodices filled the shop. "This is a very interesting display. It seems so simple."

The woman sang out proudly, "Aye, 'tis father's design in accordance with our new queen's taste. She does not favor the excess and frippery, which has been such a nuisance and a waste of fine materials for several years."

"You have seen the queen then?" Mariamne asked with her back to the woman.

"Nay, King Edgar seems to be keeping her all to himself. It is said she is from a far-off land, possibly as far as the Asterie Islands, and he is allowing her time to gain familiarity with our tongue and customs so she can make the best impression when he presents her to his people."

"And what do you reckon is the truth in the tale?"

The merchant paused for a moment to consider. "I think our queen is lonely."

Mariamne turned to consider the slender woman.

"She has been brought here, far from home with naught but a bunch of men to accompany her, to marry a man she never met. There is naught but one lady of the court with whom to socialize. King Edgar waited far too long to marry. Now he plans for war and rides around the country leaving our poor queen alone in a foreign castle."

"What a heartrending existence," Mariamne mused, feeling the loneliness resonate in her like a plucked harp string.

Cy inclined his head encouragingly.

"Mayhaps you should be invited to the castle to cheer me."

The young lady laughed, until realization of what Mariamne said strangled the noise in her throat.

Mariamne slid open her cloak to reveal her chemise and patchwork bodice as she extended her bejeweled left hand. "'Tis my greatest pleasure to make your acquaintance."

The woman fell from her stool in a deep curtsy. "Your Majesty, forgive my ignorant presumption…"

"Oh, goodness." Mariamne stepped forward, pulling the woman to her feet. "You are going to soil your lovely gown if you cower there, dear lady."

The woman continued to gaze at the floor and tremble, and Mariamne moaned. "Fie, I have spoiled everything. We enjoyed such a lovely conversation. And, as you intimated, one of the few I have been afforded the pleasure of since I arrived. Now I have ruined it by revealing myself."

The woman looked up at her with more calm, "Thank you, Majesty, you are too kind."

"I am, Mariamne."

"Aye, Majesty," the woman answered in awe.

Mariamne laughed gently. "And do you have a name, dear woman?"

"Oh, aye, Your Majesty."

When she said nothing further, Mariamne laughed all the more.

"Oh," the poor woman exclaimed as color flooded her face. "Annabel, Your Majesty. I am called, Annabel."

Mariamne curtsied to her, "It is an honor to make your acquaintance, Lady Annabel."

Annabel stood, jaw hanging slack and staring most improperly.

"Your father did a most excellent job of reproducing my favorite attire, do you not agree?" Mariamne opened her cloak more so Annabel could compare the two outfits, and the woman finally smiled.

"Yes, I would say he did, Your Majesty."

Church bells rang. Cy stepped to her elbow. "Forgive me, Your Majesty, but the time…"

Mariamne smiled contentedly, "Of course, my promise to the captain." Looking to Annabel, she said, "'Tis the Lord's Day in two days, and I assume your shop is closed?"

Annabel nodded.

"Then, if it would not be a great burden, might I have the pleasure of your company at the castle. If it is amenable, we could have tea after the midday meal?"

"Your Majesty," Annabel said, "it would be a great honor."

Mariamne smiled at her, "Be assured, my lady, the honor will be all mine." She glanced at Cy as he opened the door.

"I will see to all the details and Lady Annabel's transportation, m'lady."

She said her good-byes, mounted her horse, and headed toward the castle. But Mariamne remained lost in thought. It confounded her and filled her with trepidation to think she set fashion for a whole group of women she had never met.

Cy, as always, understood her unspoken thoughts. "They have never met you, and yet they seek to emulate you, m'lady. It is a great responsibility your position affords you. Think of the changes you could perpetuate to sweep across this kingdom with but the simplest action."

She shuddered at the notion.

"The queen could assure the abolishment of oppressive servitude, the respectful treatment of women, and any other thing which stirs her passions."

She nodded her silent understanding, still unable to form words on her confounded tongue, and hurried into the hall to see to the serving of the meal, without changing from her riding clothes.

Chapter 28

The events of the day replayed as Mariamne retired later. She drifted from the frustration of her lessons, to the freedom of the ride, to seeing the copies of her attire in the shop, to the sweet merchant woman, and finally to the matters Cy had discussed. They overwhelmed her. She struggled to make sense of it all as the shadows of fear and doubt assailed her yet again.

The familiar angst called from the darkness. *It will be oppressive to have the whole kingdom forever watching what you do so they might mimic you. You will lose your own identity. They will all be like you, and you will no longer be special or unique.*

Lying in the dark on her pallet in the nursery, she shook her head to clear it of the strange ramblings. "I have never wanted to stand apart. I seek always to fade into the crowd."

The darkness took a new approach as she groped for the truth. *You will always be singled out. A land can have but one queen. No one will be your equal. You alone stand at the center of Veronia.*

"I clean bedchambers and serve at tables with servants, even with the title queen. I am no honored jewel locked away in King Edgar's treasury to only be looked at and admired. I serve with my hands, my mind, and my heart."

The darkness struck again. *You are locked within these walls, for has not the king begged you to stay. He has chained Cy to you to see you remain within his castle. He claimed to free you, then wrapped you in fetters of his fleeting kindness and affection. You are bound as surely as in any of Jarel's chains.*

"No! The king gave me the choice. He hopes I will stay, but provided Cy to go with me if I choose to leave," she shouted to the darkness filling her. She gripped her head and moaned, "God of this land, silence the lies. *Please.*"

The room fell silent. Moonlight returned and with it came the peace. *Rest, Daughter, I am with you and will watch over you.*

Mariamne slipped under the thin cover, filled with the quiet she could not understand from a God she did not know. Yet He answered when she called.

The next day passed quickly, and then the Lord's Day dawned bright and full of promise. The entire castle gathered in the great house of the God of Veronia. Now as queen, Mariamne was expected to sit in the front row across the aisle from the king's empty seat.

Mariamne groaned as Cy fell into step beside her.

"What troubles you, m'lady?"

"I struggle to know what to do with all those who could serve as examples hidden behind me. The only saving grace is the fact I am not expected to participate."

"Has it not been explained that it is the custom of the Veronian churches to assess a new member's understanding of the great truths of God before one is allowed to participate in the service, receive the holy sacraments, or take any action?"

"Aye." This unseen God took His religious observances seriously. "He is unlike any other god," Mariamne wrung her hands. "It is as though this God, like King Edgar who serves Him, gives the people a choice to worship or not. He fully accepts all who choose Him and denies all who reject Him, but no middle ground exists for one to believe He lives, and yet still choose not to worship."

"And therein lies the strength of God above all other gods. He does not need us for anything, but He desires relationship with us. Is it not most wonderful?" Cy stopped at a pew on the right as she continued to the front row on the left.

As she sat struggling to comprehend the ministration of the priest, his eyes fell on her reminding her of their pending meeting. She would only be afforded the leisure of ignorance until she met with the priest.

These people concerned themselves far more with doing things in a holy manner for the sake of the soul than doing them quickly. The knowledge brought her both frustration and peace.

Her mind wandered from the message again. How controlling of this narrow-minded God to only come to the aid and protection of those who followed Him. But He had answered her pleas.

She shifted in her hard pew, struggling to concentrate on the words Father Paul read from the sacred Scriptures. A new message penetrated deep into her wounded heart: "If any of you lack wisdom, let him ask of God, which giveth to all men liberally, and reproacheth no man, and it shall be given him."

She sat still as stone, rolling the words around. She barely noticed as the faithful came forward for the holy sacrament. They talked of eating and drinking the body of their God—horrifying. She did not wish to dwell on the morbid rite. The words of seeking wisdom still occupied her musing when the congregants filed out.

Father Paul approached her quietly, "Your Majesty, does anything trouble you?"

"No Father, I merely hoped to stay and…" Well, she knew not why.

Father Paul smiled, "All are welcome to seek God, Your Majesty, for whatever thee has need of. I will leave you to your prayers,

Majesty, and when you are finished, mayhaps we could set a time to begin your interviews?"

She nodded but did not look at him, and he moved off with silent steps. Mariamne's gaze rose to the altar and the great gold cross resting there, and she considered it. Then she bowed her head. "God of Veronia, if You are willing, may I have wisdom? Would You give it to one such as I? For I need to know the truth of things before the lies capture me."

The gentle warm breeze swirled about her. *Ask, and it shall be given you: seek, and ye shall find...*

"Thank You," she whispered. Wisdom did not pour out of heaven at that moment. When she needed to discern a truth from a lie, would she know? Comfort eased her cramped muscles as she rose.

Cy smiled in the back row and stood as she drew near. He never spoke as he escorted her to the hall for midday.

"Good afternoon, Your Majesty," Annabel greeted her with a tremble in her fair voice.

A squire escorted her to the small table prepared near the front of the garden. Mariamne stood as she approached, and Annabel curtsied deeply. Annabel was several inches shorter than Mariamne and a few years younger, but she was just as slender and shapely. Rich brown hair, generously highlighted with bright golden strands, framed her fair complexion. She wore it in a gentle chignon bound with a ribbon matching the blue of her simple linen gown.

Mariamne sighed as they both sat silently.

"Have I displeased you, Your Majesty?" Annabel's voice quaked.

"Not at all, dear lady, but I would beg a great boon of you."

"Anything, Your Majesty," Annabel agreed before she knew what would be asked of her.

A great sadness filled her Mariamne. "Would you kindly afford me the simple pleasure of not recognizing my status as queen?"

Annabel's eyes opened wide and words strangled in her throat.

"I so greatly enjoyed our short conversation when we met, before you knew who I was. Can you act as if I am still a simple customer from your shop?"

"Do you wish my father to create a special garment, Your Majesty?"

Mariamne laughed, "No, dear. King Edgar has made sure the royal seamstress is at my disposal. I want a friend, my lady," she told the woman honestly. "Someone who will speak to me plainly without observance or flattery. Someone who will call me by name." She turned to Annabel hopefully.

But the woman dropped her head, "Your Majesty, I am but a humble merchant's daughter, how can such favor be showered upon me?"

Oh, if Annabel but understood the reality of her much greater social status than her own—the false queen. Annabel would likely refuse on the grounds of her social status being far above Mariamne's.

She did not put voice to her secrets. "Because, dear lady, you understood my plight, though we had never met. I suffer from profound loneliness, and I would eagerly welcome a woman with such keen insight to ease my burden."

Annabel raised a bewildered gaze, "Are you sure, Your Majesty?"

"Only if you will stop calling me majesty." Mariamne chided her good-naturedly.

"Yes—Mariamne," she finally said with the nervous smile of a child who has just gotten away with something naughty.

"Thank you, Annabel." Tears threatened from her gratitude. A flutter of joy touched her aching heart like a balm on the open wound that she had long refused to even acknowledge lay deep within her. "Do you take honey in your tea, my friend?"

"Aye," she giggled as her cheeks flushed brightly. "My mother is forever saying I like more honey in my tea than actual tea."

Mariamne laughed. "I completely agree. Most teas can be so bitter."

Annabel nodded.

"Perhaps we should have a little wine instead," Mariamne whispered with a mischievous giddiness dancing on her insides. Who was she? Had she ever giggled before? She seldom recalled even smiling. Why did everything here feel so—right?

Annabel raised a demure hand to cover her sweet laughter. "Mayhaps so."

Mariamne joined her with a boisterous guffaw. She poured their tea as Annabel looked around. "Who is the broad-shouldered blond warrior sitting deeper in the garden?"

"My constant shadow," Mariamne handed her the tea. "King Edgar requested the poor man remain chained to me while he gallivanted off to assess his kingdom and lords."

Annabel took a sip with a raised brow.

"He would glory to fight at the king's side, though he is too kind to say as much."

"Would it not be an honor to defend any member of the royal household?"

"He spoke those very words, but he carries a warrior's heart, and warriors must, by their very nature, have something to war against. I fear my many antics are not befitting of his skills."

"The queen behaves badly?" Annabel flashed a roughish grin. "So it is true? You threw a tray at the king's head?"

Mariamne could not contain her loud laugh. "No, I did not throw anything at him or yell at him. In fact, I spoke not at all to him the first three days following my arrival."

Annabel's brows rose higher.

Mariamne leaned in close to admit with great embarrassment, "I did drop a tray full of meat in his lap that first day, though."

Annabel covered her mouth and then giggled. "Oh, you did not? What did the king do?"

"At the time, he dismissed me, but later he apologized for not paying me more attention. I should have seen the man's concern over the treaty he sent to King Harthacnut and the conditions at the border, but to my shame, I did naught but add to his concern by acting the spoiled child."

"How did you regain his favor?"

"I started acting my age," Mariamne said full of mirth, and Annabel laughed.

"If it is not too presumptuous of me, might I ask—What is King Edgar like?"

"He is tall, strong, dark hair—" Mariamne broke off at Annabel's snickers.

"I am aware of the king's appearance, Mariamne. What is the nature of the man?"

Mariamne's cheeks heated, and she chuckled at her own dullness. She struggled to put voice to her conflicting thoughts. "He is kind, easy to give praise." With the first few words off her lips, the rest came of their own. "Hard to provoke to anger. He is the only man I have known who seeks forgiveness of someone he feels he has wronged. He favors laughter and he holds the respect of his men."

"He is a blessing."

Mariamne hesitated. Old fears rallied to stop her praise of a man.

"Remember I have known him but less than a week, and one cannot learn much in such a short span of time."

"True, but you know his manner when he is angered. There is great information in such knowledge."

Mariamne considered the young woman closely and said in awe, "A sentiment I have used more than once myself."

"When do you expect his return?"

Mariamne sipped more of her tea. "He thought at least a month, and mayhaps even two." She shrugged. Turning their conversation to shake off her disquiet she said, "How long have you had the dress shop?"

"Oh 'tis Father's. I just help when I might, to lighten his burden." Annabel studied her tea as if it held some grand mystery.

An air of untruth hung between them, but she wondered if it was her own or Annabel's. Letting it be, Mariamne let their conversation turn to matters of fashion, and all else fell forgotten at their feet.

"I see you are still wearing the skirt, chemise, and bodice,"

"Yes, the women of Wiltonshire presented the chemise and bodice as a gift, and I cherish the garments, for they remind me of the women's kindness. Though, apparently the king has commissioned Edda, the seamstress, to make me a few more gowns. I struggle to comprehend how many dresses one needs to sit about the castle and twiddle her thumbs. How dirty or worn can a garment become is such idleness?"

"I thought you served at King Edgar's tables?"

"Three times a day I traverse between the long boards with food from the kitchen. It is not as if I slave in the kitchen preparing the food," Mariamne said with unbridled exasperation.

Annabel smiled. "So what manner of gowns are you commissioning of Edda?"

"Why, Annabel, my friend, are you hoping to tell your father that he might complete a new display in time for the debut of the queen's new gown?"

Annabel replied with an innocent bat of her eyelashes. "Such an action would make the other two dress shops so envious."

"So you do not care to know?" Mariamne snickered playfully.

Annabel's laughter would not be contained, and she burst out, "I never said such! What good is there to having royal friends if—" she stopped abruptly as she realized afresh who she spoke to and what she implied.

"Indeed. What good is it to have friends in high places if you cannot share a little in their glory?" Mariamne completed her sentence with a great laugh, and Annabel chuckled softly again staring deep into her teacup.

The two women talked and laughed for more than two hours before Annabel took her leave with the promise of returning the following Sabbath afternoon.

Over the next week until Annabel came to visit again, Mariamne returned to her reading lessons and attempted to look for something to occupy her hands. At one time she had worked a loom and a spindle and had become competent at both, but she could find neither for her to use here. Embroidery and knitting had long been pastimes reserved for the nobles, unfitting for a slave's hands.

Here no one could instruct her on such matters. And she dared not let her deficiency be known. They might deem her "royal" upbringing lacking. Such scrutiny could only reveal all the areas in which she failed to meet the expectations of her station.

At their next tea, Mariamne let slip her desire to embroider, and her friend happily offered to teach her.

"You know how to embroider?"

"I am not nobility, 'tis true, but it is something I have need of in my line of work. My father always praised my tight stitches." Annabel bit her lip as her own secret tumbled from her lips. "I must confess, Mariamne, my father has been dead near five years. I alone labor in the shop to support my mother and young sister. It is not proper, but we have no other way to provide for ourselves if not for me continuing to act on his behalf."

"I understand. I will never breathe a word."

Chapter 29

The next week when Annabel arrived, Mariamne had everything they would need ready in the queen's sitting room.

They sat, and in a short time Mariamne rested her work in her lap and looked at her friend. "I am amazed at the ease with which I grasp these first simple stitches, after failing so miserably at my reading lessons. I have worked daily with Sir Hugh, but I cannot comprehend the Veronian script.

"You are a good student, Mariamne. I trust the reading will come." Annabel encouraged her and introduced a new stitch.

As the day proceeded, Mariamne wondered if in truth reading befuddled her or the instructor. She voiced her musings to Annabel.

"I have learned to read, though I have few opportunities to use it outside of business notes. I would be honored to act as your tutor, if you wish."

"I would like that very much, Annabel."

In a matter of hours with Annabel, something finally clicked in Mariamne's stubborn brain, and within a few lessons she showed more progress than in her weeks with Hugh. Soon she spent her time with the chancellor discussing Veronian law.

She now filled her idle hours with embroidery tasks and reading. She asked Tye one morn, "Sir, do you think it would be permissible for me to select a few books from King Edgar's library? I have read all the items Hugh has at hand.

Tye's face filled with a huge smile. "I know our king would

welcome you to borrow any of his volumes you wish."

"Thank you."

As she entered the king's inner chamber, her insides twisted with unexpected longing to see him again. It took her several moments to shake the repugnant feeling off before she mindlessly jerked three random books from the shelves and raced from the room. She dropped them on the dresser in the nursery and fled to the fresh air in hopes of setting herself to rights again.

But as luck would have it, at the same moment she stepped into the bailey, Father Paul exited the church. Seeing her, he turned and approached. "Good afternoon, to you, Your Majesty," he said with a stiff bow and a tense tone as he looked up at her. "You have kept yourself quite busy, for I have not been afforded the time to meet with you for your interviews."

Mariamne stared at the bare skin on the top of his head as she struggled to turn her mouth in a smile. "Forgive me, Father. I have been seeing to the Lady Ingrid's recovery, and my duties in the king's absence weigh on me."

"Well, I have seen the Lady Ingrid supping in the hall for the last many days, and there seems to be enough time for socializing with the merchant's daughter and completing embroidery. Surely there is a moment in your day, Majesty, when we can speak of the serious matters of your soul?"

"Yes, Father," Mariamne conceded, feeling like a chastised child.

"I am available now, and it seems as though there are no pressing matters for you to attend to at the moment?"

She followed him to a room at the back of the chapel. Father Paul lumbered around his desk and directed her to a chair with a swish of his brown robed arm. "It will be good to sit a spell and talk, my child."

The simple intimate title he used stirred images of haystacks and the sensation of floating in the air. She shifted in the hard chair and gripped her hands together.

"I am the only priest in the castle since my predecessor, Father Bartholomew, died during the winter. King Edgar promised once the roads became passable he would send to the holy hermitage in the west for more brothers to assist me." He smiled at her kindly. "But then you came, child, and King Edgar seemed rather preoccupied. He sent me away on what he called an urgent errand over the Kestron Ridge. I did not see the need for me to be there, but I do as the king bids."

Father Paul continued to smile as his eyes studied her like they did his holy book. "I scarcely recall getting a glimpse of you in the hall before King Edgar sent me away." He crossed himself. "I bless the Lord Almighty I missed the upheaval of the dukes' arrival. If the gossip can be believed, it was dreadful business."

He leaned forward, resting his stout arms on his desk, and interlaced his fingers. "I celebrate with all our people Edgar's taking a bride, though you did well at avoiding me, my child." His smile grew, "But now I finally have you here in my office. Shall we begin?"

She swallowed hard and tried to moisten her lips, but her parched tongue grated over the dry skin like a stick along a fence.

He poured them both small goblets of watered wine, stood, and handed one to her across his desk. "How long have you known your Savior, my child?"

Holding the cup in both hands to quell the trembling, she took a long draft and answered without stammering or evasion. She spoke only the truth, though quietly. "I do not know Him, sir."

Father Paul nearly dropped his cup, and she grabbed at it to keep it from spilling. He staggered back from her, sitting hard. "What?"

"I came to Veronia with no belief in any god."

"But you are wed to the king," he sputtered and grasped at his chair.

"The king has chosen me, aye," she answered.

"But you are wed, my lady?" he asked as more question than statement.

She could not lie to the holy man. "No marriage has been preformed, Your Grace, and no vows have been said."

He gasped. A babble of sounds and half words tumbled over his lips, but nothing comprehensible.

She stood. "King Edgar made the decision for the welfare of Veronia, and he has the support of his most trusted advisors. I believe your absence from the castle would assure you suffer no guilt nor could you be held complicit in any wrongdoing surrounding this matter. King Edgar should return any day, you can administer to his soul concerning this at such a time, but I beg of you not to reveal the lie until after you have done so. Please respect your king and his decisions until you can convince him of a better course."

Mariamne did not wait for a response as she walked quietly out of his office and back into the sunshine. Her heart pounded, driving away the peace from every corner within the castle walls.

Cy approached her, his brows knit together. "M'lady?"

"The priest knows, but I know not what he intends to do with the information."

"I will have Tye speak to him."

She shook her head. "Let it lie, Cy. There is no need to stir the issue further."

She did not see Father Paul at supper and wondered anxiously what he would do with his new knowledge.

As she cleared the boards at the conclusion of the meal, Cy approached her. "I know you asked me remain silent, but I thought it prudent to speak with Tye. He assured me he will tend to the matter but failed to explain what he meant."

She nodded and continued to see to the cleaning of the meal.

Tye appeared as Mariamne turned toward the stairs to retire for the evening. "We need not fear," Tye reported. "Father Paul has sequestered himself away in deep prayer."

Chapter 30

"Your Majesty?"

Mariamne turned to see Corliss running to her through the inner gate the following morn.

"King Edgar and his men approach, my lady. He will be here before midday."

While the castle ignited with a flurry of activity to prepare to welcome the king and his men, Mariamne's heart leapt into her throat and she fought to breathe.

Cy stepped forward, and she took his hand to steady herself. Sweat filled her palm. She glanced at their entwined hands, her gaze flew to his face, and she released him. She pulled away, struggling to control her rapid breathing and hoping her heart would calm as she moved to the battlements.

Edgar smiled to see his home in the distance. His trip had gone well, and he had found no more of his dukes infected. He secured the promises of great numbers of fighting men and even successfully fought a few skirmishes with the enemy as they surveyed the border.

Yet even with the good news, his heart remained heavy. He feared coming home to an empty castle. He laughed at himself yet again, for he needed to continually remind himself nearly fifty people lived within the castle itself and another two hundred resided throughout the rest of his inner and outer walls. His home could never be considered vacant.

He glanced up at the growing rock his home sat upon and sighed. It would be profoundly empty if she did not greet him, though. If she seized the freedom he offered and left—. He sighed yet again.

Nothing could be done if she no longer resided within. Dwelling on the possibility served no purpose. He would know the truth soon enough, for they already approached the outskirts of the town sprawled at the foot of the rock.

Halton led their group and had pushed for a faster pace all day. Edgar watched again as he reined in, turned, and waited for them to catch up. The man's impatience grew.

Edgar offered many of the townsfolk a gracious wave as they came to greet the company and welcome them home. But his heart longed to see another. He rode on without stopping, as he did on occasion, taking the most direct route to the castle.

As he wound up the path toward the gatehouse, a movement on the battlements caught his eye. When he turned to look, nothing appeared at the crenels. A switchback turn hid the wall from view for several moments. When it came into view again, Edgar again thought he caught a glimpse of something before another turn blocked his view.

He spurred his horse to move faster, nearly coming abreast of Halton who also scanned the battlements. For his reward, he glimpsed a long raven-colored braid disappearing behind a merlon. His heart fluttered wildly. Mayhaps she did not merely wait in the castle. Could she be watching his return from the walls above? Without another glimpse, he feared his hopeful imagination made sport of him. But as he entered through the outer gatehouse, he again caught sight of her atop the inner wall. Mariamne remained in his home.

Mariamne slipped from the preparations and went to the battlements to watch him return. Unfamiliar feelings tickled her insides, as her heart seemed to leap at seeing Edgar even at a great distance when he entered the town. She watched enthralled and filled with a strange excitement she could not understand as he made his way past the town and to the road below.

She hid like a child caught spying when he looked up at the walls —twice—and raced to the inner wall before he entered the gate. She waited there for just one more glimpse of him before she scurried down the nearest tower and into the hall. Many of his people waited in the ward to greet him and welcome him home. She would not make the same mistake she had on that first day.

What ridiculous behavior. *Fool, what is the matter with you?* Darkness touched her. She cared nothing for any man or what he thought of her. Her mind protested, but her heart could not be convinced of her disapproval.

Preparations claimed her attention. She needed to be about them and throw off these foreign notions assailing her. She would not demand his attention. Let him talk with all his men and inform them of the condition of the land. She would see to the work without giving him another thought. As she moved toward the kitchen the dark voice whispered to her.

Look at you. What a fool you have become. Swooning over the attention of a man—you, who knows best what men are about. He has ensnared you and trapped you with his kindness. You have been with him for only a small pittance of time and you think you know him? He will turn on you and rip you to shreds.

She shuddered but could not shake the thoughts besetting her.

Racing in Halton's wake, Edgar charged into the ward. He scanned the space and dismounted, apprehension making sweat form above his lip. Mariamne could not be counted among those gathered. He continued to look around as he absently listened to his people's greeting and shook their hands without thought.

Halton moved up the steps to the hall. Edgar called to him. "Halton?"

The man turned, a scowl turning his lips.

"Find Tye and Hugh. Have them ready to meet in my study in an hour."

His fist clenched at his sides, and he did not move for several minutes. At last Halton stomped off toward the southern tower where the two men resided.

Turning his attention back to the crowd, Edgar's gaze landed on Cy at the back of the crowd, and he raised a questioning brow to the man. Cy tilted his head toward the hall, and Edgar broke away from those gathered tight about him before greeting most of them.

He took two stairs at a time in great strides and burst through the doors, scanning the room with an anxious heart. He let out a sigh of relief as his quick steps moved him toward Mariamne. He intended to kiss her hand or just stand and look on her lovely face, but when she stepped to him, he suddenly found her in his arms. She trembled, and when he pulled back from the embrace tears danced on her cheeks.

As people poured into the hall, she stepped with a toss of her head and squared her shoulders. "Welcome home, Your Majesty." Her formal greeting slapped him in the face as much as her disappearance into the kitchen.

Edgar stood rooted to the spot, stunned, for he did not expect her to run into his arms and then she withdrew just as quickly. Had he done something wrong?

Father Paul appeared at his side. "We must speak."

"Aye, as soon as I am cleaned and fed, Father, we can sit and discuss all manner of important things."

"This will not wait, Majesty."

Edgar did not move.

"It concerns *her*!"

Edgar understood and led the man to his study, encouraging his men to eat with a promise to join them momentarily.

Mariamne waited for Edgar to enter the hall at his leisure. But she was unable to move, caught by the darkness assailing her. It would take time for him to greet those outside. Then only moments later he burst in the doors alone and seeking something. Then his fretful eyes fell on her. She watched him sigh with such relief, all thought fled from her startled brain. But he asked her to stay. Should he be surprised?

He raced across the hall toward her.

Her thoughts dashed around like a crazed hummingbird, for it occurred to her that he left all his men standing unacknowledged for her. Now he came at her.

As he approached with his arms outstretched, she clutched her arms to her chest and her thundering heart pounded. Then—as if pushed—she vaulted into his arms. They closed around her with an incomprehensible gentleness. No unbridled passion, no possession battered her—but a mere sweet embrace. Filled by his utter relief and overwhelming gratitude to know she yet remained, still his pretend queen, Mariamne fought against tears.

The world broke in on them as the hall flooded with his noisy men. She pulled away abruptly, uttered a restrained greeting, and dashed into the kitchen as his intoxicating scent lingered about her.

She now stood against the inside of the door, trying to calm her erratic heartbeat and collect herself. The truth of his embrace communicated to her soul with profound clarity, it wiped the lies from her mind. The truth told of how he missed her, looked for her, and when she had not come to him, he had neglected all others to find her. Her presence alone satisfied. He asked for no more. She was enough.

Her heart thundered out of control, drowning out the noises of the kitchen around her as it pounded. She managed a couple quick breaths, collected two trays, and reentered the hall. She caught a glimpse of the king disappearing into his study with Father Paul close on his heels, and her stomach lurched so powerfully within her she nearly collapsed on the reeds at her feet. She stopped, steadied herself, and delivered the food to the tables.

New whispers from the darkness assailed her. *Now that you seek to stay, he will force King Edgar to send you away. You are going to lose everything. The father is a powerful man, and when he opposes you. Edgar will have to tell his people the truth and send you away.*

She returned to the kitchen as an unimaginable pain ripped her open.

She turned and nearly collided with Halton. His eyes bore into her and added to her discomfort.

"Blessings, my lady. Are you well?"

She nodded. "Quite, Sire. Do you require something?"

"I merely wished to spend a moment with you and know all remained well. You like your new home?"

"It is the finest place I have every stayed, and I am treated far above my station. The people are kind."

"And the king? You are still amenable to being his bride."

She shifted her weight, swallowed hard, and lowered her gaze. "In name I am who I can be to aid him."

"And if another path can be offered to you?"

Her head shot up. "I do not know what you are suggesting, sir. I have tasks to attend. If you will excuse me." She stepped around him and entered the kitchens. With her heart pounding and sweat covering her skin, she slipped out the rear entrance and into the warm afternoon sun. Scanning the ward for attentive eyes, she ducked into the nearest tower and hid in an empty room. Siting on the floor, she buried her face in her knees and cried.

Chapter 31

"Your Majesty, how could you think to have unholy relations with that heathen woman!" The latch on the king's door barely sounded before the holy man's angry words burst out.

Edgar staggered to the chair behind his desk and plopped down—though his backside wearied of sitting from the better part of two months in the saddle. He unbuttoned his doublet and pulled his tunic to free it from where sweat and dust glued it to his skin. His stomach growled, and he plopped his heavy arms on his desk.

He forced his eyes fully open and sighed heavily. Edgar indicated the chair, hoping the man would sit. "Your Holiness, who has been spreading ugly rumors that I have had any kind of relations with the Lady Mariamne?"

"The whole castle knows of her amorously entwined with you in your own bedchamber."

Edgar clenched his fists as the anger of the event rekindled. "The schemes of evil men forced the Lady Mariamne into my chambers. Perpetrated by a man who gave himself to the black poison. I was fully clothed, and she stood wrapped neck to toes in a nightshirt and robe. I did my best to shield her from the vulgar attempts by the duchess to besmirch her honor. The dear Lady Mariamne placed a single hand on my shoulder and implied a great untruth to rid us of the disgraceful intrusion before I could lash out and do the duchess harm.

"With doors closed, I slept in my breeches and under-tunic, on a mat, behind a screen in the corner of the chamber. The Lady slept, however, several feet away, *alone*, in my curtained bed. For all that is holy, Father, she slept closer to Halton and his men on her journey here!"

After several moments, Father Paul lowered himself to the chair and Edgar asked bluntly, "Who told you we are not bound as husband and wife?"

"It came from the lady's own lips, Your Majesty. I have sought to conduct her interviews since I returned, but she mastered the art of avoiding me. The reason is now apparent." His words dripped with disgust. "Your Majesty, you cannot continue to lie, for God will not be with you if you so blatantly break His holy commandments."

"If I have broken His commandment, then let Him deal with me, Father." Edgar jerked back to sit fully in his chair. "For in my eyes she is my queen, the one who I have given my promise in marriage. My men know her to be queen, and the people I serve know this truth as well. It is only the Lady Mariamne who cannot see her own destiny as yet, Father." Edgar sighed again and rubbed his neck as his stomach rumbled riotously. "May I ask you, Father, how is it you have determined she is an unbeliever?"

"She admitted it readily." Father Paul barked his defensive reply.

"What did she say, exactly?" Edgar again leaned forward.

"I asked her how long she has known her Savior, and she told me plainly that she knew Him not."

Edgar's arms again rested on his desk. "And what did you say to her then?"

"I—I did not think to say anything, but I asked her about her marriage to you—"

"You did not invite her to meet her Savior?" Edgar sprang from his seat, nearly topping his chair. "You did not tell her of the Lord and instruct her in His great truths?"

When Father Paul only blinked at him in stunned silence, Edgar paced behind his desk speaking with great animation. "Good Heaven's, Paul, she sat right there in front of you, telling you she knew naught of our God, and you spoke not a word to her! Are we not told that the Christ Himself came to seek and save that which is lost? And is she not lost? Are we not instructed, as those who He indwells, to go and make disciples of all men? Why did you not try to make her a disciple, Father?"

Edgar came around the desk, sat on its corner, and leaned into the holy man. "You need to know, Father, the Lord God Almighty has His hand on this precious one. He led Halton to her in a sea of faces in a slaver's dungeon. He protected her on the journey here, for when the evil surrounded my men, it went with murderous intent after her and her alone. The evil one also knows she is chosen by the One True God, who showed her how to use the light she does not yet possess to reveal the ploys of our enemy. He has a great plan for her, even when she does not yet know Him. We cannot fail to teach her in all matters concerning Him."

Father Paul's head dropped. "It is my greatest disgrace, for I have profoundly failed my God, my king, and the woman who—it seems—is destined to be my queen. I sought the Lord in prayer, focused on the wayward heart of my king. I did not allow God to speak to me and show me the truth." He stood trembling. "I must return to my prayers, Your Majesty, for I am in desperate need of absolution for my failings. When I have received a clear direction from our Lord, I will meet with you again."

Edgar stood and placed a comforting hand on his shoulder. "I understand, and if it is any help to you, Father, I have brought three of your brothers back from the holy house to assist you in your service to our people. You may even return to the sacred halls of the monastery for a sabbatical if it seems good to you. You will always be welcome at my table and serving before God's holy altar in His church here."

"Thank you, Majesty. I will seek the Lord's will on the matter." They nodded to one another and left the study. Father Paul did not remain to eat, choosing to return to his prayers instead. Edgar nearly inhaled his plate, eating with great vigor of the food Mariamne left on his high table.

As Edgar's great hunger abated, he again glanced around the hall for Mariamne, but did not see her. He bypassed Halton without a word and went up to see if she occupied the queen's chambers, but he could not find her anywhere inside the castle. He looked in the gardens and the ward but could not find her. Finally, he spotted Cy and called him over. "Where is the Lady, my friend?"

"The last I saw of her she served at boards, Sire."

"I have just looked in the queen's chambers and the kitchens and the halls…"

"Perhaps she is with Ingrid, Sire?"

The king raised a shocked brow to the soldier.

"After Carrington successfully rid the lady of the spawn, Lady Mariamne moved her to the back of the second-floor apartments to minister to her as she recovered."

"But the poison lay so thick upon her?"

"Aye, Your Majesty. Our lady prescribed a new treatment for the black infestation, and it has proved to be most effective. I understand Carrington has written down the particulars of her instructions and has begun to distribute them to the towns, shires, and villages. He says it will save many lives."

Edgar could not contain his smile, again amazed by this woman fast becoming part of his heart. He turned back to Cy. "She has been well, then?"

"Aye, Your Majesty. She has made a good friend of a tailor's daughter from town."

Edgar again shot him a wide gaze.

"They met on a return from a ride in the king's preserve."

Mariamne had ventured out of the castle? How far did she roam? Did she wish to go further? Edgar could not stop the questions leaping through his head.

"She became quite frustrated with her lessons and having little of purpose to do with herself. She requested I escort her for a short ride. I thought the protection of your hunting grounds best, and we have found opportunity to repeat the excursion." Cy considered him for a quiet moment. "If I may speak freely, Sire?"

"I will accept nothing less," Edgar urged.

"Our lady is ofttime restless, and if something is not provided to occupy her idle hours, she is prone to wander or be stirred by the evil that seeks to claim her."

"Thank you for your candor and your service, Cy." Edgar gave him a friendly slap on the back as he went back to the hall.

He noticed Mariamne on a bench—alone—she startled when he entered. She wore a new gown, something he had not seen when first he greeted her. Made of fine linen with a deep-blue brocade sleeveless overdress and round gold buttons tracing their way from her neckline to her ankles, it fit her every curve.

As he approached her teeth worried her lower lip, and her eyes flittered anxiously over his face. His own fear grew.

"My lady, whatever troubles you?" he asked, kneeling in front of her.

A tear rolled down one cheek as she whispered to him, "When has Father Paul said I must leave?"

Speech failed him as his overwhelmed heart lodged in his throat.

She sat consumed in fear she would be forced to leave. The very notion that she did not wish to depart filled him with such hope, his heart nearly burst.

He took both her trembling hands in his. "Never, my lady. Father Paul understands the truth now, and he has no desire to have anything happen to you."

Tears streamed from her eyes, and he pulled her to her feet. He wrapped her in his arms again, but this time she stiffened. His heart ached. She did not wish to go, but still she was not his. He released her.

"Will you walk with me and tell me of your time here in my absence and of your new friend?"

She wiped the tears and turned to the door with a nod.

They walked the battlements for some privacy, and Mariamne told him of her slowness to acquire the skill to read. She spoke of Annabel and their teas and embroidery lessons, Ingrid and her recovery, and her rides in the preserve. When she finished, she asked of his journey and what he learned. He told her everything to the smallest detail.

As they descended a tower to head back to the hall for supper— for they had talked all afternoon—Edgar asked her, "Is there anything you require, my lady?"

Mariamne shook her head. "Your Majesty has already been exceedingly generous, I could ask for naught more."

Edgar stopped a few moments later outside the hall and turned to her again. "It gives me great joy to provide for you, my lady. Is there nothing you desire that I could provide you?"

She chewed on her lower lip. "If it would not be a great burden, Your Majesty, a loom and spindle would give me something to occupy my days and would not require much instruction."

Edgar smiled and offered his arm, "It would be my delight to provide you these things."

They entered the hall. Then she curtsied and turned to the kitchens, while he bowed and turned to his gathering men. He greeted many and then turned to Halton, "There are faces at my boards I do not recognize, old friend."

Halton nodded. "Aye, Sire, it would appear your bride has invited Stanley's men to sup with us. She is a woman and thinks we will all fight more effectively if we know one another better. She is a woman and fails to comprehend we train so we can fight with any of a hundred different swords by our sides and be assured they know the commands and how to guard us."

"True enough, my friend, but there is no one I would rather have at my side than you, for we have trained and fought for so long together we know how one another thinks instinctively. Without time to contemplate, I know in most any given situation whether you will turn to the right or the left. Familiarity does afford another level to the training, and mayhaps this is what she hoped in inviting so many hungry mouths to board."

"Probably so, Sire. At least she only invites them for one meal a day," he offered with a slim smile as he took the king around to introduce the new men.

They enjoyed a good meal, and at last Edgar sat with Hugh and Tye and saw to the business of the realm and heard reports of what transpired in his absence. The hall lay dark and empty when Edgar concluded his dealings for the day. He lumbered his exhausted body up the stairs to his long-awaited bath and his bed, where he slept late into the next morn.

The next few days proceeded unremarkably as Edgar's affairs of state confined him to his study. When not trapped within, he met from his throne on the dais with citizens who needed his judgments.

Mariamne saw little of him, save at meals, as she found ways to keep herself hidden from everyone for hours at a time. Cy never drifted far away, even now. But he kept her confidences.

King Edgar's return left Mariamne unsettled. She secluded herself away for long periods, hoping with a growing desperation to regain some balance to her conflicted emotions. She managed well with the memory of the kindhearted King Edgar in his absence, but his return set her emotions into crazy disjointed waves.

She had watched his approach but then hid from him. She had not greeted him as the darkness taunted her. But relief overwhelmed her to see him looking for her, and she let the man embrace her. Now the mere memory of his touch sent her to trembling.

She next hurtled from the embrace and into the all-consuming terror that she would lose all. Then back to the heights when she learned she could stay. A second embrace followed, and terror yanked her back to the mire.

Halton took opportunity to speak with her as she attempted to avoid the king. His kind words and smile comforted her, but as he sought her out each day, her uneasiness grew.

After talking with Halton, she returned that first night to her pallet and chastised herself for not leaving the castle when the chance presented itself. But she drifted to sleep, caressed by the memory of that sweet time walking the battlements in cordial conversation with Edgar.

She woke the next morn assailed by her thoughts until she could no longer concentrate. When Edgar passed her, arriving late to the boards, she nearly dropped a tray of food. She stole away to the nursery and tried to do some embroidery, but her quaking fingers could not hold the needle nor her fluttering mind the pattern.

She next sought escape in the Veronian tale of a great hero, but Edgar's book only served to set her mind to comparing the similarities of the ancient hero to the current king.

Mariamne dropped the book on her pallet and ventured down to the second floor apartments to see Ingrid. The young woman now fully healed and long beyond need of her care usually met Mariamne's need for feminine conversation, though not this day. Mariamne excused herself with apologies and wandered out for a walk in the gardens. They did little more than reminded her of Edgar. Truth be told, nowhere within the king's walls was there a place that did not in some fashion remind her of him and further stir her inner turmoil.

In exasperation she made her way to the church and sat up in the dark gallery from midday near to supper. She tried to focus her thoughts on anything but the infernal man who so tormented her. Peace remained elusive.

It would be best if she left the castle and King Edgar, if only to escape what he was doing to her. She still remained free and could leave anytime she chose. She had fulfilled his request to remain until he returned. Now nothing more prevented her from going.

Then it came. The quiet whisper. *Be still, and know that I am God.*

"Be still? How can I be still when my thoughts are at war?"

The wisdom of the Spirit is life and peace.

"Spirit? What Spirit? I understand naught at all," Mariamne complained, but the whisper said no more, and the bell rang, sending her back to the hall.

Cy waited at the doors of the church. Somehow he always knew where she roamed, and he never failed to watch over her.

"The king has returned, yet you have not been released from your duty, sir?"

"You are in need of me, little sister."

He used the moniker anytime her mood turned dark. She stopped, stomped her foot, and planted her fists on her hips. "Why do you call me this?"

He turned away from her, looking far off in both place and time. "You remind me of another." The words carried such weight they dropped to the ground between them and kicked up dust.

She reached out and placed her hand on his arm. "You have a sister? You have never spoken of her."

"Once. A very long time ago." A slim smile turned his lips. "Beauty graced both her features and her spirit, not unlike you. Full of life and wonderment, she turned every head in our village and tickled every ear with her wit and her intellect." Cy cleared his throat. His next words trembled. "She was rebellious and stubborn. Like you, her own worst enemy. I saw the danger for her, but she would not heed my council. She resented my protection, seeing it an intrusion on her merriment." He lowered his head and squeezed his eyes closed. "She used her beauty to manipulate others, and it resulted in her end."

"Cy…"

He sniffed and straightened, returning his gaze to her with a steely determination that made her shudder. "I failed once to protect a precious one left in my care. I. Will. Not. Fail. Again. Promise me, m'lady, that you will not go without me."

She stepped back from his intensity. "I will not go without you."

His shoulders loosened, and he gave a quick nod as they proceeded to the meal. Thus he remained her faithful and loyal shadow. Somehow he understood her need to work things through in solitude, and he provided her every opportunity she required. He never asked for explanations of her wanderings and never shared her hiding places with anyone—not even King Edgar.

Chapter 32

Days later, Edgar approached Mariamne after the breaking of the fast. "Good morrow, my lady."

She curtsied.

"I have seen little of you since my return. Cy says you like to ride —would you join me through the preserve?"

She gave a quick silent nod of her head and turned toward the stairs. As she climbed to return to her chamber to change, she chided herself. *You are a fool, you have been seeking to hide in places you have never shared with the man, and now you are going to take one of those options away by sharing a ride with him.*

She changed quickly and met him at the stables.

Cy brought her horse, his brows drawn together as he stepped close to speak privately with her. "Are you sure of this, little sister?"

"I need the freedom of flying on the back of a horse, Cy. I am unsettled."

"Aye, but do you wish King Edgar to see you in this state?"

She grabbed the reins from him. "It is time he learns the truth, do you not think?"

He looked up at her. "This is not the truth, little sister."

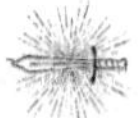

They turned east at the base of the castle, and Mariamne found herself riding between Edgar and Cy. She remained silent. Too many thoughts rattled within her to pluck one free and put voice to it.

As they neared the entrance, she shot Cy a quick flash and they thundered off together, leaving Edgar with Halton and a small contingent of knights looking after them.

The wind caressed her cheeks. She closed her eyes and released the reins, extending her arms out at her sides. The freedom stirred her soul. She could take flight. What would it be like to soar over the trees and escape the confines of walls and thoughts of men?

An arm encircled her waist and drew her from the saddle. She opened her eyes to find herself in Cy's steady grasp as her horse ran under a low branch and through thick brush.

"You are being overly reckless, little sister." He placed her safely on the ground before he gave chase to her mount.

The drumming of hooves approached, and she turned as Edgar and the others crested a rise behind her. She whiled from his smiling face, crossed her arms, and stamped her foot.

As Mariamne and her guard sped away without saying a word, Edgar turned suspiciously to a knight.

Nyle, a knight who remained in the castle, frowned. "They have spent much time together in the last months, Sire."

"Mayhaps leaving the foreign knight with your bride was not wise, Sire. Her heart could have strayed," Halton said.

"Sire, do not misunderstand me. Cy is loyal to his king. He would never betray you or forsake what he sees as a sacred duty," Nyle added.

Halton leaned closed to Edgar. "I should see to her care from now on, Sire."

Confusion fluttered in Edgar's mind like drunk butterflies. Halton never spoke against someone without cause. Mayhaps… he looked up as Mariamne came into view. She turned from him and stomped her foot. Cy did not accompany her, nor did her horse.

"Sire, Cy would never allow any harm to come to her," Nyle spoke again, "but the two share an understanding from their time together. It is no more than this that you see now, Sire."

The king grimaced and determined to watch Cy and Lady Mariamne closely. Cy returned in short order with her horse and scowled at her as she mounted again. An unfamiliar possessiveness twisted his insides as he noticed that Mariamne looked flushed. Did her cheeks color with shame from getting away with something torrid, or merely from the excitement of the race? Anger sprang up, which he did not fully understand.

They rode side-by-side, before she turned to him seriously. "Tell me of your God, Majesty."

His troubled thoughts fled. He sat straighter, and words tumbled from him with eager ease. At her furrowed brows and pursed lips, he reined in his excitement and began again. "God is the one God. The creator of heaven and earth, all knowing, holy, and loving. He sent His Son to earth—"

"God has a Son!"

"God is one and three. He is God the Father, God the Son, and God the Spirit, and they are all one God."

She stopped her horse. "I do not understand, Your Majesty." Her eyes held his with such intensity and hunger that his words failed him for a moment.

"Think of water, my lady. In the depths of winter it is solid, firm, and unchanging. This is like God the Father. But at the same time it can be frozen, water can flow, cleanse, refresh, and bring life. This is like the Son. And finally, water can be steam, hot, without form, and it seeps into your skin and warms you. This is like the Spirit. This is not a complete illustration, but it is the best our finite understanding can grasp. All together they are one, indistinguishable from one another and yet distinctively different at the same time."

She tossed her head and released a frustrated sigh, spurring her horse forward. "This God has a Son…"

"God sent His Son to earth to live among us."

"To force us by His mighty power to follow all of Him?"

Edgar smiled. "No, He came as an infant. A helpless babe born of a woman who never knew any man."

Mariamne stopped again and stared at him eyes wide and mouth agape. "How can a woman have a child if no man…"

"God is God of the impossible. If He created the earth and moon and stars and man and woman, why would creating life in an untouched woman be too difficult for Him?"

"But why a helpless baby, if He is God?" she asked as they continued along the trail.

"Because He wanted to live among us, love us, and experience the trials and pains we suffer so we could call on Him and know He understands. He grew and taught others about the God who loved them so much He would send His Son to earth to die for them."

"God died?" she nearly shouted. "How powerful is a God who can be killed?"

"He allowed Himself to be put to death to pay for our sins. All of us have broken the prefect laws God created for us to follow. We have: taken what is not ours, hurt others, been angry, coveted." He turned to her. "And lied. All of these things and many more are a great affront to a holy and righteous God, and we cannot be in His presence unless we are holy. So God's perfect Son, One without sin, came to earth and gave up His life to pay for our transgressions, that we might be restored to a relationship with God.

"God sees us as being perfect like His Son when we accept Him and live with Him in our lives. God looked down through history, from the creation of the world, and he saw me and wanted me with Him for all eternity, and He chose to die for me. He looked and He saw you, Mariamne, and He could not live without you, so He died that you would not be separated from Him."

"Where does the Spirit come into it all?"

"After Christ the Son died, He stayed not in the grave. Three days later God raised Him from death and He again walked with people on earth for a short time. When He left to sit beside His Father in heaven, He sent the Spirit to be with us, live in us, and help us."

Mariamne nodded without looking at him and said no more. She remained quiet for several minutes before she looked at Cy. In unison they stepped from the path, and he helped her dismount. She gave him a kind smile as she bounced off to pick some wildflowers, looking more like a child playing in the sunshine than a grown woman. The king caught Cy smiling at her.

Cy looked at him as he helped her remount, and he shook his head. When Mariamne talked with Cy easily and neglected Edgar, Cy's gaze held Edgar's and not Mariamne's.

Then she spurred her horse to speed once more.

"Nyle, please follow Her Majèsty," Cy as he remain beside Edgar.

"Your Majesty," Cy told him bluntly, "I would never do anything to come between any man and his wife."

"That may be true, Cy, but…" Halton left the accusation hanging between them.

Cy picked up the pace to a trot as Mariamne disappeared out of sight around a bend.

With some distance between them and the knights following, he turned back to Edgar. "She is most assuredly your wife, Sire. She may not be ready to admit it, for she has no desire for any kind of relationship with any man. Men are still the enemy, violent creatures who hurt and destroy and are definitely not to be trusted.

"She may look to be comfortable with me for the basic reason she has not been out of my sight other than when she is in her private chambers. Furthermore, you have been away for months. But she most assuredly does not trust me, Sire. I see her watching me as I look after her, and she often trembles. She will watch me as if looking for some sign I am about to turn on her. She quakes at my touch when I help her in and out of the saddle, Majesty.

"That woman has been profoundly wounded by a number of men, and it will take more than a few months to heal her from such deep pain and rend the defenses she has created, if indeed it can be done at all."

Cy shook his head and sighed deeply. "If I know her at all, Sire, she is using this day to show favor on me so you will turn on her and prove her right about all men, thus giving herself a reason to stop falling in love with you."

Edgar drew up his horse. He motioned for the men to move ahead and follow Mariamne, still several long strides ahead of them. It took even more urging to get Halton to follow them and not stay at his side.

Once alone, he turned back to Cy. "You believe she has feelings for me?" Edgar fought to keep from choking on the hushed words.

"I know she does, Your Majesty," Cy said with an easy grin. "But they are completely foreign to her, and she has no notion what to do with or about them, for they utterly terrify her."

"Surely the feelings of love are something all women long for," Edgar said. Enraptured by the mere thought Mariamne could love him.

"Most women, aye. But your Mariamne is not most women, Sire," Cy chuckled.

Edgar looked back on her as she again ran through wildflowers.

He let the truth of Cy's words pour over him. It washed away the jealousy the enemy tried to stir within him. "Thank you, Cy, for being such a good friend—to us both."

Cy nodded, and they rejoined the others.

With the dark envy silenced, Edgar rode easily with his men and let Mariamne talk and banter with any she wished. He only responded to her with a kind smile, which seemed to further confound her.

Finally she spurred her gentle gelding to great speed, racing out of the preserve with Nyle and Shaw a half a stride behind. Edgar let her go, giving her the space she asked for, and Cy leaned toward him with a roguish grin. "Halton named her rightly, Sire, for she is most assuredly rebellious."

"Indeed," he commented with some mirth.

Once clear of the trees and out in the bright sunlight, Mariamne slowed her horse to an easy canter and pulled the cowl of her lightweight cloak up to shade her eyes. As they neared the town, she noted a great number of people gathered in front of Annabel's shop, so she rode to investigate.

A wiry red-haired man with a face full of freckles stood screaming at Annabel as the crowd around them continued to thicken. "Your father is dead, woman, and has been for years. You know the law does not allow women to own businesses or property. I demand you close and vacate this shop immediately!"

"The law does allow a woman to continue to run a family business after the death of a father or husband. She is allowed to support other family members until such time as she is wed or her family can support themselves." Mariamne spoke firmly from atop her mount, her face hidden by her cowl.

"Woman, this does not concern you." The man turned back to the crowd as if he had dismissed her. "Martha, the girl's mother, is too old and withered to remarry, so they must get out of this shop."

"The daughter is just as protected by the law as her mother. She may run the shop to earn a living for her aging mother and her young sister until she, herself, is wed or her mother is deceased and her sister married."

"And what do you know of the law, woman?"

Mariamne threw back her cowl to reveal herself. "I would hope a very great deal," she ground out angrily.

The red-haired man stared at her uncomprehending.

"Your Majesty," Annabel called out, curtsied to the ground, and remained there.

A buzz erupted in the gathered crowd as word spread to those who had not heard. Every knee bowed low and remained there. Every tongue greeted her with such awe and wonderment in their airy, "Your Majesty."

The red-haired man took a knee last. Once he paid his observance, he rose stubbornly to his feet but kept his eyes averted, "Your Majesty, now that the town knows Annabel is the one running the shop they will no longer support her business, for everyone knows a woman's work is far inferior to a man's."

The king joined her to the left, and Cy on her right as her eyes narrowed on the man. Her voice trembled with quiet fury, giving each word the point of a dagger. "I will have to remind the king's own personally appointed royal seamstress of her shortcomings the next I see her. And if no one is inclined to purchase the Lady Annabel's fine garments, then the queen herself will have to be her only costumer." Mariamne looked at her dear friend and smiled kindly to her. "In fact, I am of a mind to purchase the exquisite green satin overdress you have on display, Lady Annabel."

"Your Majesty," the man stammered. "If you favor only one of the town's tailors, all the people will follow."

She leaned in the saddle, and he glanced up at her fearfully. "If this is what you fear, sir, might I suggest you treat your competitor's shop and the woman who runs it with a great deal more respect. Perhaps then the queen will see fit to show you her favor as well."

"Aye, Your Majesty." The man bowed again and moved back from her.

Mariamne looked up to her friend again and raised a quizzical brow. Annabel understood her unspoken question and nodded her consent. In a clear, strong voice, Mariamne asked, "Lady Annabel, would you be a dear and have the dress with you when you come to our weekly tea tomorrow?"

"It would be my pleasure, Your Majesty," Annabel said with a quick curtsy as another rumble meandered through the crowd.

Mariamne's leg became pinned between her horse and Cy's. He looked past her to the king, "Your Majesty." His voice was harsh with concern, and Mariamne became aware of the throng advancing to crush them.

Edgar glanced around, and Mariamne's eyes followed. The crowd surrounded them. There remained no room to maneuver their horses without hurting someone, and the people pressed ever closer. Panic rose choking off her breath.

Her gelding began to toss its head and stomp its feet as it reacted to the swarm of hands reaching out to his rider and her growing tension on his back.

Cy reached for his bridle, but the nervous horse shied away and knocked Mariamne into Edgar and his horse. Cy tried again; this time he grasped it and held firm.

From somewhere at the back of the crowd, a shout drew Cy and Edgar's attention. "Your Majesties, could you do with a little assistance?" one of Stanley's knight yelled out.

Edgar gave him a quick nod, turning to Mariamne and Cy. "The men on foot will have more success than we can on our horses. Be prepared to move when they make a path for us."

Stanley's men maneuvered, with some difficulty, to the horses then promptly turned and pushed the people back until they created enough room for Cy and Edgar to pull their horses away from hers. She turned her anxious mount in the tight space between, and they followed her through the corridor Stanley's men opened for them. Once clear of the crowd, she looked to the men on either side. "Why did they do that? What did they want?"

"They wanted to say they saw, or even touched, their long-awaited queen, my lady." Edgar's voice shook with fear, and Mariamne saw the shadow it cast on his face as he exchanged a glance with Cy.

She reined in and turned to see the great throng crushing together. They stood dejected at her apparent rejection of them.

Cy reached out for the halter of her horse.

She smiled at the people and raised a hand to wave at them.

They rewarded her kindness with waves, great smiles, and loud shouts of, "God save the Queen!"

She continued for several minutes before Cy cleared his throat. She turned back toward the castle, and they proceeded home in quiet reflection. "You may need to plan something for the people, Your Majesty. Allow them to satisfy their curiosity. Otherwise I will be accosted and crushed anytime I wish to venture into town."

"I will see to something right away." Edgar's tone and demeanor spoke of lingering fear. Somehow his distress moved her, but the emotions unleashed were at odds with her restless spirit.

Chapter 33

"These loyal men of God will serve you faithfully. After the long months working alone, I go to seek renewal and refreshment with the brothers at the holy hermitage, leaving you in the care of Father Gregory."

Father Paul introduced the three new priests the next morn. Father Benedict, a great round man; Father Francis, a tall and stern man with hawklike features; and Father Gregory, a rather ordinary man except for his unnaturally orange hair, which stood like flames around his head.

Cries of dismay wafted from the worshippers, and their eyes pooled with tears. Mariamne was flooded with guilt. When the service concluded, she again remained behind, and Edgar stayed with her, his brow raised in curiosity. Father Paul approached her, and she dropped in a deep curtsy before him. "I am deeply sorry, Your Reverence. I did not mean to so disturb you by my unholy ways that you would find it necessary to leave."

"No, child, you have done nothing to send me away."

His face, creased with lines, framed dark rings under his eyes. His gaze never met hers. "It is I who needs your forgiveness, dear lady, for I have thought things most unbecoming and untrue about you. I have failed you miserably, both with my accusations and my silence."

Mariamne reeled once more at a man who apologized to any woman. It left her speechless. This holy man, who held the respect and love of all Edgar's people, believed he hurt her or had done her wrong.

He wanted her absolution. Her mind would not process such a foreign thing.

He asked her again, more directly, "Will you forgive me for failing you, Your Majesty?"

Though he addressed her as such, she knew she was not his true queen and so she could not form words on her lifeless tongue.

Her look must have explained something of her feelings, for he lowered her to the pew and sat beside her. "In my prayers since I met with King Edgar, God has revealed to me you are the rightful queen of Veronia, my lady. He is seeking to comfort and restore you so you can fulfill the destiny He has chosen for you."

A great torrent of fear roared through her.

The priest took her hand and patted it tenderly. "Fear not, for God is with you and He will never leave you."

She sat unable to move as he rose to leave. He took several steps before the stone in her mouth reverted back to a fleshy tongue. "Yes, Father, I forgive you, and I thank you," she whispered through her tears.

He bowed and continued on his way.

When Father Paul disappeared into his study, Edgar approached and offered his arm, but she sat staring at the spot where Father Paul had vanished. "I do not understand the men in this strange land," she muttered more to herself than to the king.

King Edgar led her without a word to the hall. She served in a fog of her own thoughts, and when Annabel arrived she still had not cleared her mind of all the ideas assailing her.

"Mariamne, are you hale? You have asked to the same thing thrice."

She took Annabel's hand and led her up a tower. They walked east on the battlements to where they ended at the rocks; there they sat on the bricks.

Her friend joined her, twirling a lock of hair around her finger and watching her intently. "What is distressing you so, Mariamne?"

"Oh, Annabel, I understand naught of what troubles me. Since the king returned, I have been most perplexed. Coherent thoughts flee. The very world has been upended," Mariamne bit at her lip and wrung her hands.

Annabel's shoulders dropped, she sat straighter, and a playful smile tugged on her lip. "It sounds as though love has captured your heart."

Mariamne shot to her feet and nearly yelled, "What!"

"Mariamne, whatever is the matter? Do you not want to be in love with your husband?" Annabel trembled.

Mariamne bit back her rage and ground out, "I will never love a *man*." She spit out the last word with such disdain and contempt that Annabel drew back from her. "Men are horrid beasts, and I will never allow one to claim such a hold on me."

Annabel slid down to sit on the bricks and wrapped her arms tightly around her legs.

Mariamne writhed with an uncontrollable fury and paced with stomping steps in front of her.

Cy turned to look squarely at her. He crossed his arms and scowled at her behavior. When their eyes met, his gaze scolded her as surely as if he spoke the words. She glanced back to her friend trembling beside her.

Mariamne turned, and the dark shadow lost its grip on her. She fell to her knees and cried, "Annabel, I am so sorry."

Annabel pulled her close, and Mariamne wept on her shoulder. Her friend allowed her to cry herself out before she spoke. "We have all been hurt by one man or another, but they are not all beasts."

Mariamne pulled away as the darkness seized her again. "All the ones I have ever met are foul, depraved creatures no woman should be forced to suffer."

"King Edgar is foul and depraved?" Annabel asked softly. "What of Cy? Has he been anything but kind and tender toward you?"

Mariamne shook as a battle between the darkness and the truth raged within her. The darkness claimed victory, for she could not—would not—accept the truth that some men could be good. "They play a wicked game, Annabel. They speak in sweet, honeyed tones till we let down our guard. But the bitterness of what they offer next bites more painful than any viper. They say and do what they must to gain what they desire most—our ruin."

"Why will you not see some men are good and kind, tender and loving? Why does the very thought scare you so, Mariamne?"

Mariamne sat back and leaned against the rock at the end of the battlement, considering her friend's question. The word *why* reverberated in her mind like a mighty shout echoing in a cave, to the point it chased the shadow away. The darkness feared her knowing the answer to that question. It knew that when she understood this single answer it would be rendered powerless to stop her.

Annabel leaned forward and gently took her hands, "Are you well, my friend?"

"I am unsure—of a great many things. Nothing makes sense to me, Annabel, for things are so different here. Men behave oddly, and people are kind. I do not know what is truth and what is lie, and I am tormented by prophecies of a great destiny I am afraid I do not even want."

Her friend pulled her close again and held her in a fierce embrace. "You cannot look at the whole of the future and embrace it all at once, my friend. You must take one day at a time and live in it, slowly and deliberately. Do not worry about tomorrow, for tomorrow will worry about itself, do what you know is right for this day. God will see you through to the completion of all the rest."

Mariamne lay cradled in her dear friend's arms for some time as the peace again washed over her. They later walked the battlements, and Annabel spoke about her father and how kind he had been. Before they parted, Annabel told her, "The Lord God Almighty lives in the souls of men, and He alone can change a heart. The way of a man or woman will be immeasurably different when it is indwelled by the Spirit."

Mariamne hugged Annabel and returned to her room before attending the evening meal. All the memories of the last two days came to her mind in a rushing whirlwind. Memories of being told of a God who created her, loved her, and died so He would not to be separated from her. A Spirit of God who would live within her and change her and lead her to fulfill the destiny He planned for her. And ideas of the Spirit creating kind hearts in the men in which He lived.

The truth of these things reverberated in her soul with such profound assurance that she could not deny them. But the darkness pulled up other memories of hateful lusts and brutal beatings and whippings, which had left her in agony and near death. The pain sprang up again, and she could not accept the truth or the healing it offered.

Mariamne closed her disillusioned heart to her unwanted destiny, the God who pushed her toward it, and the men who sought to pull her into it. She set her heart against their way and determined she would decide her own fortune.

She rose each morn and went about her day without emotion, locking her feelings within herself until she could no longer hear their sweet words. She would not be hurt again.

"Your Majesty, what has you out so late?" Cy looked up as the king approached him atop the inner battlements late one evening.

"Mariamne," Edgar said with a weary sigh as he too looked out over his darkened land.

"Aye, Sire, I fear for her as well. She came so near the truth. Fear of what she knew in the past and what is now created such conflict it has driven her inside herself. She will not speak of God, and Lady Annabel confided in me she will not even allow her to speak of Him. She is in full retreat, and I fear the evil one will now have the power to claim her."

"That is my great fear as well, Cy, for if she does not claim the protection of the Almighty, she will be exposed to the trappings of darkness."

"The Lord has been faithful to her thus far. We must trust Him to complete the good work He started in her. We should not stop praying for her protection either."

"I entertain no other thought than to pray for her, my friend," Edgar said, resting a hand on Cy's shoulder.

Chapter 34

Edgar ventured from the castle once more, drawn by a skirmish to
the east. The conflict entangled him for almost three weeks. When he
returned, Mariamne did not await his arrival atop the walls. She did
not greet him. When the meal came, she dropped his tray before him
without stopping.

"Will you walk with me, my lady?"

"I have other pressing matters to see to, Sire."

He asked her day after day, but she remained distant and cold.
Compelled by God, Edgar drew near to her, though it wounded him
far worse than any battle injury.

"Is there something you need, Lady Mariamne?"

"Time alone with my friend is all I require." She brushed past him
to meet with Annabel.

"My lady, have I done something to offend you."

"No. I have no thought of you."

Each kindness he extended was flung back at him, each tenderness
answered with a sneer of disdain.

Tye approached him late a few weeks after his return. "All
arrangements have been finalized for the grand celebration of the
queen. Announcements have been placed inviting all those in the town
and in the nearby shires and villages. Tables are being prepared in a
meadow to the south of town, and I am told some have already begun
to gather in great excitement to see Queen Mariamne."

"Thank you, Tye."

"Sire, the items you requested arrived today, also."

Edgar sought after Mariamne and found her striding purposely across the hall. He quickened his steps to greet her.

She passed him without acknowledgement or word. Almost at the doors, Cy stepped before her. He blocked her path with his intimidating presence, his arms folded and his gaze hard on her.

She hastily averted her eyes, clenched her fists tight, and stomped her foot.

"You have wrapped a lovely gown around a rebellious countenance of late, m'lady."

Edgar watched as Cy's tender chastisement caused her to tremble.

Cy did not move from her path, and she seemed unable to go around him. "Be at peace, little sister," came his anguished whispered.

She raised her head to look at him.

He smiled weakly, "Remember her pride and belief that she could do anything. Forget not her end."

Edgar's heart ached at the great pain in Cy's warning.

When he spoke again, his voice trembled. A tear slid down his cheek. "I will not lose another sister. Tell me now if you can no long bear this place, and we will leave, or stay and let us help you."

She looked at him for a long moment until a gasp tore from her. She turned and ran up the stairs. She did not return for the evening meal.

Edgar found Cy sitting at the top of the third-floor stairs. Edgar opened his mouth to speak, but Cy shook his head.

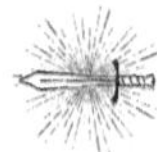

The following day Mariamne walked once more among them, controlled and silent. Her faithful guard walked in her shadow. Edgar watched her work on many things throughout the day in preparation for the coming day's celebration.

Edgar approached her cautiously. "It will be a grand festival in your honor, my lady."

"'Tis but an excuse to be put on display and gawked at. But mayhaps it will be better than staring at the walls of your home."

A dagger through his heart could not have hurt him more.

Edgar watched her push Cy away and race for the stairs again. Pushed by God's hand, Edgar sought her later. He stepped over Cy's long legs and lifted his hand to knock on the queen's door.

"Not there, Sire," Cy said with his eyes closed as his weary head rested against the wall.

"The Lady Mariamne is not in her chambers?"

"She is, but those are not her chambers."

Edgar scratched his baffled head.

Cy directed him further down the hall. "She stays in the nursery, Your Majesty."

"Nursery?" Edgar repeated, befuddled. "We have a nursery?" he mused.

"Last door on the left, Majesty," Cy told him. His eyes were still closed, and a slim roguish grin curved one side of his mouth.

Edgar moved to the last door and stared at it, mystified, for several seconds trying to remember the last time he even noticed the slim entrance. At last he knocked, and the door opened a crack. Mariamne sighed and looked at him blankly.

"Good afternoon, my lady. Something has arrived for you, and I wanted to know where you wanted it placed," he greeted her with hopeful cheer.

Mariamne looked at him for a long moment. "Wherever seems best to you," she answered coolly and began to shut the door.

He pushed the door open and looked inside at the stacks of

cluttered furniture and her pallet at the far end. "Whatever are you doing in here, my lady? The queen should be in the queen's suites."

"I did not wish to offend the woman who would one day be your real queen by presuming to sleep in her bed, Your Majesty."

A great anguish washed over Edgar. He crossed his arms over his breaking heart and leaned against the doorframe. "You, my dear lady, are the only queen my reign will ever see, for I will take no other." He managed to smile at her. "The nursery is full of furniture because no children will ever use it."

He watched a light tremor race through her at the mention of children. Her back straightened, and she stepped away from him.

Edgar raised a hand to calm her. "No, my lady, you misunderstand, I cannot sire children."

She relaxed as he continued to confide in her. "A deep fever befell me as a young boy. My mother attended me and became ill as well. Many in the land fell ill, and many died. When the illness had run its course, those who survived learned they could no longer bear or sire children, and that is why I have no siblings. I have known I would be the last of my line for most of my life, and I chose not to marry and leave my bride with such emptiness."

He paused and looked at her as his heart wallowed in pain. "I admit I dared to hope when you arrived that mayhaps God sought to bless me. For in you I saw the possibility I might yet know love." Tears stung his eyes. He stood tall, straightened his doublet, and let his arms drop to his sides. He forced a smile back to his lips. "I will have to learn to be content with loving you from afar." He turned and hurried down the back stairs before she could see him cry. Once he slipped alone into his dark study, Edgar sat at his desk and folded his arms. He rested his face into them and wept for several minutes before he called out to God. "I love her, Lord, but she is so hurt I know not what to do for her."

You love because I first loved you. Keep loving her, My son. Let My love in you soothe her troubled soul until she can hear My voice again.

"It hurts so much to keep loving her this way, Lord."

My grace is sufficient for you, Beloved. Rest in Me and let me heal you both.

Edgar let God minister to his soul and praised Him long through supper.

Edgar's words beat at the walls around her heart like hurtled boulders. The weight of his pain—pain she had caused—crushed her. She slumped to the floor and sobbed. All her emotions burst from behind the dam she had build within her. It could no longer contain them, and the torrent threatened to drown her from the inside.

She'd broken his heart, ripped it beating from his chest, and laid it open. She had become the cruel and vile beast she always imagined him to be. Footsteps drew her attention, and she looked up to see Cy in her doorway. She leapt up, throwing herself into his arms.

He embraced her gently and stroked her hair with tenderness, "Yes, little sister, cry. Let go of the pain and be healed." He pulled her to sit on the floor of the hall, wrapped her in his arms, and let her sob for hours until she started to drift into sleep's sweet abyss. He cradled her and carried her to her pallet. He laid her there, saying a prayer over her before he left.

Chapter 35

Mariamne descended to the hall a changed woman the following morn. During her weeping in Cy's arms, she resolved to be kind to King Edgar and to cause him no more pain. She did not want to love him, but surely she could find a way to be at peace with the man. She owed him, for even in her emotional turmoil, the last months had been the best of her life.

He had freed her to do as she pleased. She lived in a beautiful castle and wore the finest gowns. Granted all manner of respect and showered with utter kindness, she could not ask for better. She never dared dream such a life for herself. The man deserved better than her disdain, so she determined to find a way to be a better person, if only for his sake.

With her resolve set for the good of her king, a dark curtain lifted from her soul. She wore the deep-green overdress she'd purchased from Annabel. She passed Cy with a genuine smile, and the smile he returned glowed.

She brought Edgar his tray, "Forgive me, Your Majesty—"

He fervently grasped her hand. His eyes filled with love, "Think no more of it, for I never shall."

His quick and complete forgiveness brought tears. He kissed her hand as if the last many days had never happened. She finished serving, bathed in his unconditional kindness.

Before midday, the king helped her into the seat of the open coach prepared for the special day. He sat with his shoulders squared and his chest out and a contented smile. They rode in the bouncy contraption behind Cy and Halton, and were followed by Shaw, Eldon, and the rest of the king's knights and men-at-arms.

He sat apart from her. His forbearance touched her. They rode through the town as the latecomers raced to arrive ahead of them. They stopped behind the large dais built south of town. It held a table for seven, not merely the two she'd expected.

As Edgar offered his hand to help her from the coach, the crowd bowed low. Halton also stepped in and offered his hand as well. Edgar turned with an odd furrow creasing his brow. Halton bowed, stepping aside as Mariamne stood before a throng of silent kneelers.

Edgar led her to the center of the large platform and announced to his people in a clear and resounding voice filled with love and pride, "My good people, I present to you, your queen. Love her as I, and our land will know peace. My people, Queen Mariamne."

Stillness followed his words.

"God save Queen Mariamne!" She jumped at the sudden eruption of their shouts.

Edgar held tight to her hand as he smiled and bowed to her. The people cheered with wild abandon. Then before she could comprehend the spoken adoration of the moment, the benches cleared and a great line formed in front of her as one by one the families came forward and greeted her personally.

Edgar took one step back and stood with the four knights smiling proudly as the people lavished her with kindness, praise, and love. Some laid humble gifts of flowers or music boxes and precious trinkets from their limited means at her feet. Their outpouring of gifts and love overwhelmed her until she leapt down from the protective platform to greet them face-to-face. She touched the children presented to her. She took the hands of the adults, many of whom kissed her hand. The men behind her stepped nearer but did not bring her back atop the dais. The people waited patiently for their moment to be personally recognized by her.

A familiar face came to the front of the line, and Mariamne threw her arms around the man's neck. "Garrick, my friend, how are you?" the queen squealed with delight.

When she released him, he bowed low with a broad smile. "I am quite well, Your Majesty."

"You look fabulous!" she exclaimed at seeing the formerly rotund slave almost half the man he had been. His tan and muscular arms, and broad shoulders framed his firm chest. He surely turned many a maiden's head.

He leaned into her with an impish grin and whispered, "And you *sound* fabulous, my lady."

She smiled as he waved to Cy and Halton and made way for the next in line.

So many people came to greet her she lost all sense of time until at length the final few made their way to the line. Annabel now stepped and hugged her friend fiercely, whispering, "How are you?"

"Better than I have been in weeks, my friend."

Annabel gave her a little squeeze and turned to introduce those with her. "Your Majesty, this is my mother, Martha, and my sister, Olivia."

Mariamne greeted them both with a hug. She loved them as family, as she did Annabel.

As Martha and Olivia turned to take their places at the tables, Edgar reached out a hand and pulled Mariamne back onto the dais. She startled to see Cy extend his hand to Annabel, and she joined the men with her.

Edgar called Father Gregory, and he stepped forward to bless the day. "Heavenly Father, we Your people come to You in great joy as we celebrate the holy union of our faithful King Edgar and the woman You have chosen to rule in righteousness beside him. We pray Your many blessings on their union. May their reign be marked by Your justice, love, and humble service. We pray the added blessing of many children to Queen Mariamne and King Edgar, that his rule may be long under Your blessing."

Edgar's hand jerked, and she squeezed it a little tighter.

"Give those gathered here cheer, fellowship, and satisfied bellies, as we celebrate You, our Mighty God, and the provisions of Your hand. Amen."

"Amen," those gathered echoed.

Then Edgar led her around the table and they took the center seats. Halton stepped to her other side until Edgar and Cy motioned for Annabel to sit at her right. Cy and Shaw took the seats further beyond her friend. Halton moved to Edgar's left, with Eldon beyond him.

Mariamne turned with a quizzical brow to Edgar. "I thought you might like the company of more then insufferable men, my lady." His sweet smile spoke of him making sport of himself and not her ill behavior.

She smile, inclining her head with a grateful heart. "You are too kind to me, Majesty."

He held the tray for her to choose some delicacies. After Edgar filled his plate, she passed the tray to Annabel. She caught a look passed from Cy to Annabel. The two talked amiably, she noticed. Mariamne could see clear as the nose on his face the love in Cy's eyes for Annabel. When Annabel turned to receive the tray, Mariamne could also see the love reciprocated by her friend.

When the tray passed to Cy and he busied himself with filling his plate, Mariamne playfully elbowed her friend and whispered to her, "You little minx, why did you not tell me you set your cap for my personal guard? I would have found ways to give you more time alone."

"My lady," Annabel gasped as her face flooded with bright color.

"And it seems to be a shared feeling," she said as Cy turned back toward them and his glance again fell on Annabel.

Annabel seized her hand fiercely and leaned in to whisper, "Do you think he feels so?"

"Most assuredly!"

As always, Mariamne's words had been ill timed. Annabel turned from her nervous giggles, and sighs followed as she gave all her attention to Cy. Mariamne turned to Edgar on her other side, but he sat deep in discussion with Halton. Neither of her companions realized she sat neglected to stare out at the people who gathered to celebrate her.

She glimpsed Garrick and grinned at him when their eyes met. His face filled with a great smile, and he lifted his cup to her. The tailor who had challenged Annabel sat among those gathered, and she inclined her head to him. He had presented her with an exquisite bolt of satin fabric. She also noticed a handful of servants arriving late, followed even later by Tye and Corin. She turned to Edgar to ask after the matter, but the plates were cleared.

Villagers pulled the tables below them to the sides, leaving room in the middle. A small group of minstrels took their places to the left of the dais. And at last Edgar turned to Mariamne, "Will you dance with me, my queen?"

Terror gripped her. "I know not how, Majesty."

He smiled and stood, offering her his hand. "Follow me and have no fear. We will be with you."

She gave him her trembling hand, and he led her to the cleared space. He beamed at her as he took his place with the line of men facing her and the women in her line. The music started, both lines stepping toward one another, hands raised. Mariamne mimicked Annabel's movements beside her and mirrored Edgar's in front of her. They glided to step forward, to the side, back, and then to the other side. Then they repeated the pattern.

Edgar smiled at her. In a turn where her right hand was raised high in his right hand, and his arm draped around her waist, he whispered, "You are doing beautifully, my lady. Relax and enjoy." As the pattern became predicable, she relaxed and even laughed with the others.

The music ended. He bowed to her, and she curtsied. He invited everyone to enjoy a dance before he led her back to her seat and watched his people.

Mariamne tried to encourage Cy to join Annabel in the dancing, but he refused to even acknowledge her many glances.

Her conflicted behavior made laughter bubble to Mariamne's lips. For in one moment, she rejoiced for Annabel and Cy, in another she rejected her own feelings. She longed to see them united in happiness and love though she still did not wish the same for herself. This land and its people turned her every thought and feeling on end, and continued to confound her.

Chapter 36

Mariamne and Edgar to retired long before the revelers went home. The pleasant night of late summer encouraged many to stay out late and enjoy themselves.

When Mariamne enter the nursery, she gasped and the sound echoed down the hallway. All the extra furniture was gone, and her pallet had been removed. In its place under the window sat a slender feather bed with a beautiful brocade coverlet. A huge brightly colored rug lay on the floor, and the blue chair sat on it uncovered. A narrow table sat near the chair with a small lamp on it. The mirror now hung on the wall next to wardrobe and the dresser.

On the right wall, where all the furniture had been stacked, hung a huge tapestry of a dark-haired girl spinning in a field of flowers. On the left side of the room where the chair once sat, a dark hunting tapestry had been moved to reveal double doors she'd never noticed. The doors stood wide open to the queen's bedchamber, and between the door and the queen's great curtained bed sat an exquisitely carved loom and a spindle made of rich dark wood.

Beauty and wonder filled every corner of the small room—so much larger now that it was cleared of the clutter. Edgar had been unaware that she was staying in the nursery until yesterday. Cy said as much. Edgar planned all this for her in a matter of hours and at a time when she had been at her worst. How could the man find it within himself to be so thoughtful and kind when she acted the beast? Hot tears of shame and gratitude threatened.

"Do you like it?" Edgar stood in the doorway.

Her voice failed her as tears cascaded. "How can you be so kind when I have been so cruel?"

Edgar respectfully remained outside her door and smiled, "My love for you is not measured by anything you do, my lady." She fought to make sense of his words and actions."It is something God has taught me. For He loves me mightily, regardless of what I do or fail to do for Him." He bowed to her and left.

Mariamne raced to her door, "Thank you. 'Tis all very beautiful."

He tossed a contented grin over his shoulder and disappeared into his chambers.

She closed her door and slipped into the chair, savoring his care for her. Passion, desire, lust—these things she understood. But the unconditional love he showered on her was something altogether foreign.

By the next morn, the castle buzzed.

"Why did your Saul arrive late?"

"He stayed behind to help clear the nursery," two maids whispered. They stole furtive glances of Mariamne as she passed.

"Well, being in a motherly way would account for her moodiness of late," the other giggled.

Mariamne continued as though she had not heard. She stumbled upon another cluster of servants making wagers as to when the blessed babe would arrive and the likelihood of it being a boy.

Edgar drew her off alone. "My lady, I am so sorry. I never thought of what cleaning the room would imply."

"The fault is all mine for refusing to stay in the queen's chambers. I have brought this on my own head, and you will pay the price for it,

Sire. What do you require of me?"

He stood slack-jawed for several moments.

"We could do nothing. Sooner or later they will concluded the truth," she said dryly. "If anyone asks, you can tell them I wished to be prepared when the blessed event did transpire, but for now we still wait."

He smiled.

"Whatever are you grinning at, Sire? I have brought great trouble upon you."

"You will never bring me trouble, my lady. We will say nothing, for God will make a way for us."

Mariamne could not fathom how such a thing could be possible, but she curtsied and left.

As Edgar and his men contended with various skirmishes with the horde over the remainder of the summer and into the early fall, Mariamne remained in the castle. Almost daily she noted someone's eyes dropping from her face to her flat belly as they wondered when it would become apparent she carried Edgar's heir. She fretted over what Edgar's people would do when they learned no babe would occupy the nursery.

Soon fall painted the valley in vibrant golds and reds. The barns filled with the last of the year's harvests. Edgar returned to prepare for winter. He sent Stanley's men home, and Father Paul returned.

"Things are falling into a comfortable routine again, Cy," Mariamne mused one afternoon.

Cy gazed out over the land, searching intently for something. "That is oft when trouble begins."

Chapter 37

"Sire, a small band of men-at-arms arrived at the castle carrying news for their king," Halton told Edgar late one afternoon as winter neared. "They say they have knowledge most important for you, claiming to have learned of a way the evil can be defeated. They insist on speaking with you at once."

"Halton, allow the men in. I will dine with them and hear what they would tell me. See their leader eats with me at my high table."

"Sire, do you think it wise? We know naught of the origins or intentions of these me," Cy warned.

"They come with news of our enemy. I will hear their words and decided what is to be done."

Edgar ate, enraptured by the dark-haired man with keen eyes and a fast tongue. "It is a wonder to behold, Majesty. To see evil flee with great terror. What a reward it is to be rid of them."

"Tell me of this weapon, that I may use it to secure my kingdom from this terrible threat."

"It is more a strategy than a weapon," the man hummed with a shrug as he munched on a leg of mutton. His gaze fell over the hall and lighted on Mariamne. He smiled.

"My wife is quite beautiful." Edgar said with pride.

"She is a rare treasure. A king with her at his side could do great things—great things indeed."

An uneasy tremor rumbled through Edgar.

"This strategy, Majesty. Might there be a place to speak in private?

You know naught where spies lurk. Would be a shame if this information fell into the wrong hands. It is vital to your survival, Majesty.

Edgar brushed aside the caution tickling his brain and led the way to his study.

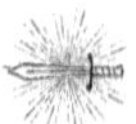

Mariamne skirted between the boards and delivered refilled trays. A hand slid along the back of her thigh and between her legs. She jumped. One of the newcomers smiled. She brushed off the affront and returned to the kitchen. On her next pass down the aisle, again another hand ventured where it should not. She bit back a yelp.

"That is our queen," Shaw snarled at the man.

"Oh, do forgive me," the rough man gasped.

Mariamne noted his smirk.

"Who would have thought the High Queen of all Veronia would serve at boards like a common wench. It is unheard of."

"No woman is a common anything in King Edgar's kingdom, sir," Mariamne snapped at him. "I would expect men of his realm to treat women with far more respect than to accost them at their work or anywhere else."

"Again, Your Majesty, I beg your utmost pardon." His slim sneer and slight wink sent a shiver down her spine.

She shook off the threat. Both Edgar and Cy sat near at hand. She finished laying tables and enjoyed a pleasant meal with Lady Ingrid.

Mariamne yawned, sleep pulled at her tonight more than normal. Edgar disappeared into his study with one of the men. The group had yet to leave. On the morrow, he would be sure to tell her all he had learned. She glanced around the hall as she moved to the stairs. Cy was not among those preparing to sleep on the hall's rushes. The tickle of unease hummed on her skin as she climbed the stairs, her legs heavy and her mind murky. She passed no one, but the sheets of her bed looked ruffled as though someone had sat upon it. Another yawn assailed her. Why was she so tired?

Brushing the disquiet away as nothing that a good night's rest would not cure, she reached for the pitcher of water to fill the basin. She stared into the empty vessel. She yawned again as she snatched it up and headed down the back stairs. *I filled this early this morn, did I not?* No matter. One more task before the end of another day.

Hands clamped around her arms and slammed her to the ground. Air rushed from her lungs, blood from her heart, and thought from her head. Mind-numbing shock turned her limbs to stone as a myriad of hands explored her curves.

An old familiar threat within King Edgar's safe walls? How could this be happening again? How could it happen here? Her defenses sprang to life, clearing her head of the sleep clouding it. With skills neglected, but never forgotten, she fought against the men holding her. She kicked.

Vile names battered her. Brutal hands assaulted her. They spoke of all the evil they intended to do to her.

Panic made her thrash and strike out, wild and frantic. She clawed at eyes, punched at noses, struck at throats, kneed offending organs, and all the while writhed in the men's iron grasp.

Her dress rent.

Hands explored beneath her skirt.

Terror tore loose in a scream.

Chapter 38

Edgar! A pot shattered. A voice rumbled fiercely through his head. *Edgar! Where is your wife?*

Edgar sat bolt upright.

A shriek tore through the night.

He drew his father's sword mounted on the wall behind him and raced to find Mariamne. Cy met him, sword in hand, at the doors of the hall, and they burst into the ward together, filling the space with holy light.

Others, dressed in their nightclothes and rubbing sleep from their eyes, stumbled from every door. How did it get so late?

"Lord, where is she?" Edgar called to the heavens.

Another terrified scream rent the air.

Edgar and Cy raced toward the sound. "Unhand her." They slashed at the men attacking her.

Mariamne gathered her tattered dress.

One man lay dying on the ground, Cy pinned another, and Edgar's boot and sword held the third. He dared glance at her. Terror-filled her eyes shone in the light of the glowing swords.

He stepped toward her.

She jerked away, shrieked, and raced into the hall. In the moment of distraction, his captive escaped and jumped to his feet. The man pulled his own blade. Edgar caught the glint of swinging metal.

"Edgar!"

Edgar blocked the blow stumbling over the dying man, but the fallen one vanished.

Edgar clashed with his opponent. Cy knocked his man unconscious and leapt to Edgar's aid.

"Do not kill him. I need information," Edgar ordered over the clanging of swords.

Lowering his shoulder, Cy barreled into the man, grabbed him, and slammed him to the ground. Edgar stepped on the attacker's sword arm as Cy used the hilt of his own sword upside his skull.

A handful of servants stood agape. Where were his fighting men?

A man-at-arms ran in though the inner gate. "Sire, the man you dined with has started several fires in the homes and buildings in the bailey. We fight against the flames, but the man escaped."

Edgar looked from his soldier, to the fallen attackers at his feet, to the door to the hall. He should go to Mariamne. He needed to assure she escaped unharmed.

The men at his feet stirred. Edgar bathed them in the light of his sword. Their garments covered all their flesh save their hands and face, but the poison showed in their eyes.

"We will take them to the dungeon." Edgar pointed to the man under Cy.

"As soon as they are secured…"

"Aye, we go to her," Edgar nodded.

Cy bound both men before he and Edgar yanked them to their feet shoving them toward the cells.

Flickering light shone through the crack round the door within the inner gate. Smoke choked the air. Muffled orders wafted over the wall.

"Mayhaps we should see to those efforts." Cy's features were drawn.

The empty dungeon had no guard waiting to accept their charges. The captives laughed. Edgar threw one in a dank cell, slammed the door, and set the bolt.

"Put the other there," Edgar said, pointing to a set of manacles mounted high in the wall. Once the man's arms and ankles were secured, Edgar sheathed his weapon and reached for a torch. He brought it to lick at the prisoners' skin. "Go see what may be done to aid with the fires, then check on her."

"Forgive my disobedience, but I cannot leave you alone with this vessel of evil, Sire. They possess unnatural strength and mysterious powers."

Though the flame bit as his flesh, burning away his clothes, the attacker only smiled and chuckled softly. "Surely you are man enough to face me alone, Edgar."

"Man enough, aye. Foolish enough, nay. If you want me alone, 'twill be the last thing I do."

Cy stepped forward and slammed the man's head against the wall. "Why do you hunt the queen?"

"She is a beautiful creature. What man does not want her?"

Flesh struck flesh again. "Do you rape every woman you meet?"

"Any I can," he said with a boisterous laugh that threw back his head.

Cy yanked his sword from his sheath, and in one swipe removed the man's head. "Forgive me, Sire. I could not…"

"Had you not struck first, it would have been me."

They returned to the cell for the other man, only to find him lying on the floor. His wrists oozed blood and he drew his last breath.

They returned to the ward. The bailey lay dark and quiet. Heavy clouds bellowed over the valley and blocked out the moon.

A tremor raced down Edgar's spine.

Chapter 39

While Cy went to see who served as guard when the strangers entered, Edgar went to Mariamne's door. She would not open it, and he feared terrifying her further by going in uninvited. He tried to reassure her through the wood barring him, but no sound came from within.

He met Cy in the hall as he led two guards toward his study. The two men-at-arms dropped to their knees in the rushes "Sire, we did not light-search the men when they came to the gates. Naught has happened within the castle in months. You return victorious time and again from any skirmish with our enemy. We saw not the need for extra searches."

"Your queen now languishes in her quarters because of the violent attack of these men. Do you now see the need of completing your duties as ordered by your king?" Cy bellowed.

"I will see to them, Cy. Go see if mayhaps our lady will open the door for you." The men passed each other. "Do not go in unless invited," Edgar called over his shoulder.

"Aye, Your Majesty." Cy left Edgar to mete out punishment to his men.

At the end of the following day, Edgar wandered across the quiet cold hall. A maid's quiet whisper filtered through his dark mood.

"Queen Mariamne is being treated to remove the poison."

Edgar trudged up the stairs. Mariamne remained locked in the nursery. He did not know the extent of her injuries. Cy posted himself outside her door and waited for her to summon the courage to emerge once more.

"It has been too long, Sire. What if she lies injured? I perish the thought of breaking down her door when she suffers from such a fright, Sire, but if indeed the poison infests her, she could be too far possessed to help if we wait. My fear for her grows unbearable."

"We must see to her safety," Edgar said.

A heavy autumn rain swept up from the south and deluged the valley as Cy broke down her door. Her chamber lay empty.

"Cy, Tye, Halton—search every room!" Edgar waited. He could not imagine a sword thrust hurting so.

After near three hours, the rain-drenched searchers stood dripping before him.

Cy reported first. "I searched the battlements, the chapel gallery, and every empty room in the north tower of the outer wall. I could not find her. I questioned the guards who served the night of the attack. I have been assured the queen did not leave through either the inner or the outer gate, though the fires distracted many."

Halton spoke next. "I searched all the buildings of the inner ward. I overheard a servant's strange complaint, which sent me racing to Mariamne's chamber. I found this." He dropped her torn gown on Edgar's desk and a length of black hair a couple of dozen digits long. "I took extra care to search her wardrobe before racing to find Tye. I informed him of my suspicions."

"She is gone, Your Majesty," Tye announced with a groan.

Cy fell to his knees while Tye and Halton would not meet Edgar's stare.

"She stole one of the groundskeeper's breeches and tunic from the laundry and fled into the night." Tye concluded his report.

Cy's voice quaked with his great grieving heart. "A knight sent from Lord Dawson sought entrance in the dark hours the night the enemy assaulted our queen. A guard offered a vague recollection of a servant with black hair, slipping out the gate at the same moment of the messenger's admittance. Your Majesty, I have failed you and her…" Cy sobbed.

"No, Cy, I failed her. This is my home, and I resided at the time of her attack. I allowed myself to be beguiled by these men and their promise of news of how to defeat my enemy. I welcomed the threat into my own walls with open arms. I allowed myself to be drugged by them, and I failed to save her from the one thing she feared most." Edgar became lost to his own great breaking heart.

Through the clamor of the pain rending him asunder came Halton's desperate plea. "We must go after her, Your Majesty,"

Tye attempted to reason with Halton. "Heavy rains have fallen all day, Halton, and the sun has long since set. There is no hope of finding her. Three days' journey now separate us, and we know naught of the direction she headed."

Halton addressed Edgar once more with even more urgency.

Edgar put his hand up, "God holds her now, for I gave her the freedom to go as she pleased. She found my safety insufficient to her needs and sought it elsewhere," he groaned, dropping to his chair. "But, should the good Lord see fit to clear the skies on the morrow, we will do what can be done to find her."

Each of his men staggered from the study.

Chapter 40

Days after Mariamne was discovered missing, Annabel stood at the gate, and Cy came to escort her home. "The queen was attacked."

"Aye, this I know. Is she hale?" They walked down the mount and neared her shop in silence.

"She has been lost to us," he choked.

"She is dead?"

"Nay, she fled into the night."

Annabel touched Cy's arm. "The fault was nay—"

He jerked away as if she burned him with a hot iron. "I accepted as my sacred duty her guardianship. I alone was given the responsibility of keeping such an atrocity from befalling her," he roared. "If 'twas not my fault, than why did she break her vow and leave without me. I would have gone with her, anywhere…" he trailed off as his aching heart shattered anew.

"She ran because it is the only thing she knows. And she did not call unto you because fear blinded her to the need. Well I know her, Cynric, and she does not blame you. For you, above all, she did trust and care."

"She feared me. Her anxious gaze searched me each time she glanced my way. I could be capable of doing unto her what…" again the pain stole his words.

Annabel's fists planted on her hips as the rain soaked her. Her firm words adopted the sting of a blade. "'Tis not true! She cared overmuch for you. It resided there in the manner she spoke of you, the way she worried over you being forced to stay behind with her. 'Twas confusion which distorted your gaze, for she understand naught of your unwavering tenderness—even when she behaved the child. I tell you truly, Cynric, the only thing which could separate Mariamne from your care lay in the schemes of evil itself, for never would she have left willingly."

Cy saw her to her door without further conversation and turned to leave. "Yet, I have failed once more to protect one left in my care, and I will not be placed in a position to fail again."

He left Annabel standing in the doorway of her home dripping wet as tears mixed with the rain on her face. He plodded back to the castle, the gloomy afternoon swallowing his hopes to find his queen, his honor, or even love.

Chapter 41

"We must go after her!" Halton slammed his fist on Edgar's desk.

"Heavy, oppressive rains have deluged the land for near a week. The waterlogged earth and swollen rivers make any manner of travel impossible. Now early snows have leapt on the heels of the unusual rains. The deep snow has not only cut off the Kestron Ridge but covered the valley floor as well." Edgar glanced at his friend. "I cannot remember so deep a winter. Never has the whole valley been trapped indoors."

Halton flew from the room, slamming the door.

Edgar cast a weary gaze toward the fog-covered window. Shapeless white forms blurred his vision. He stood trapped within memories of the woman he loved even more than he realized. His memory filled with her terror-stricken face. Taunting whispers kept sleep at bay. *Why did you not save me?* Despair, like a mythical dragon, devoured his appetite, his joy, his soul.

In the king's silence, conjecture permeated the castle as to the fate of their precious queen. Whispered theories swirled around him.

The first whispers said, "Serious injury has confined our queen to bed."

As time passed, the concern for their queen's welfare grew. "She has lost the babe in the attack and remains abed to mourn."

When no one had seen the queen or heard anything of her for a month, they grieved. "Poor King Edgar, he has lost them both."

Edgar did nothing to stop or change their assumptions. He rarely ate, and as he grew more thin and drawn he slipped further into his own silent grief.

The whole castle grieved with him and for him. They too held Mariamne close to their hearts. Soon the gloom outside seeped into every room. Servants took to speaking only in hushed whispers, if at all.

As his world became dark and colorless, Edgar noticed Cy carried a matching pallor of gloom about him. Halton, however, grew more angry and agitated by the day.

"You fool, you belong in the dungeon where I found you!"

"Halton what are you doing?" Edgar barked after overhearing the cruel rebuke.

"Reminding the boy what we have lost."

"Do you wish to remind me as well?

Halton raised his chin proudly and looked as if he would oblige him.

"Do you think any soul in these walls does not know the great price we have paid for *my* negligence? And your hand in it as well."

His thane sputtered. "I had no hand in—"

Edgar stepped toward the man, standing near nose to nose with him. "You, Halton, brought those men to me. You spoke of the message of deliverance they claimed to carry. Did you light-search them? Test their claim? Nay, you brought them to me. And I failed her from that moment forward. So now we know our failings, has it lightened your spirit?" Edgar leaned in further, causing Halton to retreat a step. "And since you wish to assign blame, where were you when the enemy roamed about our walls, drugged me, and attacked my wife?"

Halton's eyes went wide. His shoulders squared as he stammered, "I became detained on that dreadful night. A strange complaint arrived at the same time as the visitors. An urgent missive came from one of the alehouse owners in town. It had been alleged one of your men drank too much and did damage to the establishment. The drunkard refused to pay for the destruction or his ale, and the plea came to me to deal with the matter immediately."

"And did you deal with it?" Edgar snapped.

Halton's shoulders slumped. "When I arrived in town I could find no alehouse with any such complaint. By the time I completed a thorough investigation and returned to the castle, you had the matter concerning our lady well in hand. The surviving attackers had been executed and, as we know now, our Mariamne had already left our protection."

"So, Halton, evil led you away, drugged me senseless, and detained Cy from reaching his post. The enemy worked a great web and pulled each of us away from our precious lady. None can blame the other without the guilt falling soundly on himself. We each fell victim, but none more so than Mariamne."

With the light of truth on the matter, the three men took to avoiding one another as winter wore on, deep and dark.

Father Paul called Edgar to his office. The dark cold months of winter locked them off from everyone, and the Christ Mass loomed but days away. He entered, surprised to see Cy and Halton waiting. He spoke naught to either man and sat sullen as the holy man looked over them with a slow stare.

"Gentlemen, it has been three months since the Lady Mariamne became lost to us." The good father spoke with soft caresses. "The castle is mired in deep mourning over the loss, but she is not lost to God. It is time you break free of this self-deprecating wallowing and help your people. We *will* be celebrating the coming of our Lord Jesus in days, and *none* will celebrate without the three of you."

"Then there will be no celebrating," Edgar said dully.

"You would deny your God for the love of a woman?" The father's incredulous questions caused Edgar to raise his gaze for a moment.

Edgar buried his head in his hands. "By removing her from this land, God Himself has removed His hand of blessing from us. The very sun refuses to shine without her."

Father Paul continued with a gentle prodding. "Then many of your citizens died in the flooding as the rivers overflowed their banks when the rains came?"

"No, none died," came Halton's terse report.

"Oh, mayhaps 'twas the crops lost to the rains causing your people to starve in this long winter, which weighs overmuch upon your heart?"

"No, an overly large harvest was completed and stored in time, so the people are eating well." Edgar straightened, considering the man with growing interest.

"People are dying of the extreme cold, then?"

Halton leaned forward now. "No, while the wood is wet it will yet burn, and there have been no reports of any deaths."

"But do not some usually die in the most mild of winters from the cold?" Father Paul asked with a perplexed glance over them.

"Indeed, as you well know, Father, for you are asked to perform the last rites, so what is your point?" Edgar demanded.

Father Paul directed his next question to Cy. "How far would she have run or could she have been carried if the weather remained mild?"

"She would not have stopped!"

Father Paul sat back on his desk, rubbing his chin thoughtfully. "But the rains and the snows enfolded the whole land when she vanished, preventing all manner of travel. That is odd, is it not?"

Each man eyed the other as the idea took root.

"Have you not all told me—and has not the Lord Almighty, Himself, revealed to me—the Lady Mariamne is the queen of Veronia?"

Each man nodded his silent agreement.

"Has not God used each of you to show her His love that she might come to Him and be healed of her pain?"

Again they nodded.

"And is not it just possible God Himself has her now safely in the palm of His hand to such a purpose?"

"What evil meant for her destruction, God will use for her good," Edgar whispered.

Father Paul finished with a sharp clap of his hands. "Now, is not such knowledge sufficient reason to celebrate the Lord, gentlemen?" He opened the door of his office for them, and a beam of sunlight burst through the door, the first to be seen in months.

Edgar walked with Cy toward the chapel, his steps lighter and a smile once more on his lips. He set a hand on Cy's shoulder. "Let us thank God for coming, for us and for her."

Cy nodded. "She will be returned soon. God is faithful."

The weather broke, sometimes for only hours and sometimes for a day. The turn of the year lacked great revelry. Many still mourned their queen, as they carried an insuppressible hope this year would see their joy restored in some new way.

Edgar guarded the flame of hope Father Paul lit in him. *Lord, please let Paul's words to us be truth. Please be with her and protect her as I did not. Heal her and return her to us, to me. I need her, Lord, near as much as I need You.*

The weight in his home lifted as his people believed his time of deep mourning lay behind him.

But the first month of the year saw the end of the rains and the drying of the land, and no word of her came. The darkness within him pulled him back into despair. The second month came with unusually warm weather melting the remaining snow in the valley in a matter of days and clearing much of the Kestron Pass in a matter of weeks. The one-year anniversary of Mariamne coming to his home neared, yet no sign of his beloved revealed itself.

Edgar again refused to eat. He took refuge in bed to escape his tormented thoughts in the oblivion of sleep. There he dreamed of flying across the valley and up through the high snowcapped Kestron and down the far side. He would sweep left avoiding Lincolnshire and rush into the woods in the east. But always he would awake to a heart filled with such longing it brought tears to his eyes.

Chapter 42

Mariamne scrambled from those who attacked her. Edgar's hand struck out for her, and she drew back from its bite. She raced to her chamber, holding what remained of her gown to her trembling body. She bolted both the door to the nursery and the one to the queen's chamber. Falling beside her bed, her body racked with uncontrollable sobs she could not move. Great heaving cries tore through her and left only one thought. *Run!* She must get away, for not even here could she be safe.

There is nowhere safe for you, the sinister voice taunted. *Run. Run until you can find a safe haven. Run far from the desires of wicked men. Run. Run now!*

Oh, baby girl.

Mariamne froze at the familiar voice. Where did it come from? How did she know it?

Run!

She ripped the tattered dress from her shaking body and discarded it on the floor. She threw on a simple under-dress. Staying in the shadows, she raced down the back stairs and to the laundry. She found what she sought. A male servant's dirty and well-worn breeches and tunic lay waiting to be washed.

She grabbed them. In the deserted hall, her eyes caught on a flash in the torchlight. She crept closer. Her senses now hummed with alertness. A dagger was left on a table, discarded because of a broken tip. She took it.

Run! The mantra beat as she yanked on the stolen clothes. The dagger trembled as she sliced through her bound hair. She threw her hair on the floor with all the other items destined for the fires. She looped the short length that remained into a common warrior's knot.

Her heart set a frantic pace. The sun would rise in hours. She must be away before first light. She crept out and followed the wall to the inner gate.

It stood open a crack—unguarded. Why?

She slipped through. Smoke greeted her. Fires. Her feet moved as fast as her pounding heart. She skirted the main road, racing in the shadows between the buildings scattered in the bailey. The outer gate loomed above her. It mocked her fear. The solid beam held it closed in a sadistic laugh. The guards would never open the gate. They stood with blades drawn.

"Who goes there?"

Her heart froze.

A muffled call came from the other side of the gate.

"Who is it?" a guard at the gate called up to the man on the battlements above.

"A knight of Lord Dorset."

"What does he want at this hour?"

The muffled voice of the man came from without.

"He brings word from Dorset of the Black Knight. He is on the move."

The two guards at the gate discussed the matter between them. They lifted the beam and tugged open one of the heavy doors.

Mariamne watched a silhouetted form enter.

"Dismount!" one guard instructed him at the point of his blade.

As they light-searched him and confirmed his identity, Mariamne slipped out. She fled down the rocky outcropping. At times she ran straight down the side of the steep hill, avoiding the winding road for a more direct path.

When her feet hit the valley floor she ran for the trees, which lay several leagues away. She charged through the thin tree line before the first glow of the sun touched the sky. Cramping muscles forced her to slow her pace.

Oh, my beautiful girl, where are you running?

She spun. Drew the dragger. No one stood nearby. She pushed the phantom voice aside and surged forward, far from the main road. The pounding of her heart and the memory of groping hands drove her until midday. She dropped beside a stream, plunged her face into the cold water and drank deeply.

Baby girl, look at you. Covered in mud. You were supposed to be washing the clothes not painted with grime, my heart.

She sat back on her aching legs for but a moment. Memories. Old long-lost memories flared to her mind. Strong hands lifted her high in the air spinning her around with great joy. His raven-black hair caught at the nape of his neck in a simple thong, and his deep green eyes shone with pride.

Run! Get away before they find you. She swallowed the image, compelled back to her feet. She trudged through the underbrush and thickening trees. Each step harder to take than the last. Her muscles quaked and cramped.

By nightfall she came upon a place reminding her of the spot she camped the last night before arriving at the castle. She shuddered. It took her since before sunup to walk what horses covered in hours. A twig snapped. The searchers were already upon her! Fear drove her to charge forward through the night.

She refused to slow for the cramping in her overworked legs. She would not stop for the bleeding blisters on her feet. Nothing could hinder her progress. The singular drumming thought remained. *Run! Run! Run!*

She stumbled upon another stream as light kissed the eastern sky. The foothills materialized a few leagues in the distance. They would carry her up into the high ridge.

She sat for a spell and drank deeply.

You promised me, my heart. Have you forgotten your promise?

She ignored the pleading memory, seeing a few late berries hanging invitingly beside her. She yanked them free, cutting her hands on the thorns. A new fear gripped her. She pulled up her tunic to examine her skin and found three black scratches and their accompanying tendrils. Fear drove out the wasting exhaustion. She knew if she slept she would be lost to its dark ends, with no one to protect her.

She built a fire the way Bray had taught her. Remembering the knight who lost his life at the hands of the horde made her shudder. She could be next. Her hand quaked as she heated her dagger to a bright glow. Covering her nose and mouth with her sleeve, she burned the poison from her body. When she could see no more traces on her skin, she leaned over the brook. She splash cool water on her burning skin and sweat-drenched face.

Another look over the rest of her body revealed a cut on her leg. She burned it away. Dousing the fire, she lumbered to the foot of the ridge. The inevitable exhaustion overtook her. Her body would not move another step. Forced to find shelter among a tight cluster of tall trees, she slept fitfully. The noises of the waking forest jarred her awake. Heavy raindrops and crushing fear woke her. Pregnant clouds covered the sun. How long had she slept?

Too long, the dark voice taunted.

She looked at the trail snaking up the tall ridge. If it took two days on horseback it would take her twice as long on foot. Glancing back at the grey clouds hanging low over the valley, she set her mind. Scanning the mountain once more she made out a route. It would take her nearly straight up. She started to climb.

Her aching legs and raw feet protested. She refused to hear them. Now as she used her hands and arms to pull herself up the sharp rocks, they too bellowed complaint. Rain fell, heavier each hour. The wet rocks caused her to slip and fall, leaving her aching body covered with cuts and scrapes. She would not entertain them.

Stopping to catch her breath, she remembered again the invading hands against her flesh. Do not stop. Move. The wind drove against her. Like an icy hand, it tried to hurtle her back down the mountain. She pressed upward until the day's light failed. Forced to stop or fall to her death, she surrendered. She took shelter in a cleft in the rock.

Run!

"Without light it would mean certain death," her voice rasped through her aching throat.

It laughed.

At first light she drank water collected in several deep gouges in the boulders. She ate the last of the high mountain berries she'd found. The rain fell in a never-ending torrent. The bitter cold further stiffened her muscles as she approached the summit. A frosty wind lashed at her and made her sore fingers numb. She continued on undaunted.

Remember your promise.

"No!" she screamed. "I will not listen to you!"

By afternoon of the third day on the mountain she started her descent. The downward slope quickened her pace but proved no less dangerous. She placed her foot on a rock, and as she shifted her weight to it, it dislodged from the soil and she slid on her backside for the length of a rod. Rocks cut her as she banged into them. She lay gasping for breath.

Run!

Exhaustion pulled at her senses, wooing her to sleep no matter where she perched. She fell several more times. Each time it grew harder to get up. Late in the afternoon of the fifth day she stumbled upon a small cave and took shelter in its dry interior for the night.

Waterfalls over the cave entrance woke her the following morn. She tried to stretch her sore and tight muscles, but they bellowed their objection at being moved at all. She worked her legs until they would support her. The compulsion to continue drove her out into the driving storm. She staggered on raw feet.

Run!

As nightfall approached, she could see the lamplight of Lincolnshire. Did she dare go there? Find help? They knew her to be the queen. They would remember. A flash. A flicker. Something caught her attention to the east in the woods. It did not last, but she turned toward it. She stumbled over the forest debris in the failing light. A solid dark shape loomed in the middle of a tight clump of trees.

She crept closer and a tiny windowless cottage took solid form. No smoke billowed from the chimney. Dust lay thick on the porch. She knocked. No answer. The latch gave with ease, but the door stopped before it opened. She leaned against it, tear springing up yet again. The wind lashed at her like a whip. Snow started to fall. With the last of her strength, she threw her feeble body against the door. It gave with a groan and fell to the floor. The dark space engulfed her. A stale, dusty smell filled her mouth. Her fingers searched the room and her hands discovered a hearth. Kneeling in front of it, she found dry wood stacked nearby.

It took her longer in the dark with stiff painful fingers, but at last she had a fire lit. She tended it until it burned large and hot. In the light of its glow she looked around at the utterly bare single-room wattle and daub space surrounding her.

She sat on a wood floor, slate shingles formed the roof above her, and both served to keep out the snow and the cold. Fatigue overtook her and she curled near the fire.

Mariamne assured herself her eyes were open, though she could see nothing. Not an ember remained of the fire. Darkness thicker than a starless night surrounded her. Cold embraced her like a deadly friend leaving her as brittle as ice. Whether Mariamne slept for hours or days she could not tell, but the excruciating pain in her empty belly pulled her from the black abyss. She attempted to move, but not one stiff muscle would respond. It was as if she had turned to stone. Panic seized her. Her mind raced but nothing else would move. Frozen tears stuck to her cheeks. *Help me.*

Chapter 43

When she woke again, she found her muscles still painful and stiff as stone. Slowly, she worked to drag herself to the woodpile and from there to the hearth. She laid another fire.

As it grew, her rigid limbs melted. Drinking in the heat, she stretched and worked her tight limbs—her hands and arms first, then she sat and moved down to her legs to her feet. Oh, her shredded feet. They were swollen and raw, and the lightest touch sent bolts of pain charging through her whole body. Mariamne's mind bellowed orders like a military commander. *Remove the shoes. Examine the feet. Clean the wounds. Wrap them in clean cloth. Do not allow them to fester.*

She shuddered and scanned the barren room. No water, no clean cloth, and worst of all—no food. Soon the condition of her feet would be the least of her concerns.

The fire crackled and popped its merriment, sneering at her pain. She spun on the dust-covered floor and placed her feet as near to the flames as she dared without setting them ablaze. The heat would not aid the swelling, but mayhaps it would prevent the rot.

She lay on her back and closed her eyes. Memories drifted gently through her quiet thoughts. *The God of Veronia wants to heal you.*

If only she could ask for such healing. Stinging tears escaped. Tears of regret. She rolled to her side and pushed the unseen God away. He had brought her to this land for a destiny she never sought. She had disobeyed Him. The pain. The sores. The cold. The silence. They served as her punishment.

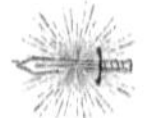

Mariamne marveled at waking once again as her body continued to weaken from hunger. She reached for a log and moved with ease. She placed a fresh piece on the coals and examined her feet. No swelling remained. She gingerly removed each shoe and looked in amazement at the thick scabs covering both feet. No sign of disease could be found. In fact, her skin looked well on its way to healing. She stared at them, bewildered.

"Peace, little sister. God wants to heal you."

Mariamne's head shot up. Cy's voice had filled her ears, yet she still remained alone.

Cy. Her heart seized and she doubled over. She had failed him too. She had given her oath that she would never leave without him. He would bear the blame for her absence. More guilt-ridden tears tumbled and dampened the dusty breeches.

"I do not merit Your forgiveness, God of this land, but Cy should not suffer for my actions. Please do not blame him."

"Peace, little sister. God loves you."

Quiet tears erupted into gut-churning sobs. He sounded so near.

"I am sorry, Cy." She rocked before the fire, tears finally slowing, only to return afresh.

When the tears at last subsided, she crawled to the door. Outside, low clouds rested on the treetops and a gentle rain again soaked the land. She spotted a discarded iron pot upturned and partially buried near the corner of the structure. She freed it and crawled toward the nearby roaring stream to clean it.

The rush of water brimmed high on the banks from the recent storms. Mariamne scooped some into her hands and drank deeply. Relief flooded her, and she drank more, remembering not to take too much at once or her stomach would reject it. Filling the pot with water, she used sand to scour it clean. She rinsed it several times and filled it with water to bring back to the cottage.

As she neared the small dwelling on her hands and knees, she noticed the remains of a forgotten garden. Finding several roots and tubers, she pulled up one slightly shriveled cassava and carried it inside. She cooked it on a stone of the hearth and ate a small piece. She ate two more bites before she sat the remains down and curled by the fire.

By the following morn some of her strength returned, and she ate what remained of the tuber. In the afternoon she crawled to the stream for more water and collected a leek, an onion, and some beans. She added them to the water and hung the pot over the fire. While it simmered, she found a slim piece of smooth birch bark to use as a spoon.

Rain fell in never-ending waves. She placed the empty pot outside the door for a time and drank the rainwater collected in it, but the rest of the time she sat near the fire to rest.

She lay staring at the dancing flames. What now? She needed a plan, if she was ever able to walk again, and if the rain ever stopped.

"Peace, little sister."

Cy's words came often. At first they had frightened her, but now these kind words stilled the restlessness.

Remember your promise.

Another familiar voice tickled her memory. It belonged to the dark-haired man who spun her in the air. An old memory; one she could not call to the surface.

Chapter 44

Light the fire. Fix one meal. Sleep. Remember all she left behind. Every few days Mariamne tried to stand. It seemed as though weeks passed before her feet would again bear her weight. By then rains had stopped, only to give way to snow. Before it piled too deep, Mariamne ventured out to investigate her surroundings.

She found a great amount of cut wood behind the small structure and took to bringing in some of the pile regularly to allow it time to dry before she needed it. A meadow stretched out not to the west and she pulled up armloads of tall grass. She dried the grasses by the fire and bundled them together for a soft bed. It did not seem to matter where she went, near or far, she never failed to find something she could use or eat.

In one trip she brought back a long evergreen branch, which served well as a broom. On another excursion dragged back an odd-shaped portion of a fallen tree for a chair.

Now safe and warm inside the little hovel, the nagging urge to run lost its appeal. Soon the silence and loneliness churned her memories. These forgotten images and conversations comforted her as dear friends. They drove out the darkness and served as a balm to her soul.

Most often the soft memories spoke with Cy's voice. Somehow he still protected her. She often talked to him, as though he sat with her.

"The Son of God came to earth to experience everything you did, m'lady, to understand you better."

"Surely, Cy, no man ever experienced my torment?"

"The Scriptures say, 'I gave my back unto the smiters, and my cheeks to the nippers: I hid not my face from shame and spitting.'"

Cy never said those words. Where had they come from? The priests? Possibly. They read every week from the Holy Book. How many Sabbaths had she sat unhearing? Maybe she had heard after all. More words sprang to mind. "And when they had scourged him, they will put him to death."

Mariamne reeled at a God suffering the same beatings and whippings as she. She stood in the open door the world lay blanketed cubits deep in white. But why would God, in any form, endure such treatment?

"But His wounds were for our transgressions, He was broken for our iniquities: the chastisement of our peace was upon Him, and with His stripes we are healed."

"Cy, honestly, how can wounds on God heal me?" She sighed heavily. She returned to her mat and lost her concerns in sleep.

Her imagined the conversations with Cy continued each day. They only served to stir more questions than they answered. But in her soul grew a deep hunger that no food could quench.

She pulled the last tuber from the garden. The snow numbed her fingers. Nothing grew now. She may have healed only to die of hunger.

Father Paul's words before he left on sabbatical sprang to mind. "God is with you and will never leave you."

Would the God who created a destiny for her still watch over her after she had run away from Him—and it?

Her mind listed her provisions: The cottage appeared in the darkness to protect her from the storms. The wood lay prepared both within and without for her warmth and to cook her food. The food she found readily, even in this deserted place. The complete healing of all of her injures.And the evil had not found her here.

Her heart thundered. Each gift spoke of divine protection. Her breaths rapid gasps.

God knew where to find her, and He had provided all these things. Her tears startled her. She staggered under the weight of such a great love. Pleasant memories, met needs, the profound touch of a God who continued to pursue her—the tears came in answer to all these things.

As she stepped out the door, she nearly stumbled over a basket draped with an oiled cloth. She stared at it, afraid it might vanish if she moved to touch it. Her senses leapt to the surface and she scanned the area for danger. Footprints, already partially buried in the lightly falling snow, led to and from the west in the direction of the shire, but no one remained in sight.

She brought the basket inside and uncovered it. She gasped to find it stuffed with several loaves of hard dark bread, a collection of vegetables, and a hunk of salted meat. A tremor coursed through her body as the message came again, "God is with you and He will never leave you."

She did not deserve His favor, yet He bathed her in it nonetheless. "Thank You."

Fresh tears of wonder and gratitude tumbled were offered to the God who had not abandoned her, even in her desperate flight to escape Him. His tender peaceful touch soothed again as she prepared a small portion of the food.

Rationing her precious supplies with care allowed them to last nearly a week. Yet when they ran out, new provisions mysteriously appeared at the door. She took to placing the empty baskets back outside, and they were replaced sporadically throughout the long deep winter. She never glimpsed the bearer of the much-needed gifts. She imagined God Himself brought them, and it made her smile.

The snows stopped falling. Trusting in God, His care, and provision worked an unusual result on her rebellious heart. New memories surfaced. Hard remembrances she struggled to face.

"What are you so afraid of?" Annabel's words challenged her again, jolting her from sleep. She could not shake free from the fear or the question all day as it rattled around inside her like a toddler's toy.

After days of the tormenting question, she buried her face in her hands and whispered to the God watching over her, "I know not what frightens me so, God of Veronia. I fear a great many things, but I know not the answer to this question. You must tell me."

Again peace comforted her. The day saw a rare spot of sun and warmth. The bright orb set to work unburdening the trees of their heavy loads. She sat contentedly in the doorway listening to the large clumps slip from branches and plop loudly to the ground.

Her eyes caught on a mound in the distance. A collection of debris had pushed in a heap when the river ran high. Now dressed in a thin layer of snow, it reminded her of a haystack. The image stirred a memory.

"Baby girl," the dark-haired man rushed to her as fear etched deep lines in his thin face. She might have been six or seven. "Listen to Daddy." Her father. The man that spun her in the air was her father. He looked—old. His black hair was laced with grey, and great wrinkles covered his drawn and hollow features.

He knelt and grabbed both her arms almost painfully as he spoke strained orders. "My heart, you must run to the field and hide in the great haystacks. Hide there until I come for you. Do you understand?" He spun her around and pushed her toward the field. "Run, precious girl!" She had only gone a matter of steps when he moaned his last words, "Choose the light!"

Mariamne blinked, and the plopping of snow drew her gaze to the debris mound. An eerie shudder slithered up her spine. She remembered the far-flung day now. And she wanted to forget.

She moved to the fire and stared into the flames as they became the fires that consumed her village. Curled there she listened to muffled shouts and terrified cries. Daddy never came.

Hunger drove her from the hay the next day. Her village lay destroyed. Wisps of smoke drifted from the smoldering shells that had once been homes. Bodies littered the ground. It did not take long before she stumbled to her house and found her beloved father, covered with cuts and bloody wounds as he stared blankly at nothing. The old loss cut fresh wounds in her heart. She curled onto her mat and pushed the hateful memory away. Her tears rocked her to sleep.

Remember your promise.

Larks and finches sang her awake. She opened the door to a bright spring day. New flowers burst open through the last of the snow and flooded the meadow with a rainbow of colors.

Remember your promise.

"Daddy, please. I cannot remember. What promise?" she whispered.

Remember your promise, my heart.

She remembered the tall man who loved to spin her in the air and hold her hand. A forgotten sense of joy and safety filled her until it nearly crushed her.

Oh, baby girl, Daddy loves you.

The child within stomped her foot in infantile annoyance at being called a baby. But now as a grown woman, she treasured those sweet words and longed to hear them again.

Tears came. "Daddy, please…"

At last the memory of another day he knelt before her returned from a lost corner of her mind. His words came fresh to her ears. "Oh, little warrior, someday you will be asked to make a great choice. It will determine everything which follows and it will either lead you into a great destiny or great destruction. My precious girl, you will have to give up your will in order to follow your true path."

Mariamne jerked from the recollection, her heart pounding a furious rhythm. She had her answer. Give up her will, her stubbornness, her notions to control her life. This is what she feared now. The thing she dreaded above all else.

A falcon screeched overhead. Her heart longed to be as free, to soar above the troubles of this earth, out of the reach of pain.

"Little sister, 'If that Son therefore shall make you free, ye shall be free indeed.'"

Snap!

She turned.

Snap! Snap. Snap.

Someone approached. She could not move. She could not breathe.

"Hello, precious."

She shuddered at the ghost of a memory stirred by evil. "No!" she screamed , her voice ragged from disuse.

"Precious, you know you have a destiny. Accept it. Come."

"I would not surrender to you as a child. I will not surrender now!" Cold dark wisps threatened to break her resolve, as evil brought back memories of the man who came and buried Daddy.

So many thoughts besieged her she lost track. Yet her skin, even now, lay covered in gooseflesh thinking of him. Her would-be rescuer. And his vile touch. How many times did he speak of her special destiny? How many times did he say she needed to choose to obey?

She had promised Daddy she would give up her will. But this man's touch made her sick, twisting her stomach. The touch of evil.

Choose the light.

The distant memory of a horse's whinny echoed in her mind. A black figure on a rearing horse stood silhouetted against the flames of her village. The Black Knight. The same Black Knight who lay on Veronia's border also destroyed her village years ago. The evil killed her father. It had sought her death since her childhood. It hunted her still.

Now it taunted her with memories of men's evil desires. Its purpose was clear. To keep her from her destiny. Fists pummeled her, whips laid open her back again and again. *Surrender and this will be your fate*, it sneered.

Choose the light, my heart, Daddy called.

Chapter 45

Mariamne's vision cleared. A bright shaft of sunlight pointed at the meadow as the clouds parted. She stumbled forward and dropped to her knees in its warmth. Eyes closed she lifted her head to the brightness and threw her arms wide. She attempted to join the birds' songs. "You have revealed the truth, Lord God of Veronia. I can feel the great chasm that separates the truth of Your love from the hatred of the evil one who seeks me. I choose You."

His gentle wind swirled, warming her skin as it rustled the branches and played with her loose hair. A now familiar voice came with it. *You will surrender yourself to Me, Daughter?*

"Yes, I do surrender my will, my destiny, my life, my dreams, my very breath. Take it all and do as You will, Almighty God."

Why Daughter?

"You are the creator of the heavens and the earth. You paid the price for my sins. You bought me long ago and I want to worship You all my days."

What are your sins, My Precious Child?

"I have cursed Your name, denied You. I have been willful and rebellious, hurt people, run from my destiny, been unkind, ungrateful, unforgiving, unloving, hateful." Great tears rolled as she listed every evil thing she could remember.

When she completed her shriving, the wind swirled faster about her. *Welcome home, Beloved. Take My Spirit and be healed.*

The wind seeped into her skin until it filled her with such warmth and peace she feared her lowly soul could not contain it. She sat back on her heels, dropped her arms into her lap, and reveled in her God and the sweetness of His holy presence within her. Her soul sang unending praises when her voice gave out for she could not keep her grateful spirit quiet.

She sat thus for most of the morn as awe, wonder, and love filled her beyond measure. Finally her Lord spoke to her again. *It is time to go home, Beloved.*

As the third month of the year dawned, the dream flew Edgar through the valley over the ridge into the woods and to the door of a tiny little cottage.

Go find your wife, Beloved.

Edgar woke with a start.

He sprang from bed with such exuberance he nearly knocked over the lamp on the bedside table. The sun not yet visible in the east, he dressed in haste, yanking his boots on so quickly he injured several toes. Ignoring the pain, he ripped his wool cloak from the wardrobe and flew down the stairs.

He woke a squire. "Saddle my horse, as well as Cy's, Halton's, and the Lady's."

The squire rubbed sleep from his eyes with a mumbled agreement.

Edgar ran two at a time up the narrow stairs to the barracks. Finding Cy first, he laid one hand on his shoulder. "'Tis time." He did the same with Halton, and both men followed on his heel moments later.

"I go to wake Tye and tell him his charge. Halton, gather supplies. Cy, collect the items she may need."

The squire led out the horses as the first glowing of the rising sun burst over the horizon.

They mounted, secured the gelding's lead to one of the saddles, and thundered through the gates.

Wanting to prove her readiness to do His bidding without hesitation, Mariamne raced to the cottage. She rekindled the fire, grabbed her dagger, and headed for the stream. Using her knife she dug up a soapwort root she had noticed some time ago, cut it into small pieces, and mashed them before she stepped fully clothed into the frigid water of the deep stream.

The cold nipped at her toes and made her legs ache. When she knelt to submerge herself, she whimpered at the pain. She had noticed in the last few days her bosom had grown swollen and tender. They pained her more so this day. The cold water added to her discomfort. She could not understand what ailed her but did not dwell on it as she hurried to clean so she could return to the warmth of the fire.

She scrubbed her clothes, hair, and skin before her cramping muscles and chattering teeth drove her to the fire's blessed heat. She wrestled with the tangles of her matted hair without any form of brush.

Her rations had run out yesterday and no more had arrived. "God will provide," she croaked with a confident grin. Content in her trust of Him, she curled next to the fire one last night, praising God as she drifted off to the sweetest sleep she had ever known.

Chapter 46

She rose before first light, wanting to be on her way back to King Edgar. The old evil tried to prick her fear, attempting to sound like her God, *When you give yourself to this king, he will behave as every other man. You will never escape the pain.*

She did not speak to it. "Lord, you told me to go. To King Edgar. There will be safety and love there, for You love me."

Evil may have lost the battle for her soul, but it still hoped to destroy her future.

You think Edgar will accept you back?

"Lord, You sent me and You will make a way and go before me."

She cleaned the cottage of her rough furnishing, leaving only the makeshift chair and the pot. She brought in the last of the cut wood.

Bang!

The door burst open, jerking her to her feet with her dagger ready.

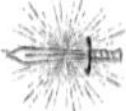

Edgar, Halton, and Cy rode all night, as Edgar urged them on at a crazed pace. Both men shot him sideways glances as he turned from the path to Lincolnshire into the woods, but he pressed them forward.

When they spotted the hovel with a thin wisp of smoke snaking from the chimney, Halton spurred his horse ahead of them. The first to leap from his mount, he charged toward the door as though going into battle.

Edgar watched from the doorway as Mariamne whirled and pulled a dagger to defend herself against the unwanted intruder smashing down her door. The sight of her—alive—rooted him to the floor.

Halton took great strides toward her. His back rigid, he grasped hold of her upper arms until his fingers went white.

Mariamne raised a bewildered brow.

"Mariamne, are you hale? Are you *well*?" Desperation made his voice uncommonly harsh.

"Sir, Halton, whatever are you doing here?" she said in a hoarse whisper.

"I love you, Mariamne."

Edgar choked on his startled breath.

Mariamne gasped and pull away.

Halton's determined countenance melted. His head dropped and his shoulders sagged. A visible shudder raced through him. "Forgive me, Your Majesty," he groaned in near inaudible words.

He stepped from her with his hand raised for her to take, which she did with some reluctance. As he turned to lead her, Edgar found the will to take a few steps inside the door.

Mariamne's eyes did not leave Halton's face.

Edgar too stared at his dear friend, dazed by his shocking admission.

Halton led her to Edgar, where he placed her hand on his and left the room.

The warmth of her hand filled him with joy. She blinked wide-eyed several times as if trying to make sense of things.

As Mariamne's muddled thoughts shifted from the thane to his lord, the appearance of the man in front of her caught at her heart. This once healthy and hale man now stood thin with immense dark circles under his great brown eyes, which seemed to bulge out of his drawn face. In those sweet brown eyes lay the immeasurable pain she had caused him. Her head dropped, much like Halton's, as deep remorse stirred.

Edgar placed a trembling hand on her fallen cheek. The tenderness of his caress soothed, and she nuzzled into his hand. Her eyes closed with a sense of rapture at his touch, his acceptance, his love. It left her overwhelmed.

Compelled to reach out to her, to touch her, Edgar let his hand hang trembling in the space between them. Would she pull away in disgust? Would she allow the caress? His pounding heart nearly burst free when she not only did not pull from him, but leaned into his hand further.

At last she lifted her head and looked at him with a tenderness he had never seen before. "Please forgive me, Your Majesty. I have caused you such pain, and I deeply regret it."

Tears trickled down her thin cheeks, and he brushed one away with a thumb. "I do not want you as my queen any longer," he said stiffly.

She straightened, and her beautiful eyes grew wide in fear. She gasped, and her breath caught.

"Mariamne, I need you as my wife. These last months have taught me I am incapable of living without you by my side."

She relaxed as a smile parted her lips. She slipped her arms under his to encircle him and lay her head on his chest. Shocked, he did not immediately respond to her embrace. When he came to himself, he wrapped his arms securely around her and pulled her even closer. But she tensed. He loosened his hold, but she did not pull away.

Edgar could barely find his voice. "Will you marry me?"

"Aye."

A euphoric whoop escaped him. He kissed her on the forehead and drew her close again. Her muscles tightened, but she did not resist him. All would come in time, for now she agreed to be wed. He would rejoice in that.

They remained for a time until Mariamne drew from him gently. "I feared you would not wish to see me again after I vanished so abruptly." Her lips turned in a radiant smile and her eyes flashed. "But God assured me I belong with you. I am ready to step into His destiny, and I will try to serve you as a good queen, Sire."

"You are an excellent queen, Mariamne, but I hope you will take pleasure in being my wife as well." He watched as uneasiness dampened her bright features.

She slipped from his arms, and he held out his hand for hers. He replaced her emerald ring. "You left this in your haste."

She smiled and closed her hand around his. Something near the door drew her attention. She gasped, a joyous smile on her lips, and rushed to meet the one standing in the doorway.

Edgar did not fear the bond she shared with this man. She had spent the majority of her days with him, and Edgar knew it to be a bond of family and not romance—unlike his friend Halton.

Mariamne stood before Cy as a giddy child, but he would not look at her. His arms remained crossed. His head hung low. He did not acknowledge her.

She stopped a step away, chewing her lip. Then she stepped close to him and rested her forehead against his tenderly, her hands on his arms.

He still would not look at her.

"Oh brother of my heart, forgive me for breaking my vow. You are not to blame. You were always good and faithful and dearest of all to me. I acted wrongly, not you. But our God would not let me run far, and He kept the memory of you and your words ever in my ears."

Cy raised his head. His brows knit tight together, and he searched her face.

Joy of her newfound faith bubbled through her, and Cy could not help but share her smile.

"You may believe I left you, but you have been here with me every moment of every day. You watched over me, for I felt your prayers, I saw your smile, and your voice filled this cabin. God used you to bring me to Him, brother, so please forgive me and celebrate with me."

Cy finally relented, kissing her on the forehead, and his tight smile relaxed.

A foolish grin tickled the corner of her lips. "Tell me, brother," she coaxed him playfully. "How is the Lady Annabel?"

A shadow of pain washed over Cy's face. "I have not seen the lady since just after you left, little sister."

He bowed deeply and turned away.

"Cy," she called. "Do not blame Annabel for my horrid behavior. She is a good woman. She will never treat you as I have. Forgive me for all the ways I have hurt you."

"I forgave you long ago, little sister. I am overjoyed to know you are well and serve God."

"Will you see Annabel again?"

He walked to the horses. When he returned, he handed her a bundle of clothes.

"Annabel?" she asked again.

"You must to change."

A light bubble of laughter filled the heavy air between them. "Do I understand this to mean you approve not of my attire?"

"Filthy servant's breeches do not become the queen, m'lady."

She laughed again, and he drew her brush from his belt. "Oh, you know me well and the things I most need." She stepped forward and kissed him lightly on the cheek.

Cy made it but one step when she called to him again. "Brother, would you do me a great kindness and collect some more wood? A great quantity sat stacked behind the cottage when I arrived. It saved my life. I would like to leave some for the next soul God sends this way."

He smiled, bowed low, and left.

Edgar laid a tender hand on the small of her back, "I will help him and allow you to change."

Mariamne worked the brush through her unruly hair before she removed the tunic and donned the chemise. She again became aware of her sore bosom and noticed how swollen they appeared. *What is the matter with me?*

She cut the legs from the breeches and converted them into an undergarment before pulling on her riding skirt and bodice. She marveled at how loose the garments fit, except for her breasts, which seemed to have doubled in size. She never noticed the weight loss. Brushing aside the change, she joined the men.

She spotted her gentle gelding first and laid her cheek alongside his face and rubbed his muzzle affectionately. As she pulled from him she noticed a small length of leather cord and cut it free from the saddlebag to bind her plaited hair.

She followed the steady hacking of axes to where the men worked. They chopped a tree they had felled. She collected the logs they created and carried them to the growing pile behind the cottage. As she returned for another armload, her stomach roared.

Edgar looked up with a bemused smirk. "Are you hungry, my lady?"

Heat crept up her cheeks, but she smiled and nodded.

He dropped the ax and led her back to the horses. Reaching into the saddlebag, he provided her with some biscuits and a little dried meat. "Stay and eat, we will be finished soon."

With the wood stacked and Mariamne's stomach quieted, they turned to the horses. Cy draped her warm cloak about her shoulders before he lifted her into the saddle.

He slipped her foot into the stirrup. "Little sister, you are in sore need of new shoes, for these are too tattered and stained to be on the feet of the queen."

Mariamne ruffled his hair, "It shall be my first task when I arrive home." *Home*, how good did the word taste on her tongue.

Chapter 47

Mariamne closed her eyes to contain the tears. She bounced uncomfortably, bracing her arm under the unbearable leaping of her bosom. What ailed her?

Halton took the lead, though almost a half a league separated them.

"Tell us of what God has done," Cy said.

"Aye, tell us," Edgar encouraged with a smile.

"God brought back memories of my father. He seemed to know of the call on my life. And even then, the Black Knight tried to keep me from attaining it." She explained what she had remembered. They marveled at God's hand throughout her journey.

Thank You, Lord. Their love is Yours given with human hearts. I praise Your name. Mariamne praised God for reuniting them and for the horse to return upon. She had not been eager to walk back over the mountain. She settled into a tolerable rhythm as they came to the foot of the ridge near midday.

Something stirred in her. She reined in and sat, eyes closed, listening.

"Halton, hold," Cy said

"My lady?" Edgar asked.

Both Cy and Edgar spoke at near the same moment.

The rustle of the horses quieted. She listened. There. Something faint. Something distant. Something drawing her.

"Mariamne?" Edgar asked again.

"This way." She turned to move around him and headed east, deeper into the forest, away for the mountain.

The men regrouped, Edgar and Cy again flanking her with Halton behind.

"Little sister, where are you going?"

She turned to him, filled with wonder and awe. "I know not, but I am told to go this way."

Mariamne rode as unbelievable contentment washed over her in response to her obedience. She swam in it and savored it as her God's touch continued to soften her calloused heart.

She drew up her reins again and listened.

"What is it?" Edgar's voice held a nervous edge.

"I only know God wants me to go this way." She turned her horse by a degree and led them farther into the forest.

Twigs snapped. Forest litter, sodden from the winter storms, squished beneath them. In other places, mud sucked at the mounts' hooves. Entwined in those sounds, something called. It tickled her ears like a precious whisper. It pulled at her heart, causing it to beat out an excited rhythm that grew in intensity as she drew nearer.

Mariamne stopped again to listen. The creak of leather turned her head. She looked at Cy. His eyes narrowed and focused on a small clearing several paces ahead. He leaned forward and turned toward the sound.

"What is it?"

She smiled at him and shrugged.

Mariamne and Cy spurred their horse forward at the same moment.

"I hear it now too," Edgar said of the warbling sound wafting through the air.

Cy kicked his horse to greater speed and moved out ahead of the rest. Halton galloped past her, and Edgar and joined him. Halton and Cy raced neck-and-neck as they entered the clearing. Cy drew up and leapt from his saddle. He leaned over something in the leaf-litter, drew his sword, and promptly light-searched it. When the light hit the unknown object, it fell silent.

Halton dismounted and picked up the mystery, revealing a tiny baby.

He held the still infant out in front of him as Edgar helped Mariamne dismount. He approached Edgar with stiff arms stretched straight out in front of him. He pushed the babe at Edgar. A deeply perplexed look crinkled his face into a tight pinch. "'Tis a babe, Your Majesty."

Edgar did not take the naked boy from him but scanned the surrounding area apprehensively. "We should try to find his mother."

As if responding to the king's rejection of him, the infant let out a shrill wail of frustration and began to squirm wildly in Halton's hands.

Mariamne gasped at the sudden outburst and her chemise became damp. She stepped from behind Edgar, took the babe into her arms, and turned away from the men. She worked frantically to unlace her bodice with her free hand as the famished infant struggled to find her. As she finally opened the bodice and pulled down her loose-fitting chemise, the babe seized onto her with such eagerness that a whimper of pain escaped her tight throat. She watched in wonder as the small boy ate hungrily. She covered both of them with the edge of her cloak before turning to the men.

They each stood slack-jawed and wide-eyed, but none uttered a sound. Did they still breathe? Finding her own voice, Mariamne whispered with profound awe, "It appears God has found his mother, Sire."

"But how…" Edgar stammered.

One fist sat perched on her hip. "If the Lord Almighty can create life in the womb of an untouched maiden, can He not likewise create milk in one not a mother?"

All heads bobbed in awe-struck agreement.

Edgar cleared his throat, and his tongue ran across his lips. "Nevertheless, we should search."

Cy and Halton mounted and made concentric circles around them, scanning the ground for a trail.

With the men out of sight, only the suckling sound of the hungry babe filled the clearing. Mariamne looked up at Edgar as he drew near, his steps slow and unsteady. "He is truly not yours, Mariamne?"

She rested a hand on his arm. "Those wicked men did not succeed in their attempt, Sire. I promise you. God alone led me here."

Placing a hand high on her back, he led her to a stump where she could sit.

As she nursed the babe she glanced up at him. "God has made a way for you, Sire. You have an heir."

Edgar dropped to his knees with a gasp. It seemed as though the air had been driven from his lungs.

"Majesty?"

"You are quite right," he said. Awe kissed his words. "God has provided me a son to raise as my own blood." Edgar sat back on his heels and ran his hand over his short hair. "Within the span of hours God has fulfilled the two great longings of my heart—to have you as my true wife, and to have a son. It is too much to comprehend."

Heat washed her face. "We must praise our great God who loves you so much." The babe grew heavy as he drifted off to sleep, so she covered herself and pulled him from under her cloak. She raised him to her shoulder and patted him gently as she had seen other women do with their newborns.

Cy and Halton returned. "We found no sign of anyone else in the forest, Sire. Not a trail or even any evidence of anyone passing." Cy stepped from his saddle and rent a blanket in two long strips. Then he took one of the lengths and tore a small portion off to create a square of cloth for a diaper. Mariamne laid the babe on her lap and began to secure it around him as Cy ripped another length and handed it to her. "Use this to swaddle him."

The babe woke with a jerk and began flailing his arms before she had him completely wrapped, so she again tucked him into her cloak and fed him until he slept. When at last his belly was full, she wrapped him and gently placed him in Edgar's arms. "Your son, Sire." She smiled as he stared with wide eyes and slack jaw, first at her and then at the babe asleep near his heart.

Cy continued to work with the torn blanket. "He is darker skinned than you, Sire, but not as dark as our queen. His hair is the same, for it grows in wispy deep-brown tufts."

"He cannot be more than a day or two old," Mariamne said.

Edgar cradled him in a loving embrace. "He is my true son. I know it as I know my own name. Already it seems impossible to think this infant is not of my blood."

Cy held the longer length of the rent blanket toward her. She tipped her head confused. He wrapped it around her in the form of a sling that lay diagonally from her hip to her opposite shoulder. He measured off the appropriate length and ripped away the excess. "We can use this for diapers later."

She removed her cloak, and Cy tied the sling securely about her and she remounted her horse. Edgar handed the small babe to her pride straining against his buttons an infectious smile filling his face.

The men joined her in their saddles, and they turned back to the trail. "Does our son have a name, Sire?"

Edgar somehow managed to sit even taller. "Our son," he echoed staring off through the distant trees. "Our son will be called, Shane."

"It means gift of God, my lady," Halton called, already moving toward the trail home.

They proceeded up the great ridge, stopping every couple of hours to allow Shane to feed. As darkness approached, Mariamne called to Halton, who rode as far removed as he dared. "There is a cave near, sir, where I stayed to shelter from the rain."

Halton glanced over his shoulder to see where she indicated. Once they dismounted he disappeared and returned some time later with vines from the hillside. He used them to kindle a small fire near the entrance.

Mariamne left Shane in Edgar's arms and began a small meal for them.

As they lay down to sleep, Mariamne noticed Cy had no blanket and realized he had sacrificed his for the babe. She smiled and carried hers to him and covered him. He stirred, pulled it away, and opened his mouth to protest. She knelt down and laid a calming hand on his powerful shoulder. "Peace, brother. My husband will share his blanket with me, take this and rest well."

He placed his hand over hers and squeezed it tenderly.

Edgar lifted his blanket to welcome her into it. Her heart fluttered at flashes of old memories. She swallowed the lump lodged tight and took a slow calming breath. She pushed a smile to her lips, curled with her back against his warmth, and pulled her son close. Edgar dropped the blanket over them and let his arm rest on hers as they drifted off to sleep.

God clearly directed her. This man was her husband, though no rites had been said. Yet the darkness still gripped her. It flooded her mind with cruel and unwelcome touches until she could no longer feel the tenderness in Edgar's hand. Her heart shuddered again. After a lifetime of running, she had surrendered to God. Would it now take as long to surrender her heart, and her body, to the one chosen for her?

The gentle rise and fall of his chest brushed against her back, and the soft sigh of his rhythmic breathing filled her ears. He slept in the joy of her presence. Why could she not do the same? She squeezed her eyes shut, groping for the peace God gave. *Lord, help me.* Another memory brought another shudder, and the king tightened his hold. *I cannot call the man by his given name. How can I be his wife?*

I have heard thy prayer and seen thy tears: behold, I have healed thee.

Her stomach still twisted in tight knots, but she clung to the promise of the One she trusted above all her fears.

Chapter 48

As they spent another day inching over the great Kestron Ridge, followed by another across the valley, the strength of Mariamne's voice returned, and all of them gained back the vitality lost in the dark mournful months of winter. Hunting proved good, and they ate well even at the summit and returned to the castle radiating the glory of the God who indwelled them.

As they approached the foot of the castle, Mariamne drew her horse very close alongside Cy's and slipped her foot from the stirrup. She placed her tattered shoe on his horse's shoulder blade and gave it a great shove. Her unexpected action forced the horse to step from the path to the castle onto the path into town. She raised great pleading eyes to him in an effort to encourage him.

He looked at her, a sad frown disfiguring his fine face, but he nodded. "I will tell Lady Annabel you have returned."

Mariamne again grieved for what she had done to him. She turned to Edgar. "He is not going to make amends, but as a lowly sandesman. Oh, the damage I have wrought."

Edgar wiggled his brows, and a wide grin appeared in a most odd fashion, as if he held some great secret but had no intention of sharing it.

She continued to stare at him, but his gaze would not turn her way and his chin rose defiantly to her silent pleas. The grin became a mischievous smirk as they proceeded up the steep outcropping and entered the gate to thunderous shouts.

"The king has returned. Long live King Edgar!"

"Look, Queen Mariamne is with him!"

"Long live Queen Mariamne! Long live Queen Mariamne!"

Her heart leapt at their cries. Many reached out to her. More waved and bowed and stared. Tears flowed like waterfalls.

"Long live Queen Mariamne! Long live Queen Mariamne!" They sang again and again until she entered the inner gate.

Tye rushed from the hall and greeted them with a hasty bow as Edgar dismounted. "You have visitors, Sire."

Edgar tossed the reins to a squire as he turned back for her. "Go, Majesty. I will follow."

Edgar continued to reach for her.

Tye urged him. "Sire, please. They are most impatient."

Mariamne nodded to him as Halton moved to help her down.

She followed him only moments later. Edgar sat in his throne, a small band of knights stood before him. He sat straight and stiff with his lips drawn in a harsh line.

Mariamne bit at her lip, and her muscles tightened.

The knights righted from their observance and one spoke in a tone which grated on Mariamne. "It is good to see you well, Your Majesty, for the land is astir with rumors of you wasting away after the death of your beloved queen. There are many who fear you are too weak to lead us in the upcoming battles with the Black Knight. Therefore, we have each been sent from our respective lords to measure your fitness."

Mariamne quickened her steps. The tattered soles of her slippers crunched angrily over the rushes filling the vast space. She passed the knights and stood proudly beside Edgar. "As you can see, good sirs, I am anything but dead." She flipped back her cloak to reveal the babe in her arms and handed him to Edgar.

Edgar stood and held up the swaddled infant, "You have the honor of being the first to be introduced to my son and heir, Shane, Son of Edgar, Son of Mather, Prince of Veronia."

Every knee in the hall bowed. Edgar handed Shane back and returned to his seat as the knights stood again. "King Edgar has an heir," they cheered, looking to one another.

"We shall return to our lords and carry word of the good news to all we pass." They bowed again and sped from the room, talking excitedly.

"How is it exactly they know the king's mood when travel throughout the land has been impossible for months? It would seem we have someone within our home who sees fit to share all manner of gossip and intrigue with any who would dare listen," Mariamne said.

"Come, let us celebrate. We are hale, you have returned, and you carry our son. A son who has been given to us by God's own hand." Edgar brushed her arm with a tender caress.

Mariamne lowered her head in prayer. "Forgive us, Lord. We know Shane is part of Your plan for Veronia. But others would not be so accepting. If we are to speak the truth of him, let our mouths be open. We trust in You alone."

"Amen." Edgar smiled. "God has been gracious to us. He has brought you home safe, with our son, a son of such miraculous wonder," Edgar spoke again. "He will see us through whatever is to come."

"Let the securing of the kingdom delay not a moment longer, Sire. Call the war host that your reign might continue for your son."

"We celebrate this night. Then all will be made ready. Now that the Knight has lost you, he will not delay another year. We will meet on the battlefield soon."

Chapter 49

"Welcome home, Your Majesty."

"Oh, we have missed you, Majesty."

Mariamne moved into the queen's chambers, placed her gowns in the queen's wardrobe, and laid Shane in a hastily provided ornately carved cradle placed near the queen's curtained bed. An urgency, born of her inner excitement, pushed her. She changed into a deep-blue, long-sleeved woolen gown and left Dawn, a faithful maid from the kitchens, in the outer chamber in case Shane should wake.

Now, as a child thrilled to show a new treasure to a friend, she tried to race across the ward to find Father Paul. But her eager feet slowed as each inhabitant of her home stopped to greet her with blessings and love.

"'Tis good to have you back, Majesty."

"Welcome!"

"The Lord will bless us now that you have returned."

She paused, reining in her desire, to accept the greetings filled with love. She waded through the precious faces until she caught sight of Father Paul some distance away and shouted at him, raising the heads of many around her.

The holy man turned, a smirk tugging his lips as she ran eagerly to meet him. He stepped back and straightened. "Your Majesty?"

Her childlike exuberance caused her to abandon proper decorum. She took a steadying breath, unable to contain her smile. She drew closer to share her news in confidence. "I have known my precious

Savior for four days, Father."

Father Paul's shoulders fell, and his firm spine became a gently bent reed. His hands rested on her shoulders as his lips brushed each cheek with a holy kiss. "Come, Daughter. I wish to hear about your time away from here." He led her to his office.

Mariamne barely felt the strength of the chair beneath her before she erupted in a long breathless recitation of her time since she fled the castle. She concluded with her prayer in the woods the day before King Edgar arrived.

Father Paul turned his eyes toward the heavens. "Lord God, Mighty Father, we praise Your name for this precious one who has chosen Your will above her own. You are mighty, Lord, to change any heart."

A ripple slid down her spine.

"We ask now for Your leading hand on this, Your daughter. Accept her confession and her profession of faith in Your Son. Aid her, as You have King Edgar, to rule well with all wisdom and honor. Mighty God. Amen." His gaze dropped to her once more, his face filled with a radiant peace.

He moved around his desk. The corners of his mouth turned. He cleared his throat. He leaned back, straightening. He looked heavenward for a moment, then came forward, words tumbling from his lips. "Is it true you have returned with King Edgar's heir at your bosom?"

Mariamne moved to the edge of her seat, excitement bubbling afresh, tossing aside the holy man's concern. "Fear not, Father, the Lord Himself has provided for King Edgar. God has given him an heir." Father Paul continued to frown. "I assure you, the farce of our marriage was in title alone. The Lord Almighty has made a way for King Edgar, Your Reverence, Shane is not blood of our blood, but a child to be the rightful heir to the king." She detailed the leading of the Lord, how God prepared her body days in advance, and of her being drawn by Him to the abandoned infant, and thus how Shane came to be Edgar's heir. "Shane is the son of my heart, if not my flesh, Father, and he is as surely a gift to King Edgar and Veronia as I have been to them."

Father Paul heaved a deep sigh of relief and gently touched the queen's head. "You are truly a gift, child, for the castle suffered in your absence. I rejoice with all Veronia to know you have accepted God's will for you."

He stood and swept out his arm for her to join him as they moved to the church. She knelt before the altar and partook of Holy Communion. Father Paul prayed over her, and then she stood before his great smiling face.

Heat filled her cheeks, and she struggled to pull the stammering words across her confounded tongue. "Father, King Edgar has expressed his deep desire to make our wedding authentic and wishes to inquire if you would be willing to perform the ceremony at your earliest convenience?"

"It would be my great delight, Your Majesty, anytime you so choose." He paused a moment. "Should we also plan to christen Prince Shane on the Lord's Day?"

"Yes, thank you for thinking kindly of him."

She left the church and found Cy exiting the stables. The dusty crown of his blond head filled her eyes. His arms hung lifelessly at his sides. As her shadow fell on his dirt-crusted boots he glanced up at her. A slim smile forced his lips upward.

The small ward closed in on her. "Is Lady Annabel well?"

"Aye, she is quite well now she knows you are safe and returned to us." His shoulders heaved and sank even lower. If he crumpled much more they would be at his waist. "The lady has suffered through a long winter without the queen's patronage. Only recently has she received requests for her garments."

His eyes caught her. They swam in his unspoken pain. "She hastens to fill the needed orders, but she sends her love and promises to arrive on the Lord's Day, if you wish to continue your afternoon socials as before."

No cheer filled his words, though they bore good news. Mariamne knew the brother of her heart and shared his great despondency as her own. Guilt threatened to fill her soul and blot out the new light growing within.

"Oh, brother, please forgive me. God directed my steps. I am well. No fault lies in you."

"Aye, little sister, our God has made such clear."

"Then what stops you from following your heart?"

His mouth twisted in a smirk, "Not *all* my troubles stem from you, little sister."

Mariamne laughed, "There are yet miracles in the land."

Cy would speak no more concerning the matters of his heart as he lumbered off and she turned toward the heavens. *Lord, forgive me for hurting him. Please make a way for him as You have for King Edgar. Cy is Your faithful servant and is dear to me.*

With preparations already underway for the evening supper, she popped her head in the kitchen.

"Your Majesty!"

"Esther, it is good to see you, my friend."

Color filled the woman's already red cheeks until they reminded Mariamne of rosebuds from the garden. She should not have referred to the servant so familiarly. "I know it improper, Esther, but you have truly been a dear friend to me. And I have missed you." Mariamne squeezed Esther's flour-covered hand.

Esther drew from the touch and curtsied nearly to the floor. "You honor me far beyond my station, Your Majesty."

Knowing her attention only distressed the dear woman, Mariamne turned to the sumptuous feast well underway. "I have missed your cooking as well," she stammered as her stomach rumbled. "Everything smells quite marvelous."

Esther rose tall. "'Tis all in celebration of your return."

"How can I assist?"

Every spoon stilled. Every knife ceased. Glances turned, met hers, and dropped respectfully toward the floor. "Majesty, may we request at least this one night you not serve but join King Edgar at the high table as the guest of honor?" Esther asked.

"I will ask King Edgar if he wishes such a thing," she said holding still to stifle a tremor. She turned and left the kitchen. She gasped as she nearly collided with Edgar.

His warm smile caressed her face and made her heart stuttered. He reached out and cradled her face again, and her heart stopped beating altogether. Would the flames filling her face burn his hand? She could not refuse him, but when would she feel she could accept him?

His hand dropped and he stepped back.

She wet her lips and took a breath as the strong beat of her heart return. "The kitchen staff requests I be served at your table this evening—if it seems desirable to you, Sire."

He took her hand and kissed it, "This night and every meal henceforth, if you are agreeable."

A slim smile turn her lips, caught by the warmth now filling her. *I belong here, to him, but still... Oh, Lord help me be the wife he needs despite the past that still haunts me.* She leaned closer. "Father Paul has joyously agreed," she grinned, "and he is also making preparations for Prince Shane's dedication."

"As always, you are one step ahead of me, my bride." He drew near again but only kissed her hand. "And where is our beautiful son?"

She swallowed her buzzing nerves. "In his cradle in the queen's bedchamber. I am on my way there, Sire. Would you care to escort me?" The words washed from her lips before she could stop them, and her fear bubbled to the surface. He held tight to her hand as he stepped to the side and made a wide sweeping motion with his other hand for her to proceed.

They talked as they traversed the stairs. "I tried numerous times to speak the truth of how Shane came to be ours, but I was interrupted with congratulations, praises to our God, and topics changed before the words would pass my lips," Edgar said.

"If your heart is willing but the words could not be spoken then it must be the hand of God. We will determine to speak the truth if ever given opportunity. But we will wait for God to open such a door."

"Aye." Edgar followed her to the cradle.

Chapter 50

With Shane nestled in her arms and Edgar close at her side, Mariamne returned to the hall. Edgar paused to hold her still while those gathered took a knee. As she stood awestruck at all the bowed heads, Edgar called out, "Men of Veronia, noble lords, brave knights, and faithful servants—welcome the return of our precious queen."

"Long live Queen Mariamne!"

"And let me present Prince Shane, crown prince of Veronia and heir to the throne."

"Long live Prince Shane!"

"Long live King Edgar! Long live Queen Mariamne! Long live Prince Shane. May God bless them. May they always rule in His wisdom and love!"

Tears slid down her cheeks. Her heart could not contain all their love. *Lord, I am going to fail these people.*

Edgar's firm, steady hand pressed into the small of her back. She turned to him.

Oh, Lord, I am going to fail him too.

His countenance radiated love and pride. No doubt of her shone there. She drew strength from his confidence. Her lungs filled again with refreshing air.

"Join me," he whispered. Her feet followed his with ease. "I will savor this festive meal with you beside me after so many mournful ones alone. Listen to our hall hum with excitement and delight as every soul celebrates you. God's blessings are on our land with you beside me."

Mariamne turned to those gathered to escape the doubt gnawing at her thoughts. "Halton is absent. He said little on the way home. Is he well, Sire?"

"He will be fine—soon."

Mariamne turned to look at him again, but he would say no more. "It is as if you are hiding some wonderful secret, Your Majesty." Again sadness pulled at his smile for a brief moment, but he only patted her hand and returned to his meal.

Soon lively entertainment followed the meal, sweeping all other thoughts away in their merry melodies. A small group of minstrels serenaded them. The young prince squirmed and fussed during their performance, and Mariamne stood to take him to her chambers.

At the back of the hall, near the stairs, Dawn met her, "May I take him to be changed, Your Majesty?"

Mariamne hesitated, but the entertainment had been part of her celebration. "Thank you, Dawn. Please wait in the chamber with him until I return. He will be hungry soon, so I will not linger long."

When the minstrels concluded a short time later, a roar engulfed their fading notes. "Long live King Edgar! And long live Queen Mariamne!" Cheers rattled her ears as every cup raised toward her. Her tears would no longer be constrained; they trailed down her cheeks as she stood and curtsied to the floor before them. Cups and dagger hilts banged out a rhythm on the boards as Edgar pulled her to her feet and the courtiers chanted their well-wishes without end.

"It is good to have you home, my lady," Edgar whispered.

The hall emptied, and Mariamne went to her suite and fed her son before she turned to her bed for the night. The long day wore on her. She found comfort in the great curtained bed. *Thank You Lord, for— everything. Help me be the woman they need.*

Chapter 51

"Your Majesty, I am unable to express the depth of my shame over my behavior toward your wife, my queen, and I am here to receive the punishment you deem appropriate." Halton slumped to the floor, his head so low it nearly touched the tiles.

Edgar set aside his work and leaned back. "And what great offense have you done me, Halton?" Edgar asked with a kind sigh. "Have you stolen the queen's heart, or engaged in an affair with her?"

"No, Your Majesty," Halton sputtered, which caused his entire body to tremble. He gulped several quick breaths and moaned. "But I have admitted to loving the wife of my king, and my friend."

"It is right that all the queen's subjects should love her," Edgar soothed, conveying to his friend he bore no hatred or animosity toward him.

"This love I feel for Lady Mariamne, my queen, your wife, is not a wholesome respect for her, but an unholy desire for her as a woman." As Halton continued to reveal the true nature of his struggle, he withered further.

Edgar regarded him thoughtfully, "And what do you propose as the best way to help you not fall to this temptation, my friend?"

"If it seems enough of a punishment to his Majesty, I would request I be sent from the castle to find another way to aid my liege from a great distance. If I am not about, then I can do my king and my queen no harm."

"Very well," Edgar conceded. "I have but one condition of your exile, however. I wish for you to have a good night's sleep within my walls one last night, and I wish you to break fast with me on the morrow. I intend to send you off as the honored friend you are and not allow you to slink away in shame."

Edgar stood and pulled Halton to stand before him. He smiled and laid a hand on the contrite man's shoulder. "Halton, my brother, you are a man and as such susceptible to the temptations of the flesh, but being enticed is not a sin. Christ was tempted, but He was without sin, as you are now. You may have desired the Lady Mariamne, but you never fell to the sin, and I will not allow you to bear such shame. I will send you out as the honest, loyal, and trusted friend you have ever been to me and our people."

Halton bowed and said with a tremor of emotion edging his voice, "Thank you for your graciousness." Halton turned and left as Edgar returned to his paperwork.

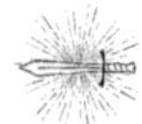

The next morn dawned bright, and Edgar all but danced down the stairs. Mariamne once again slept under his roof with a child to claim as an heir and call his son. Could one man be more blessed? As he sat atop the dais, he noted Mariamne again served the long boards before she sat at the high table beside him. As she took her place, he rapped the hilt of his dagger on their table to garner everyone's attention. When the hall fell silent, he stood.

"My friends, it is another glorious day blessed by God in Veronia." The hall resonated the confirmation with the thumping of dagger hilts. "There is one among you on whom I wish to bestow special honor this day. Sir Halton, knight of Veronia, trusted thane, and loyal friend—step forward." Halton came forward and stood before him on the dais, his eyes darted about as a small shudder seized his body. "Sir Halton, take a knee."

Halton's eyes widened. Worry crinkled his brows, but Edgar nodded for his compliance.

"Sir Halton, you have been found to be one of the honorable company of the most noble of our fair land. You have never failed in your service to me or to the people of Veronia, so I have chosen this day to bestow on you, as is my right as your king to do so, the title of duke." Edgar saw Halton startle in front of him and knew his friend wanted desperately to jump up and refuse the honor, but he could not do so without offending his king in front of his men.

Edgar smiled and continued. "I am bestowing to you the fief of the Summerlands, which Lord Richards held, with all the wealth, the manor, and all the holdings bound to the estate." Edgar drew the long sword and tapped each of Halton's shoulders gently. "Arise, Lord Halton, Duke of the Summerlands, and receive your king's favor."

Halton rose slowly as Edgar extended his hand, and when the new duke grasped it, Edgar turned toward those who cheered. They showed him their approval with great thunderous poundings of their daggers and loud cheers of huzzah.

In the racket, Edgar leaned near, "Will the Summerlands be far enough away to assure you keep your honor, my friend?"

"I could travel no further and still remain in Veronia, Sire," Halton mused dryly.

"Good, then you will be safe, and my lands will be strong, for I trust you to return with a good number of knights soon. I will have need of you yet, my trusted duke," Edgar released the overwhelmed man to allow him to be congratulated by those present.

Edgar returned to his seat until the excitement diminished and then thumped his dagger on his table again. The hall fell silent once more to hear what further news he would share, he glance to

Mariamne. "Friends, there is one other I wish to honor this day. Cynric, step forward." As Cy walked forward, Edgar could see his lady's face brighten with pleasure.

"Take a knee before your king, Cynric."

Cy dropped.

"For your faithful service to me, to the queen whom you love as a sister, and to the good people of Veronia, I do bestow upon you the title of Knight of Veronia."

Tye stepped forward and placed a heavy woolen red cloak bearing the king's insignia over Cy's shoulders as Edgar said, "I place this cloak on you so that you may find the strength to stand alone. May your acts of chivalry be the warmth for others colder than yourself."

Next, Tye lashed gold spurs to his boots. "The spurs represent the right of a knight to ride unhindered throughout the land, dispensing justice tempered with mercy, protecting the weak, defending the defenseless, and helping the needy. By wearing the precious spurs near his feet, the knight shows his disdain for earthly treasures in favor of spiritual ones."

Tye secured a belt around Cy's waist. "I place this belt on you as a symbol of your chosen path. May it always remind you of its importance. The belt represents the unity of chivalry. The blue color reminds the knight to be ever faithful in his duties, to be pure of heart, and to be respectful in his actions."

Tye then handed Cy a shield bearing Cy's coat of arms dominated by a tall, powerful bear. "This shield stands for the honor and renown of you as Knight of Veronia. Use it and remember to guard yourself well."

Lastly Edgar handed Cy a finely crafted sword. "I give this sword to you as a symbol of your own actions. The sword represents the knight's right to dispense justice. The double edge of the blade ever reminds him to temper justice with mercy. As the steel must be tempered by fire and water, so must the soul of the knight be tempered by adversity and compassion. Never draw this in anger, and only use it for the service of God.

"Do you, Cynric, formerly of far-off lands now swear an oath as a Knight of Veronia in the faithful service of King Edgar and Queen Mariamne?"

"Upon these gifts, and before God, my king, my queen, and those assembled, I swear to be a good and true knight, to uphold chivalry, its honor, rights, and privileges, to uphold the laws of Veronia, and to remain faithful to my sworn word, to hate evil and love good, to temper justice with mercy, to defend the weak. This I swear upon my honor, Cynric, formally of lands which no longer matter and now Knight of Veronia." Cy's oath rang out proudly in the silent hall.

Edgar drew his sword again. "This we do hear and shall never forget nor fail to reward that which is given: fealty with love, service with honor, and oath-breaking with vengeance. Arise, Sir Cynric, Knight of Veronia, and accept your king's honor."

Cy stood to a great proud height. As Edgar clasped his arm, those gathered again filled the hall with cheers. Edgar again took advantage of the noise. "Now you are free to pursue your lady fair, my friend. But I warn you, should you fail to win the lady's heart you will bear the wrath of your dear sister."

Cy's grin grew. "Then I will not fail, Sire, for we know how unpleasant the woman can be when she is displeased."

Mariamne caught the look exchanged between them and wagged a finger at them in warning. But her smile told Edgar of the joy she shared for Cy.

Cy did not remain long, shunning the congratulations and food to seek the Lady Annabel's hand.

Chapter 52

Cy raced from his knighting, saddled his horse, and charged down the rocky outcropping to Annabel's shop with a pounding heart. As his luck would have it, when he arrived a woman being fitted for a gown kept Annabel in the back of the shop.

"Be with you in a moment," she called.

Annabel continued to work, remaining behind a curtain, forcing him to wait. By the time she finished and the woman had left, Cy had melted from an eager suitor to a nervous lad beset with frantic pacing and hand-wringing.

Annabel waved her customer farewell and shifted her gaze to him. She studied him. "Good sir, whatever is the matter? Is there something wrong with Her Majesty?"

"No, Queen Mariamne is quite well and impatiently awaiting your Lord's Day visit," he stammered breathlessly.

Her head tipped to one side. She smiled, "Sir Cynric, is it now Good Knight?"

"Aye, King Edgar has seen fit to bestow his great favor on me, a renegade and former slave," he confessed and then resumed his nervous pacing.

"Well, I congratulate you, and I know 'tis well deserved, for you are the most loyal and trustworthy man I know." Sadness shaded her words. She stood far from him, her arms entwined loosely before her. She swayed, shifting her weight from foot to foot. "Was there something else, sir?"

"Lady Annabel, do you think you could find it desirable to marry a man such as I?"

Annabel became still. Cy noticed the pulse in the tender swoop of her neck pounding a furious rhythm. Her head dropped, and she blushed as the corner of her mouth curved in a sweet and bashful smile.

Cy's heart thundered. Could she possibly be any more beautiful?

"I know not, good sir. Are you asking me if I would marry someone *like* you, or are *you*, yourself, seeking my hand?"

His wobbly legs struggled to carry him across the room. He took her hands. "I would be most honored if you would consent to being my wife, dear Annabel. I am now a knight of the realm and can be a proper provider for you. I have been given a small fief, and you could oversee it, and your mother and sister would be welcome there as well."

"The good Lord saw fit to call Mother to her reward after the turning of the year."

"I am so sorry."

"I think she worried herself over the shrinking income without the queen's favor on our little shop."

Cy squeezed her hands tightly, "Forgive me for being so consumed by my own shame and loss that I saw not to comfort you, my lady."

He jerked up as though poked. "Oh Annabel. The most perfect notion just struck me." He stood before her but said no more as the idea rattled about.

"Well, sir, are you going to keep grinning like a jester or do you intend to share this great idea?"

"If you would agree to wed such a man as I, with my nefarious background and failings, we could make our home in the castle. There is ample room in the north tower, and the queen would be delighted to have you so close at hand. Lady Olivia could be hired as Prince Shane's nurse, if she would be agreeable, until we could arrange a proper union for her."

She looked at him lovingly but did not answer him immediately, and finally he could not tolerate her silence any longer. "What say you, Lady Annabel?"

A strange shadow passed over her face and she pulled from him. She turned and would not look at him. "I fear you are now beyond my station, as it is clear you once thought I lay beyond yours. I am but a lowly orphaned merchant's daughter, and you are now an honored knight of the realm, favored of the king, and protector of the queen. I am called 'lady' only because the honor of the queen's favor has fallen upon me, sir."

Cy saw the tears slide down the fine curve of her cheek, and he could not contain his love for her any longer. In the space of two quick strides he enclosed her in his adoring arms. "I love you, Annabel. I care not for station, neither do our king or queen. They can promote any they so choose, and I, dear lady, choose you. I want nothing more in this life than to honor God and have you as my bride. Please consent to be my wife."

She tipped her head, "Yes, good knight."

He let out a resounding whoop of joy that brought her little sister running from their apartment over the shop. When she entered, Cy went to her animatedly, picked her up around the waist, and spun her around boisterously. "Hello, little sister, we are soon to be family, for your sister has agreed to wed me."

He placed the startled Olivia back on the floor. "Congratulation, Anna," Olivia said, hugging her tight.

"I have asked Annabel to move into the north tower with me, so she may be a lady-in-waiting to our queen. I wonder if perhaps you would care to join us and serve as nurse to the prince."

Olivia squealed with delight. Cy looked bewildered to Annabel.

"She means yes, she accepts," Annabel explained as she grabbed the bouncing girl by the arm and pulled her close.

"Oh, yes sir, thank you kindly."

"If it is agreeable to you, I will ask Father Paul to plan the announcement of our betrothal on the coming Lord's Day."

Annabel nodded with a smile that melted his heart.

"Then I will send a coach for you so we may attend services together."

"It would be my honor, Cy."

"We will need to make some preparations, for the rooms in the north tower are rather spare…"

"I still have a few orders to complete. It should take me at least another few weeks. If we wait the customary forty days after the betrothal to be wed, we will have plenty of time to make the preparations."

Olivia bounced about again. "A spring wedding. Oh, how marvelous."

With all the preliminary arrangements made, Cy kissed both women on the cheek and returned joyously to the castle.

"I am sad to see you go, but you will be doing me a great service by securing the Summerlands, and I know the Lord will be with you and bless you, my friend," Edgar told Halton.

Edgar turned as Ingrid joined them. "Lady Ingrid, I know it has been difficult for you here, especially over the long months as the only lady in the castle. As Lord Halton assumes control of your former land, I wished to know, might we return anything to you? The men-at-arms who escort Lord Halton will return immediately. They can bring back anything you wish, my lady."

Ingrid curtsied low before him. "Thank you, Your Majesty, you are ever kind. I will make a small list of my personal belonging and a few of my mother's family heirlooms I would be very grateful to have with me."

"Good, hopefully these things will make you more at home here until I can see to proper arrangements for a suitable match for you, my lady."

The young woman's eyes flew wide open as she stared back at him. She stammered, "Your Majesty, why would you so generously concern yourself to see to the needs of an orphan?"

Edgar's heart ached. "Because I am the individual responsible for making you an orphan, my lady. And I am your king, and you are a woman of noble bloodlines. The sins of your parents should not be borne by you, for you are a lovely and honorable woman. You would make any nobleman a fine wife." He paused and smiled at her sweetly. "Is there mayhaps a beau in particular who has caught your eye, my lady?"

Ingrid's cheeks flames brilliant, "No, Your Majesty, there is no one I favor overly much among the noble houses. I but pray for someone who will love me, as you do the queen."

He smiled and left her with Halton to construct her list and joined Mariamne a few steps away. Mariamne waved her good-byes to Halton, and he bowed humbly to her.

Chapter 53

Cy rode back into the bailey as Edgar and Mariamne approached the church. Mariamne stopped and waited for him to dismount so he could tell her all the news.

"She has agreed," Cy's joy could not be contained. It bubbled like a mountain spring.

"Annabel? Annabel has agreed to what?"

Cy pinched her cheek. "To wed me, of course."

She hugged him excitedly, and Edgar extended his hand in congratulations.

"In my eagerness to bring my bride to me, Sire, I am afraid I have gravely overstepped my bounds. I have told the Lady Annabel she can move into the north tower, and I have offered Lady Olivia the position as nurse to the prince. Please forgive me, Sire. I allowed my excitement to get the better of me," Cy admitted as regret tainted his words.

Edgar slapped his shoulder good-naturedly. "Peace, brother, for it sounds like a grand idea. Mariamne will not complain at having her dear friend so close."

Mariamne offered a bright smiled. "Lady Olivia will make a fabulous nurse, Cy. I did not think I wanted anyone looking after Shane other than myself, but I have seen the logic in not carrying the lad on my hip at all times," she laughed.

Cy bowed to them both with a relieved smile. "Thank you."

"Would you care to return a little of that kindness, my friend?"

Edgar asked him with a mysterious smirk. "We are on our way to meet with Brother Paul, and we would welcome someone who could bear witness." Cy smiled and waved his hand for them to proceed as he followed and secured his horse to a post outside.

Father Paul welcomed them with joy before saying a prayer to bless them. Then Edgar took Mariamne's hands and said his oath, "I receive you as mine, so you become my wife and I your husband."

Cy thought about those words with new excitement.

Mariamne likewise willingly and with noticeable joy proclaimed her oath, "I receive you as mine, so you become my husband and I your wife."

"I take Mariamne to be my wedded wife, to have and to hold, from this day forward, for better for worse, for richer for poorer, in sickness and in health, till death us depart."

"I take Edgar to be my wedded husband, to have and to hold, from this day forward, for better for worse, for richer for poorer, in sickness and in health, to be meek and obedient, in bed and at board, till death us depart."

Cy cleared his throat, trying not to laugh as he imagined Mariamne as meek and obedient. She shot him a warning glance. He stood straighter, clearing his throat again still struggling to control his laughter.

Father Paul said a blessing over them, and they exchanged rings. Mariamne moved her pear-shaped emerald to her right hand, and Edgar replaced it with a lovely solitaire diamond. She placed a matching understated diamond on his left hand, and the good father said one final prayer for them.

Cy thought that forty days plus three seemed forever until he and his beloved would stand and exchange their own vows. He groaned at the thought.

The ceremony ended with the pronouncement over them of being *officially* husband and wife. Edgar leaned forward and tenderly kissed his bride.

"Congratulations, little sister," Cy said, taking her hands and kissing both cheeks. He clasped Edgar's arm, "Your Majesty, I wish you well. May your love only grow."

"Thank you, Cy. You know, now that my thane is a duke, I am in need of a good man…"

"Thank you, Sire, but if I have found favor in your eyes, my heart is set on the safety of my queen."

Edgar smiled, clasped his arm, and slapped his shoulder, "Agreed, but I will need you on the battlefield at my side in the coming fight."

"You shall have it."

The couple left, while Cy stayed behind and informed the priest of his need to announce his betrothal to Lady Annabel on the Lord's Day. Father Paul agreed with boisterous joy.

"Having the queen returned, a babe, weddings—oh, God's blessings shower on this kingdom in great abundance."

"They do indeed, Father."

Chapter 54

Mariamne's heart stuttered, and her hands trembled as she prepared to go to her husband's bed at the end of the day. Dawn slept in the nursery, and Shane lay peacefully in the cradle near Mariamne's bed. Shane would need to be fed before the sun rose, but it would be best if she went to the king.

She crossed the hall on quaking legs that barely held her and entered his outer sitting room. Steeling herself, she approached his inner door and managed a timid knock. Edgar opened the door and stepped back on his bare feet in a short nightshirt. Her gaze lingered on his well-cut legs sprinkled with dark hair. The nightshirt hung thin on his fine frame, and she soon found her eyes meeting his. He seemed surprised to see her, but he invited her inside with a wave of his hand. She walked on numb legs into his bedchamber.

She wobbled as he approached her with slow, calm steps. He laid both hands on her face tenderly. Could he feel how she trembled?

"You may be called Rebellious by others, but you are my Beloved." He pressed a gentle kiss to her forehead and then took her hand and led her to the bed.

He threw back the great covers and indicated she could slide in. Once she settled, he lay next to her. He turned on his side beside her, laced his fingers with hers, and promptly fell asleep.

Mariamne did not know what to think, but as his breathing became more relaxed and even, she too drifted off to sleep. Unfortunately she found she startled awake every time he stirred, but he never touched more then her hand.

She slipped from his bed in the middle of the night to feed Shane and returned. As she slid under the coverlet, his sleepy whisper greeted her, "How is our boy?"

"Good, Sire. He is fed and sleeping again."

Edgar chuckled pulling the covers more tight about him, "We are married, dear lady, and you are sleeping in my bed. Do you not think it time you called me by my Christian name?"

"Yes… Edgar," she stammered.

He let out a contented sigh and slipped back to sleep.

Edgar did not share the bed when she awoke the next morn. She returned to her chambers, fed their son, and went down to the meal.

Again the day proceeded with nothing of interest to note, and it ended with her lying next to her sleeping husband. When she woke on the third morn and he had yet to exercise his husbandly prerogative, a new fear took hold. She moved to sit on the end of the bed and waited for him to exit the bathing chamber.

He stepped from the room and flashed her a ready smile. She noted afresh his fine-cut feature, even more so in a sharp linen tunic and the satin doublet he often favored for the Lord's Day. He paused to look at her.

"Have I displeased you, Your Majesty?" she moaned.

He came to her and placed a loving hand on her cheek, which her grateful heart accepted. "Never, Beloved." He laid his cheek alongside hers and whispered into her ear, "Not until you desire me as much as I desire you, my love." Then he kissed her cheek and turned toward the door.

"What if I never…"

A broad smile filled his face and love dance in his eyes, "I will love you until I take my last breath, Beloved. I swear it to you." He left, and Mariamne returned to her chamber as great tears of appreciation tumbled down her face. His kindness and gentleness overwhelmed her. She wanted to reward him with the desire he deserved. *Lord, I fear such would never be a part of my life. Will You grant this request for him? Create me to be the woman he needs.*

Chapter 55

Annabel arrived early to participate in the formal betrothal rites with Cy. Mariamne greeted her with a blissful hug as the two women took their seats in the first pew. Father Paul began the service by leading heartfelt worship that soared to the rafters, as everyone within celebrated the work of God in returning their queen and the babe. His message was about the blessings of God, and for the first time Mariamne not only attended every word, she now grasped the message they carried.

"Saint Luke says, 'Blessed are ye that weep now: for ye shall laugh.'"

The whole flock sent up a most uncharacteristic shout of joy and affirmation of what God had done. The outburst caused Father Francis's stern face to look even more disapproving. Mariamne did not believe such a thing possible and stifled a wayward giggle behind a demure touch of her lace handkerchief.

"Aye, it is right we honor and praise our God for what He has done for us," Father Paul said softly.

Mariamne could only smile while contentment flooded her.

As the service drew to a close, they partook in communion, and Mariamne eagerly joined those who came forward. Then the priest called her and Edgar forward with their son. The holy man took the babe and quoted from the Scriptures, "Behold, children are the inheritance of the Lord, and the fruit of the womb His reward. As are the arrows in the hand of ye strong man: so are the children of youth.

Blessed is the man that hath his quiver full of them: for they shall not be ashamed when they speak with their enemies in the gate."

He then placed a bit of salt in Shane's mouth to represent the reception of wisdom and continued by praying another passage of Scripture over the young prince as a blessing. "The Lord bless thee, and keep thee, The Lord make His face shine upon thee, and be merciful unto thee, The Lord lift up His countenance upon thee, and give thee peace."

Next the father made the sign of the cross on the prince's forehead, saying, "In the name of the Father, and the Son, and the Holy Spirit, I christen you Shane, son of Edgar, son of Mather, Crown Prince of Veronia."

Following the christening, Father Paul presented Sir Cynric and Lady Annabel and their betrothal. When all the joyous rituals were concluded, the priest gave the benediction. As the congregation exited the church, many stopped to congratulate both couples.

Prior to the midday meal, Annabel and Olivia accompanied Mariamne up to the queen's suite. The two friends mused over their time apart while Mariamne nursed Shane, and Olivia settled herself in her new quarters in the nursery before she joined them.

Mariamne smiled at her, "I am so glad you are here, Olivia, and I know you will be a great help to me. Dawn helped, but the girl did not have the gift of childcare for such a young babe. She will be much happier returning to her duties in the kitchen. You, however, have been an invaluable help to several of the ladies in town with their children. I will put your experience to good use and possibly seek your advice on occasion," Mariamne said with a wry smirk.

Olivia's petite face flooded with color, "Thank you, Your Majesty. I will ever strive to live up to your opinion of me."

"My dear friend, I may be queen outside these chambers, but in here I would ask you to call me Mariamne, please. There are no titles in these rooms, only treasured friends."

Olivia smiled brightly at her and nodded her consent as a knock sounded on the door.

Mariamne laid the babe in his cradle as Olivia went to open the outer door. Mariamne finished tying the bow in her red satin bodice as she exited her bedchamber to greet Edgar and Cy standing in her sitting room. She smiled at both men as Annabel followed her, "Sire, brother, it is good to see you again so soon."

"We hoped to escort the ladies of court to the hall for midday," Edgar said, offering his arm to her.

Great mischief filled Mariamne and she turned to her friend. "I know not, my lady, do we dare be seen on the arms of such rogues?"

Annabel covered her laugh with a demure hand and managed to speak through her giggles. "We had better accompany them, for no telling what waggery they will get themselves into without us near."

Mariamne laughed as she accepted Edgar's arm, and Cy and Annabel followed close behind. They parted near the long boards as Annabel followed Mariamne into the kitchen to help with the serving.

Mariamne paused before collecting the first of the trays. "Dawn, will you please prepare a plate for Olivia and deliver it to her?"

The two friends served the men before they retired to the women's table to eat with Ingrid. The table of friends talking with great merriment added even greater balm to Mariamne's heart. She savored every moment and tried to push aside the dread of the coming battle.

Her gaze turned to Edgar, and the fear gnawed at the edges of her peace. Two men she cared about had already lost their lives at the hand of the Black Knight. Did she dare love another, only to have him likewise taken from her too soon? She shuddered. The concern came too late. The sight of him raising his cup to her made her heart flutter.

Chapter 56

Spring burst forth with a flourish of activities. Mariamne had attempted several more evenings to be more approachable to her husband, but now she took to sleeping each night in her own bed. Though he loved her for trying, Edgar delighted when she stopped, for he found having her so near, covered in naught but a thin night rail, inflamed his desire. He slept easier with her across the hall. One day, mayhaps, his passion would be answered by hers.

"I think Annabel has finally moved everything she needs into the north tower," Cy mused, drawing Edgar from his thoughts.

"Mariamne tells me of all manner of detail on the wedding plans, though in truth I see little of her. Our women are forever working with diligent hands in the queen's outer room. Who knew weddings could entail so much work?"

Cy laughed at his joke. "Indeed, how could one have known?"

"Now she finds me to ask after trifling matters, seeking my thoughts on a color, styles, and my opinion on the offers of the meal."

"It sounds encouraging. She is taking an interest in you, Sire. Mayhaps she hopes to speak of something more than superficial ideas about my wedding?"

Edgar stopped and looked up at Cy. "There does seem to be purpose in her seeking me."

"I know she enjoys the time she spends with you. Annabel has said as much, and I can see it when you are together."

"Thank you, Cy." They concluded their business, and Edgar left his study with him.

Edgar went to her sitting room and gave a soft knock. Olivia opened the door and stepped aside for him to enter. Mariamne looked up from her embroidery with a peaceful countenance. "My lady, would you accompany me on a stroll?" She set aside her work and came to him.

Quiet words wafted between them like the gentle breeze sailing over the wall. As they returned from their walk, he turned to her. "I have enjoyed my time, Beloved."

"As have I, Edgar. Perhaps we could make it a regular appointment?"

He smiled at hearing his name on her lips. "I would find such times most pleasurable, Beloved."

Olivia and Lady Ingrid attended Annabel with Mariamne. The bride wore a soft blue satin gown, the last of her creations. The day dawned warm and bright, a gift from God's own hand. Two young pages, with bride laces and rosemary tied about their silken sleeves, led Annabel to the church. A young maiden carried a bride-cup of silver, adorned with ribbons of all colors before her. A fat branch of rosemary filled it.

Musicians came next, then a group of maidens—some bearing great bride-cakes while others carried garlands of wheat as they passed into the church. Cy, dressed in crisp black cotton breeches, a linen tunic, and crimson doublet, arrived with his fellow knights following close behind. Edgar presented the bride to her groom with the dowry of the money, which came from the selling of her shop.

Cy and Annabel stood before Father Paul as he asked, "Do you, Cynric, take Annabel to be your wife?"

Cy stood to his full height, chest full and broad, head held high. "I do."

They exchanged oaths, spoke their vows, and exchanged the rings. The pronouncement of husband and wife was made and accompanied by many cheers. Revelers spilled out of the church and into the king's hall to an evening of celebration.

Edgar ate with Mariamne, giving his high table to the newlyweds. When the feast concluded and the long boards were cleared, minstrels played long into the night as dancers littered the floor. Edgar again coaxed Mariamne to dance. His gaze never left her, but a sadness pulled at his features.

"What troubles you, Edgar?" she asked as they climbed the stairs.

"I am sorry, Beloved, for you were never celebrated properly as a bride, with a beautiful wedding and joyous feast."

Mariamne laid a tender hand on his arm, "'Tis of little importance, for I know God celebrated with us, as did Cy and Father Paul. The only regret I bear is that I am unable to be your true wife in all ways, for you deserve much better of me, Edgar."

He opened his arms to her, and she stepped into his embrace and held tight to him. "I can only imagine what you have been through, Beloved, and I fault you not for your fears. I love you, and I pray one day you will trust my love for you enough to risk loving me."

She clung to him.

Chapter 57

Mariamne returned to her chamber and let his words wash over her. As she drifted to sleep, she listed the numerous reasons she could trust Edgar, and love him, and she prayed again for God to vanquish her fear.

A scant number of days later, as Mariamne sought to open her heart to her husband, a great number of knights, men-at-arms, and yeomen descended on the castle from all over the kingdom. They pitched their tents to the south of the great rock that supported their home and prepared for the coming war.

Edgar and Cy spent most of their days with the men, running drills and honing their skills. Their wives saw little of them. Edgar's absence stirred Mariamne's heart far better than anything her mind ever did to convince her. She missed seeing him during the day and grew impatient awaiting his return each night with a longing that deepened by the day.

Not only love grew in Mariamne's heart. Apprehension for Edgar and Cy's safety festered in equal portions. Mariamne's restlessness stirred her to take action. One day, she dressed in a simple gown and stomped out of the castle. Meeting Annabel in the bailey, she took her hand and pulled her along behind her.

"Mariamne?"

Without explanation, Mariamne led her friend up to her secret spot in the dark gallery of the church and plopped into a pew.

"Mariamne?"

She bowed her head in a quick prayer to calm herself before she spoke in quiet whispers, "The darkness which is on its way to engage our men in battle has visited me in my dreams."

Annabel nodded. "I too have sensed an oppressive feeling of dread—nay—evil."

"The men are training and preparing for this battle as best they can, but I am of a mind the impending war is not of flesh and blood only. It will pit those of the light against those of the darkness, and such a battle cannot be won with steel and brawn."

"I agree, sister. So what do you propose?" Annabel asked.

"We must pray. We must seek God, for only He can bring victory in battle. We should meet here every morn until God has granted our request or this building no longer stands."

"Father Paul has said praying Scripture is powerful, and fasting can release the power of our prayers."

Mariamne held tight to Annabel's hand. "Will you pray and fast with me, sister, until God answers?"

Annabel covered their hands "Aye! We will meet every day and pray."

Wasting no time, they bent their heads and prayed until the midday bell interrupted them and they went to the hall to serve the meal to the few who remained within the walls.

Mariamne met Annabel every morn. They ate no meat or sweets and partook in no fermented drink. And Mariamne found that God's presence surrounded her.

"Healer, we have come to help." Mariamne, Annabel, and Ingrid arrived unannounced at Carrington's door one afternoon.

"Your Majesty?"

"What preparations must be made for the wounded who are sure to come?"

"We need more cloth for bandages…"

"We have at least one loom available to us," came Annabel's quick offer.

"I will send word to the town for work to begin there as well. What else will you require?" Mariamne asked.

"There are herbs to crush and mix for the poultices, salves, and medicines I will need."

"Collect the various ingredients, sir," Ingrid said. "I worked with a healer for a time, I will assist you."

A deep sigh slipped through Carrington's lip. "Thank you, ladies, this will all be most helpful." He turned and pulled a few small satchels from the shelves behind him. "We can gather the medicines and bandages in these to carry to the battlefield."

They parted, each seeing to their new task, and Mariamne shoved aside the darkness trying to trigger her despair.

Stepping from Carrington's home, Annabel went one way and Mariamne looked up to see Edgar coming in the main gate. "Welcome, husband, how fare you?"

"Majesty!"

They whirled as three men-at-arms charged in behind him.

"Majesty, the enemy horde is on the move. Coming down from the north. It is killing all those in its path, and those who survive are being driven south."

"Send word to all the lords: Assemble Veronia's remaining war host," Edgar ordered a squire.

Mariamne laid her hand on his arm. "I will see to the preparations for the displaced."

Within days the survivors of the northern shires and villages flooded into the town below the castle. They arrived under the protection of the northern lords and their remaining retinue.

"There are so many, Edgar," Mariamne said as they stood atop the battlements watching them stream across the valley.

"Many of the knights have already vacated their tents to share with others or sleep out under the night sky. Room will be made for all the displaced families. Lord Gyles believes the horde will be drawing up siege lines within two days."

"A siege," Mariamne trembled.

"I have no intention of allowing our home to be placed under siege. Not without a fight."

She laid her hand over his. "Lord, protect us."

"Amen!" He left her and joined the warriors in the valley.

Chapter 58

Edgar called his war council, which consisted of his most trusted knights—Corin, Eldon, Shaw, and Cy, and the nobles who had arrived. Halton still had not returned, but Edgar knew he traveled the furthest. He trusted God to bring his faithful friend back to him in his hour of need.

"We will form our divisions north of the town, on the south side of the great valley. We will use the wide-open space between the castle mount and the forest as our battlefield. The mount and the town will protect our flank. Captains need to be assigned to serve under each of you." He spread out the skin with a crude map of the valley drawn on it. "Here is where each is to be posted. Tell your men. We assemble at first light tomorrow." He pointed out each man's location, and they took the word to their men.

The afternoon became consumed with last-minute armor adjustments, sharpening of weapons, filling of quivers, and many prayers. Edgar did not return to the castle, choosing instead to sleep with his men. At the break of day they would take their positions to await the enemy.

"Is all in preparation, Sire?"

Edgar looked up from his map at Cy. "I thought I told you to organize the men conscripted from the town in defense of the castle and those inside."

Cy nodded, "It seems Queen Mariamne and my wife have conspired with God. They insist I must remain at your side. If I may be so bold, Sire, I am of a like mind. They have two thick walls atop a massive rock, not to mention the Lord God Himself. I think they can spare me, Sire. I am unconvinced the same can be said of you."

Edgar did not hesitate in his response, "In truth, Cy, I welcome your sword at my side. Halton has yet to join us, and I fear he will not arrive before the battle begins. Please find Nyle among all these men and tell him to go to the castle in your stead, then return and pray with me, my friend."

"I have one final word from our ladies," Cy said with a foolish grin, causing Edgar to straighten and look at him. "They say if we both do not return to them, they shall never forgive us."

The momentary levity in the dark hour brought a smile to Edgar's face and refreshed his spirit. "Thank you, Cy. God with us, we will return to them."

"God with us."

Chapter 59

The next morn dawned to a clear mid-spring glow and found all those who had answered Edgar's call arrayed and ready for battle. But the evil fog accompanying the Black Knight, and his horde now covered the Kestron Ridge. Mariamne's heart beat in such an uncomfortable cadence she struggled to focus on her prayers. The malevolent vapor advanced on the Veronian lines. It obscured much of the forest and some of the northern edge of the valley by mid-morn. Her heart leapt to her throat as small dark figures materialized from the fog to draw up their lines just beyond its wispy tendrils.

Mariamne prayed over the king's army. She spotted Edgar with ease, for his bright-red standard bearing the cross and a raised lion waved prominently at the center of the Veronian troops. As she prayed over him and his men, something stirred in her, subtly at first, then it grew until it captured her breath.

Memories of Edgar flooded her mind. His great gentleness, his fierce strength tempered with tenderness and mercy. He dispatched justice, he grieved, and he cared for the welfare of every soul who crossed his path.

Every moment of their time together lay filled with a deep and abiding respect for her. He never pressed for more than she could give. He offered, but never took. He gave his love but never commanded she give hers. Her husband above all had earned her trust.

Her gaze swept over the valley. The evil he would soon face advanced. Hideous black warriors gathered into ranks now, and a wild tremor raced through her.

Edgar could die in this battle.

The thought rocked her so hard, her breath caught painfully and her heart seized. Violent tremors raced through her body. She dropped to her knees as she gasped for air. She loved Edgar.

Gathering her shattered thoughts, she called out to her only source of hope. "Oh, Lord," she moaned, "do not allow him to die without knowing that I love him deeply."

Air seeped back into her lungs as the dark fear melted away, and all the evil ploys disappeared. She stood confident once more. The Lord would fight this battle. She trusted His mighty hand would be victorious. God had been faithful to provide her with a husband who loved her with tenderness. He would not fail to make a way for them. She closed her eyes and resumed her fervent prayers.

Chapter 60

The horde entered the valley in unrelenting numbers. The fog did not accompany them.

"'Tis God's power alone which holds back the evil mist and renders it unable to surround us in its murky malevolence," Cy said.

"By my calculations we are already outnumbered approximately three to one, and the enemy still gathers." Edgar cast a glance over his men.

"Gideon had but three hundred when he killed one hundred and twenty thousand warriors. It matters not the size of your army but the strength of our God, Sire."

"Thank you, my friend. The enemy intends to engage in a battle for our minds long before he ever draws his sword." Edgar eased his horse out from the line and turned to his men. He repeated Cy's wise words, and the men passed it down his lines until all drew strength from the truth in them.

At the midpoint between the rising of the sun and midday, the horde stopped gathering and tightened their formations. The Black Knight took this moment to come into view.

Wickedness. Hatred. Dark thoughts and emotions slithered in the shadows of doubt and fear dancing about Edgar's brain. They would continue to encroach if he did not do something.

The Black Knight was justly named for the black that covered him from the plumed top of his black helmet to the black spurs on his black boots. He sat atop a great black warhorse. He advanced to the center of his lines and rallied his troops with great shouts.

Edgar placed his hand on his sword and looked to his men. Veronia prepared itself.

This battle would be like no other. Great battles, by necessity, started at first light to allow as much daylight as needed to secure victory, or at least the advantage, before it became impossible to fight. Much of the morn lay spent, and neither side had yet struck a single blow.

Edgar surveyed his troops once more. The contrast in the armies gave him pause. From skilled yeomen to heavy cavalry and a few conscripted farmers and merchants, all his men carried weapons and wore some fashion of armor.

The enemy, on the contrary, had only a couple hundred bowmen and a few handful of mounted warriors. Most of the Black Knight's fighting forces were barely dressed infantry. He could not trust in the skill and battle technology his men possessed, for the poison the horde carried in their bodies and the unnatural strength it gave them would make them formidable.

The Black Knight bellowed, and the horde advanced.

Edgar's men held their lines as the yeomen launched a barrage of artillery into the air. At first glance it seemed to be an effective first volley. The enemy ranks dissolved under the bombardment.

Edgar's cavalry leapt into action in an attempt to exploit the break in the opposing lines. A well-practiced tactic he had used a hundred times. He prayed they could slay the infantrymen with ease from atop their horses. But by the time the mounted knights and nobles fell upon the seemingly disheveled ranks, the enemy had miraculously found unity, again forming an impenetrable wall.

Those in the lead called a retreat.

The horde screeched and slashed at the horses, bringing down both mount and rider.

They cut down a handful. The screams of his men torn apart stole Edgar's breath and chipped away at his courage.

Veronia fled to reform its lines. How many fallen? Ten? Twenty? Too many. What now? Battle strategy rattled around. As Edgar's formations congealed, his men gasped.

The horde ripped open the fallen horses and their comrades and ate of their flesh.

Edgar and his men looked away. Young warriors retched.

The gruesome feast concluded, the Black Knight bellowed another advance.

Edgar's yeomen answered raining arrows on them.

Many enemy fell only to be replaced with more enspelled men. Where did they all come from?

The mounted warriors did not advance. The archers unleashed another volley.

The enemy advanced without slowing.

Yeomen launched another aerial attack.

This repeated several more times as the front lines of the enemy warriors continued to close the gap between the two armies.

At one point, a rank of enemy warriors came very near Edgar's line further to the west. The mounted men in Lord Randolf's retinue broke the Veronian lines and engaged them. The knights actually struck down a good number of the enemy with their light-filled swords before the horde reformed and drove them back.

The battle was haphazard. Hit-and-miss. The hours ticked by. Edgar's wounded limped to the back of the fighting men. The vanquished enemy soldiers vanished in a puff of ash. No advantage came. No matter how many they killed, more met their blades.

Edgar's arm ached. His heart pounded. Air rasped through his lungs. Sweat drenched his body. Yet they came without end.

Early afternoon the enemy advance stopped.

Edgar's senses buzzed as if bees lay trapped under his skin. He scanned the enemy lines looking for movement. His mind rattled with plans for the counterattack. And his stomach churned in painful lurches. Heads bowed around him. He joined them.

"Lord, give me wisdom. Protect Your men. Father, save us."

The horde's ranks shivered and undulated until it formed a myriad of separate units of about a hundred men each. Between each of these tightly bunched units a spacious breach formed several feet wide. The Black Knight's roar shook the ground and startled the Veronian horses and their riders.

Edgar held his breath. Then came the sound. Muffled and indistinguishable at first, it grew. Out of the fog burst black enspelled eagles, hawks, falcons, and owls. They soared high overhead, screeching. They dove down at Edgar's men, menacing talons at the ready.

Great demon bears, wolves, and forest cats followed the poison-filled birds. The animals filed down the gaps between the enemy ranks and charged toward Edgar and his men. Quick on the heels of the large animals came rats, badgers, fox, raccoons, and slithering snakes.

The larger animals caused the horses to shy, sending them to flight. Edgar and several around him fought to hold their chargers fast. The cavalry splintered in near disarray before any of the hateful animals had an opportunity to lash out with a spawn-filled paw.

The smaller animals had a similar effect on the foot soldiers as the dangerous creatures slipped between their feet to attack men further back in the lines. Unable to see what terrifying enemy advanced on them, and possessing much less battle experience, the men on the backlines ended up wounding more of their own men than the beasts did.

Edgar shouted orders to his men. "Use the light! Keep them at bay. Hold your ground!"

Chapter 61

Mariamne watched the smaller animals and birds pass through and over Edgar's lines. They advanced up to her home, climbed the rocking side, and bolted up the great walls she hoped would protect them.

She called to the few conscripted men guarding them, "Prepare your weapons, men!" She flew down the tower stairs and burst into the ward as the first birds sailed over the walls above her.

The refugee children of the northern villages taking shelter in the ward shrieked as razor-sharp talons of the enspelled raptors plummeted toward them.

The few guards within the ward filled their swords with holy light.

Children screamed and huddled in bunches close to the ground.

"Come quickly. Save the children!" Mariamne yelled for more men.

As the men arrived, several of the smaller creatures breached the walls.

Annabel grabbed a long stick. She fought off many of the vile animals. The men dispatched a few.

"The light seems to have more of an effect in keeping the animal at a distance," Mariamne shouted.

The animals snarled and circled. They worked in concert. One distracted while another attacked. But each creature managed to stay just out of reach.

Mariamne joined Annabel in a clumsy defense with a rake.

Horrified screams came from the hall.

Shane wailed.

Mariamne leapt over a knot of hissing snakes and burst into the hall.

Olivia stood atop a long board. Shane bawled as she clutched him. Olivia kicked at the rats nipping at her ankles.

Servants seized whatever weapon they could wield, valiantly keeping the hideous creatures away from the younger children who sought shelter inside the king's hall. Frantic cries filled the room.

Falcons entered behind Mariamne. They dove at Shane.

Unheard over the din of cries and screeches, Mariamne prayed in desperation. "Lord God Almighty, I have no weapon to fill with Your holy light, and even if I had one, there are too many for us. Save us, Father, I will give my life to save these innocents You have entrusted to our care."

A thought flooded her mind, and she threw out her arms and her head turned to the rafters. With her eyes closed in complete abandon, she whispered, "I am Yours, my God. Use me to vanquish Your enemy."

The Spirit, Who resided within, rose to her skin. He filled every pore of her flesh. The gentle warmth of His presence and unbound strength filled her with immeasurable peace. Over the rushing roar in her ears came the muffled scream of Olivia. Again Mariamne opened her eyes and turned to the young girl holding her son.

A bright glow obscured her vision. She watched amazed as the light washed over everything it touched. The holy light the men called up to fill their swords now filled her and overflowed out of her eyes, her open mouth, and her fingertips. The light released every person touched by the poison of the spawn.

The animals fled to avoid the light's power.

The light freed any creature touched by evil's grip. The animals, created by God and given no will to choose to be used by the Black Knight, did not die at the touch of the holy light. Once free of their imprisonment, they sang and chattered as they escaped from the castle.

Following her example, those around her opened themselves to be filled by God's light in the same manner. They too joined the holy battle as His mighty weapons. With the hall spilling over with the Spirit's combined light from so many, Mariamne turned to the bailey and those still under attack outside.

She entered the frantic courtyard and called to those wildly attempting to ward off the demonic creatures. "Put down your weapons and allow God to fill you with the only weapon which will be victorious—Himself."

She opened her arms again and welcomed the Spirit back to the surface of her being. It took only seconds for those around her to understand and fling their useless armaments aside to welcome the holy light.

As those in the ward freed the enspelled animals to flee back to their homes, Mariamne allowed the Spirit to slip back to her soul. She raced to the stables, surprised to find her gelding still in his stall. All the other horses stood on the battlefield, but God made a way for her in advance. He had left her horse for such a time as this.

She slipped the bit into his mouth, led him beside a tall hay bale, and pulled herself onto his bare back. She sped him to the inner gate. The guards at the first gate had seen how God used her and allowed her to pass into the bailey to tell those on the other side.

Many still positioned on the walls had also seen the new use of the holy light and now instructed those of the outer courtyard in God's powerful deliverance. She proceeded at a full gallop to the outer gate.

"Stop, Your Majesty, 'tis not safe," a guard yelled, but he could not disentangle himself from the enspelled animals scurrying between the buildings.

"Open the gate," she ordered a trembling squire.

He shook his head.

"Those on the field must know how to unleash God's power."

He would not move.

She wagged her finger at the youth. "If the king dies because of your delay, his blood will be on your hands."

The gate swung open, and she fled down the outcropping until she came to a switchback turn overlooking the battlefield. Mariamne's breath caught as the poisoned animals drove back Edgar and his men. Their lines broke. The army horde advanced.

Chapter 62

Edgar, Cy, and several of the knights around them jostled for ground among the retreating yeomen. The enemy pushed them back against the great rock. Edgar slashed out and killed a fox as it sprang at him. He shook a weasel from his mail-covered arm.

"Your Majesty!" Cy moaned in a panic.

Edgar whirled about him, frantic to find the danger. When he only saw his own men surrounding him, he looked up at his faithful knight. Edgar followed the man's gaze until it rested on Mariamne as she slipped from the back of her horse and stood on the edge of the rocky shelf only a handful of rods above them.

Not only Edgar and Cy noticed her. Three mounted enemy warriors broke through the Veronian lines and raced toward her.

She looked down on Edgar and opened her mouth to speak.

The Black Knight bellowed, another jaw-rattling roar eclipsing her words.

Mariamne stood above the din. She leveled her gaze upon her enemy and spoke. Though none but God could hear. "Mighty God, silence him!"

The Knight was inexplicably made mute.

She turned back to her beloved. "Men of Veronia," her voice rang out loud and clear. "This battle belongs to the Lord, and it will not be won by your valiant arms or the strength of your steel. Give God the glory and allow Him to fight through you." She again opened herself to the power of her Lord, and the light flooded from her, evaporating the enemy soldiers thundering toward her and releasing the horses to trot harmlessly past her with joyful whinnies.

Edgar and Cy cast a stunned look at one another then turned toward the enemy. Their swords dropped. The Spirit filled them. Every man possessing the Spirit in Veronia's war host followed him in abandoning their weapons. God's light alone cut down their enemy.

The horde screeched and fled in full retreat.

Edgar cast a quick glance back up the ridge as a castle guard came to his beloved's side. He put Mariamne onto her gelding.

Chapter 63

The tide of battle turned. Edgar and his army charged to the offensive. The far wings of his lines forged ahead and began to encircle the enemy before they could flee into the forest. Halton and his retinue appeared, sweeping down from the eastern Kestron foothills and cutting down many fleeing enemy soldiers with their swords before they saw their light-filled brothers and emulated them. As Edgar's troops dispatched more enemies, the menacing fog thinned by proportion.

"The enemy is decimated," Corin remarked, drawing alongside Edgar.

"Some did manage to escape into the forest and foothills," Cy corrected.

"The dark lord among them," Edgar groaned. "Sound the horn. Bring the troops back to regroup," he ordered the nearest man.

"All the Spirit-filled cavalry—with me. We go in pursuit of the remaining enspelled men. The infantry will stay under the direction of Lord Stanley. See to the wounded."

Edgar turned his charger, and the mounted soldiers followed him into the forest.

Mariamne saw to the preparation of the meals for the weary troops. She watched as Carrington and Ingrid tended to the wounded.

"Not many are in need of medical attention," Carrington said.

A warrior with a bloody gash in his breeches but no wound explained. "Once the Spirit rose to the surface, all poison vanished from my body. The Spirit healed me."

"The only injuries which remain are broken bones," Ingrid gasped in awe.

The good healer assigned several of the field-trained men to set and bind broken bones.

He looked up and called to her. "With all the work you and your ladies did afore the battle, I have more than enough supplies for my few patients, Majesty."

Later the survivors gathered in the church to celebrate God for His miraculous deliverance with roof-raising praises. When their great joy finally calmed, Father Paul led them in continued prayers for the safety of King Edgar and his valiant mounted men.

Mariamne slept well, trusting her God's strong and long arm to watch over her husband and woke rested to mill aimlessly about the castle. With the battle over and no preparations to see to or wounded to attend, nothing remained to occupy her. Finally late in the evening, shouts from the battlements announced Edgar and his men's return.

Mariamne waited, though she could not stand still. Her heart thundered as they wound slowly up the rock to the gate. Standing high atop in the wall, she greeted him with an excited waved. Annabel waved likewise to Cy before she raced down the nearest tower steps to greet him as he entered the gate. Mariamne knew his men and those living in the bailey would demand Edgar's attention first. She moved to the inner battement and watched him wearily accept the accolades of his people. He turned all praise for him to their great God, as he made his way with slow purpose to the inner ward.

Mariamne waved again from high above as he passed through the inner gate. Here again cheerful servants, attendants, sheltering children, and officials greeted him. Once he dismounted and handed his horse to an eager squire, he proceeded through them until he at last came to her.

Mariamne stepped forward, and everyone parted to afford them a moment of solitude. She smiled broadly at him as a new excitement burned over her skin. She reached up and slipped her arms around his sweaty, dirty neck and ran the fingers of one hand through his drenched hair. She pressed close to him, feeling his bumpy mail under his over surcoat until she could lay her cheek tenderly alongside his. She savored his musky scent as she whispered, "I love you, Edgar, Son of Mather, King of all Veronia and Beloved of my heart."

He let out a tremulous gasp as his strong mail-covered arms encircled her waist. He held her a long time, unwilling to release her. Mariamne turned her head slightly and kissed his cheek. She slid off her toes and into his loosened embrace.

"You must be tired and hungry, my husband. Come and let me see to your needs."

Chapter 64

Edgar filled his hand with her smaller one. His heart pounded, fluttered, flipped, and did a jaunty dance as she walked with him to the stable. She left him with his armor-bearer, who helped him out of his heavy mail, but her absence after such a greeting made it feel as if she carried away his heart, lungs, and every thought.

Free of his encumbering armor, he went up to his chambers hoping to find her. Only a warm bath greeted him. He slipped into the blessed water, grateful for the thoughtfulness of the one who provided it.

He woke in the cooling tub when his outer door eased open, followed by shuffling in his sitting room. He stood and dried, donned his robe, and staggered out to see who awaited him. He was overwhelmed with joy to see Mariamne laying a simple meal on the long table before one of the divans.

He leaned against the doorframe to his inner chamber and happily watched her for a time before she noticed him. "I knew you would be tired and thought you might prefer to eat in the quiet of your chambers," she said.

He came toward her, and again his heart thrilled when she met him without a trace of fear. He laid his hand on her face and leaned down to kiss her sweet lips. They were warm and supple. He drank deeply, and she answered with equal hunger. He kissed her more deeply and she readily melted into him, causing his heart to soar on wings of pure ecstasy. He savored her sweetness until he could no longer breathe.

Her lips left his, her cheeks flushed with color and her eyes deep. "We can see to all your needs in due time, husband, but for now you need some food in you." He kissed her again before moving to set to eat hungrily.

They spoke in quiet conversation of the success in dispatching many of the enemy soldiers who escaped the battlefield, but not the Knight himself. When he finished eating, Mariamne returned the trays to the kitchen.

Edgar entered his inner chamber to wait for her.

Mariamne found Edgar fast asleep. She covered him and pressed a light kiss to his temple before she went to her own chamber. She fed Shane and curled contentedly into her own bed, thinking of Edgar's kiss. His hunger stole her breath, but she did not fear him. Her tongue traced her lips now at the memory of his taste. His kiss stirred feeling from deep inside her. The foreign sensations made her head spin and her limbs tremble. Her heart pounded with excitement at the thought of sharing his bed again.

The next morn Edgar woke late, well after the meal. He dressed with haste and exited his bedchamber to find a tray of bread and meat and a cup of wine. Edgar downed the wine and grabbed the bread and a bit of meat as he raced down the stairs. He finished the bread while a squire saddled his horse. He let his eyes roam wherever he went, hoping to catch a glance of his beloved. She worked nowhere about. He sighed on the way out to oversee his men in their encampment below the castle.

Cy greeted him, "Good morn, Majesty."

"How are the wounded?"

"There are not many."

"Mariamne told me of the healing effects of the Light."

"Aye. Those who remain are this way, Sire." Cy led him to the injured first and then to his fighting men.

Edgar spent all day with his war host as he arranged payment for their services and saw to any of their needs.

"Who among my fighting men will join the masons and craftsmen I will be sending north to rebuild the churches and manor homes of the north? I promise any man-at-arms a small fief for his service."

Many stepped forward, eager for the promise of their own land.

"Arrangements are made for the gathering of materials and beginning of construction," Cy told him later in the afternoon. "Many of the displaced village men are preparing to join those returning to rebuild. They wish to know if their families may stay in the knights' borrowed tents and be cared for by the castle and the town until their men send for them."

"See if each of the lords can leave a few of his knights to help with the extra burden and protection of the refugee families."

"I will ask for increased provisions from them as well." Cy nodded and left.

The moon crested the horizon when Edgar finally returned to the castle. He entered the empty hall, his steps echoing his passing as he ascended the stairs to his chamber. His one thought all the way up the rocky outcropping had been to see his Beloved, but still weary from the battle and the following chase he turned to his own chamber. He again relished the memory of holding Mariamne and her sweet, passionate kiss. But how would she feel to find him in her chambers?

He turned from her door and opened his own. Mariamne assured he had provisions. A tray of meats sat waiting for him on the long table with a full cup of wine. He sat and had some of it before continuing on into his bedchamber.

He removed his jerkin and pulled off his tunic and a tiny knock sounded at his inner door. Before he could cover his bare chest, the door cracked open, and Mariamne slipped into the room in her thin night rail.

"Am I disturbing you, husband?" she whispered from the door, her eyes caressing his bare skin.

Edgar could not suppress his delight, "Never, Beloved." He reached out a hand toward her, and she slid into his arms. He kissed her and drowned in the passion flowing between them. His blood burned where her hands caressed his skin.

He pulled back the covers and welcomed her into his bed.

Afterword

Shane raced about the inner ward with Ethan, Cy and Annabel's two-year-old son. The young prince took advantage of his nearly year seniority over his young playmate. He bossed him around and pulled him down when Ethan would not comply with his demands.

"Shane, stop," Mariamne scolded, sending him crying to Olivia.

Annabel shook her head. "Olivia does not think it her place to spank the crown prince. And even at his age, Shane uses her respect for you and King Edgar to prick your jealousy."

"Yes, he clings to Olivia, saying he loves her. He uses those words sparingly with me." Mariamne sighed at his continued antics. She sat on the edge of the gardens with her ladies-in-waiting as the boys played at their feet.

Annabel remained ever near at hand, but Ingrid had been wed to the son of Lord Bathmore nearly a year ago. Now the Lady Kimberly, who married Shaw about the same time, joined them. As more of Edgar's knights chose to follow Cy's example and bring their families into the castle, more ladies joined her small group. Early this year, Eldon brought his wife, Lady Gayle, to the castle, and Corin's wife, Lady Edlyn, followed her only last month.

As the ladies sat about watching the two toddlers play, Kimberly put down her tea, perspiration glistening on her face. Gayle reached a caring hand to her, "Oh, Kimmy dear, are you sick again?"

"Not again," Kimberly moaned. "Still, and the good healer says it could last another month."

Everyone looked at her bewildered except Annabel, "That would mean a fall birth," she announced matter-of-factly. Everyone looked between Annabel and the now smiling Kimberly.

"Indeed," the radiant woman agreed as she dabbed at her wet face.

"Oh, congratulations, Kimberly," the others sang out, and talk turned to babies and all the joy they brought.

Mariamne sat lost in thought, listening absently as she watched the son she had not borne. Her own wonderings drifted with unease to her ill health of late. She suffered a few weeks of not being able to keep much more than bread down. The smell alone of certain meats made her retch. Now she could not remember the last time of her monthly.

"Would you excuse me, ladies?"

"Of course, Majesty."

She climbed to the battlements as she considered the ramifications of indeed being with child. She turned to stand over the inner gate and noticed Annabel followed her.

She offered her dear friend a slim smile as they leaned over the wall to watch the activity of the bailey below. "I should also think the next royal heir will be arriving around late summer or early fall," Annabel commented without looking up.

Mariamne stood straight. Breath caught. Before either woman could say more, Mariamne grabbed her hand and led her to the back of the battlements near the rock.

"But, Anna, how could you know? I have only now begun to consider the idea."

A wide smile tickled the other woman's lips, "Oh, Mari, you are aglow and have been for months. Then you add the sickness, which beset for near two months. It could not be more obvious. But surely you recognize the signs of being with child?"

Mariamne's cheeks colored, as the Lord loosed her tongue to share the long-held secret. "Anna, I did not give birth to Shane."

Annabel did not react. "I concluded as much," she said calmly.

Only when Mariamne raised a questioning brow did she explain.

"You had none of the signs of being with child before you disappeared that winter, and I knew your feelings concerning men. I honestly did not believe you had allowed the king to touch even your hand before then."

Mariamne nodded the truth of it and told the miraculous tale of how Shane came to be Edgar's heir. "But, Anna, how am I to tell Edgar? He is convinced he cannot sire children. What will he think of me?"

"The man adores you. He will celebrate another miracle of God. Fear not."

"Anna, I near thirty, what if…"

"God is faithful, Mari. Stop worrying your lip and go share the good news with your husband."

They parted ways, but Mariamne went to see Carrington to confirm her suspicions before she informed Edgar.

When Edgar came to her bed, he found her standing not far inside the inner chamber waiting for him. She seemed tense when he kissed her, and he pulled back to consider her with concern.

"My love, I have some news I pray you will see as a blessing," came her ominous whisper. She paused and opened her mouth a few times to speak, but no words came forth. Then they tumbled from her as a swollen river bursting its banks. "I am with child, Edgar. Your child," she said.

Edgar smiled, understanding the root of her fear, and he pulled her into a tender embrace. "Of course it is my child, Beloved. We share a bed near every night, and you are busy about the castle all day. When would you have time to see another?" He sighed and squeezed her. "God has again blessed us most wondrously." He kissed her soundly.

As he led her to bed, she asked, "If you have a son of your own flesh, what will become of Shane?"

"Shane was a gift from God, my chosen heir, and he will ever remain so. Fear not, Beloved."

The next months flew, and they savored their secret together. Not until his queen wore loose-fitting gowns did Edgar announce their coming blessing to their people. Celebrating continued throughout the summer until the time of her laying-in.

Once Mariamne was confined to her chambers, only Edgar, Annabel, and the midwife were allowed to visit. Trapped within her chamber, Mariamne felt her apprehension growing as her delivery drew nearer. Father Paul came and prayed over her one day, and then the midwife took up residence in her outer chamber.

When Mariamne's time came, Edgar paced with Cy in her sitting room for hours late into the night. Edgar could hear her great cries of pain, and his anxiety grew. Cy prayed, but Edgar could not hold a coherent thought. His heart broke.

Then before the dawn broke, a deafeningly quiet invaded the castle.

Edgar charged the door, but Cy leapt to stand between him and the barrier.

"Cy, get out of my way!" Edgar tried to force his way aside.

"Sire."

They wrestled until the tiny whimper of a child leaked through the door, and they both froze.

Moments later Annabel opened the door and allowed Edgar to enter, as though she could have stopped him. He flew to Mariamne's bedside and found her wet and weakened from her great efforts. He laid his hand on her face, and a weak smile pulled at her lips. "You have a daughter, my love," she whispered.

"Are you well, Beloved?" he barely acknowledging the child.

The midwife spoke as she continued to clean the chamber. "'Twas a very hard delivery, Your Majesty. She is quite weak and will need to be looked after until she regains her strength. The babe is healthy, though also tired. They need their rest, Your Majesty."

Before the woman finished, Mariamne slept. Edgar turned to the midwife. "Thank you, Katherine, for your faithful service. I will see to them for a time myself."

The woman curtsied and left the room. Annabel reentered, and Edgar thanked her likewise before telling her to go and rest, for they would have need of her later.

Edgar took his daughter and cradled her. A tiny babe again lay in his warrior arms. Her skin was warm and sun-kissed like her mother's. A crown of ample black hair adorned her head. He cooed at her, "Hello, little one. Milana, my precious one."

The Lord's Day following her birth, Father Paul christened Milana at but two days old. Mariamne did not attend, as she recuperated. Several weeks passed before Mariamne emerged to be seen about the castle. In time she regained her strength and returned to all her activities.

Prior to Milana's second birthday, Mariamne gave the king a second son after another difficult delivery that required the physician be summoned.

"Here is your son, Sire."

"Mariamne?"

"She is alive, but she will bear you no more children, Your Majesty. I am sorry."

Edgar smiled wearily. "Carrington, I have been blessed with three beautiful children. I only need my beloved wife to help me raise them now."

Again Edgar lovingly tended to her throughout her long convalescence until God restored her to full health.

He christened his second son Jak, for the name meant "God is gracious." With three unexpected children and an adoring wife who yet remained at his side, Edgar could think of no better description for this latest blessing.

As the royal princes and princess grew, a lasting peace settled over Veronia and continued for as long as Edgar and Mariamne reigned. God continued to bless them and their kingdom as they faithfully followed Him and instructed their people to do the same. Edgar and Mariamne's love grew every day, and they showered it on each other, their children, and their people.

The land saw only rare sightings of the remaining enspelled men, and the Black Knight was not heard of again until after Shane came of age.

Glossary of Terms

Cassava – a root tuber similar to a sweet potato
Chignon – a large smooth twist, roll, or knot of hair worn by women at the nape of the neck or the   back of the head
Conviviality – feasting, drinking, and merry company
Crenel – any of the open spaces between the merlons of a battlement
Digit – A measure of length equal to 10.48 mm
Dentris – money of the realm *(my word)*
Divan – a long cushioned seat, usually without arms or back, placed against a wall
Fief – a piece of land, formerly granted by a feudal lord to somebody in return of service
League – a unit of distance, in English-speaking countries usually estimated roughly at 3 miles
Long house – varied with the wealth of the builder; typical size might be 50 feet and would be
divided with part making up a byre housing the farm animals, agricultural produce, or perhaps brewing equipment
Merlon – (in a battlement) the solid part between the two crenels
Mummers – masked or costumed merry-makers or dancers at festivals
Night rail – a woman's loose garment
Retinue – a body of retainers in attendance upon an important personage
Rod – a distance equal to 5.5 yard
Sandesman – old English for "man who was sent," a messenger
Slottering – old English for the making of snorting, animal-like sounds while chewing
Steward – the man responsible for running the day-to-day affairs of

the castle when the lord was
> absent

Thane – originally meaning a military companion to the king, a thane was a man holding
> administrative office

Tonsor – medieval barber

Unshriven – not granted absolution: not having confessed sins to a priest and been given absolution

Yeomen – English and Welsh farmers who owned their own land (hence the term "yeomen") and
> were paid by the king to train in peacetime and to answer his call when he needed to raise an
> army. For hand-to-hand fighting they usually carried a sword, an axe, or a mallet, but their
> principal weapon was the longbow

About the Author

Michelle Janene (Murray) the office manager/secretary/go-to-gal her her church by day
and writes Christian fantasy and historical fiction in all her free time.
She lives in Northern California with two crazy dogs and the characters of her imagination.

If you enjoyed *God's Rebel* please review it on your favorite site.

Join Michelle's email list and get a free novelette at
MichelleJanene.com
You can also connect with Michelle:
Facebook: Michelle Janene-Author or Strong Tower Press
Twitter: @MichelleJaneneM
Instagram: michellejanene_author
Pinterest: www.pinterest.com/michellejanene
Goodreads: Michelle Janene
StrongTowerPress.com

Other Books

Check out these books also by Michelle

Mission: Mistaken Identity

The Changed Heart Series:
God's Rebel
Rebel's Son
Hidden Rebel

Seer of Windmere

Barbarian Hero

Guardians of Truth

Culling a Miracle

Lost Stones

The Last Good King

The King's Vengeance

Thice a Bride

Dragon Fire